Revolution Calling

Advance Praise

"It's obvious Ray knows his metal, but it's also obvious he knows his wider pop culture history and his politics and world events, as Van Horn, Jr. snaps us right back to life as a goofy metalhead in the pressure-cooker that was the late '80s—or as Morrissey called it, *The Haties*. As well, he delivers action events, concepts, and plot in a rock-solid writing style that shines with clarity. Dialogue is mapped-out with similar confidence, allowing Jason and his exquisitely drawn buddy Rob, as well as the tale's other characters, to take shape quickly. Completing the circuit and keeping the tale fizzy and effervescent are endless flashes of place names, band names, and brand names."

> —**Martin Popoff**, heavy metal journalist and author at BraveWords.com, VH-1.com, CMJ, Goldmine

"A story of everyday heavy metal folk and how their everyday pain is real."

> —**Joel McIver,** author of *Justice For All: The Truth About Metallica* and *To Live is to Die: The Life & Death of Metallica's Cliff Burton*

"Ray Van Horn grew up during the '80s metal upheaval and associated culture wars and was clearly paying attention. *Revolution Calling* captures what it was like to be a metal fan when the music was still dangerous. The book has a vibe that will remind readers of Joe Lansdale and Robert R. McCammon. If you ever wanted a novel that mapped *Stranger Things* favorite Eddie Munson's inner life, this is it. Die, posers!"

> —**Justin Norton,** *Decibel* magazine

Revolution Calling

A NOVEL
RAY VAN HORN, JR.

Raw Earth Ink

2023

First paperback edition December 2023

ISBN 978-1-960991-15-7 (paperback)

Published by Raw Earth Ink
PO Box 39332
Ninilchik, AK 99639
www.raw-earth-ink.com

*With love and respect
to Geoff Tate, Chris DeGarmo, and Queensrÿche*

*To the Class of '88 NCHS
and my brothers and sisters in metal*

Stay gold…

Author's Note

North Carroll High School, Hampstead, MD
Photo by the author

AS WITH ANY STORY, there has to be a bad guy.

When you're a teenager, the lines between good and bad, honorable and immoral are blurred. Or to be more accurate, transparently disregarded.

Revolution Calling is a semi-autobiography amplifying the trials brought on by the waning moments of adolescence, that foreboding anticipation preceding both the freedom and accountability of adulthood. Teenagers carry with them an inhibited sense of rage and panic as they try to discover themselves and what their place in the world is. Worse, they're expected to check that pubertal lava down at every turn a grownup is lurking. As a parent, I've always said if your kid can present him or herself upright in the public, you've done half your job, since the omnipresent combustion is reserved for and aimed directly at you.

Lord knows how much angst I swallowed as the real-life Jason

Hamlin and Rob Martino from this story, who are both me and who carry all my silent truths from the times in which this story is set. Lord also knows how the tables have flipped as a father from a teenager who had to digest divorce and remarriage, relocations and peer exploitation in some rough trenches while *Revolution Calling* was written. My son has had his own share of bad guys in his short life.

The core bad guys of this story should be inherently clear, even if teenagers at-large have the propensity to be perfect assholes upon the drop of a dime. Usually when their piss smells its strongest. Teenagers need somewhere to project all their integral belligerence, usually at one another, most focused upon target groups who don't fit their own outward molds.

This story has its share of mean-spirited, hollow clowns and its share of kind souls, plus all those in-between, be they rebellious or compliant to the school caste system, which is basically the same in any generation. No matter your age, you may recognize people you knew in high school, even these Gen X'ers I parade as the peer set I knew. I have the beautiful people and the dweeby scags inside *Revolution Calling* and this story is intended to speak for all, not just the adolescent exiles wringing out a hard-earned comeuppance.

I will offer more insight and caveats in the afterword but let me say in advance of your reading *Revolution Calling* that I have nothing but love and respect for the farming community of our great country. I lived on a farm for a few years and drew significant insight as to what a crop-raising family endures in subservience to the land to make ends meet. Even my wife, TJ, was raised a tomboy farm girl and her latent green thumb talents are evident all over our deck. Nobody makes finer mint tea, just saying.

The Future Farmers of America is a valuable organization met with its own challenges of recruitment in modern times, much like the United States military. Yet, farmers are the irrigating backbone of our civilization. Without them, you see what we'd have to resort to, synthetic-grub-raising as seen in the opening minutes of the eco-decimated world of *Blade Runner 2049*.

With full disclaimer, I have no disrespect intended whatsoever to the FFA. However, as I said, every story worth bleeding over needs a totem bad guy. A gang of them, in the case of *Revolution Calling*. The caricaturized bruisers of this story were based on a knotty crew from the local farming community who'd jacked up my personal Fahrenheit over a prolonged dispute, and that's not even hitting it inside the park. I'm glad to say cooler heads later prevailed after some ugly exchanges.

It was hard enough fighting an alcoholic father and fighting for my right to belong in high school as a mullet-cropped metalhead, the latter being a lesser struggle after a first year period of torment. Both Jason and Rob's school-bound victories in this story were my own and I delighted in recreating them. They plant the quite real seeds of my life's devotion to writing, music, and fitness. By graduation, I can easily say half the school knew me and half of those were friends. A large number are still my friends today.

The built-up conflicts in this story are mostly true; the violent consequences are outright fiction. After all, we hardly need to hold out for another hero in another stupid, anticlimactic tractor chicken-run ala *Footloose*. I wasn't about to dance my way with a lit cigarette in my mouth to draw resolution in this thing.

There are bad guys all over the place aside from my primary heels in *Revolution Calling*. If you ever walked the headbanger's path, you'll know exactly what Jason and Rob go through in this story. The 1986 shlock horror film *Trick or Treat* nailed it to the sheets what high school can do to a metalhead's will to live, much less toss the horns in the air without being branded a de facto devil worshipper. Nobody accused Texas Longhorn fans, much less Parliament and Funkadelic of being Satanists for using the same pronged hand gesture, the latter's intent being to summon their imaginary mothership of bliss to heal a racially divided Earth. Let us *all* ride that sweet chariot.

I hope you, as the reader, will see I attempted to paint my antagonists with a minute sense of empathy. Namely through the vehicle of Bud Curry, constructed from a real-life biker-farmer music store owner, Ron Curry, a dear older rocker friend from the past who gets his due in this story. You're forgiven all those crappy cassette tapes you peddled us, brother. There was still manna, including your ability to close the generation gap with us, your handful of loyal customers. You also called it before anyone; Metallica *did* end up ruling the world.

Ron broke down the agrarian dynamics of the region I grew up in nearly the precise way Bud does in *Revolution Calling*, scratching for coin by cross-selling Harley Davidson merch and blasting the music we loved so much in his store. The real Curry's Music was as much a sanctuary as a place we forked over most of our part-time earnings to. Ron (aka Bud), and his sidearm cashier, Kelly, made our young, confused lives real.

The blue-collar farmland which my ancestors plotted themselves in the mid-1800s, Carroll County, Maryland (renamed George County here) had a tough digestion period of industrial permeation during the 1980s. This courtesy of suburbanite transference into land-gobbling subdivisions, back then a third the size of what they are today. I did a ton of walking around my hometown of Hampstead back then and I saw flagrant violation of the lands plus the occasional upper-middle class douchery cast toward our farming neighbors.

The anger of the farmers was palpable, and I understood where they were coming from, despite being put into a near-death experience one night walking home after work in the dark. A scene well-replicated inside this story.

The whole brouhaha with the FFA posse who'd had it out for me started over a heated exchange of cocky forechecks in floor hockey during Weightlifting class, of all things. They were angry, so was I. I got planted and laughed into my face. I retaliated. My friends made a bigger deal of it than it was. Considering I covered the NHL for a year, forechecking can be simple dustups, or they can lead to nastier, gloves-off scrums. What Jason endures in this story until the climax rings like the truth. I saw a blue corduroy jacket back then, especially at my grocery clerk job, I automatically went on the defensive. At that age, they were my real-life monsters, even with the few FFA guys and girls I was on friendly terms with.

It was dumb crap we all got over. Maybe one day we'll have a beer together like men and bury said dumb crap where it belongs instead of my dodging brewskies thrown at me (us being minors) from a snarling steel dragon charged with .289 fury. After all, metalheads and farmers had more in common nobody but me ever knew.

It wasn't just a shared love of Rush and Skynyrd. Farmers became as much of an outcast in their own native turf as we longhair grits were.
~Ray Van Horn, Jr.

Prologue

1988 Anno Domini.

THE INTERMEDIATE-RANGE NUCLEAR Forces Treaty banning transitional range missiles between the United States and the soon-to-be former Soviet Union has gone into effect. The peaceniks breathe a collective sigh, while Big Business shrugs its Armani-covered shoulders and ploughs on with rallying refrains of diversification since armaments now spell profit loss. Rocky Balboa chopped Ivan Drago and his whiffle cut down to the canvas inside an enemy-blurred land of confusion, fostering a wind of change the Scorpions would score big with once the era of perestroika comes two years later. It's a no-nuke utopia except in the heavy metal community, which continues to issue bombastic, game-over prophecies of fissionable doom, because corrupt governments and thrash music make for good bedfellows. Ozzy Osbourne had already called the button-hovering cold war out on its xenophobic ass with "Thank God for the Bomb" and "Killer of Giants" two years prior.

In Childress, Texas, the body of 17-year-old Tate Rowland was found hanging from a horse apple tree. Ruled a suicide after two reported attempts to take his life, a subversive stink of foul play in the name of the devil propagates a hypersensitive American "Satanic panic" due to Rowland's rumored affiliations with a cult. Keeping in mind Judas Priest is currently making big bucks swooning about turbo lovers after finding themselves in the legal crosshairs in 1985. It was when two teens made a suicide pact after spinning "Better By You, Better Than Me" from Priest's *Stained Class* album.

The metal society, by de facto, is ripped by the moral majority and their Corvette-peeling offspring as being in league with Satan, a fact being played in the scene as both a joke and in all earnestness — depending on what extremity of the genre's numerous sub-classifications the artists subscribe to. Fervent, born-again homebodies swear on their King James bibles Tate Rowland's death was a homicide committed by a reputed Satanist faction, even as their high priest televangelists fall from grace in the middle of a power hour. By attrition, Jessica Hahn becomes an instant celebrity hopping off the end of Jim Bakker's ordained dick. Also by attrition, VHS porn sales and rentals have spiked by 122% from the prior year.

The thrash, death, and black metal underground gains steam in an inquisition-style backlash against commercialized hard rock, dividing the scene into hate-filled sanctions unseen by any other subculture. Comic book nerds arguing to the bitter end, who is mightier: Thanos or Darkseid have nothing on thrashers versus party rockers.

"Death to false metal" becomes a unifying mantra to a losing cause. MTV's *Headbangers Ball* has sold out to the glam-banged likes of Bon Jovi and pale shades of Mötley Crüe and Def Leppard. Record labels are after the next "You Give Love a Bad Name" cash cow single and any band wielding an edgy guitar is subject to watered-down revisionism. Even Slayer, of all bands, slows down by corporate mandate with their newest album, *South of Heaven*.

An insurrection of "true metal" bands like Bathory, Danzig, Carcass, Forbidden, Saint Vitus, Candlemass, Voivod, Flotsam and Jetsam, Helstar and the newly formed Anal Cunt become the talk amongst the metal hip, all believing they have borne witness to the long-term future of music. Never mind that honor will be claimed by N.W.A. and Nirvana, hardly Nuclear Assault.

It is in this spirit of fist-banging mania in which two alienated, horror-freak metalheads in their senior year of high school find their comeuppance.

Chapter 1

"IF THERE'S A NEW WAY...I'll be the first in line..."

Pifffff...sploossssshhhh...

"Asshole, you did that on purpose!"

The BB missed its target wide right, breaking the glassy plane of the millpond with a throb of undulating ripples. If the groans from skittish bullfrogs hiding amidst the grassiest spots around the pond's perimeter weren't loud enough, the sweaty and willful 17-year-olds teetering on the edge of the soggy bank put them to shame. They sounded as piqued as they looked beneath the late August bake.

"Did what, Rob?"

"You screwed up my shot, Jason."

"I wasn't talking to you, so don't pin your sucky aim on *me*, fart knock."

Rob snarled at his friend, blowing upwards, as much to push away a soaked strand of hair as much as to vent before fuming, "You freak me out sometimes, the way you always talk to yourself."

"But it better work this time," Jason sang instead of said this time, doing a rugged, teenaged impersonation of Megadeth lead guitarist and vocalist, Dave Mustaine, snarling the chorus to the title song of his band's thrash metal anthem, "Peace Sells, But Who's Buying?"

"Meh," Rob droned in response to Jason's snarky up and down jutting of his eyebrows. He swung the barrel of the Daisy air rifle he was holding back toward the pond for another shot.

"Gimme it, putz," Jason sneered with a bitter dip to his tone. It was evident he was done with his larking. Jason swiped slavers of sweat from his damp eyebrows with an already slickened forearm. "I'll bet your cassette copy of Testament's *The New Order* I can nail the bastard with no problem."

The air around them was as brutal as the Bradenton Jaycees' meat smoker running full on through carnival week. Tense farmers praying for respite from the long summer drought had little use for wishing upon stars through the hazy, wearisome nights. Nary a gray cloud teasing the potential of rain had been seen all week. It was the kind of prolonged heat sending most of Bradenton into the shield of their air conditioning if they had it; it was also enough to drive those with lesser grips on control to the point of destructiveness. In five years, a movie starring Michael Douglas called *Falling Down* would summarize the whole sweltering exasperation better than anything. Right now, rentals of his hot ticket flicks *Wall Street* and *Fatal Attraction* were still indoor pleasures, a year after their theatrical runs.

"That fatso meteorologist on Channel 12, Chris Ball, says this stinking heat wave's finally gonna end next Monday with a projected thunderstorm," Rob noted with a look of defiance about him. He held onto the stock of a Daisy air rifle, resuming the point of the barrel at the water. "Not enough to end the water ban, though."

"Last day of summer vacation, go figure," Jason retorted with a hasty grab for the BB gun and missing from a similarly hasty jerk away by Rob.

"Chris Ball's gonna shank it like he always does. My dad says weathermen have the best job security; they can be wrong any ol' time and not get fired."

"I can say the same thing about my idiot bosses at Super Thrift. Now give me the gun, already."

"Hold your horses," Rob said with a broil matching the simmer around them. He turned his gaze toward the surface of the pond and with his target lined up to his own estimation, he pulled the trigger. This time, the BB soared well past its mark, plinking the other side of the water with a faint dash.

"Christ, Rob, I'm down to my last canister and my ma's been in no mood to take me shopping for BBs. Anytime I want to use the Daisy, she acts like I'm fantasizing about going down into the east side of Baltimore City with an Uzi."

Looking at the shaggy haired teens, Jason Hamlin and Rob Martino from behind, even the blackness of their respective Manowar and Metal Church concert tees divulged soaked splotches at the centers of their backs.

In Rob's case, the thinner-haired between the two, his shoulder-length, chestnut follicles looked like they'd been dunked into the slime-choked drink in front of them. Jason's thicker beige-blonde mop was darker than its norm with the added film of sweat. Right now, Jason could double as a less-stalwart William Katt, the gallant, if ill-fated escort of Carrie White, Tommy Ross, as well as the loveable bumble bum in tights and cape, *The Greatest American Hero*.

The scruff building around Jason's chin was the only thing on his body he kept systematic other than his heavy metal attire. Jason's poofy hair had grown so much it swallowed the pronged diamond stud piercings lodged in both of his ears. At home, his mother had nagged him that a trim of his shrubby locks would turn him into a "real looker," advice he'd rejected quicker than any dinner she served featuring liver, onions, and peas.

"Alright, smartass, you got a bet," Rob's said, handing over the Daisy with a perturbed leer. "What'll you put up if you miss?"

Rob's unkempt eyebrows furrowed as he needled his friend in return. Without thinking and provoked by a coating of fluid above his lip, Rob's tongue glazed the smidgeon of his golden-brown hair overtop, "peach fuzz," as others his age called it. His first attempt to coax his stubble at the beginning of summer vacation with a Delco electric razor had only produced an annoying blast of acne which had taken more than a week to get rid of. The lip nape had become a quiet, mid-August victory for Rob, almost as satisfying as the battle won against his parents a summer ago for the shark tooth earring dangling from his left lobe.

Now in his possession, Jason clutched the carbine rifle as if it would take nothing short of Armageddon to pry it from him. A look of determination ignited his flint-colored eyes. If he'd wanted to enlist after high school, Jason already had a war stare Uncle Sam would've gotten a hard-on over.

"Ahhh, geez, I dunno, man!" Jason exclaimed as he punted a loosened rock from the perimeter of the pond into the grubby water. The *sploosh* echoed around the empty farm, quieting any frog with the intention of sounding off.

The homestead was void save for the lumbering skulk of the owner, Farmer McGruder, shambling about his parched fields many yards away. John McGruder was his actual name, but "Farmer" was how the newcomer suburban transplants staked within the surrounding Bradenton Hills development referred to him. It was condescending, but nobody, not even the poor smallholder himself, made much to-do about it. It was just a part of the community's daily grind, like one-upping each other with their above-ground pools and comparing the tube sizes of their floor model televisions like obsessive 14-year-old boys did their penises.

With no commercial bumper crops to brag of the past couple seasons, the lonely widower Farmer McGruder was content to let the neighborhood kids kick up scratch football and soccer matches in the open, grassy section behind his barn. The only thing the sun-bombed land-tiller asked was that kids take their emptied water and Gatorade bottles with them, a simple request often overlooked. Gracious to a fault inside of his seventy-whatever years, Farmer McGruder had been seen numerous times during the smoldering summer season collecting trash off his pasture.

McGruder also allotted the neighborhood youth to tool about his pond, which he kept tediously mowed and edged. It hadn't taken much effort during July and August. Fishing, skipping rocks, and pinging copperheads and cottonmouths had become the summertime thing to do for Jason and Rob.

"I'm not kidding," Rob said, pooching his lips to once again cajole the dangling follicles away from his glassy brown eyes. The moisture slicking his eye sockets morphed his shifting gaze toward the object of their focus, a coiled copperhead snake lazing at the fringe of a small, overgrown island in the middle of the pond. All summer long, the boys had called the grassy key "Alcatraz."

"Seriously, man, whattya after? *Seventh Son of a Seventh Son? Leprosy?*"

"What self-respecting metalhead wouldn't have those already?" Rob taunted with a wave of his bony arm. The flap of his t-shirt waggled in tandem.

"How about the uncensored version of *Open Up and Say Ahh...* You know, the original cover with the tiger girl and a tongue that can yummy down harder than even Gene Simmons. It wasn't out long before K-Mart and Camelot Music pulled the album and reissued it with those stupid black bars covering most of her face once the PRMC butchered it. Tipper, get bent, already. *You* could use a good yummy down."

"Are you trying to insult me?" Rob prattled, though he looked less offended than he sounded. Unlike a moment ago, he was about to bust a seam in laughter. "I can't believe you even own a Poison album."

"A moment of weakness," Jason returned with a roll of his clammy eyes. "Sue me. I know, how about The Plasmatics' *No Hope for the Wretched?* Wendy O. Come on, Rob, that's gold, right there."

"You know what I want," Rob said, folding his arms like a seasoned dealer with negotiations going in full swing.

"Fuck you, Martino. No way."

"Way. I want *that.* Unless you're fulla shit and can't hit the stupid snake, which I don't think you can. Dude, you won't even reach Alcatraz."

"Hell no," Jason refuted, holding the BB rifle barrel up and out in front of him, as if giving it a thorough if needless inspection. "No way I'm parting with my Slayer *Live Undead* picture disc."

"That's because you can't hit it. Put up or shut up, Jason. You think I want to give away *The New Order?* Last time I made a bet, I lost my lunch money to Eddie Neubauer taking the Pats over the Bears a couple Super Bowls ago."

"That's your dumb ass fault."

"Worth it to see that punk McMahon catapulted."

"Point," Jason acknowledged with a faint smirk. "Still, forget it. Pick something else."

"I want Slayer," Rob mocked with the repeated derision, "Put up or shut up."

"No," Jason said in as stoic a voice as he could muster with his black Manowar t-shirt featuring a hoary eagle avatar beginning to mold itself to his muggy form. Jason used to be as skinny as his friend; however, the past five months working as a grocery bagger at Super Thrift had added some musculature to his arms and rounded out his shoulders. In this clammy state, however, the creased and wrinkled eagle looked as googly as one might see it after dropping an acid tab.

"Jason Hamlin, whose first concert was freakin' Sha-Na-Na," Rob egged. "Jason Hamlin, who secretly likes to listen to Madonna and freaking Wham…"

"Madonna, yeah," Jason spat. "You're a total dick beyond that, and don't think I didn't see that copy of Duran Duran's *Seven and the Ragged Tiger* on your shelf."

"Duran Duran rocks," Rob said, shrugging his shoulders. "So does a Coke-flavored Slurpee. I'm only human."

"Forget synth pop and forget *you,* man," Jason said in a more even tone while drawing the Daisy barrel forward, pointing it toward the sprouting islet. "It's not happening."

"Neither is your shot, jerko," Rob said, pressing his advantage. One thing he knew about Jason, his friend could become unbalanced if you kept the throttle engaged.

"*Live Undead,* then, huh?" Jason huffed as he lined up the Daisy barrel with the copperhead seemingly paralyzed in his distant control. It hadn't moved, even with two gilded pellets whizzing by it earlier. "Okay, screw it. I'm not even worried."

"Rad, you're on, then," Rob sneered, rubbing the sweat of his palms down the sides of his baggy, knee-torn, Levi 501s. His left foot, clad in a battered black and white Nike high top begging for death, pumped up and down with anticipation. "I call you, Hamlin. Shoot."

Jason fell silent for a few seconds before he began murmuring, as if Rob was nowhere in sight. His closest friend of three years had a point; Jason was prone to uttering out loud with nobody around. The few who caught him nattering to himself must have felt he was a ripe candidate for the funny farm, *ho ho ha ha hee hee….*

"Did you run down to the front, did you queue for your ticket through the ice and snow…"

"Now he's reciting Saxon's 'Denim and Leather,' Jesus wept," Rob objected. "Hold still a few minutes while I run back home and get my boom box. You're no Biff Byford."

Only a couple miles away, a faint emission of brass horns and thumping drums carried down from Merriweather High School. The marching band was ramping up for the upcoming fall sports season in a late summer practice session.

"Those poor schmucks must be roasting out there with all those instruments strapped to them," Rob said. He looked off to the horizon for a moment as if he could see the band itself, grunting and drizzling all over their instruments.

"Their fault for signing up," Jason sniped, doing his best to steady a fresh wobbling that was mucking with his aim. "Shush, already."

Somehow, the speckled serpent sensed something was awry. Its tail pulled closer to the rest of its helix and its head raised an inch, now alert to the danger coming its way.

"Dude, pull the damn trigger," Rob harped as the copperhead signaled its escape. "It's getting ready to dive back into the water."

"I know, I know."

A welcoming breeze cooled the tension between the two teens. To anyone else, it was a pedestrian reprieve from the heat, but to the boys staking a bet over the shooting of a snake, it penetrated the humidity long enough to lick Jason's drape off his ears for a brief second. It also stopped the dripping perspiration on Rob's forehead before it could pool into his scruffy eyebrow.

Even from afar, the boys could see the copperhead dart its wiry, forked tongue out before it began its retreat into an aquatic deliverance.

"That picture disc's mine," Rob ridiculed, looking more confident than he felt in that very second. Lining his stare at the slight dip of the Daisy's barrel, Rob's expression suddenly quashed, knowing he was about to lose his Testament tape.

"Like hell," Jason declared with all the confidence he needed. He pulled his index finger backwards, now with full composure.

A sound of compressed air punctured the bake around them. This time, no *ploosh* into the water.

The snake not only flinched; it launched from the basin of the tiny mound. The copperhead, still alive after being plunked by a Daisy BB, dunked its enraged head into the water and submerged its blood-pocked midsection. The tail wriggled angrily behind the rest of the submarining snake.

"Son of a bitch!" Rob yelped, despite coming up on the bad end of the bet. As a good sport, he flicked a pair of horns-up salutes with both of his hands and thrusted his pelvis in exaggeration, as if a phantom prankster had goosed him from behind. "You nailed it, man!"

"Damn if I didn't."

Jason gleamed with full appreciation of his mark, even though a part of him felt bad for goring the snake. He brought the BB gun back to erect, leaned the stock into his shoulder, and pointed it toward the sky with the dry joke, "Hands up, God."

"Did ya see the way that sucker leaped a mile?"

"I didn't kill it, at least," Jason whispered, matching the hiss of summer's pissy purr around them.

"You win," Rob sighed. "Let me tape a copy and *The New Order* is yours."

"Ehhh, keep it, I made my point."

Jason lowered the gun with the point aimed at the ground, as his Uncle Steve had once taught him in a long-ago hunting lesson which never stuck beyond that.

"Credit where it's due, killer shot."

"Thanks, man," Jason said, glancing back at Alcatraz, then the water's plane to make sure the snake hadn't been heading their way to mount some payback. "Think Farmer McGruder might toss me a buck for chasing the snake away?"

"Doubt it. Mom says she sees him selling tomatoes, squash, and zucchini roadside on Route 62. I think most of his soybean's been torched, the broke bastard. He must be growing his crops in the greenhouse since there's nothing to speak of around his land. Hell, the cornfields all over George County look bankrupt."

Changing subjects, Jason said, "My dad's taking me to some stupid antique car club event when he picks me up this Saturday if you want to keep me company. Rich guys stroking off around their restored Model A's and Ford Coupes. They call it Depression Era for a reason."

"Your dad has a Duesenberg SJ, right?"

"Virgin cherry," Jason affirmed.

"Didn't know he was so rich."

"The bachelor life's been good to him. He cares more about that dumb convertible than he ever did me and Mom. When they got divorced, I wanted to take a knife and cut the shit out of that folding roof tarp. I almost did."

"Jason, you've been my bud at least longer than Madam X has had a career, but you've got issues."

"I suppose, but I told Mom once I start driving, I'll decide when I go to see that drunken douchebag. *If* I go. I'm half scared when he drives me home in his regular wheels."

"Shelby Charger '83, right?"

"You know your cars."

"Not really," Rob said. "My old man traps me in his man cave all the time walking me around his framed pics of classic cars and Fifties singers. He thinks I don't give a crap, but I pay attention. I never say it out loud, but my dad's kinda cool."

"No mystery how I feel about mine," Jason said with a tart in his voice reflective of his scoff. Now it was his turn to look off in the distance, not toward the Merriweather marching band's emissions, but somewhere beyond. "Hard to like a guy who tells his own son while shitfaced he should've pulled out and shot me into my mom's bush."

"Harsh, dude."

"He also jabbed me in the forehead at age seven over and over when I couldn't get my division homework. I can still hear him... 'Dummy!' 'Dummy!' 'Dummy!' My mom threatened to leave him back then. I wish she'd had."

"Your old man's a fucker, agreed, so are we done here?" Rob asked with a heave, trying to find a casual way to ease out of the dark turn of their conversation and knowing he likely sounded unsympathetic right now. Rob wiped the back of his neck beneath his hair and scowled in disgust at the dampness left upon his palm. "We can cool off at my place; maybe kick on *Night of the Creeps* or something. My folks won't be off work for another few hours. They bought a fresh bag of Cool Ranch Doritos, the family size. Mom joked you'd be good for half the bag."

"Gnarly," Jason said with a faint crinkle. The scant smile wiping itself away just as fast, he dropped the Daisy barrel against his right shoulder. He aimed the point behind his head, almost passable for an infantry dress parade. "The marching band sounds miserable, and they only have a week until school starts. The band director, Mr. Hyde's gotta be crawling out of his skin. I know I am."

"Me too, just thinking about the new Bon Jovi album coming out in a few weeks. Talk about Depression Era."

"Heh," Jason chuckled. "Random thought, no way do we put up with the same shit we have the first three years of high school. It ends now."

"And your proposal against metalhead persecution to the entire student body of Merriweather High will be what? Do tell."

"You better beware," Jason caterwauled in the shrieking Teutonic key of Accept vocalist Udo Dirkschneider through a rendition of the band's "Fast as a Shark." "You better take care...be prepared for the shock..."

Chapter 2

"SUCKS WHAT HAPPENED to Greg Boedecker and his punk crew," Jason said to Rob a few days later, pulling out a blade of grass and shifting it between his fingers back and forth. He was just as skillful at the gliding motion with a coin.

"School hasn't even started and the FFA bulldogs are on the prowl," Rob groaned, snapping his loose hair away from his right eye. He turned up the volume on the Emerson boom box positioned between the boys. It was turned up to four, now latched up a level. Inside the cassette deck, *Taking Over* from New Jersey thrash upstarts, Overkill, was spindling.

"I saw their cars hitting Mach 10 as I got to work," Jason said. "I'm surprised Greg could get a decent lead on Sam Shaffer's '67 Nova in that turd bucket Escort he rolls around in."

"Whattya think started this whole thing between them?"

"Because they're punkers, duh. It's not like Greg and his gang goes around starting shit. They're straight edge."

"I like them, don't get me wrong," Rob said, leaning so far back against his planted hands behind him both his wrists and shoulders popped from the strain. "They can be hypercritical clowns, and not just because they rag on heavy metal. I can get with no smoking, no drugs, and especially no fighting. I mean look at us. We're not taking down The Hart Foundation at Wrestlemania anytime in this life. Well, you might be able to scuff up Jim Neidhart's knees a good bit."

Jason guffawed at that one.

"Ian MacKaye's heart is in the right place, but no alcohol, though? No sex? Where's the fun in that? I mean, Lori Phillips runs with those guys. She looks like Siouxsie Sioux waking up on the bad side of the coffin, but what a body, right? None of those dudes are parting her meat curtains? Come on."

"She split Phil Barber's lip last year for calling her a skank, if you remember."

"After he'd told everyone he'd petted her panty hamster, of course," Rob snorted with combined laugh-cough.

"Phil might be a bigger spaz than Sam Shaffer."

"I hear a lot of the straight edgers are vegetarians, too. Guess that's why they're not down with the fur burger."

"Jesus," Jason said, cracking up. "Where do you get this stuff? You have a book on 101 ways to say 'vagina' stashed somewhere in your library? If so, can I borrow it? I can only say 'Egg McMuff' so many times before it loses its flavor."

"I just might," Rob cracked. "Hidden next to my contraband 45 of The Who's 'Squeeze Box.' My mother lost her mind hearing that song come out of my room, but not as much as when she caught me saying 'gorilla in the washing machine' on the phone to my cousin Andy. I was stunned she even knew what that meant."

Their laughter kicked up a notch, so much they drowned their music for a moment. One might think the sound of thrash metal had capriciously outshone Eddie Murphy's sidesplitting, profane *Delirious* concert film, a total rage amongst their generation.

"Anyway, the punkers are harmless," Jason said, settling down and bobbing his head to the grooving crunch of the opening track on the tape, "Deny the Cross." "Greg was at Super Thrift with his folks the next day after they got jumped. His punkling kid brother, Joey, was with him, wearing that Germs tee Greg had on all last year."

"Makes you wonder if Sam Shaffer has a kid brother to groom as a punk beater-in-training."

"No, and kudos to the Shaffer parentage for stopping at one."

"So, what about Greg? How's he doing after the beatdown he took?"

"Pretty pissed, as you might expect. He helped me bag his family's groceries, so we got to talk for a minute, though Joey kept nosing in. Greg's face looked like it got wrecked by Tyson in half a round. The bruises all over his arm hurt to even look at. He went and flattened his liberty spikes. His mohawk's all compressed to his scalp, like the old 82nd Airborne you see in the war textbooks. No green or purple in it, either. It's not like Greg's sold out or anything, but he's..."

"Conceded," Rob finished for Jason with a sharp nod.

"Exactly. All Greg said under his breath was, 'Those inbred sister fuckers are getting theirs one day.' So much for straight edge."

"They only verbally harass us," Rob logged for the record. "Guess Lynyrd Skynyrd and Rush make us shaky allies with the farmer kids, though if Emily Haney calls me a geek one more time..."

"She'd be kinda hot if she wasn't such a bitch all the time," Jason wheezed more than said, surveying the close-clipped expanse in front of them while Overkill bulldozed the austere air around them.

The Hanford Mansion was alive with a bustle of galvanized metal shimmering upon the American Georgian-styled estate. The five-part symmetrical building had, only a decade ago, been given the uplift of a thorough restoration of its pilaster, cornice, and woodwork through a National Park Service preservation program costing more than an appropriated sixty-five thousand dollars. The landmark manse had originally been built by a relocated maritime merchant-turned agriculturalist from Portsmouth, New Hampshire, Nathaniel Hanford in 1841. His Maryland estate spread across a reported 19,000 acres, once used for soybean, wheat, and corn growth. After the uplift, the Hanford Mansion was re-opened for tours, banquets, weddings, holiday parties and rented out for other social gatherings like the periodic meetings of the Chesapeake Mopar Motor League.

The early afternoon warmth was reaching its apex at a merciful 83 degrees. Fall was teasing its inevitable coming, given the first sneezes of browned leaves scattered around the base of the estate's hardy elms and hemlocks.

One would still think the brutal summer hadn't altogether finished its chokehold by the way the all-male members of the Chesapeake Mopar Motor League were pawing at their brows while they tugged on cans of Schlitz and Colt 45 beer. The meager handful of women to be found were clustered on the great patio of the mansion. The auto club's bored, ignored, squawking wives fanned themselves and poured lemonade from blue-tinted glass antique pitchers in frequent intervals. The timbres of laughter to be heard were skewed toward the men.

"You know, Nathaniel Hanford had slaves here," Jason said, letting the grass blade float back to the ground. "That's the overseer's house right behind us near the edge of the woods. Our forefathers make me sick."

"Here in Maryland, no less."

"If I learned anything in American History that stuck, Rob, many northern whites owned slaves, including our so-called neutral turf here at the Mason-Dixon. I've probably listened to too much Impaler, but I can feel the pain and suffering just being here. Doesn't feel like much has changed. Case in point, you see what I see?"

"Yep," Rob said with a shake of his head. "So blatant."

With his extended forefinger, Jason was singling out a lone, chubby black man hovering at the edge of the closed circle of likewise overweight white men. He was dressed in plaid slacks, a green polo shirt, and white flat cap. He was holding a beer like the others. Laughing like the others, yet he looked almost desperate to be noticed through the deliberate stonewalling from the rest of the group.

"They could give two fucks about that poor guy," Jason said with a rumble. "Any idiot can see they're snubbing him. My dad's no better, the prejudiced jerk."

"Your old man has a sweet ride," Rob said in deflection. "Though I can't believe he kept going on about how AC/DC rules, like he's trying to impress us. Anyone knows that band's done. If *Blow Up Your Video's* the best they got, you can kiss their Aussie asses goodbye within two years, max."

"You know, my dad once told me he'd gone golfing by himself, and the tee starter was going to place him in a group of three black men. He'd made up an excuse to go back to his car, then he came back once he was able to be lumped in with a white couple. He told me this story like he was proud of himself."

"Those snobs are probably cheesed the black guy's SS Jaguar outclasses them all. Probably dusts their cracker asses, too."

"See why I don't wanna be here?" Jason said with a sour pucker.

"If you wanna stay in theme, this is same reason I told you I didn't want to be in the pit at the Grinding Gristle show last year."

"Right," Jason agreed. "Total disgrace."

"What that skinhead prick did to Rod Jones... The poor guy paid for his ticket like anyone else."

"Rod knows metal and punk better than most," Jason said, tapping his knee in time to the music. Also from a growing agitation. "Talk to the dude sometime if you can find him. Rod knows the underground, *fact. Hit Parader* or *Rip* should have him writing for them."

"Just not *Circus* mag," Rob ridiculed. "Unless he'll take mascara products for his pay."

"True," Jason said with a quick grin, yet swallowing down the urge to bust out as they had over their pussy talk moments ago.

"I remember that swastika-tatted fucker shoving Rod harder than anyone else in the pit," Rob went on. "I heard him yell at Rod to get out of the club and go listen to Slick Rick."

"That Nazi waste of sperm used the phrase 'jigaboo shit' at Rod, I'll never forget it," Jason said. "You know what's hypocritical? That sicko despot had the balls to wear a Bad Brains shirt to the show."

"No peace and love for Jah's children," Rob added grimly.

On the portable stereo, the song changed to the faster-paced "Wrecking Crew," snapping the boys out of their funk.

"Aww, hell yeah!" Jason exclaimed, springing to his feet. "Mosh!!!"

Without needing a prompt, Rob turned the boom box up two notches and was likewise up in a fluid motion. With years of slam dancing practice, Rob stomped all over the parched grass and pumped his fists in time to the pounding rhythm.

The boys looked like a pair of lunatics in the thrall of dual seizures as they spasmed, crashed off each other's backs and sides, pushing one another, but not so hard as to spill the other to the ground. They twirled and kicked up a mini circle spin around the boom box as vocalist Bobby "Blitz" Ellsworth ralphed how his thrashing cronies would walk all over you, because they were most decidedly a wrecking crew.

Jason and Rob roared with glee, looking even more insane without a full throng of people to whirl up a proper circle pit at a live heavy metal or punk gig.

As the song ended, the boys flopped to the grass, chortling like they had the inside scoop to the hottest joke in the country as the breath-catching power metal marcher "Fear His Name" decelerated their ruckus.

"Turn that freakazoid shit down over there!"

"Leave it alone," Jason muttered between breaths as the boys rose up to see Jason's father hollering at them. He was pawing his can of Schlitz like he wanted to mangle it, but he didn't give the boys a second glance as he turned to the other men. The group had created a tighter formation to fully impede the black man in the green shirt and flat cap. Jason's dad pushed a wave of dismissal in the direction of Jason and Rob.

"Excuse my retard son and his loser friend," they both heard Jason's dad say to everyone but the obstructed black man in their midst. Even with the bombast of Overkill in their proximity. "Their taste in music says everything you need to know."

All the other men laughed in response. All save the black man, who turned with a perturbed expression. He pulled away from the group and glanced at the gaggle of women who likewise ignored him.

"Rotate, you assholes," Jason fumed, as he lifted a middle finger toward the car club. Only one person saw it, and for the first time since gliding his golden Jaguar onto the estate, his laughter became genuine.

"No use wasting a volume crank on a slow cooker," Rob said, scratching both of his arms from tumbling in the grass before he turned the volume down.

"Dad used to be cool," Jason seethed, also scuffing about his arms. "You see that beer gut on him? He was thin only a couple years ago, and he had a lot more muscle tone. He traded his t-shirts and Wranglers in exchange for those stupid short-sleeve button downs and slacks. Worse, he wears them around his condo all the time, like he's still at work. Rob, my old man only just turned forty and I don't think he's had a date in forever. He leaves a ripped open Trojan wrapper inside his bathroom trash can, which he hasn't emptied in months!

What a fake."

"Poser."

"He leaves his *Hustler* magazines all over the coffee table and there's a couple of phone numbers written on a piece of loose leaf with the names Trish and Barbara tucked beneath his ashtray. I even found a Polaroid wide out in the open on his dresser when he asked me to go fetch him a hand towel. I know he left it there on purpose for me to find. It has this naked chick sitting on his bed, parting the velvet seas. It's like he wants me to think he's this supreme swinger, like he's over my mom and having the high life of bachelorhood."

"All that excessive drinking and smoking, he's likely to stay a bachelor."

"He's up to a pack-and-a-half a day," Jason said, frowning at his father who didn't see one iota of it. "Try waking up and listening to someone on the verge of puking for nearly an hour before he settles down. That was even before he rolled out on us."

"Both of my parents started the nicotine patch in May," Rob said, trying to spool a thread of empathy. "They were total basket cases at first and it was hard watching them trying to wean off the smokes. They'd sneak one or two behind each other's backs and ask me to keep their secrets. My dad keeps telling me, 'Never start smoking, Rob, whatever you do.' They eat a lot more, but you know what? They've been a lot more affectionate with each other. My dad's so loud in the sack these days he sounds like he's wrestling a bear when he busts a nut. Good for him, though."

"I used to worship mine," Jason said in a bitter voice.

Neither boy had seen the man approaching from their side, and both Jason and Rob were startled by the sight of two unopened Schlitz cans pushed into their immediate view.

"Go take a long walk, boys," a robust, grizzly voice said beneath the white flat cap. His smile looked as congenial as devilish as he handed them the beers. There was such kindness to the man's brown eyes and his curvy, spotted cheeks he could've offered the boys quaaludes and they might've risked acceptance and stuffed them into their pockets, only to be polite. "I never gave you these, and you never saw me."

"N-no, sir," Rob stammered, taking his beer with a precarious grin, smuggling it beneath his plain black tee. "Thank you, man!"

"Mmm hmm," the man said, jostling the other can slightly at Jason, who took his with greater caution. He needn't have worried, since the car club and their hope-stripped wives were in their own worlds.

"How'd you get these brewskies past those buttheads?" Jason asked, doing the same with his beer as Rob.

"They never saw me, either," the man said. He sounded equal parts despair and conviction as he fired the boys a wink. "Not since I got here, the stuck-up sons of bitches, and I've been breeding thoroughbreds since the days of the Martin Luther riots downtown in '68. They never see me at Pimlico, Timonium, or Laurel, either, but I win. A lot. I'll be withdrawing my club application, just to make a point, though I doubt it'll make a dent in any of their days. Y'all be good."

"Wow," Rob whispered before the man turned away from them and, with a casual stride nobody else gave notice to, slipped into his SS Jaguar. Nor did anybody make comment of his deliberate gunning of the engine before pulling away.

Chapter 3

"THINK MY PARENTS smelled the beer on our breaths earlier?"

"I doubt it," Jason said, pushing a bravado to Rob he really didn't feel. The truth was, he'd been at odds with himself even accepting the beer, much less drinking it. "That's why I pinched some of my old man's Life Savers for us to cover up with. That's taking a page from his trick book."

"Hnh," Rob said with a scrunchy look of half-acceptance. Suspicion was clearly hanging about him like the oversized gray Champion athletic shorts wilting in silk pools beneath his undeveloped legs. "What's wrong, then?"

"Nothing, man."

"Bullshit."

"Bull true," Jason said, already losing the battle with Rob. "Alright, fine. Call me a wimp or whatever, but I feel like a fraud."

"For drinking the beer when your old man is…"

"An alcoholic," Jason said, squeezing his eyes shut. The mere admission of it caused him great pain. "I mean, you saw him driving, Rob. I felt guilty asking you to come, knowing my dad puts his own life at risk, much less ours. It's gonna happen one day, I promise."

"What?"

"Drinking's gonna kill him. I'm glad nothing bad happened while we were with him, but Jesus, he nearly fell asleep behind the wheel! Then I go ahead and have a beer as well? You see where I'm coming from?"

"You can't beat yourself up over it, man," Rob said, trying to ease, if not tame the growing tension inside his best friend. He reached across and shook the shoulder closest to him a couple times, the way an older brother experienced in baseball would console his younger sibling striking out at the plate in Pee Wee League.

Rob and Jason were potted cross-legged on opposite ends of a cushion-crushed couch stationed against the far wall in Rob's bedroom.

The old Bridgewater they faced each other on had been replaced by Rob's parents earlier in the year by a new sectional with a foldout in the family living room. The repurposed Bridgewater had recently taken the place of Rob's childhood bed, which he'd outgrown to the point he'd needed to hoist his feet into a fetal position just to fit upon the single size mattress.

The walls surrounding them looked as if heavy metal musicians got sucked into a battle royale slasher film. The bands all but ran for their lives surrounded by the menacing forms of Jason Voorhees, Leatherface, Freddy Kruger, Pinhead, and a gazillion zombies. Posters, extracted foldouts, magazine pages, and covers had been torn loose, and in some cases, trimmed down to half pages.

All of it was thumb tacked with little white space to be found in Rob's room. Iron Maiden gathered the most musical real estate with their shaggy-haired, psychotic mascot, Eddie, featured in various scenes. One poster, Iron Eddie was caped and flashing a ripped torso in a vast fantasy realm, slamming his fingers down upon a futuristic organ with a base carrying his crazed image in the middle. In another, he was coming for the viewer brandishing a wakizashi. Another, Eddie looked like an amalgam of Clint Eastwood's western antihero, the Man with No Name and Harrison Ford as Rick Deckard from *Blade Runner*. Another, Eddie was snarling in his cockpit in the middle of a World War II dogfight. Yet another, he was deified upon an Egyptian temple.

"I was more worried your folks were gonna come downstairs while we had *I Spit On Your Grave* playing," Jason said, trying to play it cool as he gazed upon a poster across from his view. It featured an unseen assailant jamming a pointed shish kabob into the gaping mouth of a victim. An original movie poster right out of the theater for *Happy Birthday to Me*.

"It's why they sprung for an extra VCR," Rob stated, as if proud of himself more than his parents. "It keeps me out of their hair when we disagree on what to watch on the tube. I'm pretty sure they're onto us, but yeah, if my mom had seen us watching all that gang raping, castrating and hanging a guy with his pants down, she'd probably take the basement VCR out for good. That went too far. I kinda feel gross about myself right now."

"I had to pony up two bags of Hershey's miniatures to that wasteoid, Chad Rowland, at Bradenton Coast Video for holding me the tape behind the counter."

"Like we have an actual coast in this farmstead burg," Rob said, rolling his eyes up.

"If they'd just quit marking the tapes 'adult audiences only,' we wouldn't have to go through all this sneaking around."

"I had to bribe Rowland with pepperoni Combos to get us *Texas Chainsaw Massacre, Evil Dead 2,* and *Pieces,*" Rob susurrated, riffling through a stack of comic books he kept inside a drab, cross-barred resin milk crate stationed between them. "My mom was there each time. I'd had to fib the bags were full of paperbacks I'd 'gotten in trade' with snacks for with Chad. She didn't think anything of it, coming from a 23-year-old man child who still wears He-Man and Inspector Gadget t-shirts. I hate lying to my parents, but when the needs must..."

"Your ma and her prejudice against chainsaws," Jason joshed, nearly spritzing the Sunny D he'd been chugging out the corner of his mouth, feeling better and less culpable than he had moments ago. Nonetheless, he clamped his hand over his lips before he spewed all over Rob and his comic collection. "Mine's never recovered from that head exploding bit in *Scanners,* but dude, we're almost able to fly the coop. This censor shit's for the birds."

"So's trying to get your own apartment at age eighteen, ask my cousin Beatrice," Rob said glumly. "I mean, I don't even have a job yet, Jason. I'm not going anywhere exciting beyond the toilet and my parents' fridge."

"Heh," Jason chuckled, running his hands up and down the femoris and vastus muscles beneath his jeans like a nervous tic. Or like he was subconsciously giving himself a massage.

"I think this film and *Make Them Die Slowly* might be my threshold," Rob groaned, getting up from the sofa to pull down a record from his shelf across the way. Deep Purple's *In Rock* album. He dropped the unsheathed vinyl platter onto the turntable and set the needle into motion against the grooves of the 33-rpm spinning platter before flumping back onto the couch.

"*The Land Before Time* is what gives me the heaves," Jason said in a stiller though sarcastic voice. This while plunking his knees in a frenzied rhythm matching the one-handed southpaw double strike rolls of Deep Purple drummer, Ian Paice. Rob's room was packed with a percussive bluster, even with the volume on his stereo turned down to three after his mother had come in an hour ago telling him to turn down the "racket," as she'd called it. The boys began bobbing their heads, then accelerating their hair-flopping neck snaps in time with "Speed King."

"We're lucky my dad recorded all of *North and South,* much less talking my mom into watching it again," Rob said, pausing from the head flailing. "The only reason she even agreed is my dad took the time to hit pause on every commercial break while taping it."

"Now that's dedication."

"Plus, she has googly eyes for Swayze."

"All the chicks do," Jason said with a sour expression someone might show in the presence of an opened slab of limburger cheese. "Him *and* Cruise, those pretty boys. The rest of us peons don't measure up."

They crooned together along with singer Ian Gillan as guitarist Ritchie Blackmore hijacked the stereo speakers with the song's titanic riff. Even at reduced decibels, the cloth over the woofer vibrated.

"Dork," Jason teased his friend.

"Space cadet," Rob sent right back before laughing. He pulled out a *Flash* comic book from the milk crate.

"Cloverland," Jason said warily, tracing his finger along the bottom of the crate's embossed logo. "I believe I've seen one of *these* before. My employers at Super Thrift may press charges if they find this."

"Dude, I spotted it all the way on the other end of the shopping center, near Ames," Rob said in protest. "The only thing they have constituting food is Halloween candy and those nauseating fruit cakes at Christmastime. Ames doesn't sell milk, I assure you. Besides, even my dad said, 'finders keepers,' before you go trying to nark on me."

"I never took your old man for an enabler," Jason sassed, glancing over at Rob's alarm clock, which reflected 11:43 in glimmering red digits. "Seventeen minutes until *Headbangers Ball*, man."

"Sponsored these days by Revlon and Aqua Net," Rob joked.

"Riot," Jason said, cracking up. It felt tremendous to laugh right now, Jason mused. He was glad he'd let Rob talk him into staying the night after the shit show of a day spent with his father. "Rocky Horror's infiltrated heavy metal."

"So, what do you figure our chances are people will stop riding our asses at school this year?" Rob posited, dropping his *Flash* comic back into the crate.

"About as likely as *Headbangers Ball* showing a Carcass, Possessed or Dark Angel video. Or another *Star Wars* movie. Or Wendy's coming up with something to beat a Whopper or a Big Mac. Rap may take over the world one day, though. I'm kinda scared about that."

"Ian Paice may be out of a job with drum machines getting so popular," Rob lamented. "Can you imagine music without real drums, much less guitars?"

"Not one I want to be part of," Jason said with a mock sagging of his face which shifted to pensive. "I don't want to be out of step with the world once I'm able to buy a guitar. Ma won't hear of it until I buy my own wheels first, but it's happening. Watch me."

"Hear, hear," Rob said with a sharp nod.

"I hope to sock enough money from Super Thrift to get a Gibson Marauder by the end of the year," Jason stated, throwing his left hand into the air and dancing his fingers as if noodling along a fretboard. He dropped his right hand near his waist, making strumming motions. "It has a sweet blend control between the neck and bridge pickups. Bud Curry has a brown Marauder in his music shop, and I hear he's giving lessons."

"No kidding," Rob said back. "I thought his gig was Harley Davidson along with selling us bad albums."

"Still pissed about those Pantera *Metal Magic* and *Projects in the Jungle* albums he talked you into buying?"

"Pawned them, is more like it," Rob groused. "Like that band'll go anywhere."

The stylus on Rob's turntable had already breezed through "Bloodsucker" and neither of them noticed "Child in Time's" arrival on Side A of *In Rock* until the effervescent organs of Jon Lord caught their attention.

"In answer to your earlier question, Rob, no I don't think our peers at Merriweather High will ever accept us, not even if we come in wearing slate colored Cotler suits with double reverse pleats and a lime-colored button down. Ick, did that really come out of *my* mouth?"

"In that getup, we'd still get harassed. Don Johnson's run his course."

"So has everyone's bullshit. I don't care if the Populars, the princesses, and the jocks ever like us, but this bullying business going all the way back to freshman year when we came to school wearing Mercyful Fate shirts? Rob, my friend, that is all going to stop. At whatever cost."

"Just wait until they see our Senior photos," Rob objected. "Headbangers in suits, just wait for the crucifixions to commence. I'm pretty sure my tie's crooked."

"My hair was all frizzy in mine, I just know it," Jason said, looking all around the busy walls of Rob's bedroom to deflect. "I half-walked, half-ran from work lugging my dad's old suit over my back to get to the photo shoot at school, and I looked it. I was sweatier than Gene Simmons' codpiece."

"Foul," Rob returned with a snicker, unlodging a piece of phlegm he promptly swallowed back down. Rob never saw the crinkling of Jason's face. "*My* dad's suit fit him in 1975 much better than it did me. It was hanging all loose down my shoulders. Would've been even more catastrophic if I hadn't buttoned it. I'll never do a hand-me-down again."

"They can vote us Scags Least Likely to Succeed for the yearbook."

Rob busted out laughing prior to saying, "I give it five more minutes."

"Give what five minutes?" Jason questioned. "There's only four until the *Ball*."

"Until my parents call this a wrap and send you home. Dad's making his famous blueberry pancakes for breakfast. You don't want to miss out on those."

"What's so special about them?"

"He was an army cook," Rob responded without the reciprocal hilarity. "You make it to the morning here, you'll never ask that again."

"Your words to God's ears," Jason said.

"And whatever God did with our summer, I'd like to register a complaint," Rob said, splaying his hands out for dramatic purposes. "Gone way too fast."

"First person to call either of us 'Satanicus' this year's gonna get decked," Jason vowed amidst Ian Gillan's hypnotic woolgathering. He stood up in his spot as Rob cringed to find Jason's zipper undone.

"XYZ, man!" Rob chided him, covering his eyes.

"It was a hell of a piss, what can I say?" Jason said with lewd grin, tugging his fly back up.

It was 11:58, two minutes to midnight. It wasn't Iron Maiden but Deep Purple taking the boys into the new Sunday and a new episode of *Headbangers Ball*. Ian Gillan's enthralled chanting was joined by the lesser-abled warbling of Jason and Rob.

Chapter 4

"WELCOME TO YEAR FOUR of this shit parade," Rob scorned, snapping his head forward then backwards to fan his still-drying hair away from his cheeks. He could smell the strawberry-scented Herbal Essence shampoo he'd nicked from his mom, since he'd run out of Prell two days ago. The extent of his strands whipped across his shoulders then settled behind his neck. The shark tooth pendant shimmied beneath his left earlobe, looking as nervous as he felt. Judging by the condemnatory stares coming his way inside Merriweather High School, he had reason to be on edge.

"Gag me," Jason groaned back.

The boys trudged more than walked down the corridors of the east wing of Merriweather High. Their identical, once-white Nike high tops scuffed the carpet in the English studies section. Most of their peers came to the first day of the new school year in choice new sneakers. Despite the deterioration of the boys' unreplaced shoes, the soles squeaked along the linoleum of the main floor corridor. They clacked with each step from the scores of pinned band buttons raining down their respective denim vests. Their "armor," as Jason had dubbed their torso scheme a couple years ago. The only thing that might've been considered primping for their first day of Senior Year, Jason and Rob wore clean Levi's jeans devoid of their usual splits at the knees.

"Preppie army: *march!* Rank and file," Rob said like an armistice drill sergeant grown bored with his robotic regiment.

Most of the juniors and seniors were dressed to impress on day one in their Jordache and Sasson acid wash pants, Ralph Lauren polos, pastel crewnecks and in the case of the nouveau riche progeny, tweed blazers. A striped pattern in anything, any brand, dictated the norm. Jason and Rob counted aloud the number of girls wearing banded, collared long sleeves with the Coca-Cola imprint swooshed across their abdomens. Not even five minutes at school, they were up to four.

Rob swung his shoulder out of the way of Jeannie Keys, the

school's All-County volleyball captain. By an athlete's prerogative, Jeannie was clad in a frumpy crimson Merriweather High sweatshirt, swathed atop her gray, thigh-hugging sweatpants. Her Puma sneakers glowed more than the veneer of her swishing, ash blonde ponytail. She'd made no effort to give ground as she barreled in their direction, gnashing the word "grits" at the boys in passing.

"Oh, no, excuse *me*," Rob sniped at Jeannie as she bulled by without retort.

"I hope that self-entitled jockette clotheslines herself over the net this year," Jason murmured. "Or breaks her ankle leading the next pep rally."

"One more year and we're out of this Banana Republic," Rob said, lining back to Jason's side.

Entering the fray of teenagers clustered in the school's promenade circling the administrative offices, auditorium, bathrooms and the entrance to the cafeteria, Rob and Jason kept their hands plugged inside their pockets and their heads upright, looking at no one in passing.

Even after the two-and-a-half-month summer break, there was the usual omnipresent aroma of bleach and disinfectant smacking down the suspect clog of grease from the cafeteria. It was like an entire decade's worth of fish sticks, tater tots, corn, and pizza boats haunted the lunchroom.

Those who were friends moved like there wouldn't be a Homeroom bell coming in the next ten minutes, much less ever. They idled shoulder-to-shoulder, making it difficult to slip around them. By contrast, some kids moved briskly, lapping everyone as if hall roaming had become a new fad sport.

"Like *Dawn of the Dead* in here, John Waters version," Rob said as the boys slowed down coming upon a pack of shuffle-stepping girls. From behind, the shocked and teased auburn perms upon the girls were not only identical; they could've passed for quintet sisters. Their denim-hugged butts wiggled from side-to-side with such verve they'd drawn horndog stares from guys everywhere. The supple, spicy vision was floundered by an unappealing reek of menthol permeating the choke of amber, musk, and honey following their every step. It was evident they'd shared a pack of Newports before school, then passed around a bottle of Poison perfume in the futile attempt to hide it.

The morning chatter was higher than normal with socialites and longtime buddies catching up one another's summer breaks. There was always a loud buzz the first day; much less the first week at Merriweather High, as there was the expected scurry of unsure and terrified freshmen, clutching their yet-to-be-used Trapper Keeper binders for dear life, lest they tumble out of their shaky grasps. Most were dressed like they were going to church instead of school, but without ties and leather patent shoes. They all carried that revealing tail spun look, no longer rulers of their preceding domain in middle school.

A dweeby looking freshman in gold wire framed glasses, khaki-colored slacks, a pine green button-down and docksiders that seemed too big for his already ungainly posture, had somehow mustered up the courage to ask Brad Stone, of all people, for directions. Now in his fourth year as snap center for the Merriweather varsity football squad, Brad was a hulking presence without his letterman jacket. With it strapped to him as tightly as his flat top buzz cut, Brad looked like a red-blazed trooper.

"Oh, good God, kid," Rob said in a hopeless tone as the boys swung around the group of girls, who had risen their nattering to an annoying group cackle. "You *would* pick the gridiron Gestapo to ask for directions."

Jason let out a boisterous laugh that startled the girls they passed.

They could hear the following exchange coming upon Brad and the noob arrival:

"Excuse me, could you tell me how to get to the southwest wing? Room 127?"

"Well, hey there, bud," Brad chirped, as friendly as anyone who didn't know him could sound. "You turn right down there, okay? Go down past the band room, which you can't miss. Hook another right to the rear stairwell. Go down one flight, take a left. Then another left. *One more* afterwards. You got all that?"

Jason kept laughing as they strolled by the trophy case stuffed with gold and silver championship statues, more for tennis, track, volleyball, wrestling, and field hockey than for football, basketball, or baseball. Rob stuck his tongue out at his own reflection in the glass.

"They should've told that nerd in orientation, never trust a lineman," Jason said. "Have fun finding your way through the boiler room, kid."

"Onnnne, twoooo, Freddy's coming forrrrr youuuu...." Rob sang off-key, coughing over the final note.

"Stick to the jokes, Rob."

"Outta the way, fuck nuts!" the boys heard as Brad Stone bulldozed his way between them. Having been used to keeping opposing defensive players off his quarterback, both Jason and Rob staggered from his shove like a human bowling ball taking out the seven and eight pin for a spare.

A few steps ahead of them now, Brad spun around and jerked both of his hands up to the sides of his face. He threw what was supposed to be mock horns-up gestures, but he'd erroneously put three fingers out on each hand instead of only the forefingers and pinkies. Unwitting, Brad was throwing them the universal hand signal for "I love you."

"Hail, Satan, ape drapes!" Brad hollered.

"Tuck the thumbs down unless you want the whole school thinking you wanna bone us in the guys' room, dumbass," Jason fired back.

"The fuck you say, dick wad?" Brad bellowed, stopping in place and lurching for Jason.

By sheer luck, Jason not only missed Brad's considerable paw, which merely grazed the bottom hem of his clickety denim vest, he'd been given a reprieve with the sudden appearance of Vice Principal Paul Newton.

If Brad was a hulk, Vice Principal Newton was his senior juggernaut. Newton, a former All State safety for Merriweather High back in 1965, dwarfed Brad. Those who'd seen Newton play for the school back then marveled how a defensive end could sprint like he did. Vice Principal Newton could still blaze the school's track today, as students often testified seeing him glide round and round after-hours, even with the globby paunch foiling the administrator's waistline.

"Mr. Stone," Newton said in a voice far calmer than he appeared. His eyebrows were ruffled and if one caught it quick enough, he'd crunched his open right hand into a fist before releasing it just as fast. The knuckles cracked gruesomely in response.

"H-hi, Mr. Newton," Brad spluttered. Considering his bravado a moment ago, he looked downright hindered.

"Boys," Newton said, acknowledging Rob and Jason.

"Sir," they responded together.

Vice Principal Newton engaged Brad further by bringing up the school's first game against one of their many state archrivals, Taylor Tech. Newton deliberately put himself between all three of them, and Rob and Jason took the silent cue to slip away. They nearly crashed into the same five girls they'd passed moments ago.

"Pardon us," Rob said to them.

"Get a clue, jerkos," one of the girls called out to them. "And haircuts while you're at it!"

"Get *bent*," Jason growled at a volume only he and Rob could hear.

"Suicidal move calling out Brad Stone, dude," Rob said when they were away from the scene. "If Newton hadn't shown up..."

"Fuck Brad Stone and fuck those prefab elitists. Fuck this school. Graduation can't come soon enough."

"We still have 179 days after this one, Jason. Right now, I'm only counting down to Christmas break."

"Ahh, shaddap," Jason fired back impatiently. To himself but no lower in volume, he muttered, "Watch for the stray bullets."

"Say what?" Rob asked, looking at Jason as if his friend had pulled a hit off a spliff laced with cocaine. Jason kept a deliberate gaze forward and he moved his lips without giving air to whatever he was thinking this time.

They said nothing for a few moments, pulling their hands out of their pockets as they ascended the main stairwell up to the second floor. The scene was more of the same as the promenade, only thicker and slower. Kids were bunched into a corner on the central landing between the two sets of stairs like they owned the spot. In the case of Eric Aldrich and Sally Stephens, they were making out in plain sight, oblivious to the hoots and catcalls around them.

"Hmm, didn't know those two were an item," Rob said, breaking their momentary silence. "Summer lovin', had them a blast."

"Whatever," Jason grumbled. If anyone but Rob had bothered to take note of Jason turtling himself into his heavy metal shell, they'd see he was on the verge of popping.

On the second floor, things seemed even louder than downstairs. This being the northeast wing of the school and their designated senior homeroom area, the din of students was enough to fill the school stadium on their own.

A brand-new year, but some things never changed. Guys were slamming one another into the lockers and yowling like lunatics with pretend bloodthirst, giggling at themselves in congratulatory fashion at the ruckus they stirred. Carl Bovill plowed Matt Larson into the orange-colored lockers, leaving a gaping dent in their wake. They looked outrageously pleased with themselves as they hustled off before anyone could bust them.

"Oh, Christ," Rob said with dread as they passed the smashed-in locker to find a new commotion developing.

"Leave him alone, you bastards," Jason sighed. "You've done enough damage."

His black eye now yellow-purple, Greg Boedecker was alone, without his punk friends to back him up. Greg was surrounded by a sea of corduroy blue jackets encasing some of the beefier members of the school's Future Farmers of America. At the center of the farmer mob was Sam Shaffer, a red, paisley pattern bandana half-dangling from his right rear pocket. From the left side, a chain belched outwards and dangled down Sam's hip, affixed to a bulky, zippered leather wallet. His oily brown hair looked like it been washed in Quaker State, if washed at all.

"I let you off *easy* last week, shit breath," Sam snarled as other passersby stalled to see the developments, a crazed sparkle flashing inside their collective eyes. The first day of school and already some drama to chew on and circulate through the day's final bell at 2:40 p.m.

There were four other male Future Farmers of America: the Metcalf brothers, Lee and Billy, Butch Hill, and Steve Fick. Billy was half the size of his husky brother, but they were easily pegged as siblings with their indistinguishable tan hair dripping beneath their earlobes. They both also carried the same browned, crooked teeth. Butch Hill could give Lee Metcalf a run for his money in the size department, yet he was slower and dumber. People tried to talk Butch into joining the wrestling team, yet he never could get rid of the pooch around his midsection, now in his fifth year at Merriweather High. Butch being a repeat customer as a sophomore.

Steve Fick was the leanest of the bunch and a good scrapper when pushed into a brawl. He was usually the last to join in, save for Sam Shaffer himself, who, most people witnessed getting his licks in after the rest of his gang had first cleaned house.

As always, the ginger haired Emily Haney accompanied them and judging by the way she was scratching Lee Metcalf's mountainous shoulders, they'd opened an FFA romance over the summer. She might have been slight in the chest the first three years of school, but it appeared she'd been visited by the boob fairy over the summer break. She'd also lost most of the freckles she'd carried for much of her life, now only wearing a sneeze of brown dots across her nose. It gave her character, even if most people despised her for being latched to a bully crew. Rolling with another crowd and wiping away her omnipresent sneer, Emily might've been able to transition into the ranks of the Populars.

The backs of the males created a semicircular wall that nearly cut off Greg Boedecker from view. Their baggy, field-stained dungarees sagged instead of hugged their wide, flat butts. Only the circular shape of Skoal chew tins jammed into a couple of their back pockets gave any impression their asses even existed. By contrast, Emily's Levis were yanked up so tight anyone could detect the outline of her underwear through the form-fitting denim. The vernacular of the day would call that "VPL," as in "visible panty line."

"Geez, Greg, say it ain't so," Jason said, as if news of an impending nuclear drubbing by the Soviets was on its way across the Pacific.

Greg was wearing a bright yellow Izod polo shirt, so new and so luminous the left breast gator imprint glowed like it was basking in an all-encompassing sun. He'd traded his customary black jeans for beige slacks. His signature combat boots, which had been passed to him by his grandfather who'd fought in the Korean War, had been stowed to a deserved resting place back home. Replacing them on Greg's feet were a pair of brown, corded docksiders. His mohawk was still apparent, but he'd made no recent attempt to shave down the sides of his head. Just that fast since Jason had last seen him, there was an easy inch of growth where bare skin had once been prominent.

"He's gone conformist," Rob said with a slack in his jaw.

"You're hot shit with a gang behind you," Greg mustered, attempting to sound stoic, but it was evident, alone against a pack of blue wolves, he was scared out of his mind. It had been nonetheless enough of a ballsy burn to summon a rousing "Ooohhhhhh" from those gathered around the escalating conflict.

"You wanna say that again, dildo?" Sam bellowed. His palm jettisoned so fast nobody knew what had happened until they saw it crack upon the left side of Greg's prickly head, and his neck snap toward the right in response.

"Where's Greg's crew?" Jason pondered at a downturned pitch.

"Should we back him up?" Rob asked, knowing how ridiculous he sounded.

Emily Haney had heard their voices more than what they'd been saying. She detached herself from Lee Metcalf as Sam Shaffer whacked Greg Boedecker upside the head again.

To his credit, Greg stayed on his feet, and the glare in his eyes advertised a fury which quickly dissipated with the despairing arrival of Lori Phillips. Lori was strapped in fishnet leggings, black shorts, and thin, lacy gloves flowering at her wrists. Her Mission of Burma tee was a size too large, but she suspiciously lacked a bra beneath as her chest rolled all about with each cautious step she took. Jiggling at her neckline was a small padlock clipped to a cheap chain. Her junk jewelry sagged out of the tangles of her chocolate-brown mop.

Lori skulked around the farmer posse and shrank altogether from Emily Haney, who flinched on purpose toward her in a mock attack. As a known cohort, Lori gave Greg a glance anyone could've interpreted as pity as she wormed herself away from the crowd. No interpretation needed for Greg's sunk and done-in look after Lori passed through.

"The hell are *you* gawking at, geeks?"

Emily had turned her attention to Jason and Rob. Only Steve Fick had spun halfway to see who Emily was jawing at before rolling his eyes upwards in dismissal and spiraling back to Greg Boedecker.

"Nothing much," Jason said in defense. "Greg's right, you know."

"Take a hike, metalheads," Emily jeered, sending them a hateful stare. Her darting brown pupils were mascaraed more with venom than L'Oreal, it seemed.

"Go on, motherfucker! I dare you!"

The boisterous challenge Sam Shaffer threw into Greg's face preceded further humiliation as he began jabbing his forefinger against Greg's forehead. Emily spread a sickening grin across her face that unnerved both Rob and Jason before she whipped her middle finger up at them and reassumed her position at Lee Metcalf's back.

A hollow-sounding chime pealed throughout the entire school, the Homeroom bell.

Most of the teenagers skittered off like insects being uncovered by a lifted rock. Steve Fick and Butch Hill sauntered more than raced off, sending Greg Boedecker their fiercest scowls. Lee Metcalf reached down and grabbed himself a good handful of Emily's taut behind before locking his fingers into hers.

"I see you off school property, you're dead," Sam taunted Greg. "I see you and your freak show anywhere on the roads, you're *all* dead."

Sam raised his arm as if he was going to backhand Greg, then let it drop, bumping into Billy Metcalf as he eased back.

"Watch it, homo," Billy jibed, playfully punching Sam in the arm.

"*Dead,*" Sam snarled, pointing at Greg one final time before pivoting and giving Billy Metcalf a return shot with half the starch as what he'd laid upon Greg.

Heaving and trembling in place, Rob and Jason could see Greg's eyes water overtop his flushed cheeks. His fists were balled so tightly his knuckles screamed jolts of white.

"You okay, dude?" Jason asked once everyone else had dispersed.

"*He's* the one who's dead," Greg wisped, flashing Jason and Rob feral articulation inside of his teared-up, flitting eye sockets. "That's a promise."

Chapter 5

"DAY ONE OF SENIOR YEAR at Merriweather High, how would you rate our service?" Rob quipped to Jason. The intent may have sounded funny, but the delivery matched the put out expressions on both teenagers' faces as they plodded through the school parking lot.

"Lookin' good there, ladies, sexy sexy!" they heard behind their backs. This accompanied by babbling, laughter, car doors slamming, engines starting and a lewd whistle blown in their direction.

"Rooooooock ooooooonnnnnn, dudes!" a female voice ridiculed them.

"Yyyyyyoooooowwwwwwwwww!!!" another girl exclaimed, presumably a friend of the other.

The first joker added his own encore:

"You guys must be carrying an extra twenty pounds each with all those stupid buttons! If that's a new weight loss program, it's working like a charm! Jane Fonda, eat your heart out!"

It was Jason who was growing more riled by the step as the boys reached the grassy knoll on the outer section of the parking lot where nobody parked, not even those eager beaver school buses which arrived a half hour ahead of time.

"Don't expect a tip," Jason said to Rob in such a surly voice it made him sound ten years older. He turned his head away from Rob just long enough to utter to the open space to his left and with no rhyme or reason, "Heaven's on fire."

"No, sir, nothing's changed," Rob went on. If he'd heard Jason a second ago, he never showed it. "Pizza Face Kenny McQueen has more cred around here than us. That's a new low."

"All...damn...day..." Jason fumed, accenting each drawn out word from the depths of his molars. He walked in elongated strides, full of steam, as his book bag bounced off his back, the crashes sounding as angry as he felt. Rob had to turn on his own jets to keep up with him.

"Got any favorite class?" Rob asked, knowing it was pointless.

"*No,*" Jason bristled, his hair catching a welcoming breeze. Thanks to a Canadian cold front half a country away, George County was breathing easier at a more seasonable seventy-three degrees.

"I just know I'm gonna kill it in Creative Writing. The teacher, Mr. Morrow, said he'd been there at Woodstock, maybe fifty feet away when Ritchie Havens kicked it all off. The guy's unlike any other teacher I've ever had. He seems to really dig what he does."

"Weightlifting, maybe," Jason said right on Rob's heels, as if he hadn't even heard him. "Jury's still in there. The one time today nobody gave me any crap. Hell, they didn't have to. The jocks never said a word to me, but I can tell. They think I'm a maggot. *How dare* the metalhead invade their turf. Maybe you should transfer to Weightlifting and keep me company, Rob."

"I'll wait until you say if there's hope for us crud balls in Lunk World."

"Yeah, sure," Jason said as a Ford Bronco slowed within reach of them and honked.

"Ugh," Rob groaned as the sight of a blubbery bare ass pushed its way out the passenger side of the Bronco at them. "Get a life, bubble butt."

"Eat shit, fairies!" the driver shouted, as his oversized comrade pulled back inside. He gunned the motor and spun his rear tread in place before tearing away. A posset of smoke reeking of burned rubber followed their wake, leaving with it two black streaks upon the road.

Out of nowhere, a police car sped in chase of them, its blue and red roof lights twinkling ravenously.

"Get 'em, Sheriff Tanner," Rob cheered with anticipation. "Make sure you ticket the other guy for George County's most disgusting glutes."

"I swear to God I'm gonna lose it, Rob! It took everything I had not to launch on someone. Only the first day! If I make it through the rest of Senior Year without popping one of those assholes, it'll be a miracle!"

"Ozzy believes in miracles, Whitney Houston too."

"Rob, be serious."

"Sorry. You gotta find the humor down a bad road sometimes."

"This one ain't all that," Jason growled as the boys reached the sidewalk flanking Route 485, the windy country junction leading right into the central hub of Bradenton.

"Whatever, man," Rob said in defeat. "I tried."

"You have no idea. You didn't know me back in middle school when I lived in Perry Hall."

"*Scary* Hall," you used to call it. "Where you…"

"Right," Jason intervened with an outstretched hand barely avoiding clipping Rob's chin. "I don't wanna go there. Never again, if I can help it, and I'm telling you, dude, it takes everything I have on a daily basis not to let shit get to me, to the point I…well, have a repeat of what went down at Scary Hall Middle."

"I feel it too, Jason," Rob said, keeping pace as Jason was starting to pull away from him again. The agitation radiating off his friend reminded him of himself when his cousin Connie dumped a jar of pickles on him at a family picnic after they'd gotten into a heated argument over the dumbest thing of all, whether John Quincy Adams was the sixth or seventh president of the United States. Rob being correct at sixth and still taking a pickle juice dousing which had clung to him all afternoon. To think of the sweaty reek of it now made him miss half of what Jason had said next.

"…if I hadn't been stopped while turning that kid's face into hamburger, I doubt we would've ever met. It would've been Juvie for me. I rammed that bastard's face into the locker so many times I could've killed him. I kicked the hell out of the other guys who'd been tormenting me at Perry Hall Middle. I nailed one in the face with the toe of my shoe, broke his nose. I can still see that fucker's blood on the floor. Another kid, I clotheslined. The fourth guy ran away, but not before I could snag his hair and yank him until he fell. I just lost control, man. I wanted them all dead. You have no idea what I went through back then."

"Worse than what we get dished at Merriweather High?"

"Funny enough," Jason replied, slowing his antsy stride and giving enough of a pause to face Rob with an earnest expression on his face. "Yeah, it was, no matter how much high school's sucked and the bullshit we've gone through, they're just words, man, when you get down to it. Perry Hall, I got a beatdown every day for the longest time until I started fighting back. It only got worse when I did. Dad, well, he thought I'd been doing drugs since I was in such a funk. He threatened to kill me as if I *was* doing them."

"Hypocrite."

"Yeah," Jason affirmed.

"Heh, check it out," Rob said, pointing at the halted Bronco from earlier, breaking the tension. The cabbed truck was now pulled into the entrance of Sizemore Egg Company with Sheriff Tanner standing outside, going over identification and registration. The one who'd mooned Rob and Jason looked downright mortified as they passed by.

With the sheriff's back turned, both Jason and Rob glanced at each other and nodded, knowing exactly what the other was thinking. Not a word said between them, both of their right middle fingers went up at the Bronco.

"Justice is served, scags," Rob said.

"I don't want to go through another Perry Hall, Rob," Jason blurted after the Bronco and Sheriff Tanner were behind them. "I feel it coming, though, words being just words. They still fucking hurt, but I'll never be pussy enough to say it to anyone else but you. We don't fit everyone else's script, but something's gotta give, dude. Something's *gonna* give."

Chapter 6

AN EMBITTERED CREASE SHOVED from Rob's lips as Celtic Frost's brand-new album, *Cold Lake* whirled upon his turntable.

"What the living hell, Tom?" he groused to the opposite side of his room where nobody was, unless you counted his Han Solo, Lando Calrissian, and Chewbacca action figures holding guard in front of his cassette tapes actual people. They, along with a paint chipped Luke Skywalker in his Rebel Alliance pilot gear, were holdout souvenirs from age eleven, when *The Empire Strikes Back* ruled his world. "As if I didn't get enough ear pollution today at school."

The Tom in question was Thomas Fischer Gabriel, aka Tom Warrior, leader of the Swiss avant garde metal band which had recently undergone a lineup overhaul since turning the heavy metal underground on its ear for much of the decade with their arcane dirge music. Given the shocking commercial rock tones filling Rob's room, it was a complete purging of their once diabolical sound.

In Rob's lap was a spiral notebook with heavy metal stickers plastered every which way across the front, yielding the band names Virgin Steele, W.A.S.P., Exciter, Armored Saint, Bitch, Grim Reaper, Crimson Glory, Lizzy Borden, and Venom. The latter, Rob had turned upside down on purpose in homage of the band's jokey hails to Satanism. Written in choppy block letters in black magic marker in the only space not occupied by a sticker was "ROB'S MINI ALBUM REVIEWS."

Even the turntable seemed to labor through *Cold Lake's* spotlight single, "Cherry Orchards," which Rob had told Jason "Sounded more ominous than anything on *Morbid Tales*, in the wrong way," when the video premiered on *Headbangers Ball*. Tom Warrior came off like a snide, grating parody of himself in the song, which told anyone beholding such lark he hadn't given a flying fuck what he'd been doing in the recording booth.

Rob tapped a pen against his knee, not to keep rhythm with the music, but in frustration as he said in the direction of his stereo speakers as if they were the ones at fault, "I actually put a deposit down for this shit."

As the stylus on the turntable made its escape of "Cherry Orchards," Rob flipped to one of his prior reviews, singling a few scribbled passages for the 1986 released, self-titled *Vinnie Vincent Invasion*:

"Kiss booted Vinnie Vincent reportedly for playing too fast. The dude scorches like he's trying to get back at Gene and Paul, though the songs sometimes get lost under the weight of Vinnie's ear-raking fret speed."

Then he chuckled at himself for thinking of this zinger: *"Consider the bad idea of torching a solo overtop a would-be ballad, 'No Substitute.' Ain't nobody getting laid to that. Vinnie smothers the intent instead of giving it juice, as if Zeus had been turned down in bed and let his rage be known, Olympus down to Earth."*

The last bit Rob scanned, he'd read for Jason out loud months ago and they'd high-fived over it:

"Robert Fleischman shrieks more than Vinnie's guitars, but hell, I've got a soft spot for this album. Vinnie can cook enough shred stew to make me forget Def Leppard's Hysteria *was ever recorded. Well, maybe."*

With a chunk of blank space left between this review and the next one for Yngwie Malmsteen's *Rising Force*, Rob clicked on his pen and scrawled this addendum: *"Not gonna bother writing up VVI's All Systems Go from this year. Vocalist change to Mark Slaughter is a kinda-sorta boost, but the album's more watered down than Krokus'* Change of Address. *Whatever."*

"Like I'll ever be a music critic," he said to all the horror and metal moguls caught in freeze frame around him. Nonetheless, Rob pictured himself backstage with a laminated pass dangling from his neck, jotting notes at the speed of light on a hand-sized notebook in front of Nikki Sixx of Mötley Crüe or Joey Belladonna of Anthrax. Targeting a mini poster of the latter band splashed overtop his closet door, he halfheartedly declared, "Ehh, it could happen."

Casting his notebook aside, Rob's mind veered from *Cold Lake's* abject misery to more hopeful prospects in the kitchen, knowing he'd left a few gulps worth of Colt Cola inside the fridge.

Outside his bedroom, Rob's mother was tugging armfuls of dirty laundry out of the hallway hamper and depositing the cumbersome wads into a carry basket at her feet. She was wearing a loose-fitting denim jumper overtop one of his dad's Fruit of the Loom white undershirts. She'd rocked an alternating set of shorts the earlier part of summer which she'd owned since Rob was a boy. They'd all gone right into the trash can at the end of August behind her self-chastising edict,

"Quitting smoking's great for the lungs, terrible for my waist and rear end."

Rob could see fatigue bogging her green eyes from behind her charcoal-tinted plastic frame glasses with lenses so wide they covered the upward pushes of her cheeks. Her raven-shocked hair was pulled into a utilitarian ponytail that flopped about with equal exhaustion.

"Ahh, he lives," she joked, playfully swatting Rob on the hip as he scooched past her.

"Maaaaaa," he huffed back with a half grin forced into his usual domestic "too cool" candor. Not that he would ever say it out loud, he liked the attention whenever his mom would pat, rub, or outright hug him in passing.

"Take a shower tonight," she called out to him.

Before he could answer, Rob heard spraying. Even after feeling violated by the first side of *Cold Lake*, his ears were sharp enough to know the spritzy emission was coming from his bedroom.

"Whattya doing, Ma? What the heck?" he pretend-protested with concentration on keeping his language clean. If it had been Jason here and no parents, the vulgarities would be prerequisite. By answer, he could smell the Lysol emission all the way from the kitchen.

Even Rob had to laugh when he heard his mother scold him, "The *funk* in your room, Rob. I pity any girl you try to bring in there."

"As if that'll happen," Rob droned back.

"Maybe start leaving your ratty shoes on the porch a while until they air out, huh?"

"Yeah, alright, Ma," Rob mumbled, already with the refrigerator door open and the near-empty two-liter plastic bottle of Colt Cola teetering to his lips. The leftover soda had long lost its fizz and he vexed in disgust while slugging the watery sugar drink gone.

"And that bad habit has to stop."

Rob jumped in place, feeling as thunderstruck as he no doubt looked. No matter how many times his mother had snuck up on him, even to the point of annoyance, he was in awe of her stealthy prowess.

"Even though it's *you* drinking our soda most of the time, we all share from that," she needled. "Your father and I want nothing to do with your backwash, especially after you've been eating Slim Jims. It's gross, Rob. Seriously. There's another bottle in the basement pantry. Bring it up, but go easy. Your future wife will thank me for this, and a hundred other things."

"*Okay*, Ma," Rob groused with an irritated frown. He closed the refrigerator door gently, but rolled the emptied plastic bottle off his fingertips, sending it midair and clunking into the trash can. He made pretend creepy-crawly twinkling fingers and a mock ghoul's face at his mother's back as she turned toward the stairwell with her laundry basket.

"I saw that," she said without turning around until she was at the bottom of the foyer. She winked at Rob from behind her spectacles as she hooked to descend into the basement.

Trailing much slower behind her with one laggard step down at a time, Rob was greeted by the reverb of a scratchy 45 record playing a fast-moving number from the Fabulous Fifties. The pops and hisses from the decades-old platter were louder than usual coming through the family's Pioneer stereo in the basement. In some ways, Rob was jealous of the Pioneer's pummeling subwoofers in comparison to the meeker Wharfdale Diamond speakers of his unit. Whenever his parents were out, Rob always seized the opportunity to jack his records on the Pioneer, and the bass he got was usually enough to knock upon the venerated doors of Valhalla, he reckoned.

He caught his parents passing each other a smooch on the lam as his mother padded her way to the laundry room with the dirty wash bouncing off her hip. The nip inside the clubbed-in cellar washed over Rob's face and neck. A couple weeks ago with the summer peak, he'd found any excuse to dawdle down here to cool off. Right now, though, it had a bipolar effect. A chill played tag with Rob, spanking the tip of his spine, and sending a tingle straight down. It was pesky instead of pleasurable.

"Quick!" Rob's father shouted, pointing at the Pioneer with a grody dust rag flapping in his paw. He filled his red-blue-green flannel shirt with squared shoulders and a proud, swollen chest he'd never lost from his army years. Around the house, he was known as "The Italian Tank," though he was all but desperate to distance himself from World War II menaces Benito Mussolini, Giovani Messe, and Italo Gariboldi.

Surrounding his dad on the walls flanking the family bar were eight-by-ten pictures of greased and primped icon rockers from the 1950s like Chuck Berry, Jerry Lee Lewis, Buddy Holly, Fats Domino and Wanda Jackson. Included, of course, was the deified Elvis the Pelvis, whose birth and death days were observed with marathons of his asinine musical movies on those bleak and snowy VHF stations no rabbit ear antenna had a chance of clearing. Cable tv had been declared savior of the *true* American pastime.

Rob tried to picture his dad with his own rendition of Presley's slicked up duck's ass do swamped over his neck while cruising around in his teal and white '56 Ford Fairlane Challenger. Funny to imagine the adolescent version of his dad gulping down vanilla shakes and triple-decker burgers known as "Powerhouses" at drive-in restaurants that no longer existed. Even right now, Rob could see his dad drowned in 164 horsepower nostalgia, waxing in silence over his car-dragging days on the legendary Route 40 in the Baltimore outskirts.

From the knee-high-sized Pioneer speakers, a cool cat of the era was philandering with his muse, talking about walking her home after school and carrying her books home too. Everything else beyond a simple courtesy coming by mere suggestion.

"Quick!" Rob's father repeated with a zealous flare inside his dark pupils. "Who's this?"

For a hundred or so Friday nights after dinner in years past, Rob's dad would play his long-kept 45 records, these days called "Oldies." Revolutionary music that had been exiled from FM radio to the static-filled tundra of AM. An hour's worth of Fifties tunes on those fun Fridays before the family settled in for *Dallas*. Rob's dad would play those timeless discs while they all lounged in the living room letting their pre-weekend meal (usually Shake and Bake-crusted pork chops or chicken) settle. Rob's mom hadn't made those in ages and he sort of missed it, even if Fridays had become favorable taco or pizza events.

After enough of these sessions, Rob's dad would quiz him without showing the labels of the 45 record he'd whisk into play with masterful haste. At first, Rob was asked to identify the artist. As Rob got good at the game, his dad made him include the song titles. The musical game stopped once Rob got older. He realized only now how much he'd missed it as well. His brain popped and wheezed in search of information suffocated by countless thrash and power metal recordings since.

Thus, Rob was rusty when his father chirped "Quiiiiiick!" a third time with his family-adored goofball accenting.

"Uhhh, Little Richard?" Rob nudged out in a hurry.

"Ohhhhhh," his father winced. "Pitiful. Just pitiful."

"Wait! Wait!" Rob exclaimed with sudden recognition. "Larry Williams!"

"My man," his father said with an approving fist pump before taking his dust rag along the brass rail encircling the bar.

Proud of himself, Rob scooted down to the pantry room and fetched the lone bottle of Colt Cola from an array of canned fruit and vegetables, bottled juices, soups, spaghetti ingredients, boxes of instant rice, and au gratin potatoes.

Now feeling ornery, Rob stopped at the laundry room and with purposeful emphasis, opened the new soda bottle pointed at his mom's back so she could hear the hiss of the CO_2 release.

"Oh, Rob," she said with a mild startle, taking his bait while pouring All detergent into the washing machine in a circular motion.

Having poured himself a fresh glass of Colt Cola upstairs with a few ice cubes and squeezing into it a smackerel of Hershey's syrup, he closed the door to his room, taking note of his *X-Men and the Micronauts* comic miniseries and a beat-up paperback copy of Robert Howard's *Conan of Cimmeria* he'd set upon his dresser to read for the fourth time each. Those, he would start tackling before night's completion.

Returning the needle to the flipside of *Cold Lake*, Rob took a few slugs of his homemade chocolate soda and licked his lips before pulling the notebook back to his lap. It took him no time to tune out, thinking about the first day of school. He'd been bumped into so many times it began to feel on purpose. A masculine sounding girl had slapped his backpack and called him a "pathetic slob" between fifth and six period changeovers. Another female voice from behind had called Rob's shark tooth earring "tacky." He was too chagrined to turn around and face her.

Then all the haranguing he and Jason had left to their backs in the Merriweather High parking lot. The mooning incident thereafter. Jason was right; enough was enough.

If he had a mirror in his bedroom, Rob might pull his hair as far back as he could, just to see what he would look like. Would everyone get off his case then? Would he finally be accepted after all these years?

A moment of inspiration or surrender, Rob contemplated it for a measly moment as he unhooked the shark tooth from his lobe and let it jiggle between his thumb and forefinger. Then he hurled it in anger across the bedroom.

The earring bounced off a tacked foldout from *Fangoria* magazine depicting the severed head of Pamela Voorhees from *Friday the 13th Part 2*. That part had made him smirk. Where the earring landed, he didn't see, nor did he care. Whether or not he would replace the earring or let the hole in his ear close up would be for another day to decide.

By the time *Cold Lake* had come to near close with the ninth track, "Dance Sleazy," Rob had had enough, already wondering if he'd be able to hock the album back to Bud Curry in trade at the music store.

Having opened an entry for *Cold Lake* in his notebook, Rob wrote two simple words, leaving his thoughts rest on that:

"Total abomination."

Chapter 7

TWO BLOCKS OVER, JASON was drifting around the back yard at his house, lost to his thoughts like his father lost himself most nights to drinking. With that lingering parallel, Jason was still feeling a hangover guilt by taking the beer from the cold-shouldered guy in the flat cap at the auto club meeting over the weekend. For Rob, it had been a fantastic novelty of getting away with underage imbibing. In Jason's case, it was more about getting even with his father than drinking the beer itself. As if his father had bothered looking for him the rest of the afternoon.

In similar fashion, at age nine, Jason once stole a sip of Heineken at a family party when nobody had been watching him. It was eight years ago and Jason could recall the brew tasting far different than Schlitz. Far better. In a way, manlier. Yet the younger Jason hadn't put things together how his father had increasingly cultivated an alcohol addiction. The dawning became apparent later when he was thirteen and Jason's father had called him a pussy, of all things, for getting beat up by two kids at Perry Hall Middle School. One of whom Jason only remembered by his last name, Schneider. That was the one Jason had rammed into the locker countless times, splitting the kid's head open in two places. It had taken the vice principal, as bald and roly-poly as Principal Weatherbee in the Archie comics, to subdue Jason. "They had it coming," was all Jason could say to the school administration and his parents. Jason remembered his father shocking the principal and his pudgy second (actual names were blocked from Jason's memory on purpose) reiterating what his son had said, adding, "If my son hadn't started giving it back to those little pricks, it would've been *me* kicking his ass."

Recounting those days to Rob on the walk home from school left a burning inside of Jason well in the early evening. The day his father had called him *that* had been cast in a stupor, an entire six pack gone as fast as it arrived from Winfield Liquors and left on the kitchen counter like a taunt. Jason's father had crunched the final empty beer can in his son's young face after verbally affronting him.

"The beer that made Milwaukee famous," Jason muttered, reciting the slogan swirled in cursive around the mouth end of a Schlitz can. "*You're* the pussy, Dad."

Jason tipped the barrel of his Daisy air rifle upwards. One of the cooler things his old man had ever done for him, the BB gun had come from his father for his fifteenth birthday. They'd even gone to the woods and taken turns firing it at a paper target his father nailed to a tree. It was a wonderful birthday, one in which his mom gave him a vinyl copy of the *Escape From New York* soundtrack and ended at Gino's for dinner. Jason had pounded not one, but two patty-stacked Gino Giants. The Giant tasted like, but was far superior, in Jason's opinion, to the Big Mac. He'd been too full to eat more than half of one of the strawberry turnovers his mom had made for his birthday dessert, but he'd had four to gnaw on the remainder of the week. It was Jason's favorite birthday to-date, and it had never crossed his mind back then his dad would be leaving in less than two years.

Swimming through Jason's run amok concerns was the pining echoes of Metallica's somber ballad, "Fade to Black."

"Life, it seems, will fade away," he whisper-sang, scanning the brushy poplars in the yard, calling to mind another family gathering just a year ago. This time, Jason had stuck to birch beer instead of pinching the adult variety. To think about it now, he never saw the signs of what was to come. The only thing which had perturbed more than alarmed him that day was his Aunt Bonnie asking Jason in sardonic fashion before the rest of the family if he was cross-dresser at night because of his long hair. His Aunt Bonnie, on his father's side, always had some snarky thing to say, usually at the expense of his dad's beloved Miami Dolphins.

Jason's mother and father seemed happy then with his aunts (the kinder ones being on his mother's side), uncles and cousins chattering, laughing, eating grilled chicken and burgers, crunching on potato chips and guzzling beer, iced tea or soda, depending on propensity. As the youngest of four in the family, his mom's brother, Uncle Larry, had infamously brought a paper bag of Molson singles with him despite an ice chest's worth of Budweiser and Schlitz already provided. Uncle Larry pounded his stash without shame before taking down an equal number of Buds. Larry's wife, Aunt Peg, had ripped him a new one as she steered his woozy, belching self out of Jason's family's fenced-in back yard, threatening to leave him for the umpteenth of many times. It seemed alcoholism ran rampant in both families on the male end.

Jason remembered his father patting his mom's butt in the open, for all to see, like she was more his trophy than his wife. He'd missed the fire in her eyes she'd later told him about, this after his father bailed on them.

In public, Jason had caught many a man ogling his mother, Uncle Larry being one of the biggest offenders. Weird to ponder it considering she was his mother, Jason had to concede her wavy flaxen hair rivaled Suzanne Somers, and her similar fondness for turtleneck sweaters and form-fitting cotton slacks complimented her figure to nearly the same effect as Somers, one the hottest women on the planet.

Before the divorce, Jason's mom had been beautiful in her own right, aged thirty-three, five-foot-two, and carrying a complimentary 122 pounds. She'd been considered a spitfire. She could and *did* go toe-to-toe against his father when he'd tie one on as bad or worse than Uncle Larry. Not one to put on a game of grab ass for spectacle, the Pamela Hamlin of the past would've dragged his dad by the wrist out of view and teed off on him behind closed doors. Hardly what that horndog country crooner Charlie Rich had in mind.

Finding out her husband, Casey, had a Philippine piece on the side had taken all the fight out of Jason's mom. His dad had thrown on the devil's smile all afternoon during that final family picnic and only just now could Jason see the disguised sadness behind his mother's artificial beaming. If she'd already known his father had been cheating on her, she'd sold an act the Jesus freaks would've sung psalms and praises over.

Right now, there was no disguising her whipped, hangdog slouching and a tired sullenness dripping from her cheekbones down to her waistline. She looked both soggy and defeated.

His father had done this to her, whittled her down, as often as he'd done the same to Jason himself. What he'd said during the Perry Hall years, what he'd said even this past Saturday at the auto club meeting…there was something far worse, less Harlequin romance novel-ish than the word "heartbreaking," but Jason couldn't come up with anything. Heartbreaking had to do, because heartbroken is how Jason felt.

Betrayed. *That* was the word he wanted, yes. His father had betrayed him. Betrayed Jason and his mother and left them in this two level split foyer not much different than Rob's house, save for beige versus sky blue siding and pine shutters instead of maroon at his friend's place.

"Drifting further every day," Jason went on from the first verse of Metallica's sullen tune while lowering the rifle barrel down to a horizontal level. "Getting lost within myself…"

A half hour ago, he'd been on the phone with his dad. It was the first weekday night Jason had off from Super Thrift in the past two weeks. This had come at his mother's insistence for the opening day of school. She meant well despite the fact she'd been sleeping more than hanging out in the living room these days. Yet Jason would rather be working than idling right now. Other than being broken into his senior year by verbal harassment from his peers (so much that Jason's litany of "metalhead" and "headbanger" had become hateful to his own ears), there hadn't been much reason to have requested the day off from work.

Not when he had both a future car and a guitar burning on his mind.

Especially not when being home tonight meant being within aural reach of his father, who'd called up asking for him. He'd bypassed Jason's mom as if she'd never held a place in his life other than to spit out a child between them.

She'd made a feeble, self-deprecating joke to her ex-husband, comparing herself to dog meat before handing Jason the phone receiver. A pale shade of the proud scrapper she'd once been. Her eyes were drowning as she'd passed Jason the phone. There was no hypothetical life preserver Jason could give his mother beyond a compassionate rub on her arm before she whirled away and disappeared to her bedroom. Any other time, the lithe spin of her snowy hair would've looked extravagant.

"I 'ave one question fer ya, kid," Jason's dad had sloshed from his end of the phone line. He sounded so goddamned *drunk* it was alarming coming at the premature evening time of 7:22 p.m. Jason's trashed progenitor didn't give him a chance to respond before he'd nudged out, "Are ya sure you ain't doin' drugs, boy?"

"What?!?" Jason exclaimed, stunned by the return accusation, so much he forgot watching his mouth. "Not this shit again!"

"You loo' li' ya fuggin' high ever' time I see ya, so 'splain *that*, huh? You an' tha other longhair fool ya hang out with…"

"I don't know where you're getting that impression!" Jason had pleaded in sudden retreat. It was if the mere sound of his father's voice, trashed or not, held such power over him it gave him empathy for his mother's teary squirreling.

"Ah fuggin' kill ya if you're doin' drugs, I mean it, boy!" his father had bellowed into his ear. Jason was so upset he plunged the call disconnect lever on the mounted phone holder, but not before he heard, "Ya hear me? Ah fuggin' killll youuuuuu…"

He lined the Daisy barrel, silently ordering the sudden wobble in his left hand cradling the bottom of the stock to get with the program and steady itself.

Jason didn't even feel the trigger pull after lining up his target with a squint he likewise hardly noticed. Only the *chuff!* sound next to his cheek signaled he'd fired the gun.

The jettisoned BB missed its target and plunked off the wooden fence marking the edge of the property. The fence had long been neglected, in desperate need of a new stain coating. Neglected, like Jason's mother, he mused. Neglected, like Jason himself.

"Nothing matters, no one else," he sang on, now beading his sight upon his target propped on the picnic table approximately fifty feet away. The picnic table, wooden, likewise in a shoddy state.

Neglected.

This time, Jason had his focus. From this far, one wouldn't be able to tell exactly what he was shooting at, but what it was gave Jason stronger resolve. It was a framed picture of Jason and his dad, each holding catfish on dangled fishing lines. Jason was dressed in his long-ago Cub Scout uniform. He'd made a sarcastic retching noise fetching the picture from his dresser and seeing a former version of himself in navy blue digs and a gaudy yellow bandana neatly tied around his neck. He'd just earned his Bear patch in that picture.

The dads all came on that Bear ceremony trip. The dads taught their sons how to fish, then to skin and grill their catches. The dads later told dirty jokes around a campfire while the boys smothered their laughs trying to sleep in their tents. Jason's dad had farted twice in the middle of the night and most of the boys cracked up like tickled hyenas, unable to contain themselves, much less sleep. The Scoutmaster, Mr. Kilgore, tried to be authoritative, but no one took him seriously through his own laughter. It was after the farting and the laughing when the beer cans popped, and the dads sighed between their slugs like it was all they'd been thinking about throughout the day while coaching their sons. The latter fact only just now occurred to Jason all these years later.

"Pathetic," he groaned, keeping the Daisy trained on the framed picture.

Scouts were for wimps the older you got, and before he'd reached Webelos eligibility, Jason dropped out. That kid no longer existed and now Jason was here with his demolished shell of a mom who'd put on eight pounds of weight despite her propensity toward anti-eating benders. She'd worried Jason so much he'd nuked a pepperoni Hot Pocket the past Saturday and forced her to eat it before she'd slipped off to bed at the ungodly weekend hour of 8:07 p.m.

Echoes of his father's garbled threats over the phone mingled with jeers sent in callous manner at him all day long at school, affixed with slighting parlance such as "grit," "slob," "denim fairy," and "the devil's butt buddy." Between periods four and five, Jason heard some feathery haired underclassman girl wearing a unisex green, blue, and white blended Izod long sleeve call him a "longhaired menace." For no apparent reason, and of course, she'd waited until she cut a corner away from him to say it.

He pulled the trigger again.

This time Jason struck true. A small explosion of glass told him so. The picture itself, punctured, floated to the grass away from the picnic table.

"I have lost the will to live," Jason continued his singing, "simply nothing more to give..."

The commotion roused a squirrel from its perch on one of two oaks in the furthest reach of the yard. It hopped off the tree and bounced a few times in the open field. Almost as a dare.

Jason stopped his singing and swung the barrel to the squirrel.

Its tail swished and fluttered a few times as Jason felt his trigger finger quiver with anxiety and indecision.

Finally sensing the threat from afar, the squirrel spread its paws out defensively, splashing across the ground like a gray, furry mini mat, glancing indecisively in Jason's direction.

His teeth gnashing with the more recent recollection of being called a retard by his own father at the car club event, Jason nearly squeezed the trigger back all the way.

"Go on, dude," he panted at the squirrel, easing off and lifting the barrel upwards again. "Get outta here."

As if the squirrel understood him without question, it bounced and skittered across the yard, leaping onto another tree and scratching its way into the dwindling foliage of the upper branches.

Jason never noticed his mother watching him from the glass door behind the patio as the tears seized him.

Chapter 8

DAY TWO, JASON AND ROB took the steps leading to the patio outside Merriweather High's cafeteria. The parking lot was stirring with young blood, some animated, others skulking and drooping their heads as if sensing a pop quiz coming this early into the new school year.

Megan Lucas and her preppie friends seemed to float out of her four-door Ford Fairmont, all closing the doors in tandem. To Rob, the succession out of Megan's car looked rhythmical. Jason negated the scene with less appreciation by sticking his finger into his mouth in a pretend puke-inducing gesture.

After this would-be monumental arrival, Jason fell into his world, or he would've seen bodybuilder Chris Majors emerge from his gleaming yellow '69 Camaro SS 396 with its twin black piping down the hood. Chris was such a massive, shredded piece of oak he'd been bestowed the nickname "Schwarzemajors" around school. Even some of the faculty had taken to using the sobriquet with all respect intended. As an eye candy senior, Chris Majors and his immense, muscular presence would be missed after Graduation. Rob had heard this proclaimed many times yesterday from the mouths of both sexes.

Chris was scarfed up by a few of the gearheads who came to school for the first half of the day, then offsite to the Eastern Vo Tech. Or, if they were skilled enough already, to an actual mechanic's job after lunch. They swarmed Schwarzemajors like paparazzi to his action hero namesake, verbally compelling Chris to back up (since not even the four of them would be enough to bodily move him) and pop the hood of his Camaro so they could all geek at his H.P. Often carrying a severe, focused look throughout his towering high school career, it was the rare opportunity to catch Schwarzemajors beaming.

In front of Jason and Rob were Duane Bullock and Marcia Sosa from the school marching band, each lugging their cased tubas. In their band uniforms, they looked larger than they really were. In their street clothes, their instruments showcased how average they were, if at least strong enough to wrap monster brass horns around their lean bodies.

Whisking past all of them, Stan Rogan wove and cut wide berths on his way toward the patio steps. He did so with his shoulders squared and his leveled arms swinging in acute interchanges. Having already committed himself to the Marines after Graduation, Stan was taking his future role serious to the point he'd begun wearing bulky camouflage pants every day since the end of junior year. Stan's gung-ho accouterments included steel shank boots and alternating red and olive plain short sleeve shirts tucked into his pants, which he buckled tight enough to heap a hint of a pudge over his waistline. Stan had even gone so far as to cop his father's red beret.

"Nobody told Stan a red beret is *Army*, sheesh," Rob mocked. "Get a clue, G.I. Joe."

On the patio were more of Jason and Rob's senior classmates, chawing and laughing while blowing smoke rings from their lit cigarettes and poking their forefingers through the holes, following those with the expected carnal gibes.

"The school governors are such frauds," Rob commented as he waved a tobacco fog away from his face. "This is the only designated smoking area on the premises. For teenagers, anyway."

"For *seniors*, get it right," Jason drudged, coming out of his momentary reverie. "Underclassmen can take a hike."

"To think we waited three long years for our turn to take over the Senior Patio. All this damn smoke, why did we all want it so bad?"

"Never mind half the faculty do it in the teacher's lounge. Hell, dude, I've even smelled weed all over Miss Batang coming out of the girls' room in the northeast wing last year. Tried to blame it on the sulfur from the chemistry room when I looked at her funny. They think because we're not yet voting age we're dumber than dirt."

Many of the kids on the patio—smoking and non—were wearing Mötley Crüe *Girls Girls Girls* tour shirts, the same trendy bunch led by party legend and reputed porn addict Jake Flanagan. Jake and his horde had paraded concert shirts for Tears for Fears' *Songs from the Big Chair* tour a few years ago, U2's run for *The Joshua Tree* after that. Often, they coordinated their concert tees for the same day, earning them the brand (from the Populars, no less) the "Cooler Than Thou Brigade."

It was Jake who'd been the first to show up wearing a *Girls Girls Girls* shirt before his flock followed suit. It was also Jake who'd led a crusade of hate against Jason in freshman year, labeling him a Satanist for wearing his shirt of the Crüe's earlier (and far tougher) *Shout at the Devil* album. It had become such a point of contention with Jason back then he'd cut the sleeves off said tee and wore it only around his house as a muscle shirt.

Jake was blathering about the upcoming senior class selections and what they should vote for their exiting theme song. Jake proposed Whitesnake's "Here I Go Again," which drew assent from the Cooler Than Thou Brigade, slouching and puffing their smokes all around him. Yes men and women-in training for futures as corporate lackeys.

"Coverdale's a legend, all respect, but what a travesty," Rob said under his breath. "Those posers would never know he sang in Deep Purple long before Whitesnake."

"Whatever," Jason scoffed. "Good song, but I'm putting down King Diamond's 'The Family Ghost' on the senior ballot. A waste of time, but worth it just to shake shit up."

"Good morning, sweeties!" Jake shouted to them.

Rob squeezed his eyes shut impatiently, while Jason was quick on the draw, as if anticipating the need to be on the offensive.

"I heard them putting your name on the callback list at Bradenton Coast Video, Jake," Jason fired back. "Your copy of *Sucking the Sailor's* overdue."

Even Jake had to give Jason style points as he did a clumsy curtsy with his cigarette extending into the air. Laughter careened all around the patio.

"Touché," Jake said before turning back to his group.

"Good one," Rob added before spotting Lori Phillips sitting by herself, tugging on a cigarette of her own.

Only the second day of school, Lori had bombed her once dirty brown hair to an inky pile of teased and tangled mud. Her fingernails matched the new color of her darkened locks, and she wore a t-shirt bearing the cover of Killing Joke's *Fire Dances* album atop a dangly, lacy skirt which would've showed her underwear had Lori not been wearing a pair of black leggings beneath. Silver anklets were draped around her ankles, given prominence by the gray moccasins she wore on her feet. Lori had strewn enough bangles on her left wrist to give Madonna herself a run for her Papa-preached derriere.

Lori pushed out a cloud of secondhand as she spotted Jason and Rob, lifting her head at them in silent acknowledgement while lingering on Jason as they headed into the school. Rob noticed this as he gave Lori a friendly wave. Jason missed her altogether.

Venturing inside to the usual chatter and the usual waft of lard and ethanol from the cafeteria, the boys schlumped their way toward the stairwell. Jason's book bag felt heavier than normal today, though all it had was the itinerary of his newly divvied textbooks, a fresh gym uniform, and his work gear for the night.

Not even a few feet inside, they heard a freshman kid, already with his dander up so soon in the day, shout behind another freshman with far less buoyancy and his brown corduroy pants hoisted high above his ankles, "Floods!!!"

The second freshman had been so startled he whirled as timid as a chipmunk into a rain spout, but not before the first kid had stomped down upon the heel of his right sneaker. It was the dreaded Nike knockoff, Zips, with its ridiculous looking "Z" slash instead of the familiar hooked swoosh found strapped upon more than half the feet of the entire school body. Only Vans sold more leisure footwear to Merriweather High's undergraduates.

"Flats!!!" the first freshman yelled in such a ravenous manner most people blew him off as the immature newbie he was. Only he basked in his own roast.

"Eighth grade is so yesterday, dweeb," Rob said, pointing to a banner recently hung wall to wall across the main promenade:

HOMECOMING - OCTOBER 7TH - SHOW YOUR COUGAR PRIDE! BEAT CENTENNIAL!

Trailing the banner to the opposite side, which dropped at the school store, the boys saw Class President Heather Belanger positioned in front. Behind her was a professionally lacquered cardboard placard summoning recruits to join the SGA, the Student Government Association. Heather shifted from side to side, waving and looking for takers, a well-polished politicianette.

Her reddish-brown hair was cropped into a mash between two eras of Molly Ringwald dos, a straight bob plowing into a medium layered coif. Hence, the easy nickname dropped upon Heather, even by her own Popular friends, "Claire." The oversized shoulder pads on Heather's peach blazer gave a wishful authoritative but inadvertently sappy look, even with the matching skirt wrapped tight around her sharp hips, cut right at the knees to show off her toned calves. Heather had played for the school's tennis team her entire school career aside from running the table in SGA and snapping photography for the student newspaper, *The Cougar's Tale*.

Heather was holding out a palm-sized button with the marauding school mascot on the front and a call-to-arms rally call in burgundy lettering: **"COUGARS WIN TOGETHER!"**

"Cougar Pride buttons!" she called out as most students ignored her in passing. "Free with any purchase at the school store! Fifty cents by itself! C'mon, guys, road game against Glenelg this week, and Homecoming's next month! Let's see that Cougar Pride at work and push our guys to victory!"

Heather paused to watch Jason and Rob walk by, rolling her eyes up at the sight of them before resuming her pitching.

"Eat it, Prez," Jason growled, sending her a mock return eyeball hoist, his tongue waggling between the middle and fourth fingers of his upraised hand, pushed into Spock-esque greeting of prosperity. In this case, a more vulgar sign representing cunnilingus. Both Jason and Rob were happy to see Heather appear shocked by Jason's lowbrow riposte as the boys wormed their way into the clogged stairwell leading to the second level.

"You're in a mood this morning," Rob told his friend with a chuckle sounding more nervous than appreciative.

"Taking no shit this morning, is more like it," Jason corrected him.

On the center landing between floors, members of the Glee and Drama Clubs were harmonizing a few bars of "Put on Your Sunday Clothes" from their upcoming fall production of *Hello, Dolly*. Tony Endrizzi, who'd won the role of Cornelius Hackl, had also earned the nickname "Tony Spumoni" the past spring by downing more of said gelato dessert than the congratulatory spaghetti dinner thrown in honor of the cast's run through *Godspell*.

Tony outshone his cast mates right now, both in voice and exhibition as he shimmied and clapped out the stress points of the cadence they'd worked up. He subsequently cracked them and everyone nearby up by threading a hysterical deviation of the chorus to "Santa Claus is Coming to Town" into "We're gonna find adventure in the evening air…"

"Alright, dude, catch you later," Rob said to Jason once they'd squirmed their way up to the second floor.

"Cool," Jason replied, finding himself cut off from approaching his locker by the interlocking spit swapping between Pat Coleman and Sandy Babb. Pat daringly, in the open, honked Sandy's right breast with a fierce clutch enough to rival Sergeant Slaughter's dreaded Cobra Clutch. This not only earned Pat an angry swat on the hand, it broke the couple apart long enough for Jason to squeeze through their hasty bickering. Sandy had been so vehement she'd drowned out Jason's murmured excusing of himself.

"Don't *even* think I'm signing up for four more years of this bullshit in college, Ma," Jason muttered as he dialed his locker combination.

He daydreamed of shredding an arpeggio onstage with a mob of stage divers climbing up and patting him on the shoulder before disappearing into a mosh whipped and whirled by his own frenzied playing.

Altogether missing the hateful glares targeting him by five guys and one girl in blue jackets.

Chapter 9

JASON FLIPPED HIS BLUE, square-cut necktie which dangled across a crate holding four plastic gallons of milk overtop his shoulder with an irritated swish. He hated ties, much less dress shirts, both nonsensical when paired with the same jeans he'd worn to school and his Nike high tops. Of course, the sneakers were relative, given the grime they'd collected all these months from his trucking on foot to work and back from Super Thrift. His mother had admonished him for their quick decline, having paid $38.50 she'd needed to flip the budget around for until that month's support check had cleared. Jason had taken her derision like anyone his age would, with a silent sneer covering up a profane response on his way to his bedroom, followed by an irate door slam.

Complying with company regs, Jason had pulled his hair into a tight ponytail, which he kinda liked, kinda loathed, though the store at least hadn't tried to make him cut it off as a prerequisite to hiring him back in spring. Things could be worse, he figured, since the deli ladies were forced to either cut their locks to ear length or wear those appalling hair nets like his break buddy, Fan, who groused to him on repeat how she despised carrying a dirty blonde "shrub" on the back of her neck. With her hair down, Fan could pass for a reasonable Kim Basinger.

The second day of school had featured less of the first's stock of incitements, but it was only until he was able to walk out with Rob and then part ways at Route 62 for Jason to head out to Super Thrift before he could *breathe*. He hadn't expected work to be full of chaos on a Tuesday, but to the plus, the first three hours had already flown by.

Jason busted a joke to himself how his nipples were hard enough to slice bread after being inside the dairy cooler for much of his five-hour shift. He'd been repurposed to work the dairy department after the night clerk, Chad Hoder, had called out with pneumonia. Jason smirked at this thought each time he passed the tacked tally sign in the stock room bragging in bold, black letters: **NUMBER OF DAYS WITHOUT A REPORTED ACCIDENT.** The number was currently sitting on seventeen.

The customers were packing Super Thrift tonight, and this without any door buster sales, except a dollar off chuck roast, plus a shave of thirty cents from Domino sugar products. The sun only having gone down forty minutes before store close, the place was nearly as clogged as Black Friday. Whatever had people's collective panties in a wad over scoring milk today, specifically the 2% nonfat gallon jugs, it had been enough for the store's assistant manager, Todd Kilgore, to pull Jason from his usual bagging duties at the cashier aisles.

The other night clerk, Dave Carlisle, was scurrying on the floor in a fever pitch. There'd be no time later to sneak in a round of floor hockey in the stock room as they liked to do on lighter nights. Just as well, since those makeshift games, using brooms and tuna cans and mop buckets for goals, had been forcibly ceased. This, given the fact Dave Carlisle, two years graduated from high school, had checked Jason plus the still-new frozen food manager, another Dave (Conway, known amongst the grocery staff as "Dave the Sequel") into a stack of cases containing glass bottles of thousand island dressing. Dave the Sequel got it far worse, so much he'd been ordered to go home and change before coming back and making up the time. Most memorable to Jason was the stench of the salad-smothering puke which had dashed his pant legs, reeking all through his two-and-a-half-mile walk home.

This same stench was pervading inside Jason's mind right now, bleeding into the comparable prompt of a sickening waft from partially emptied cases of sour cream and Colby cheese he'd tripped across earlier tonight. These he'd noticed were eight days past their expiration dates, so bad the sour cream had mold seeping from beneath the lids. These offensive, outdated items Jason stowed into an empty corner of the cooler. He would alert Todd once the mad rush slowed down.

Jason stacked the milk crate on top of another one loaded onto a green, metal hand truck. His necktie stayed in place on the shoulder of his shocked white Van Heusen button down, recently bleached of its gathered sweat stains and ring around the collar by his mother. The dress shirt was a size too big for him, but at least enough to hide his hardened "tit missiles," as guys were hyped to call to them, usually with the female variety in mind.

His lower back was beginning to smart from the twisting side-to-side and jockeying milk to the shelves, plundered as fast as he loaded it. Earlier, Todd had ordered Jason to double-time it with the implied threat of firing him if he couldn't keep up. This reproach transpired in front of Jacob Weinstein, owner of Bradenton Title and Escrow on the far end of town.

Jacob Weinstein was a serious and seldom friendly man who, anyone in Bradenton could see by his glib stature, was used to getting what he wanted. On-the-spot. Of course it had to have been Jacob Weinstein hovering at the depleted 2% milk section shelf. Todd had yanked a jug of 2% straight out of the crate as Jason dollied it out, handing it ceremoniously in deference of the disapproving scowl Weinstein had left for both with the snide comment, "I've seen last minute short sale closings better prepared than this."

Now with a new stack of five milk crates, Jason shoved the wheels of the hand cart forward, then tilted the pile back on an angle, enough to get a smooth glide toward the steel door of the cooler. He'd done the exercise so many times already tonight his right ankle had swollen. His butt had grown frosty, which he used to bump the cooler door open.

"Comin' through, chief!"

Jason heard the annoying rumble and squeaky peal of a rolling U-boat as Dave Carlisle nudged the dairy cooler door back against Jason. He was loaded, pull bars high, with boxes of Fruity and Cocoa Pebbles, Frosted Flakes, Cheerios, Raisin Bran, Special K, and Cookie Crisp cereals.

"Dickwad!" Jason hollered through the metallic closure between them.

"Sorry, dude, but I'm also not," Dave called back amidst the clatter of his trundling parcel. "They call for snow tonight or something? It's only September and a *Tuesday*, what the absolute hell? Todd's got something up his ass tonight, and it's probably Mike Fisher. Worse excuse for two assistant mangers I've ever seen."

Jason was about to answer as he bulldozed his way out of the cooler and turned his bucking load down the corridor, thinned by swamping boxes of toilet paper, paper towels and tissues. A *fwoom!* sound ricocheted as Dave blasted his way past the swinging doors out of the stock room.

Jason groaned, looking down for the umpteenth time tonight at the watery sludge festering inside an abandoned mop bucket. A dead mouse was floating in the sewage with a heap of maggots chomping away on its bloated carcass.

The same *fwoom!* commotion announced Jason's return to the main floor and lucky for him, the coolers were right outside. He slowed his roll to let three customers in a row lurch deep into the 2% section and grab what was left.

"Unbelievable," he whispered, as the third, a rotund woman tottered by with a shit-eating grin, as if she'd won some sort of game. Her fat-pocked hips looked as miserable as she signaled, wheezing past

Jason with each step. She surveyed him with a scrutinizing expression he could've let set him off. It was the same cocky look the jocks had been shooting at him during third period Weightlifting class.

When she was out of earshot, Jason mumbled, "Jabba, your wife's done ran out on ya. Call Boba Fett for a contract."

Squawking over the store intercom was Genesis' "Invisible Touch," which Jason had come to detest, if for no other reason, its reliable manifest every other hour. Though it wasn't metal, he was craving to hear Phil Collins instead spool through "That's All."

Someone in a brown leather bomber jacket came to the milk coolers, but he wanted skim, praise the grocery gods. The same person was muttering numbers out loud. When Jason caught him, the man said without a lick of concern, "Remembering my numbers for Lotto. I hear your store sold a $750.00 payout. You gotta play to win, right?"

Sparking himself back into hustle mode, Jason swung the top crate of milk jugs down and shuttled them onto the shelf. For once tonight, nobody was in his vicinity to make him stop, and he unloaded the crates in no time.

While Coach Schaub had taken it somewhat easy on the Weightlifting class the first two days, focusing more on up warm-drills and cardiovascular training, Jason had still come to work sore. Adding the full three-mile schlep from the school to Super Thrift, the walk home tonight in the dark along the train tracks he took to stay off the main drag of Route 62 would be harder than normal.

Jason's mother may have hated him taking the tracks, but the thought of her only son getting splattered on the throughway in the night had forced her to relent. Bradenton was still reeling from the death of 43-year-old townie, Abner Muller, slain roadside in walking commute by a drunk driver from Pennsylvania.

Todd scooted by the dairy cases and, at least for this round, gave Jason a grin of approbation through his brushy brown mustache as Jason slung the remaining jugs out of the fifth crate onto the shelf. Todd's plain brown tie was clamped snugly to his chest by a gold tie clip he'd fastened to the button fold of his beige short sleeve. For the moment, the 2% milk looked presentable with a reasonable amount of stock, instead of the glaring void it had shown for much of the night. Should the district manager, Pete LaCroix, show up right now, Jason would look good in the store's eyes.

"Dave up front to bag, please...Dave...to the front to bag..."

Jason raised his eyebrows in surprise at the announcement over the P.A. as he moved even quicker to get back into the dairy case, lest he be spotted by Joyce Wilczynski, manager of the cashiers and the operating teller for the store's check courtesy cashing and lottery ticket booth. If she had summoned Dave Carlisle to bag groceries, things were out of hand in the front. Jason had been hired as a bagger the past April, and he'd spent most of his work hours packing goods into paper bags and fetching grocery carts from all reaches of Super Thrift's considerable parking lot.

He'd been pulled a few times before to help the grocery clerks out, but that was always when the store was less busy and usually with time to natter with the cashiers, all who were old enough to be Jason's mom or aunt. Off during the day, they liked to recount to Jason what they'd seen on *The Young and the Restless, Guiding Light,* and *General Hospital,* soap operas, *groan.* Who the hell Newmans and Abbotts were, he didn't care.

Why Dave Carlisle had been paged to come up front and bag instead of Jason was such an anomaly Dave himself blurted his dissatisfaction while taking the extra steps to march through the stock room on his way to the front.

"Are you fucking kidding me?" Dave snarled. He tramped through the stock room, his bolo style tie, barely passable for store code, swishing back and forth at his thick chest. His pulled back black hair was thicker and a couple inches within reach of Jason's length. Much of it belched beneath his ears and swooped up and down when he moved with speed. Kids at Merriweather High had taken to calling Dave's hawkish style a "mullet." "That's *your* job, metalhead! I haven't had to bag all year! Bad enough we can't get a goddamn ten-minute break tonight!"

Jason shrugged, his response jammed inside his throat.

A good thing for him, too, since Todd emerged from a shielded empty spot on a skid holding a towering pile of cat food boxes.

"Jason's needed where he's at, Mr. Carlisle," Todd blurted with a fire lit inside of both of his eye sockets. He held a clipboard which tremored in his left hand like he would wallop Dave with it, if given one more outburst.

Everyone at Super Thrift called Todd Kilgore a douchebag behind his back, but nobody dared challenge him to his face. His shaggy hair was a tragedy, yet his wiry mustache had become a butt-end joke amongst the deli girls (Fan included) who brazenly voiced their opinion what a yummy down from Todd might feel like. All employed at Super Thrift could agree Todd Kilgore got results, no matter their like or dislike of him.

"Yes, sir," Dave said with far less starch. *Fwoom!* said it all for him, following his boisterous exit toward the store front.

"As you were, Jason," Todd said, going back to his business, scratching notes on his clipboard while counting inventory. "How many palettes of 2% do you have left back there?"

"Ummmm," Jason fumbled as he rolled the dolly back into the dairy cooler and peeked inside. The crisp, filtering coolant pounded his face. "That'd be half of one skid only."

"*What?!?*" Todd exclaimed.

"Yes, sir, Mr. Kilgore," Jason returned, holding the cooler door open in case Todd wanted to check for himself. "We're getting pounded out there."

"Good thing we close soon," Todd said with an incredulous sigh. "I'll have a talk with Chad tomorrow. There's no excuse we should be so short, even if all of Bradenton's hit us tonight. If this happens again tomorrow... Take three more crates of 2% and stagger them a couple extra rows. Leave the rest unless we get cleaned out again. Fill any gaps with the 1% and full D."

"Got it," Jason said, pushing back into the cooler. He moved as if Todd had followed him in, brandishing a whip to spur him on.

It took no time before Jason had exactly what had been instructed, his smarting back be damned, and he was already back out on the floor.

Jason lost a step, nearly freezing in place, when he saw Sam Shaffer, Emily Haney, and Lee Metcalf. None of them had anything in their hands, save for Emily's rear end inside Lee's, the same as it had been at school yesterday morning.

Side-by-side, they looked like a blue corduroy wall, clad in their plastered FFA jackets which never seemed to come off. The clothes beneath always changed, but those jackets were ubiquitous.

Jason took a deep breath, gave them a faked cool nod of acknowledgement to cover up his sudden fear, then pushed past them with his stock.

"What's up, homo?" he heard behind him.

He hadn't seen Sam Shaffer draw up behind, but Jason *felt* him. It was the hot, minty, Skoal bandits-laced breath piercing the nippiness upon his skin.

"Sam," he said, trying to eliminate the sudden shiver to his voice as he shifted to put some distance between him. Lee surrendered his prize posterior to let Emily scooch to Sam's right side, while Lee occupied the left. They'd formed a human enclosure between themselves and Jason, now flush to the dairy case.

"Soooooo, Boedecker's right, is he?" Sam objected with malice leaking through the gape of his chaw-stained teeth.

"What?" was all Jason could come up with, just now remembering what he'd said yesterday morning when it had been Greg Boedecker in the same predicament Jason was now.

"I seen you taking Weightlifting class," Sam said in a backwoods-baked tone. Jason thought how his English teacher from last year, Mrs. Werner, would have balked like the lexicon apocalypse had stormed upon her at the use of "seen" versus "saw." "You think you're all tough shit now, don't you?"

"Ahh, geez," Jason fumbled, trying to sound unruffled but losing the battle each second he stared at the farmer fortification blocking him. This morning at school, Jason was full-bravado. Right now, the complete opposite. It felt like Perry Hall again, *Scary* Hall, before he'd stood up for himself. "I don't know, man. I'm just doing my thing."

"Playing pocket pool, no doubt," Emily cracked as she chewed sloppily on a piece of pink gum, never taking her eyes away from Jason. He wanted to zing her how the slow munching guernseys on her family's smallholding probably had more couth than she did. Instead, he let it go to the cow-flopped wind.

"If he *has* any balls," Lee added in less comedic fashion. He was in business mode, his business being of the bruising and brawling variety.

"Oh, the longhair *thinks* he has balls," Sam gnashed. "You think I need a gang to beat your wussy ass, motherfucker?"

Jason didn't answer. His right hand shook as if he'd been stricken with epilepsy on the spot as he reached for a jug of milk.

"*Do* you, shrimp nuts?" Sam growled, the reek of Wint-O-Green chew slamming into Jason's nostrils. Jason would've laughed a minute solid at the phrase "shrimp nuts" if Rob had used it instead of Sam Shaffer. Right now, he was glad Rob wasn't here to see this.

"Look at him, he's pissing himself scared," Emily stirred with a cocky laugh. She may have lost most of her freckles, but Jason loathed the ones she had left, along with the rest of her scowling face.

"I'll wipe my ass with you, punk," Sam pressed, his eyeballs blaring ten times worse than Todd Kilgore's.

"We have a problem here, kids?"

If there was one time Jason had been relieved to see Todd show up, almost on cue, it was right now.

"No, Mr. Kilgore," Lee answered for all three on his side of the faltering skirmish. "We're just asking your employee here if you have any Land O' Lakes in stock. I can see you do. You know what happens with the packaging if you cut and tuck the Indian girl's knees?"

Emily stifled a chuckle with her nail-chewed hand. "You make Indian girl boobies if you do it right!" Then she tittered with a cackle even her compatriots found obnoxious.

"I know all three of your parents," Todd cautioned with a blaze in his throat. "Buy something or leave the premises at once. There is no second warning."

Todd jetted as quick as he'd arrived, but Sam, Emily and Lee remained where they were just long enough to fire Jason a gang glare.

"As muff 'stache said," Sam told Jason before they left, "no second warning."

Chapter 10

"ALICE COOPER'S RAISE YOUR FIST AND YELL *from last year may have the worst album cover of all time, but nobody with any kind of acumen for heavy metal will argue this album doesn't ROCK! Seriously, how do you go from the stroppy 'Only Women Bleed' to the sonic boom of "Freedom," "Lock Me Up," and "Chop Chop Chop" in thirteen years? Certainly a long distance from* Special Forces, DaDa, *and* Zipper Catches Skin, *which some folks say were recorded while Alice was bombed to the outer limits of his alter ego, Steven. Guitarist Kane Roberts has a good bit to do with the reason* Raise Your Fist and Yell *is one of Uncle Alice's best and loudest albums to-date, and not just because he shreds more barbells than his frets. Kip Winger's captivating harpsichord laces through the cryptic horror ode, "Gail," turning Roberts loose to blast the hell out of the song's melancholy — if cheeky — sonnets with a towering crescendo. Hell, I'm thinking both Winger (also Alice's current bassist) and Roberts are destined to have their own bands. Standout tracks: "Freedom," "Step On You," "Gail," "Roses on White Lace," "Lock Me Up," "Time to Kill" and "Chop Chop Chop." Rating: 8.5 out of 10."*

"I never did like that song," Rob's mother said, lifting her eyes from the spiral notebook she held in front of her before looking back down at it.

"Which one, Ma?" Rob asked, wondering if maybe he'd made a mistake letting her read his latest album review. He'd chosen the dining room table to write instead of his bedroom. A change of surrounding walls took his mind off the day's events at school, which found Emily Haney sneaking up on him and whispering "Geeeeeek!" into his ear before dashing off. Then there was Austin Ledbetter, a junior and one of the sound and lighting crew for the school auditorium, who'd called Rob "Iron Blowjob." As if a guy with the last name of Ledbetter had any business torching people.

Rob's mother had spotted him while coming through with a cup of ginger tea, and after asking for one himself, he'd rejected it upon the first sip before yielding to her request to read his work.

It was the first time he'd shown anyone his personal writing, Jason included. As Rob thought about it now, perhaps he'd wanted this moment to happen, even if his audience had turned out to be his mother. At this very second though, he silently cringed upon remembering the word "hell" in his Alice Cooper review. On the lighter side of the spectrum of swear words, but still enough to cause him worry. If she'd read some of his other reviews, she'd trip across far worse.

"Only Women Bleed," she responded, re-reading the entire review. Her expression was indecipherable. "Do you know what the song's about?"

"Well, *duh,*" Rob answered, halfway feeling bad for his cynicism with his mother taking an interest in his work. If noodling around for fun about heavy metal albums was considered actual work.

"I bet Alice Cooper would've thought twice about recording a song like that if he'd had to experience a menstrual cycle himself, even once," she said with a smirk, glancing back up at Rob, then back down at the spiral.

Rob chuckled at that, and in an attempt at empathy, he said, "I know that knocks you down for a good day or two. I'm sure you can't wait for menopause."

"Thank you, Rob," his mother returned with a gentle melt in her voice. "I am, but not the hot flashes that comes with it. I'm no Alice Cooper fan, though 'School's Out' always got my foot tapping…"

"*Everybody* likes that one, geez," Rob muttered, reeling himself back in before he got too judgmental. At least his mom was engaging him in conversation about music she could care less about, since the country stylings of Alabama, Willie Nelson, and George Strait were more her mountain music speed. Even better she'd thus far overlooked his minor written cursing.

"I also have a soft spot for 'Welcome to My Nightmare,'" she added, arching her eyebrows with expectation at Rob.

"Okay, *nice,*" Rob nodded, authenticating she had a surprisingly cool bone or two inside her petite, twang-loving frame.

"I really liked that bit he did on The Muppets," she added, twirling the notebook and handing it back over to Rob.

"It was corny," Rob droned, but before he outright dismissed his mother's remark, he made sure to add, "though it's The Muppets. Anyone who's anyone made it on that show."

"Stroppy," she said, shifting the tone of the conversation. "Where'd you get that word?"

"I don't know, Ma, out of some novel or I guess? It just came to mind. It fits, you know?"

"It's not a criticism," she said, spreading even more warmth into her tone. "I'm impressed, actually. I'm impressed by the whole thing."

"Really?" Rob asked with sudden bounce, sounding like his long ago six-year-old self. Around the time he'd first seen the Christopher Reeve *Superman* movie.

"Really," she affirmed. "You have a good writing voice. I could care less about the material itself, sorry, but if I was into heavy metal music, you'd make me interested in learning more about the album. 'Acumen,' that's another big-league word. It makes you sound like an authority on your topic, *and* it allows you to talk in an otherwise loose and entertaining tone. That part about eating barbells is hysterical and it has verve. 'Bombed to the outer limits of his alter ego,' that's so *brilliant!* Good job, honey. Keep at it. On that note, I have some green peppers to stuff."

She rose from her side of the dining room table and rumpled Rob's head on her way to the kitchen.

"You might want to try to some conditioner if you want to keep that long hair, though," were the words she left in her wake, already stifling them with the clatter of pans and the swish of the orbiting Lazy Susan.

Rob smiled as if a hundred pounds of air had been lifted around him, re-reading his review, and feeling good about himself.

He knew his parents tolerated his choice in music at best. On one occasion, his father had threatened to tear down an old Twisted Sister poster because he "wasn't about to have the family come visiting to find a bunch of drag queens on the wall." Rob laughed aloud at that memory now, and the fact he himself had pulled the Twisted Sister poster down last year once their tepid *Love is for Suckers* album came out. "Tepid," another good word he rolled inside his head for future use.

Speaking of the old man, his father entered the dining room, cutting off Rob from his diversions.

"Got a second, Robbo?" his dad quipped, sporting an autumnal look with the green and orange check pattern of his flannel shirt.

"I guess," Rob answered, firing a leery gaze across the few feet between them. Rob was just getting comfortable with his dad's silly play on his name, "Robbo." At first, it had plucked Rob's nerves in the way that Celtic Frost album had the day before, but unlike *Cold Lake,* Rob was finding the virtues in his dad's pet name. It sure beat what Jason's dad used for his own son. For a moment, Rob himself had taken exception to Jason's father calling them retards and losers.

"They're looking for a cleaning crew in the administrative offices at Grigsby Tools," his dad chirped, sounding so giddy he might grab his mother and Lindy Hop her down the hallway and return doing The Stroll.

"Oookayyy," Rob said, already knowing the direction this was heading and bracing himself for it. Both of his parents had been needling Rob the past couple months about Jason having a part-time job, but not him.

"I know the foreman," his dad continued as a mechanical whir from the kitchen interrupted him, the sound of an electric can opener freeing stewed tomatoes and tomato paste.

"I know you guys want me to…"

"Chuck Davis," his dad thwarted Rob before he could finish. "Good guy, used to work under me in the lawn and garden tools section. Chuck wanted his own management gig, so they let go of the current cleaning contractor and gave the job to Chuck. They lowballed three of the four people on the crew to stay on but increased their hours to make it up. If you want to call that making it up to them. You'd get $5.75 an hour. An *hour*, Rob, at twenty a week. Easy money and you'd be off work by eight. Plenty enough time to get your homework done and to consume more of that screeching ear rot you love so much."

"Hmmm," Rob paused his resistance long enough to do the math. He chortled to himself at his dad's phrasing of "screeching ear rot," dismissing it on his way to a bigger picture. Since Jason worked so much these days, it would make sense for Rob to take a job of his own. He had seventh period study hall, and that would give him the chance to pound out his homework instead of drudging through World War II books and doodling band logos on the paper bag covers wrapped in protection of his class textbooks.

"I've already set up an interview for you," Rob's dad said, matter-of-factly as he turned to inhale the waft of split-open green peppers. "It's probably a gimme Chuck's gonna hire you since you're my son. One of life's biggest truisms, son, it's all about who you know. Still…"

"Still what?" Rob asked, feeling a flood of mistrust at his father's vagueness.

"You'll probably cement the deal if, you know…"

"What, Dad?"

"Clean yourself up. Cut your hair some. Make yourself less…"

"Absolutely not!" Rob protested. His fists were already balled before he felt his fingernails dig into his palms. "Do you know how long it took me to grow it, Dad? Do you?"

"Now listen up!" his father barked, jabbing a forefinger in the air aimed toward Rob, the same as most angry parents did.

"No…" Rob fumed, lowering his voice as most well-raised children did, despite their mounting frustration at said angry parents. His father wasn't about to reciprocate, much less notice Rob had taken out his earring.

"I've kept my mouth shut a long time about this...this...*look* of yours."

"What's wrong with how I look? Do I *embarrass* you, Dad?"

Rob's mother stopped what she was doing in the kitchen to try and intervene. Out of the corner of his eye, Rob could see her shaking her head in protest at his dad. He even saw her mouth the words at him, "Don't do it." His father either failed to see it or he ignored his wife outright.

"The last time I saw hair on men as long as yours, Rob, they were throwing things and spitting at us when we were coming back from Vietnam! Do you think those flower power pussies had enough integrity to welcome us home like Americans, or at the very least, to stay the hell away from the goddamn airport?"

"Darren, stop," Rob's mother said out loud this time. "That's a poor analogy. Rob wasn't one of them."

Again, she was ignored.

"I hauled my friends off the fields with heat dropping all around us!" he stormed on, a flare rising inside his pupils, his eyeballs bulging out from their sockets an extra inch. The look of it frightened Rob more than his father's war ramblings. "They all *died!* Some lost their limbs and nearly all of them called out to a loved one for help, as if they were right there. Their mothers, their dads, their wives, or girlfriends. I was the last person they saw in this life, their blood spurting all over me. Some lost their limbs and bled out. A few had their intestines hanging out, Rob! One buddy, I can't remember his name now, because all I ever try to do is forget, he was cut in half!"

Rob remained frozen during his father's tirade. *All this over my hair?* he thought amidst his panic.

"You ever want to know what death looks like for real with all that blood and guts horror and heavy metal bullshit you love so damned much, Rob, then you step right on up and I'll give you a history lesson that'll ruin your sleep for days! You and those disgusting, ridiculous zombies. You ever fight in a war and watch guys you knew all the way from Basic get blown to bits on the front, you'll never watch another zombie film again, I promise you that!"

"All of this is unnecessary Darren, and I won't let you take it out on our son!" Rob's mother wedged herself angrily between Rob and his father. She was an easy half a foot less than her husband, but when it counted, she looked more than his match.

"I honor what you went through, Dad," Rob said with caution

before trying to make his point, fluffing out his hair in a clownish spray for emphasis. "This is just *me*, though. I'm sorry you hate my hair, you hate my music, and you hate horror movies. If you hate *me*, so be it, but I didn't cause your friends to die."

A momentary silence fell amongst the three of them with Rob's father standing at near attention in front of his wife, glaring at her, then Rob, then the ceiling. A flush crashed across his cheeks. Was it anger, humiliation, repulsion, fright from terrible memories? Rob wondered.

"And there you go," Rob's mother said as his defender. "I'll call you when dinner's ready, Darren. Right now, you should go take a few moments to yourself in the den."

"Jesus God *no*, I don't hate you, Rob! Why would you even think such a thing? Those dirtball dropouts had no right to shit on us, is what I'm saying!" Rob's dad scouted both his son and his wife for any reason to keep shouting, his eyeballs settling before he turned away from them both and steamed down the hallway. He left in his wake, "No right whatsoever, those fucking cowards!"

Chapter 11

"WHAT'RE YOU EVEN *doing* here, Hamlin?"

Jason hardly panted as he kept a respectable pace on the track. In fact, he was running in the upper ten tier of guys from his Weightlifting class of 26. An early fall chill had put the hot, dry stranglehold over George County to rest.

The new order of crispness made for a tense outdoor sight of teenage boys trucking around the quarter mile for a total of four times. Even at third period, it was *cold,* reflected by the steam belching from their sides of the boys' bobbing heads in time to their floppy, maroon color coded shorts and baggy white tees splashed with the Merriweather High logo.

Know-it-all barbell pumpers nattered how they could get the same leg muscle impact on the squat machines and dead lift stations as an excuse to ditch the run. Coach Ed Schaub, now in his fourth year at the school, grinned and shook his head at the whole thing, his sporty Ray Bans bouncing away the few glimpses of sun there were to be found. Threats of taking a zero for the day over a lack of participation got the slackers in motion.

The girls' gym class, by contrast, had settled into a fair tempo on the adjacent all-purpose field, marked by the clacking of wooden hockey sticks and coordinated shouts. They looked methodical and compliant, like an actual team despite the few non-athletic laggards delegated to defense. The latter lazed in front of their respective goals until the action roared their way. The girls' field hockey match triggered downward gazes from the boys each time they came around the rear stretch of their ovular course. Coach Schaub likewise surveyed the game from afar with quick jerks of his head.

The same wit currently giving Jason static, Bennett Walsh, whistled first at the girls in transit, then at Coach Schaub with a light poke how he should go ask out the girls' gym teacher, Delaney Camiolo.

Like he did at work, Jason had pulled his hair into a ponytail, which bobbed back and forth across his shoulders at a low berth, as opposed to the full-on pendulum swishes seen on the girls downfield.

On the first lap, speedster Neil Harper had given Jason's hair a less-than-friendly tug, jawing at him in passing, "Move, *dick!*" Neil had also elbowed Justin Necker in the chest, the second fastest guy out there, and Neil's track and field teammate. Word had it the two had become rivals for the affections of Darlene Elstad since school had started back in session. Coach Schaub admonished Neil more for his language toward Jason coming into lap two than for his foul of Justin Necker.

After Jason had somehow passed Larry Thomas, the varsity team's stealthy tight end on the third lap, he'd found himself flanked by two chugging sets of beef on either side of him. Danny Tignall and, of course Bennett Walsh.

Danny and Bennett were hulking brutes who'd started their school careers playing soccer before swelling out in sophomore year and moving on to lacrosse. They'd grown a shared reputation as bruising forecheckers and, because of said smash-and-go ethic, they'd become the school's top goal scorers. Since switching sports, they took the field to the squawky stadium entrance theme of Duran Duran's "Wild Boys." Their calves were bigger than the biceps flexing out of their wagging gym shirts.

Jason braced himself to be squished between the Lax Sandwich he'd found himself in. It felt nearly as disconcerting as his encounter with Sam Shaffer and his pals. Jason had admonished himself all night long for letting himself freeze in front the farmer posse at Super Thrift, more out of fear of getting to that explosive place inside when pounding on those four boys at Perry Hall Middle. Of course, Lee Metcalf was so goddamn *huge.* That was the other thing locking Jason up last night, picturing himself taking a knockout punch from Lee Metcalf. If Lee didn't bust Jason up to pieces first.

Sam, Lee, and Emily were last night's problem. Jason and Rob had yet to see any of them at school today. Right now, Danny Tignall and Bennett Walsh had stepped into Jason's zone of immediate concern for self-preservation.

He slowed just enough to let Danny and Bennett get ahead of him. Not to be outfoxed, however, they did the same to reassume their entrapments on each side.

"Seriously, metalhead," Bennett, well-used to moving and hollering in sprint mode in lacrosse games, said with no effort. "What are you doing in this class, man?"

"Shouldn't you be sacrificing goats behind the bleachers or something, dude?" Danny mocked, as both boys laughed and high-fived each other from behind Jason's head. The clap of their hands meeting sounded off in Jason's ears and the crack startled him. Now, more for assertion than survival reasons, Jason heard a knell of anger snap inside of him, louder than the pop of that high five.

It gave voice to that part of him saying enough to the harassment which had been non-stop the first week of school, exacerbated by the dilemma of this new, escalating conflict with Sam Shaffer and his contingency. Jason felt his guts simmer with unanticipated boldness.

"Same as you pumped up motherfuckers," he growled at Bennett and Danny, half squirming with the suspicion his sudden swagger would earn him a thumping. "Getting stronger."

Out the corner of his right eye, Jason saw Danny surprisingly shrug at Bennett in mid-motion. Checking his other side, Bennett pursed his lips and tilted his head to the side, nodding a couple times. Their silenced facades said no further rebuttal was necessary; at least not with Coach Schaub taking an interest in the situation with a quick-snapped *pleeeat!* of his stainless-steel whistle. Even the jocks accustomed to the infernal thing had complained of the shrill shriek when Schaub blew it inside the auxiliary gym during class warm-ups.

"Keep up if you can, hairball," Danny said, but this time there was no malice to his voice. Like his co-worker, Dave Carlisle, Danny and Bennett's respective sandy and chocolate colored hair was just about as long as Jason's kinky scrub. The main difference, theirs were better styled, and their mounds of muscle took away from their hair span.

Danny and Bennett picked up their speed, pounding their Adidas Fire sneakers in tandem down lanes three and four. They'd passed Kyle Boula and Chris Majors, regarded in the upper echelon of the Weightlifting class. Schwarzemajors was proudly sporting a 300 Pound Bench Club shirt devoted upon him by Coach Schaub in Junior Year. Boula, nobody's friend but certainly not inhospitable, was tramping around the track in his 250 Pound achievement tee.

The third lap around had gone so fast for Jason he hadn't realized he only needed one last round to finish. That vibe ringing inside his head, commanding him to stand up for himself against two guys who could've easily clocked him and left him for dead in the third running lane, now ordered him to pour it on with the final lap of the full mile to go.

His swelling chest, which had already begun to carve from humping grocery bags, parcel boxes, and milk crates, gorged on the adrenaline feed fountaining inside of him. His legs had become strong all these months of hiking back and forth to work, now fortified with the additional mileage traversing from school. They spurred Jason not only to pick it up, but to devour Danny Tignall and Bennett Walsh's lead.

Jason's feet smarted with each spanking thud forward. His knees rose to nearly a full ninety-degree arch and he swung his arms in mad propulsions.

"Holy shit, Hamlin," he heard in passing as he passed Schwarzemajors before Kyle Boula.

Jason barely saw Craig Brunner, whom he also had Chemistry class with. Craig offered no remark other than to glide over two lanes out of Jason's way.

Jason poured it on around the second bend of the track. Adjusting his hips to accommodate the shifting angle, Jason felt himself teeter a little, but he stayed on his feet. *Anything but that,* he fumed to himself. *They'll laugh you right off the track if you crash, dingus.*

Already five guys had finished the mile, including Neil Harper and Justin Necker, who stood far away from each other, dissecting one another like Wild West duelists. A future showdown was all but assured, depending on who landed Darlene Elstad, if either.

Seemingly content to coast toward the finish line, Danny Tignall and Bennett Walsh reduced their movements to a trot, giving Jason all the inspiration he needed.

Take 'em, dammit! some invisible voice cheered Jason on.

Now his chest ached, and his heartbeat spiked with the cool air slamming down his throat. None of that mattered. Only this split second to prove himself counted.

For a moment, Jason saw the prowling cougar of the school's mascot, painted in a skulking motion across the concrete support base of the rising stadium tiers. The view of the feral cat was blocked, only for a second, as Jason rumbled past Danny and Bennett, beating them to the finish line by a few ticks.

Jason's momentum was so great he bulled past the other finishers and Coach Schaub who gave him a crisp thumbs-up. Jason flashed a grin so wide he chided himself for his lack of coolness before coaxing his legs to simmer down with the first loop of the quarter mile track coming up again.

He slowed down, inching toward Lane 8, the furthest out. When he could fully stop, Jason felt his guts betray him. They'd seized into a frenzy to propel him as the sixth fastest guy to finish the mile, but now they chastised him for the very same thing. Jason tasted a return gorge of his apple cinnamon Pop Tart and chocolate milk from this morning. Far enough away from everyone else, he turned his back to everyone and let himself bowl over just enough to make it look as if he was merely catching his breath. With a concentrated effort not to unleash a giveaway gagging noise, Jason let an unclogged chunk of vomit spew into the spindly grass.

Jason could hear his squishy pulse worm in a throb inside his ears as another quake hit his stomach. He fought to get his breath under control, much less disallowing himself to put on a barfing show that would undo his triumph. He took a deep breath and forced his posture back up. As if Jason could scold his soured belly, it abruptly listened to him, holding the rest of his breakfast in place without further threat of upheaval.

He could see guys still jogging at half his speed around the track. These included a large chunk of the JV and varsity football players, who'd been instructed by Coach Schaub to take it easy and complete the mile at a slower pace, given their respective first game at home coming up this Friday. They came down the final stretch in a cluster, like a programmed military unit. They made no fanfare nor any attempt to bring attention to themselves as varsity squads for all of Merriweather High history usually did darting onto the gridiron at game time to the marching band's summons of tuba, trumpet, trombone, snare drum, and xylophone.

The slowest, and also the weakest guy in class, Ricky Groff, was only starting his third lap when he slogged by Jason.

"That was awesome, dude," Ricky said on his way by, trying not to cough through his words.

"Thanks," Jason muttered to Ricky on his way back to the rest of the class.

"Groff!" Coach Schaub bellowed, followed by a pleat from his whistle. "Period'll be over by the time you finish! Get back here and fall in line!" Jason chuckled to himself as he saw most of the other guys squint in misery after Schaub blew in their midst.

Feeling a normal breathing pattern resume despite the dull ache lingering in his stomach, Jason was stoked to find Danny Tignall and Bennett Walsh giving him snappy applause. It was picked up by some of the other guys, even from the football players.

"That was badass, Hamlin," Bennett Walsh said with a firm nod as Jason trotted over to the starting line without abdominal repercussions.

The approving gesture was repeated by Coach Schaub.

Inside his head, Jason embraced the bear-like ralph of Lemmy Kilmister gnashing his way through Motörhead's thrash cruncher, "Ace of Spades."

"You know I'm born to lose," he mumbled the song's lyrics as loud as he dared, "but gambling's for fools..., but that's the way I like it, baby, I don't wanna live forever..."

Chapter 12

"HOW'D YOUR DAD TAKE IT when you wanted to skip seeing him today, dude?"

The boys soared through the air, launching themselves one after the other from a toppled tree. Rob landed first, then Jason, who surpassed his friend's dismount by a few feet, playfully smacking Rob upside the back of his hooded head in mid-motion.

A swift breeze knocked around the ferns and ash and flounced the sluffed leaves about the glade like a red, orange, and yellow portal made of beech, oak, maple, and poplar fronds.

"It was fine by him, the jerk," Jason said with such passive blandness he could've been talking about chemical compounds from the week he'd long forgotten. "Sounded like he was happy about it, since he told me he'd canceled out on a classic car meet down at Ocean City this weekend before I called off today. He's there now, no doubt three sheets flying with those fake-ass old windbags. Screw him, I hope he wrecks on the way home."

"You don't mean that," Rob said, his sneakers crunching over and sifting through a bundle of white oak leaves scattered across the footpath. It would only be a few more weeks before the trail, the boys' refuge away from their development, was covered Fall true.

"Like hell," Jason refuted, poking Rob at the chest high zipper of his grey sweatshirt for no other reason than to pluck his friend's nerves.

"Cut the crap!" Rob snapped. "*My* dad went all Doug Neidermeyer on me this week."

"Whattya mean?"

"He's got a job lined up for me where he works."

"Meh, a job's alright once you get used to having one," Jason said, adding at a mumble with no intention of addressing Rob. "Domino sugar's on sale this coming week, 59 cents a pound. Cokeheads'll buy it up faster than the regular customers."

"I'm not sure what cokeheads have to do with my dad, though I heard him tell stories about some guys in the war smoking strong Vietnamese ciggies called Thuoc Lao or in some cases, toking on the jay."

"Don't mind me," Jason answered, shaking his head in rapid swishes, as if snapping awake. "Yeah, I mean, you'll love having your own money. If you put in serious hours and save it all, you may be able to get a car sometime after I do. Then again, the new Helstar and Virgin Steele albums are coming out soon. Is that what your old man's gobbling about?"

"Nah, I'm alright with working, it's time. He told me I should cut my hair, and you know, clean myself up. It's a janitor job, Jason! Why the hell should I change my look just to scrub shit out of toilets?"

"Bad enough you took out your earring," Jason said with even more defiance than Rob.

"Don't worry about it, Jason; I don't even miss the shark tooth. I did tell my dad the rest is non-negotiable. Well, sorta."

"Good for you. Never sell out. What'd he say to your insurrection?"

"It wasn't much of an insurrection. He lost his shit talking about the war. My hair became secondary. I know he faced hell on the DMZ, but he's sticking to his convictions. He hates long hair on guys like he hates Toyotas. Though the Japanese make those, not the Vietnamese. Great. Now I'm rambling like you do."

"You're not gonna do it, are you?"

"Maybe when the Anthrax guys cut their hair, which I don't see happening. Of course, those loud Jams shorts they've been wearing lately…"

"Don't do it, Martino. For the love of God."

"Okay, sure, man, but back off a little, huh?" Rob snapped. He put on a stern expression, and he raised his shoulders like he was ready to square off, yet deep down, he felt the exact opposite. Ever since his dad had pushed him about cutting his hair, it gave him extra cause to think about school and the harassment he and Jason had endured three years straight and it didn't look like this year would break any trends. Perhaps his father had a point. Not that he would say the same out loud to Jason now, if ever.

"Heather Locklear is so fine," Jason uttered, again to himself, again off-track from the conversation. "Tommy Lee, you lucky fuck."

"If I can pull you away from Planet Perv, I'm more worried about Sam Shaffer and those guys. I think the only reason they've been quiet the rest of the week is because of the rumors."

"What rumors?" Jason asked, unshaken by Rob's heckling.

"Seriously, dude?" Rob exclaimed, booting a loosened acorn into a mixed pile of sweet gum and yellow beech leaves which swallowed it gone.

"*What*, Rob? Since when are you all Rona Barrett?"

"It's all anyone was talking about yesterday. Emily Haney."

"What about that uptight bi…"

"Knocked up, dude," Rob interjected. "If you believe the scuttlebutt."

"Nooooo," Jason replied with an exaggerated drawl. If the obscure elementals of the dell were amused by Jason and Rob's physical goofery, they had to be splitting at their organic seams by the sight of two teenage boys sounding like a pair of female gossips.

"It gets worse," Rob said, his voice elevating with excitement. It was like he'd scored a scoop for the ages. "They say it's not even Lee Metcalf's."

"Get outta here!" Jason trumpeted. "Lemme guess, Sam's?"

"Don't shoot the messenger if my facts are wrong. People are saying Emily had a thing this past summer with some 19-year-old guy over in Keysville. I don't know the guy's name, nobody does. They say he'd been hired part-time by Emily's dad doing various jobs, shade netting, spreading herbicide, whatever, I don't know any of that farming shit."

"Yeah, yeah," Jason said, spooling, his hand in a rotating, hurry up gesture. "Get on with it."

"Anyway, Emily reportedly got it on with Mr. Keysville in the barn, neglecting to yield down the Trojan bypass first…"

"Whoa, she balled him au naturale!"

"And the guy didn't pull out, cue the angry boyfriend…"

"Jesus!" Jason roared. "That's rich! Lee Metcalf's the last son of a bitch you'd want breathing down your neck."

"Again, nobody knows the name of Mr. Keysville, but everyone's saying Lee put his ass in the hospital."

"Are you sure this is all true, Rob? People can't even get it right Billy Idol didn't write 'Mony Mony,' praising him like he's some sort of party genius. Hey everybody, get laid, get fucked…where'd *that* even come from?"

"All I can vouch for is what I saw yesterday afternoon. You were working late last night…"

"Which you can blame Todd for," Jason moaned. "It's nice to be doing more stocking than bagging, but it's just given the prick excuse to load me with more work than I can handle in a four or five-hour shift. He wasn't too happy with my getting only seven out of the eight tasks he'd written for me on the back of a store circular."

"Cheap," Rob cracked.

"He threatened to write me up for clocking out and leaving his dumb list incomplete, and you know what the last thing was? To load and press the cardboard baler! The thing was nowhere near filled and besides, I'd already stayed an extra twenty minutes!"

"My old man settled down and during dinner, he apologized for his tirade. Of course, he was back on my case later when I had *Night Flight* on when he wanted the tv to watch a *Rockford Files* rerun. There was no compromise in his eyes just like earlier, so I gave in and took the tube downstairs before *he* took me back to the 17th Parallel a second time. I can't begin to fathom what Dad saw over there. Mom takes a much bigger brunt than I got. My dad is so relaxed most of the time you'd never know he'd been to war, but you'd piss yourself if you heard Dad screaming through one of his night terrors. It's like he's back there, though it's been a while since he had one of those, right before they canceled *The A-Team* last year. My mom's a champ for bringing him down from the front line of his panic attacks. Decorate her with an honorary Purple Heart or whatever you'd give wives of battled-scarred soldiers. They're on the front lines right there with them."

Jason nodded, more out of instinct it appeared to Rob, since his friend jumped tracks in topics.

"I dunno, Rob, are you sure the whole Emily Haney thing's not some elaborate horseshit cover-up story to keep her dad from slicing Lee's balls off?"

"If I'm Rona Barrett, you've gone all Hardy Boys."

"Parker Stevenson, eat your heart out, but you'd think the cops would've cuffed Lee by now for first degree assault if he'd really roughed up Mr. Keysville. Hell, while we're at it, Mr. Keysville himself could hit the slammer for doinking a minor."

"*True,*" Rob granted, "but the watertight truth is Lee and Emily weren't speaking to each other yesterday. Everybody saw it. When I saw her—from a distance, of course—she'd flat-out avoided Lee, Sam, Steve, Billy, and Butch. It was the exact same thing as what Lori Phillips did to Greg Boedecker on the first day of school. Which reminds me, where *is* Greg these days?"

"Yeah, you're right, Greg's gone AWOL, now that I think about it," Jason said, throwing his arms out and tilting his back to let a fresh breeze caress him. Yet again off-topic and said only to himself, he whispered, "I need me some cat scratch fever."

"I mean, look, I'm not gonna hang the entire lot of FFA kids over a handful of assholes," Rob reasoned, tugging his hood back, off his head. "Frank Baylin, he's a good dude. We've been talking about baseball in Spanish II. His family runs that sheep farm out on Leister Road, and after a mere week, the guy speaks better español than all of us."

"Probably puts the sheep on edge after sundown, too," Jason joked.

"Dude," Rob sighed in a tetchy demeanor. "Frank's alright. So's Katie Freeland. Her family grows soybeans, but she's not in FFA. Peer Counseling seems to suit her and she's also in the IASA Club..."

"*International Aviation?*" Jason stopped Rob with a nonplussed look. "I didn't know we had such a thing at Merriweather High."

"No, bozo, Industrial Arts. Technology, mechanics. Katie's dad taught her how to pull an engine apart and reassemble it. She tells me computers are starting to become a thing in car engines, so that's now *her* thing. She's applied to go to Virginia Tech. I'm pretty sure she'll get accepted."

"Peer Counseling, huh?" Jason asked, laying more gravity into his words.

"Yeah," Rob said. "She knows what you and I have been going through this week. She talks to me about it in Civics class. Katie takes some heat because she doesn't roll with the FFA, so she understands the deal. She says her door is open if either of us want to talk to her after school."

"Nah, I'm usually working and once that final bell rings, I want nothing to do with Merriweather. Nice thought, Katie."

"Well, anyway," Rob muttered, swinging back to the topic at-hand. "Unless Emily Haney's developed a Sigourney Weaver level of acting, she's toast in school and we're not even through September. You know how those fucking savages roll at school; discreet rhymes with obsolete, which will be Emily with all the talk about her bun in the oven. I swear she looked like she was cringing more than walking from the nasty things people were saying. Dirk Gleason got in the worst lick with 'The baby's gonna be a ginger-haired hesher.' That seemed to really get to Emily. Even Jake Flanagan wouldn't stoop so low."

"Why do we care about Emily Haney, anyway?" Jason barked, dropping his arms to his sides. "It couldn't have happened to a nicer girl, though I wonder if she'll keep the kid."

"I once heard Emily say where her family goes on Sunday mornings, dude. Bethany Baptist, where they bash their bibles along with the Catholics. The same bunch puts a different anti-abortion message every month on their marquee next to Route 62. I'd be shocked if Emily's folks let her terminate the fetus."

"I'm technically Catholic," Jason said, dragging his foot through a pile of twigs and leaves.

"Technically?"

"Yeah, Mom used to make me and Dad go to St. Joseph's years ago. I think I should've taken it as a clue when we stopped going. I stopped praying to God the moment Dad had 'the talk' with me, the big speech about his taking off and deeming me the man of the house. Honestly, there's nothing the Baptists or Methodists or Hebrews, Zionists, Pentecostals, even the goddamn Church of Elvis can say to make me ditch Catholicism when I've already had the pleasure of doing it myself."

"Organized religion went right down Jimmy Swaggart's cashola crapper," Rob uttered with a scowl. "Subject change, how's your mother doing?"

"She still sleeps a lot," Jason replied with a hard shrug. "Ma's fallen into a pattern of...what do you call it, hyper...um, hyper...come on, Martino, you're the wordsmith between us."

"Hypersomnia."

"That's it. She gets up and goes to work, she makes meals, but since I'm not home in the evenings as much, she's always putting leftovers on a plate in the fridge for me. Half the time she forgets to cover up the food and the refrigerator drops a chill on the plate that dries the food and robs the taste, especially her Italian chicken which hasn't been up to its usual high standard. Otherwise, she's kind of a ghost. We mumble at each other in the mornings, but we haven't had a solid conversation in weeks."

"Hmm," Rob said, knowing by instinct to let Jason continue.

"She's taking everything hard, and I get that. You know, I forgot to tell you, when I came home from work on Wednesday night, I found Mom in my room, sitting on my bed. She had my headphones on, plugged into my stereo. She was playing side B of Dokken's *Tooth and Nail* on my turntable. Give you one guess what song she was playing."

"Damn. 'Alone Again.'"

"She doesn't even *like* heavy metal, Rob. Mom's more into that hopeless Dan Fogelberg crap. She must've been listening outside my door, as many times as I've played that album. Dokken's gone soft lately, sure, but not so much as to lure *parents*, right? It's freaky how that song resonated with her, and as I said, I get it. I've lost count the number times I've sung that lovesick jam in my room and air-guitared with George Lynch.

"Now there's a visual," Rob said with a light chuckle.

"Broke my heart when I found her like that, man."

"Did your mom even see you there?"

"No. She was pawing at her eyes and blowing into a tissue while she listened. When I saw her pick up the stylus and drop it back to the song's beginning, I just left her there and heated up the cheeseburger she'd made me until she came out of my room and went to bed. I didn't say a word about it to her the next morning."

"Sorry for all you're going through, man. I can count on one hand the number of times my parents had an actual fight, though one was brewing last night, for sure. My dad doesn't usually flip out like he did, but Mom wasn't backing down from him, either. She actually stood up for me keeping my hair."

"Thanks, man," Jason said with reservation, surveying the dropping fall foliage as it tottered to the ground in slow, rocking motions. "Today's Saturday and Ma's up and actually in a fair mood. She's ordering a large pizza and she rented *For Keeps* and *She's Having a Baby* for herself, but I had her get me *Bloodsport,* if you're up for it. Van Damme, the name sells itself."

"Videotapes are gonna put movie theaters out of business," Rob commented. "I mean, the last one I went to see on the big screen was *Friday the 13th Part VII: The New Blood* with you."

"Carrie versus Voorhees, a bigger waste than *whoever's* sperm made Emily Haney preggers," Jason sniped, this time with a grin. "I wish it had been Sam who'd done it, just to see Lee and him go at it, though Lee's twice his size. It'd probably be over in less than a minute."

"Seeing Emily Haney with her tight butt dragging along the floor, I doubt..."

"Sounds like you secretly have the hots for her, Martino, Christ. I mean, *eww.*"

Rob answered simply by pulling his hood back over his head.

Chapter 13

IT WAS THE FOLLOWING MONDAY and Health class had run a minute over the period changeover bell into sixth period, prompting a lot of students to hang halfway out of their seats with anxious groans. The knee jostling many were doing still wasn't enough to cue the substitute teacher for the regular instructor, Josie Yingling, to cut session. This soon into the new school year, Mrs. Yingling had come down with the flu. Her temporary replacement was Gary Scott, a bulbous, sweaty-looking man born with two first names who'd long earned the nickname, "Greasy Guy Gary" from his many sub stints at Merriweather High. "Triple G," as he was also known, was as infamous for wearing the same blue and maroon striped sweater as much as his dandruff-pocked, slicked down follicles.

Triple G was so soft spoken it was hard to take notes, and it wasn't only Jason who'd given up trying to jot down anything from today's lesson on the eating disorders bulimia and anorexia—which had interested him, given his mother's recent standoff against food along with her compulsive sleeping. It wasn't until Eleanor Zahn spoke up and asked Triple G to use the overhead projector and a magic marker over a slice of transparency film that anyone had been able to get the gist of the lesson: mental afflictions causing serious weight loss and, untreated with excessive abuse, heart failure.

At least Triple G had enough reminiscence to cite Karen Carpenter as a celebrity victim of anorexia. The always witty Roberta Bergman scored the lone outburst in class after spooling "Cloooose toooo youuuuuu..." from The Carpenters' enduring soft rock hit. Triple G was hardly amused, nor was his class when he dragged on with more monotony than Ferris Beuller's deadpan teacher, Mr. Lorensax, after the period bell.

"Drink more O.J., Mrs. Yingling," Roberta cracked once everyone vaulted from their seats. *"Please."*

More laughter presided, albeit nobody stuck around to commend

Roberta or even to wait for anyone else. Bodies jammed at the door out of Health class, but sanity prevailed, other than Mark Kline making the comment, "More O.J. for Mrs. Yingling, more Speed Stick for some stanky mofo in here, phewww!"

Whoever the offender was, he or she was gone, as was Jason, who wasn't in much of a hurry as everyone else, since his next class was with Pauline Prescott teaching Algebra II, only a short walk across the promenade to the southwest wing. It was his most dreaded class of the day, considering the best he'd been able to muster in Algebra I the prior school year was a C. He was already in over his head with quadratic equations and complex roots, picturing in his mind an endless lecture from his mother, much less that son of a bitch father of his, who had the absolute nerve to *enjoy* math. Of course, the way his mom had been sleeping all the time, Jason might be able to skim a D under her nose, so long as he wasn't outright failing Prescott's class.

"Outta the way, tubby!" Jason heard a few feet ahead. It was some rude underclassman Jason didn't know, a junior by his estimate, given the cocky swagger many 11th graders had about them with their finish lines for school within sight. He was a stud muffin wannabe with his silk, island print short sleeve (known around school as "Bahama Mikes") jerked open three buttons from this top of his neck. A gold medallion bounced between his considerable pectorals.

The object of his wrath was a porky freshman girl in a potato sack violet sleeveless dress. Her flabby arms wobbled with the rest of her rotund girth. Her brown hair was piled, not mounted, unconfidently atop her head, kept together by a pair of crisscrossed black chopsticks.

Stud Muffin Wannabe was already gone and catching a few glimpses from meandering girls he passed, given the tight crash of his faded jeans. The porky freshman girl slowed down to a lurk, even with her already sluggish stride.

"Hey, Fresh, to hell with that wipe," Jason said to her in passing, trying to boost the shattered girl up or least prompt her instep. Instead, she tucked her head down, the fat rolls of her neck cramming against her chin. Unlike Triple G, who nobody felt sorry for, Jason felt a prick of guilt for nothing he even did once he spotted the hot tears trickling down the girl's face.

Jason reached the main promenade where a hundred or so voices blatted around him. What stuck out the most above the topics spilled between Homecoming and Home Economics was a nonsensical shouting match across the hallway between Barb Everett, who scooted along the auditorium wall and Ernie Fleming, hovering near the announcement boards:

"Fudgepacker!" Barb screamed from her end.

"Carpet muncher!" Ernie shouted back.

Anyone would've thought an actual clash was escalating between Barb and Ernie—anyone who didn't know they were not only best friends, each were gay. They'd grown a reputation for boisterous flag bearing and now in their fourth year at Merriweather, they'd championed their causes with such fervor most of the persecution they'd experienced in the past had begun to fizzle out. Sometimes the remedy against hatred was to confront it wide in the open and with self-assured mock denigration.

Up ahead, Jason saw Lori Phillips, who'd spotted him first. She not only slowed down, she stopped to let him catch up to her.

"What's up there, Morticia?" Jake Flanagan sent to Lori's back. Jason saw her eyes squint with resentment as Jake roused his cronies into a rendition of The Addams Family theme: "Ba ba ba bump!" Two finger snaps. "Ba ba ba bump!" Two more finger snaps. "Ba ba ba bump! Ba ba ba bump! Ba ba ba bump!" Third round of finger snaps before they scooted off, pleased as fuck with themselves.

"The scum that passes for actual people in this shithole," Jason said to Lori, who wore her defiance louder than her Ramones t-shirt.

"Ehh, they're not *all* bad," Lori said back, blowing one of her spilled hairs away from her left eyeball. "Just the majority of them."

"Where are you off to?" Jason asked, trying to sound nonchalant. He'd known Lori since freshman year, and he'd always nodded or waved to her or verbally greeted her whenever they passed each other. An unspoken alliance between metalheads and punk rockers had morphed last year, drawing Jason and Rob to Greg Boedecker and his punk brigade. Since it appeared she'd split from her one-time contingency, this was the first time Jason had fully engaged Lori.

"Trig," she told him, pivoting to aim in Jason's direction for the southwest wing.

"Oh, barf," Jason groaned. "I'll be lucky to skin it through Algebra II."

"I had that last year," Lori said, not so much in a snotty tone, but something swirling inside of Jason making him want to both laugh and grunt at her. "You got Prescott?"

"Prescott," he affirmed.

"She's easy," Lori said. "You *could've* gotten Mr. Corel. More kids transfer out of his class than any teacher here. If you run into any problems, hit me up. I floated by Prescott with a solid A."

"Well, aren't you the cat's pajamas?" Jason poked, trying not to sound mean and knowing he'd failed right of the bat.

"Testy, testy," Lori sent back to him. She'd been more successful in drowning out any spite. A sudden rosiness above her grin said so. "For that remark, you can go pay Jenny Armacost for tutoring services. My offer's now off the table."

Jason let his laughter serve as his response. He'd barely noticed they'd arrived at their respective classes.

The late bell chimed over the lock of their lingering gazes. Beneath the dyed and shocked mop, there was something about Lori which Jason suddenly found appealing. More than appealing, the longer he dwelled on the reddened cheeks of her pale, untouched skin. The only makeup Lori carried upon her was the deep mascara on her eyelids. Her hardiness radiated around her on a daily basis, yet there was now an unexpected modesty to Lori's sudden downward glances and swings back up to him which stirred Jason's interest.

"Go to class, Jason," Lori chuckled, pointing at the ceiling where the bell had sounded off. "We're late. Jenny Armacost would be one of the few in our age bracket who still uses the word 'tardy,' the dweeb."

"See ya," Jason told her with a laugh, drifting into Mrs. Prescott's classroom.

"Yeah, you just might," Lori said back to his back.

Chapter 14

"WOMEN ARE GROSSER than men, foul!"

Rob pulled his latex glove as tight as it would wrap against his fingers as he leaned down inside the middle of three stalls in the ladies' bathroom on the third floor of Grigsby Tools. He'd been assigned the inbound call customer service sector, the largest zone of the building. Rob was revolted by the sight of a balled, bloody tampon on the floor, wrapped inside, and soaked through flimsy toilet paper.

Said toilet paper used by Grigsby Tools was not only cheap, it was worse than what the school used. A common gripe amongst the student body at Merriweather High was you didn't dare take a dump on school premises unless it was dire. The school's paper hand towels did a better job, though they hurt like hell to wipe with, and they'd often clog the toilets the more people used them. Those, of course, which hadn't been wetted and slung against the bathroom walls and ceilings like paper cocoons.

In that respect, Rob was grateful for the much easier, if still disgusting task of cleaning castoff pubic hair, errant piss flings and inner bowl shit streaks (which his peers hysterically referred to "chocolate swirlies") around the men's toilets. Cleaning other guys' waste had given him better appreciation for his mother's longtime nagging to watch his aim in both family bathrooms.

Being indoctrinated into the bodily release patterns on the ladies' side, however, had been a bigger eye opener to Rob than the recurring news of fires ravaging more than a third of the drought-plagued Yellowstone National Park over the summer. His mother was still talking in awe over "Black Saturday," which struck a month ago, engulfing more than 480,000 acres of the park's ecosystem.

"Ma's right about Alice Cooper," Rob muttered aloud, his face crunching in disgust, his voice a gawky echo all around him. "He never would've done that song if he'd had to *pick up* what women bleed."

Even with his fingers protected by the yellow rubber glove, Rob pinched the crimson-stained lump with his thumb and forefinger to little success. The ball threatened to unfurl its nasty contents altogether, the menstrual reek slamming into Rob's nostrils. It reminded him of the gut-churning stench of the gored, fly-ravaged possum he and Jason had found on the trail earlier in the year. Bad enough he was still carrying the barfy brew of Funyuns and Mountain Dew upon his breath from his ten-minute break earlier tonight.

"Jesus," he carped, opening the rest of his sheathed fingers to get a hold of the odious bundle. In his haste to backpedal out of the stall, he not only bashed into the partition, but the sanitary napkin disposal unit itself. A plastic bag flimsier than the office's toilet paper flapped as the lid projected open to reveal an entire pile of used tampons.

When the repulsive task of getting all those bloody discards into his rolling trash can was finally complete, Rob dashed the few feet to the nearby sink. As if the mere suggestion of contact was enough to pass on a potential virus or STD. He rolled his eyes upwards at the sight of a gray sign taped above the basin, no bigger than a postcard. It bore the engraved dictum, "ALL EMPLOYEES MUST WASH THEIR HANDS."

"Everyone else may use the sides of their pants," Rob uttered, his sad attempt to humor himself bombing like a dud around the otherwise empty bathroom.

He felt as stupid as he no doubt looked fumbling for, with his gloves still on, the cold water release knob, unable to get a firm grasp. A thin trail leaked from the spigot until he managed to get it turned all the way.

For this extra effort, Rob was pelted by a backsplash of gushing water. It soaked the bottom of his Anvil band t-shirt and, of course, the crotch of his jeans. He felt his hair whip back with the rest of him, just now feeling used to having no earring jangle about with it.

"Idiot!" he exclaimed, shirking off the saturated latex gloves in detestation of them. They hit the women's room floor with squishy splats which would have made Rob howl with laughter if had been someone else's folly. He reproved himself for thinking he could wash his gloves of the menstrual filth he'd worried would contract onto his skin.

With his freed hands, Rob turned the sink knob backwards until it pushed out a more reasonable gush. Still pissed at himself, he pounded at the bottom of the chalky soap dispenser, wondering how a company so big and respected in the power tool market could buy such shoddy hygiene supplies for their personnel. He kneaded the gritty soap into his already damp palms and scrubbed, then rinsed until he was satisfied.

He checked to make sure his digital Seiko hadn't been ruined by the water. His Aunt Trudy had all but licked her chops in wait when he'd opened her gifted watch to him, and this made him more protective of it. It was still blinking away, showing a time of 6:42 p.m. Another hour eighteen until he was free for the night.

Only three days on the job, Rob hadn't yet felt like he was one of the crew, underscored by the pervading silence in the cantina between the elevators leading up to the corporate side of the campus and the long tunnel leading to Grigsby Tools' deafening warehouse. He wondered how his father had enough hearing left to play his 45 records all the time, judging by that tinny repository din greeting employees and visitors all the way to the main lobby. Inside the adjacent cantina, it was louder, enough to smother any proper conversation between the three-man-one-woman cleaning crew Rob had joined.

Chuck Davis' personality was flatter than a wilted daffodil. On orientation day, Chuck had done little more than show each person to their respective work site, and, in Rob's case, to go over a handful of spray, wipe, swish, and mop procedures before turning him loose.

So far, Chuck had zero to say during their breaks, and neither did Rob's adult counterparts, a beer-bellied schlump in his forties named Leo Pizzillo, and the elder stateswoman of the group, Rosita Hernandez. In Rosita's case, she'd migrated into the country two years ago according to Chuck, though she offered little English to her co-workers. Her sourpuss expression indicated the basic salutations and thank yous were all she cared to learn. Nobody knew her age, nor would they. Chuck hazarded a guess at 55, which suited Rob just fine, since the best he'd managed all week from Rosita was a disinterested wave.

The common bond the three seniors had was smoking, which found them bonded at the same table closest to the vending machines, hunkered around a crinkled aluminum ash tray. Their inhalations made for most of the conversation they had for one another. Rob, being the youngest, oddest man out, outdid their exhalations and ash flicking with his Funyun crunching. Week one, Rob was already wondering when the soonest opportunity to quit this place would be without letting his dad down.

"Hello?"

The intruding masculine voice not only startled Rob, it made him feel like he'd been caught tooling around in the women's room instead of cleaning it. Rob had to retell himself he belonged in here and the added yuckiness of that thought perturbed him more than being called to by one of Grigsby Tool's late workers. One of the few things Chuck Davis had inaccurately projected on day one was the "slim-to-no likelihood" of having to interact with any of the company's direct employees.

"I hear you in there," the voice summoned again, this time giving Rob an unexpected shiver. It sounded authoritative, as if one of the company brass had come to ream Rob out for what, splatting his soggy work gloves on a floor he'd end up mopping later?

"One minute, please," Rob squeaked, crushing his eyes in frustration, not to cry, but to reprimand himself for sounding so pitiful.

"Take your time," the male voice said back, far easier this time. "I'm just looking to get this emptied and cleaned, if you would."

Rob bent down and scooped the gloves off the floor, making a mental note to mop extra thoroughly in the spot later.

What did the guy want from him? Empty and clean what? Rob had been through all the cubicles and managerial offices to empty the trash cans. It was the first task he set himself to, since a lot of Grigsby employees had the nasty habit of dumping their half-filled coffee cups and soda cans, forcing him to change the plastic bags in many cases. Only three days in, Rob already had a system down, which had him saving the partition dusting, desk sanitizing, and lastly, floor vacuuming for the last hour of his shift.

He hung the sopping gloves over the edge of the rolling trash can and then opened the door out of the women's room.

Before him was a young professional type, only five years Rob's senior at the most, he figured. His party hearty college days still hung about the guy like a clinging shadow of debauched times. The junior buck's dusky hair was spiffy and taut, even at this late hour, but his white dress shirt was rumpled around the edges of his otherwise cut waistline, and his sleeves had been rolled up to reveal his pasty yet thick forearms. He worked out, Rob assumed, since he could see veins raining into his sizable hands. He wore a claret and white striped necktie. Rob's staunch Democrat of a mother might call the conservative lined pattern "Old Guard."

"Hey guy," the overtime swinger said with a crisp smile as fake as his voice, excusable given the fact he was the last of his division to leave work for the day. He pushed a golden glass ashtray out to Rob. "You mind?"

Caught off guard being asked on the spot for something so trivial—to Rob's mind, anyway—the gesture rang of the term he'd heard in his Economics class last week, "instant gratification." If the tampon incident wasn't toadying enough, being stalked down like this was even worse.

"Sure," Rob mustered, taking the ashtray and nudging the bathroom door open with his behind. He hoped the junior executive hadn't spotted the big splotch at Rob's groin. "Be right back."

"Appreciate it, man. You're new."

"Yeah, I just started," Rob said, trying to push some muscle into his projection, but still feeling flutters of nervousness and resentment wreaking havoc inside of him.

"Looser dress code than the prior crew," the young office worker noted with a tinge of snootiness. "You do a better job, though. Those people before, they were Chinese, Japanese, Korean, ah, who the hell cares? You can't trust people who don't speak your language, you know what I mean? Never could get them to spray out my ashtray, either and it'd be *days* before they emptied it. That's just uncivilized. Also, I can't prove it, but I'm convinced one of them stole my Ron Jaworski autographed football from my bookcase. Last time I do something *that* stupid again. Live and learn, am I right?"

"Oh, man," Rob offered, since nothing else came to mind to mask his shock as he let the women's room door swing shut between them.

What was that word he'd learned in World History last year? National...*nationalism*. Yeah, that's what this was, Rob deduced. He loved his country, but this apprentice exec's boldfaced self-entitlement on top of his glaring prejudice had Rob silently thanking whatever fates ruled such things for putting him on this floor instead of Rosita.

Rob emptied the ashtray into his rolling can, feeling before spotting the blackish grit printed onto his thumb. Again he rolled his eyes up and squashed an urge to sigh out loud. Instead, he grabbed his spray bottle of sterilized cleaner and gave a harder squirt than he needed to. The jettisoned liquid pummeled the ashtray, cutting a wide hole into the pallid residue and lifted threads of it high into air. Most of it landed into the trash can harmlessly, but a glob fired up and spattered Rob's cheek.

"Motherfu —" he snarled, catching himself in time and wiping the wet soot with his left forearm. The arm now carried a dark, lined smear.

After swabbing the ashtray out with a paper towel, so clean it looked brand new, Rob left his thumb and forearm alone, knowing he'd be back at that sink to wash himself again. Remembering his soaked pants and feeling mortified it might've been detected by Young Nationalist, Rob opened the bathroom door again just wide enough to hand the ashtray back over.

"Sweet," Young Nationalist said admiringly, tilting his freshened ashtray like it was a prize. "I don't know, maybe it's those slanty eyes on the old crew they couldn't clean worth a damn. Glad we have people who know what they're doing now."

"Take it easy," Rob said, trying to hide his distaste of Young

Nationalist and hoping the guy's working overtime wasn't going to be a routine.

"You too, bud," Rob heard as the door thunked, shutting them off from each other again.

At 8:00 pm, Rob gave Chuck, Leo, and Rosita a wave bye, then an actual "See ya" to the sleepy-looking night guard, only known to Rob by the last name of "Mensah" on his brass nametag.

Still tasting the granular dust from the vacuuming, which Rob had to double-time in the last twenty minutes, he wished he'd had another Mountain Dew to wash it gone. Knowing he'd yet again offed the Colt Cola back home, he mulled his choices of drink which could best kill the dreck inside his mouth. The sugary citrus of Tang seemed like the best option, but that was still another seven minutes away.

Leaving the building to the night sky and the parking lot lights glaring overtop his father's running grey Dodge Diplomat sedan with its black hard top roof, Rob felt his body not only relax, but ease. He wasn't sure how long he'd want to remain at this job but having to rely on his dad to pick him up from work was already telling Rob he'd be in it for a long haul. It had long been established by his parents Rob would work and save for his own vehicle, much less his own auto insurance. All of that seemed so far away, especially with a foreseeable trip to Curry's Music with Jason on the horizon. The mention of Virgin Steele had stuck with and pestered the bejesus out of Rob ever since Jason brought them up last weekend. How would Rob *ever* save for a car with so many mandatory heavy metal albums coming out?

He put his hand up to acknowledge his dad, smirking at his father's finger drumming along the steering wheel, and his body rocking in the car. The Diplomat shook and wobbled in time, amusing considering its boat-like body. Only one artist ever got Rob's dad so animated, and as he stepped off the sidewalk into parking lot, Rob could hear the muffled clamor of Buddy Holly's "Tell Me How" booming from the car's tape deck.

If Rob hadn't flash-checked both sides as he entered the parking lot as one would across a busy road, he would've missed seeing the 1968 Nova in the distance of the parking lot.

It was the louder chug of its idling .289 high performance engine drawing Rob's attention to the muscle car, then it was the sight of four beefy teenager boys crammed in their all-too-familiar blue cord jackets.

"Holy shit," he gasped, freezing in place.

All four somehow fit their sizeable bodies along the front of the Nova. Billy Metcalf was the only one missing from the group, but his brother Lee was well-accounted for, occupying the entire right edge of the Nova. The car's headlight flexed between Lee's spread open fork, gleaming like a lit phallus. His arms were folded across his colossal chest; only Chris Majors or rock club bouncers could outclass him. Butch Hill and Steve Fick were tugging cans to their lips and even from this distance, Rob could detect the traditional blue-ribbon symbol, the tint matching their daunting jackets. Pabst Blue Ribbon beer.

Sam Shaffer detached himself from the left front end of the Nova and put his right hand up in Rob's direction. With a wretched grin made even more unsettling by the lamp post above him, he twinkled his fingers at Rob.

Sam's comrades began to laugh and they repeated the same fiddly gesture at Rob.

Rob's dad was carrying on too much in the Dodge to see all of this, but upon spotting his son, he leaned to the right and opened the passenger door.

Rob's legs now felt more unstable than that time at age eight, when he'd come out of the funhouse at the East Lloyd Fireman's Carnival, those shifting metal floor slats catching him unawares, trapping him for a moment as they shimmied beneath him. Only by grabbing the convenient rails on either side had Rob avoided falling altogether, but it had taken him a good minute to conquer the confounded sliding thing. Further insult, he'd toppled and gotten swept upwards a couple times in that dratted rotating tunnel at the end of the funhouse.

He could hardly stand straight then. Right now, his legs were stymied altogether. "Stymied," a funny, big money word losing its resonance in a hurry with Rob.

Butch Hill peeled off a whopper of a belch from their spot, turning the farmer gang's snickers into hock-filled laughing. Steve Hill leaned to his side and let a brown gob of chew splatter against the lot.

None of them made any motion forward. They seemed content to simply taunt Rob. How did they even know he was working at Grigsby Tools, unless they'd been stalking him?

Shaking with each step as he implored himself to move forward without further haste, Rob couldn't pull the car door shut harder once he'd dumped himself in. In past years, his father would bawl Rob out for slamming doors. Given his father's recent Vietnam invective, Rob braced himself for another loud corrective. Tonight, though, his dad was in his Buddy Holly nirvana and no scolding came. Thank God for small favors grown epic.

The music was so *loud,* but it didn't matter to Rob. Anything to drown out his spiking fear as his father put the Diplomat into drive after saying hello to him, then pulling away.

Rob didn't want to look out the window, but he was afraid not to, just in case Sam and his buddies had suddenly decided to charge them.

Lee, Butch, and Steve sent Rob a mock wave goodbye. Sam, looking far more serious, dragged his middle and forefinger across his throat with a hideous scowl Rob would never forget.

Chapter 15

THE HYDRAULIC THUD of a timecard punch never sounded so good.

An hour after his best friend got off from his job on the other end of Bradenton, Jason clocked out for the night, having first relieved himself in the back of the Super Thrift break room. He'd held himself the past two hours, determined to complete in full another one of those obnoxious task lists Todd had left for him along with an official title shift from bagger to stock clerk. Not that Jason would be exempt from bagging when the store was swamped, tonight wasn't the case, thankfully.

Todd had been in the store only long enough to monitor Jason's progress, which had annoyed more than motivated Jason. He felt like he was being watchdogged. Tonight, Jason had been on such a tear he'd finished all eight items on the list, this time written in Todd's choppy block writing overtop a sku number printout from two weeks ago. The numbers were insignificant for Jason's purposes yet aggravating to his eyes. Secondary stress he'd given no further thought to once he'd accomplished his tasks.

For break tonight, Fan Parsley (the goofiest name for the cutest girl employed by the store) had smuggled Jason a chicken breast on its way to the trash. Super Thrift's policy was to remove all unsold fried chicken by 7:30 pm, as to have enough time to break down and clean the heaters and trays. By habit, Fan pinched chicken drumsticks, wings, and breasts about to be tossed out for her boyfriend. She'd stowed an extra piece for Jason tonight, adjusting her own break time when he finally went late at 7:45. Fan was grumbling how her boyfriend, Steve, had been spending more time in downtown Baltimore than in their shared apartment on the outside of Bradenton. Steve had been reportedly coming home after midnight a lot and had dropped, by her estimation, "an easy ten pounds." Drugs, Jason almost said out loud to her, but he'd sensed no need to do so. Not even three layers of Cover

Girl could hide Fan's tired eyes, no doubt from constant anxiety her boyfriend was taking them both down a road of despair.

Jason didn't want to blame the chicken, but he was feeling queasy. He figured the heavy drop in his stomach was more from the pressure put on him by Todd and the constant core crunches from moving weighty stock all night. Coach Schaub would've no doubt endorsed this grassroots form of bodybuilding. Jason already had respectable forearm strength from bagging and hauling shopping carts into the store, as many as seven at a time. His increasing muscularity gave Jason the most satisfaction he'd enjoyed other than beating Danny Tignall and Bennett Walsh on the track last week.

He'd kept his mind off of school during shift only by thinking about Emily Haney, of all people, but most of the time, Lori Phillips. The daydreams he entertained with Lori present in all of them had him pumping fists in the air at a concert with her, to gnawing on a pizza of her choice at Salvatore's two towns over in West Lake.

As for Emily Haney, Rob's intel had been spot-on. She'd become persona non grata around school, not only toward Lee Metcalf, but the entire lot of her farmer friends. For the first time since Jason could remember, Emily had come to school in ordinary clothes. She'd nixed her FFA jacket and wore less snugger jeans with cotton blouses. Jason didn't like the girl, but like Fan tonight, Emily had looked so glum at school today, a bipolar opposite of that sneering, cackling witch who'd been in the store with her former friends to ridicule him last week.

Neither Jason nor Rob had expected Emily to send them a half-hearted jerk of her head upwards in the halls during fifth period changeover. "Shoe's on the other foot now," he'd said. "Let's see how she likes it."

Yet, there was something to Emily's torn-down schlumping Jason couldn't stop thinking about. Such defeat on a person on the outs from a pack of hellraisers she'd aligned herself. However and whomever got the girl pregnant had become such high drama, Emily Haney was paying the price beyond the frightening prospect of becoming a teen parent.

His entire day now put to rest, Jason turned to an iron partition holding squatty lockers made available for store employees to stash their jackets, purses, small purchases and anything they couldn't have on the floor. Using the same red Master combination lock he utilized in the boys' locker room for Weightlifting class, Jason rapidly turned the dial, as if someone might burst in and catch him to steal the release code. 12 right, 26 left then 9 to the right again, *click!*

Jason's locker was logjammed with his bookbag from school and "The Armor," which he always wore in and out of the store as a moderate act of boldness. In recent weeks, though, he'd come to realize nobody but himself gave two shits about his heavy metal garb at Super Thrift. Once the transformation from headbanger to stock boy was made with a simple slip-on of a dress shirt and tie and pulling back of his hair, Jason fit in at the grocery store as well as his co-workers.

Feeling proud of himself having had enough time to face the shelves in Aisles 4 through 8 (one of the most perpetually useless jobs to do during store hours, in Jason's opinion), he dragged his denim vest out of the locker with a ginger tug, so as not to yank any of the fifty-plus buttons off. Grunting as they caught the steel edges of the locker, the buttons rolling and flapping like a metallic calliope, Jason slowed his yank, learning from past lessons. He'd lost buttons before, the most recent case being a D.R.I. (a punk band turned thrash hybrid whose acronym stood for Dirty Rotten Imbeciles) button with their trademark runner street sign logo. He'd tossed a private tirade for the ages in this very spot when the stick pin fastener split apart from his forceful pulling. Nobody had been within earshot of him, at least.

The trouble button which now snagged was the cigarette toking angels from the cover of Black Sabbath's *Heaven and Hell* album. This, Jason managed to trip loose with his forefinger until the vest got hung up yet again, strange irony, on a button sporting the band logo for Ronnie James Dio's post-Sabbath solo act.

"What do they call that, kismet?" Jason asked to no one, putting out a horns-up salute. "Totally metal. Hails, Ronnie, whatever you're doing right now, singing, kissing dragon eggs, chasing rainbows…"

The vest finally extracted then strapped upon Jason's body with little effort beyond the initial wrenching, he grabbed his bookbag and hooked one strap over his right shoulder. He'd forgotten having bought a two pack of Devil Dogs earlier, leaving one for later after he'd hurriedly woofed one with the chicken breast. He'd left the remaining Devil Dog atop the bookbag so as not to have it crushed, but somehow, true to its namesake, it had obnoxiously squirmed to the rear corner of the locker. It was now a cream-exploded wad of chocolate mush.

"Pisser," Jason mumbled with a sigh, pitching the slaughtered Devil Dog into the trash can outside of the employee locker room. He adjusted his bookbag so the bulk rested firmly in the center of his back as he aimed for the front of the store.

It being 9:06 and past closing time, there were a few straggling customers who, in plain sight, ignored senior store manager Merle Alves' sickening, congenial prompt over the store intercom to bring all final purchases to the checkout.

Harriet Kapres was the lone cashier still on register and the perturbed look she fired at Jason on his way out cut him a little. The store had hired some spindly kid named Clint to take Jason's spot as the primary evening bagger. Clint, still new to the job, looked exasperated and shell-shocked as he ruffled open a paper bag and began stashing frozen foods into it. He'd been halfway through the task when the customer stopped him with a request for Clint to double bag.

Jason felt for the rook, since the same thing had happened to him countless times, much less being the short straw drawer having to stay late to accommodate the selfish clods who couldn't get their business done before 9:00 p.m.

"Have a good night, Mr. Hamlin," Jason heard as he turned the corner and pressed his foot upon the rubber mat activating the automatic swing of the main doors. He also heard a set of jangling keys announcing Merle Alves.

The medium-built manager was reported to be only 41 years old, but his gray-shocked hair and beard, plus the wrinkled crow's feet around his hawkish eyes spoke more of 61. Merle was nonetheless the trimmest of all the Super Thrift supervisory staff, a striking contrast to the pot-bellied, Viking-esque meat department manager, Bill Utz.

"Good job tonight," Merle told Jason, which stopped Jason in his haste long enough to smile and respond.

"Thank you, sir, I appreciate that."

"Todd can be hard on clerks," Merle said in the same way-too-accommodating voice he used on the intercom and when dealing with customers face-to-face. "He keeps things flowing around here, though, and we have a big shipment coming tonight. Glad to see you pulling your weight."

"Thanks again," Jason said, feeling a loft in his chest. It felt good; nearly as good as his run-in with Lori Phillips this afternoon, since it appeared something was there between them. If he'd been assessing it correctly. "See you tomorrow."

Merle nodded, then waited for Jason to leave the store before locking the glass door behind him.

Outside, the raw air made Jason realize just how warm the store was inside. He wondered how it was the temperature presiding over George County could swap from sweltering to nippy in the matter of a couple weeks so fast. Nowhere near as frigid as the dairy cooler, Jason granted, but it would be a crisp night walking from the store through the wheat field across the street and onto the train tracks.

He'd left his Walkman inside of his book bag and remembered he'd come to work from school listening to a recorded copy of Possessed's *Seven Churches*. On the flipside of his 90-minute Maxell XLII chrome cassette (the *only* brand that mattered, according to both

Jason and Rob) was Voivod's *Killing Technology*.

This tape, Jason had scored via a female pen pal named Jennifer, who lived in Matawan, New Jersey. He'd found Jennifer in the classifieds of the British-published *Kerrang!* mag, one of the few which listed fellow American heavy metal fans under the pen pal calls. Jason had reached out to Jennifer on a whim, the novelty of having a female metal friend to chat with being irresistible, since there were no female metalheads at Merriweather High. Rocker chicks, sure, plenty of those, but they were motoring with Sister Christian more than getting caught in mosh.

Even with the long waits between mailed communication dispatches, Jason had come to realize Jennifer knew her stuff. After four months of mailing each other handwritten letters talking about heavy metal music, they'd swapped cassettes. In the scene, it was lauded as "tape trading." In exchange for Jennifer recording him *Seven Churches* and *Killing Technology,* Jason sent her a tape copying Piledriver's *Metal Inquisition* and Whiplash's *Power and Pain.* Jason had razzed Jennifer for not owning any of Whiplash's albums, given the band had formed out of Passaic, her proverbial back yard.

Pulling his schoolbag off long enough to grab his Walkman, Jason thumbed the fast forward button to finish spooling the dead space on the tape after *Seven Churches* so he could begin *Killing Technology* fresh.

Flipping the tape over in his machine, then hooking the plastic latch behind the player to his right hip pocket, he fixed the corded headphones around his ears and pushed play.

This time, Jason mounted the bookbag to himself with both straps as the front door of the store, re-opened by Merle, wheezed behind Jason. The same grouchy looking woman who'd made Clint re-bag her frozen food bulled her overflowing shopping cart past Jason. He could see her shake her head in disbelief upon the mere sight of him as she wrestled the cart with exaggerated force in the direction of her car, an old powder blue Torino with a vinyl top roof.

"Whatever," he mumbled as loud as he dared when they were both far away from each other. Then, as *Killing Technology* unwound through its countdown intro, he mimicked the robotic edict, "We are connneeecteeeed....."

The anticipatory buildup of the album's title track amped Jason's sore feet, and give him the bounce needed to hike the near three miles home. Earlier, he'd kinda wanted to call his mom and ask for a pickup, but she was drowned by her own problems. Any request Jason had of her, few as they were, felt like he was infringing upon her.

Torino Lady had somehow unloaded her cart into the trunk in nanoseconds and she was already pulling away. Coming to the outer rim of the store's parking lot, Jason saw out of the corner of his eye she'd left the shopping cart next to the empty space where her Torino had been, instead of taking the time to roll it back to the sidewalk in front of the store. That would be Clint's problem now. The cart began wobbling on its way and Jason winced to see it drift, as fate would have it, then smack into a sparkly new Dodge Ram pickup.

Voivod was playing at lightspeed in Jason's ears, or he would've heard the animalistic roaring of .289 horsepower drawing upon him.

Jason trotted across the two-lane service road of 62 on his way to the empty wheat field. The ground spread before him looked chalky beneath the half-full moonbeam.

Like one of Leatherface from *Texas Chainsaw Massacre's* hapless victims being first pummeled across the dome with a hand sledge, a shocking, severe pain raged inside Jason's head. It had nothing to do with Jean-Yves "Blacky" Thierault's battering blower bass or drummer Michel "Away" Langevin's wicked blast beat patterns.

Jason came close to collapsing on the other side of the road. He staggered to stay on his feet and he thought of the word "vertigo" in confusion. The outrage bellowing inside his brain told him vertigo had nothing to do with it.

He squinted down to see an unopened can of Pabst Blue Ribbon, just as another one landed near his feet. That one had been opened but unfinished, as beer geysered out of the can, splashing his shoes and the ankle cuffs of his jeans.

His senses coming around through the twinges astounding his head, Jason yanked the earphones off and he whirled in approximation of where he thought the blow had come from. He could feel a swelling where he'd been hit upside the head as he spotted Sam Shaffer behind the wheel of his 1968 Chevy Nova. Leaning out the passenger side was Lee Metcalf, who shot Jason a victorious look. The guy was so stinking big he nearly filled out the entire passenger seat window. Someone from the back of the car handed Lee another unopened beer as he pushed his entire girth out of the car and cocked his arm to hurl it at Jason.

"Cops!" Jason heard someone, Sam, he believed amidst the swirling between his ears, shriek from inside. Despite his mounting dizziness, Jason could see the white and black boxy Crown Victoria belonging to the town deputy, Alan Bohager, making the scene.

"You got lucky *this* time, prick," Lee snarled at Jason as he sandwiched his way back into the Nova.

Instead of peeling off, Sam Shaffer had enough presence of mind to pull away and work to the posted speed of 40 miles an hour. The maneuver was ineffective though, as Deputy Bohager, no doubt accustomed to putting out Shaffer's proverbial fires around town, fish hooked in the middle of the road and threw on his cherries. In the distance, not even a quarter mile, Jason saw swirling blue and red lights on the side of the road, Sam Shaffer's nabbed Nova now parked in front of the deputy.

Whether or not Deputy Bohager saw Jason out there, it didn't matter. Jason checked the back of his head to make sure he wasn't bleeding. That much covered with a clean hand, the nasty bump developing there swelled to his touch.

Part of Jason wanted to seize the beer cans and haul ass over to Sam's car and return the favor. Part of him wanted to take those cans to Deputy Bohager to hang those farmer bullies with. In the latter case, Jason knew there was at least one beer in the car, the one Lee Metcalf had intended to pelt Jason again with. That one should've been enough to incriminate them, Jason surmised through his rising ire.

"Fucking bastards," he snarled, wanting to charge over there, but having enough presence of mind not to. Not even Deputy Bohager could stop Lee Metcalf if he wanted to finish the job on Jason, regardless of the risk of arrest on-the-spot.

Everything had happened so fast Jason found his headphones dangling around his neck as Voivod vocalist Denis "Snake" Belanger prophesized *"People are gonna progress, who knows whether we'll get more or less..."*

"Preach on, brother," Jason sneered, rubbing the back of his tingling head. "Those pieces of shit are gonna get *more* somehow, some way, I promise it..."

Chapter 16

"GOD, IF YOU EVEN EXIST, give me a filled gas can, a butane torch, and Shaffer's Nova left unattended," Jason fumed to himself in front of the vanity mirror in the bathroom. The overhead fan with its failing motor purred for a moment before cutting out altogether with a sickening wheeze. The fan had started to a die after his father had moved out and his mother never made good on her promise to hire a handyman to fix it. Jason had forgotten about the stupid, worthless fan when he'd flicked on both switches in the bathroom. He had harsher things burning on his mind.

"Better yet with all of them inside. I'll praise you, Moses, and all the damned apostles in the book of Exodus with an offering longer lasting than a burning bush."

He swabbed the back of his head with a wetted washcloth, taking his chances with a pristine white one, having little concern of his mother walking in to chide him for dirtying it. She was dead to the world in her bedroom, what did a sullied washcloth matter right now? He wasn't even sure he would tell his mother what had happened to him tonight, not the way she'd been checking out most nights these days. As it was, he didn't even want to tell Rob, at least not until tomorrow.

Spot-checking the cloth, he'd left no blood stains, only a faint grit which could be washed gone, if not bleached out, worst case. He doubted his mom would even spot it.

Jason had kept his earphones off the rest of his walk home, instead muttering assertions of vengeance to an obtuse night sky along the train tracks. Otherwise, only the sounds of his feet scuffing along the slats, the faint muffle of a dog barking somewhere, and crickets in a far happier mood than Jason. After tonight, he would never again feel safe in the open with a Walkman affixed to his ears.

The house was quiet, as he'd expected. He was now certain he didn't want to tell his mother he'd been pelted with beer cans, one unopened. Assaulted, whatever degree the police would've ruled it, had Jason run over to Deputy Bohager and reported it instead of leaving the scene. He'd been angry, yes, but scared as well. Having been attacked like that with his defenses down, ears shielded to the danger seeking out and finding him, Jason felt violated. Embarrassed, even.

For all these emotions tumbling through Jason's mounting headache, he found himself right now wishing he'd wake his mother up, drop to his knees, and put his head in her lap to sob everything out. Echoes of his father calling Jason a pussy stopped him from seeking his mother's comfort.

"You *are* a pussy," Jason condemned his teary reflection. "You should've crucified Shaffer and those motherfuckers, never mind how big Lee Metcalf is. Son of a bitch needs to pay. They *all* do."

Having no target but his reflection, Jason launched a half-punch, whiffing inches away from the mirror. It was as if he'd decked his own likeness across the chin, only the vision on the other side hadn't felt a single thing, and worse, it was leering at him, calling him a loser without ever moving its lips.

"I guess you're right, Dad," Jason spewed, lowering his fist without letting it drop altogether.

His mother had left a plate of fish sticks on the kitchen counter for him, but Jason was nowhere near hungry. He ended up pitching them away since they'd been burnt on the bottoms. He took only a swig of Sunkist orange soda which he'd left in the fridge the night before. It tasted sour to Jason for some reason, and with the remaining contents poured down the sink, the Sunkist bottle joined the abandoned fish sticks.

Smelling like beer gone sour inside a bucket of Pine Sol, all Jason wanted was a shower to get rid of the stink. Bad enough he'd had to spray down his shoes outside with the knotted garden hose after a duel of disentanglement. His saturated Nikes would still be drenched in the morning, but at least Jason had a backup pair of cream-colored Converse Chucks to use tomorrow. Not ideal for long distance walking and being on his feet all night at Super Thrift again, but the semantics of sore feet were nothing compared to the achy and enraged fulminations inside his head right now.

Jason peeled off his tie, then unbuttoned his shirt, wincing with every movement. He wanted something to kill the pain. Thinking about Lee Metcalf battering him in the head was only making things worse. He knew his mother kept both Anacin and ibuprofen for herself in the medicine cabinet, since he seldom used over-the-counter drugs. Opening the cabinet, Jason was wowed to find an old box of St.

Joseph's Children's "candy aspirin."

"Geez, Ma," he uttered, pulling the box out and finding it had expired back in 1983. For the first time tonight since leaving Super Thrift, Jason chuckled, if more for incredulity than actual amusement. The laughter came unexpectedly, and it was short-lived.

Tossing the outdated kiddie pills into the mini trash can next to the commode, he found the ibuprofen and popped four of those, slurping water from the faucet to wash it down. Remembering his mom once saying ibuprofen was good for reducing swelling, Jason hoped she was right.

After a tough swallow made worse by a sudden upsurge of bile, Jason brushed his tongue all around his mouth, grimacing at the acidic taste. The rest of his face remained hardened with all the fury of the past couple weeks, no, the past handful of years, his ire escalating each second he dwelled on it.

"Never again," he snarled, rubbing the lump on the back of his head, this time ignoring the judder from his touch as he left the bathroom.

Down the hallway, his mother's room was quiet. A bit *too* quiet, Jason considered, as he paused at her bedroom door.

The old house rule used to be Jason was to knock before entering his parents' room when there had been two of them. There was an unspoken binding to the rule with just his mother occupying the bedroom she'd shared a near lifetime with a man who'd lost his love for her. Jason was no longer a kid, however. Only a few months away from legal adulthood and more out of concern than invasiveness, he cracked open the door without invitation.

His mom hadn't undressed. She was still in her mauve slacks and tan blouse. Her opaque hair was spread like a milky tarn about her pillow, the only thing she'd pulled free.

Despite his reeling head, Jason dipped down with his ear next to her, the rouge fading from her cheeks and lipstick crusting around the creases of her aperture. She must've taken her bra off, at least, as her breasts were tumbled into a mound on her left side. Even beneath her blouse, Jason could see those swells pushing outwards in a sizable lump, feeling ashamed and yucky for looking, even though it was to make sure they rose and fell with telltale regularity. He nodded to himself upon hearing twin puffs wafting from her nostrils.

Satisfied with that much, he spotted a prescription bottle on her nightstand.

Jason didn't want to wake her, but he came close to releasing a gasp when he discovered the pills inside the clear orange canister were valium.

Chapter 17

A FEW MINUTES BEFORE HOMEROOM bell, Jason was hovering at his locker, gaping into the vacant top cubby, emptying his divergent thoughts into it. He'd felt bad snapping at Rob on the walk to school after his friend had needlessly asked him three times how his head was doing. The ibuprofen had done its job, the only thing keeping Jason's head lit up being anger. Anger from the beer beaning. Anger for an unexpected shift in soreness to his left ankle, which could've been general fatigue or he could've sprained it a hair trying to keep himself on his feet after being struck in the head.

Anger at, of all people, his mother for rolling out for work ahead of him without saying goodbye, much less good morning. She'd left the kitchen counter a mess with an unpitched empty cup of peach yogurt, a used spoon and butter knife, toast crumbs and an unwiped coffee stain with a further incriminating trail of Sweet and Low. If it had been Jason under normal circumstances, his mother would've reamed him out for the same offense.

Rob had snarked at Jason to "get off the rag" after a round of mutual sniping they both later apologized for and attributed to their encounters with Sam Shaffer and his crew the night before. Jason coming out on the more brutal end of their dual harassment.

So far, Jason hadn't seen any of the farmer gang this morning. The Nova had not yet shown in the school parking lot. Jason had made a point to slip into Mr. Budge's American History classroom (also a sophomore homeroom which gained Jason a gaggle of discomfiting underclassmen stares) to peek outside the window for Shaffer's car.

No sign, even, of Emily Haney, who Jason wondered if she was considering dropping out of school, given her roundabout circumstances.

"Earth to Planet Mongo..."

"Huh?" Jason wisped, shaken from his reverie.

He smelled the reek of tobacco on her before he saw Lori Phillips standing next to him. She'd doused her lips lilac and she'd slavered a heft of similar-colored mascara across the tops of each eye. There was a firm sprout to Lori's hair, like she'd taken the time to gel and meticulously brush out the strands to frame her usual sallow face. For once, color illuminated her cheeks and a thinly spread foundation cast a healthy glow upon Lori's skin. She could've come straight of out of a Sisters of Mercy video and later auditioned herself a makeover on the set of a Revlon commercial.

"Man, where'd you go off to right now?" Lori asked, folding her arms beneath the swell of her chest. Her bangles jangled as an accent to her question.

"Don't worry about it," Jason responded, trying to pass off a coolness he needn't have bothered with. The surprising warmth he felt in Lori's presence took a considerable weight off his shoulders as he closed his locker. Giving Lori another once-over, he rewarded her with an admiring smile.

"I hear Shaffer's got it out for you guys," Lori said, taking a step forward to block Jason from moving. She returned Jason's beam, but the mere mention of Sam Shaffer had ruined the momentum she'd gained with Jason, and she knew it. Her shoulders retreated southwards in a routed droop.

"The rumor mill runs true around here," Jason pined.

"Yeah, enough to debunk that bullshit story about Emily Haney's baby. It's totally Lee's. He even broke up with her over it, the prick. Cissy Fritsch's always been the first to hear anything from Emily, though the clueless twat never sees Cissy's the first to turn on her ginger ass. Now everybody knows and everyone knows Emily's going to abort it. Hey, at least the world will be spared another Metcalf."

"Thank God for small favors," Jason ralphed. For a moment, he considered telling Lori what had happened to him after work last night. He felt a sudden need to talk about it to someone. Someone other than Rob.

"I haven't seen any of those goons so far this morning," Lori said, looking into Jason's eyes. Detecting a point of entry back into Jason's favor, she ran her gaze down his entire body, scanning him before coming back to her starting point. "I didn't see Sam's Nova out there, and believe me, I'm always on guard for it."

"I can relate," Jason said with a single nod. He wanted to laugh, but seeing that Nova last night and Lee Metcalf raining Pabst cans upon him…it was as unfunny, if unsurprising, to know Lee had been an even bigger bastard to his girlfriend.

"Cissy's usually a reliable source, and from what I heard her telling Linda Sizemore on the senior patio, Sam and his friends got their balls broken last night. Busted for drinking and driving. *Underage* drinking and driving. Jeb Metcalf will clean up their mess, as he always does. Helps when you have a few buddies in the town planning and zoning. Poor excuse for a father."

"Yeah, I can confirm all that. I was there."

"What?!?" Lori exclaimed.

"I guess Sam took exception to my opinion when he was bullying on Greg, so now...well, you get the picture. He and his horde have been stalking me and Rob at our jobs. Lee threw beer cans at me from Sam's car after I got off from work at the grocery store. The one that was full hit me upside the head."

"Oh, shit," Lori said, spreading a loom of empathy overtop her profanity. It made her cussing sound sophisticated to Jason and, of all the weird, impossible times, it turned him on. Lori loosened her bangled arm to reach out to him and the twinkly sound calmed Jason even further. Her hand grabbed his right wrist, if only for a moment before letting go. "Are you alright? Let me see."

"I feel like I was mule kicked upside my head," he said, turning his head and pointing at the reddish swelling above the knob of his ponytail, which he'd left tied overnight. The lump had gone down after laying it on the ice pack while he watched a handful of *Mr. Ed* reruns on Nick at Night. Even dumber, Jason right now thought of that doofy talking horse nattering *Wiiillllburrrr, this young lady's pretty durned cute* into his ear. "I'll live. Speaking of Greg, where's he been lately? Nobody's seen him since..."

"I called him a couple times and he's refused to answer," Lori said, raising her eyebrows in feigned acceptance of the fact. "The other guys, same thing. Greg won't come out, much less come to school. His mom mentioned something about taking him to therapy over all this, but he's gone total recluse."

"Not that I'm trying to judge or anything, but you smoke, Lori. What's that about? I mean, I thought you were straight edge."

"Hmmph," she chuckled as the Homeroom bell rang over them. "I only skip meats. Those Ian MacKaye acolytes are boring and so is straight edge. They didn't like me smoking around them either, much less the other things I do, so we don't hang much anymore."

"Other things like what?" Jason asked with furrowed brows. He closed his locker and twisted the black combination dial back and forth. He left his backpack inside and carried only his Biology textbook for first period.

"Wouldn't *you* like to know?"

Lori didn't wait for Jason to respond. She dropped him a wink through her caked violet eye shadow and drifted off toward her homeroom. Her right breast grazed Jason's upper left arm, which had gained an inch of muscle in the past couple weeks.

She didn't excuse herself. She didn't even look back at him. There was a way her skirt shifted about her hips making Lori more of a standout, never mind the speedy vanishing act of kids from the hallways.

Jason smiled in full for the first time today.

Chapter 18

"PAIR OFF!"

The sweat was smelled as much as seen amongst the boys in Weightlifting class. The usual three sets of warm-ups consisting of push-ups, sit-ups, jumping jacks, air squats, toe touches, and lunges had been extended by an additional exercise, one that made half the group chuckle upon hearing it spew out of Coach Schaub's mouth.

Not a guy was laughing, however, after three rounds of hitting the deck like a push-up, instead thrusting the legs out, then yanking them back into their guts. The final sequence to the exercise known as "burpees" was to propel oneself into a leap with hands extended into the air before landing on one's feet. Ten reps each round had left nearly everyone gassed and raised the boys' temperatures so high, there rose a permeation of funk usually detected at the tail end of class.

Only Chris Majors seemed to take the burpee sets in stride. A few of the more athletic football players had gotten through them with minute heaving. Brad Stone, who had just transferred into the class, was downright winded, as if he'd just pulled off an eighty-yard fumble recovery for a touchdown. Brad had dropped out of British Literature and jumped to third period Weightlifting, prompting his varsity teammates to goad him in shameless, butchered English accents. The one that got the biggest roar of laughter (including a poorly covered guffaw from Coach Schaub) was from Danny Tignall, who'd dropped the following like a talking alley cat out of East End London: "Can't pronounce 'crumpets' much less *read* it, can you, old chap, pip pip?"

"Calling that Cockney would be an insult to the real deals," Ricky Groff muttered to Jason with a squint as Coach Schaub let every corner of the auxiliary gym hear his whistle. "Danny's an ethnocentric punk if I ever saw one."

Jason snickered under his breath, nearly snorting in recovery from the burpees.

The weightlifters milled around, sizing one another up and moving on to others until agreeable matches were made.

To a casual observer, this abrupt direction to choose partners seemed effortless for most of the class. Danny Tignall and Bennett Walsh were an automatic twosome. Football players teamed up since they knew each other already. Brad Stone may have become an instant class oaf by attrition, but nobody would argue he was Schwarzemajors' closest match beyond Kyle Boula. Likewise, nobody would claim Chris and Kyle were fans of one another, though outright rivals didn't cut it, either. Accordingly, Schwarzemajors and Brad became a de facto pairing. It took Kyle a couple passes around the gym until he shook hands, no fanfare or blatant enthusiasm, with the likewise reticent Bart Forney, who had on the school's 225 Pound Bench Press Club shirt.

Another taciturn guy who'd gone rogue from Sam Shaffer's bunch last year, Kerry Norfolk, was a broad-shouldered, "corn-fed mofo," as Merriweather High's clown set once derided him. Strange cosmos, Kerry had gone out of his way in the locker room before class to tell Jason he was sorry to hear about the developing saga with his former friends. The events of last night had already become public knowledge, inclusive of confirming the arrests made and subsequent suspensions of Shaffer and company.

Before warm-ups had started, Kerry had made the comment to Jason, "Not *all* of us FFA people go out getting shitfaced and busting skulls at night. Some of us just want to be left to ourselves and our land with all this industry spouting up everywhere in the county. The reason I even stay in Future Farmers is because my family wants me to take over the business when I'm old enough. There goes my dream of joining the Air Force and becoming the next Maverick."

Jason considered approaching Kerry to partner up, but Kerry ended up with Tim Hendry, a lanky if surprisingly strong kid who had Kerry in height by half a foot. Kerry had noticed Jason's advance and gave him an apologetic shrug after sealing the deal with Tim.

Which left only Ricky Groff, whom nobody had considered.

The new duos began chattering to a loud drone and were just as fast smothered by Coach Schaub's insufferable whistle.

"Groff! Hamlin!" Schaub hollered. "You're a team! Now everyone fall in with your partner, three rows!"

Already used to Coach Schaub's love of orderly lines as much as his love of teaching bodybuilding techniques, it was no effort for the boys to form three lines with proper spaced groups of two each.

"Most of you guys are repeats to my class, so you know the drill. Thanks for staying awake for the usual rigmarole over the past week."

This produced a hearty round of laughter all around.

"For the rest of the semester, the man next to you is your partner.

You new guys, here's how it works. You'll be alternating days between upper and lower body, two times each per week. Mondays and Thursdays, one concentration. Tuesdays and Fridays the other. Wednesdays are recovery days, though we don't sit around scratching our nuts. That's for the freshmen geeks in Gym I."

Again, a jingle of hilarity from the boys.

"Those of you taking my class again will be happy to know we'll still be doing floor hockey and box soccer on Wednesdays. Tomorrow, though, I've arranged a game of Dodge Ball against the aforementioned Gym I class. Tignall and Walsh, I expect you guys to be on your best behavior."

A third bout of testosterone-laced merriment ricocheted around the auxiliary gym. Danny Tignall used his thumb and forefinger to blow a roundabout whistle through his peeled lips, a close contender to Coach Schaub's.

"Alright, alright," Schaub said in good humor. "First row and the second one through Riggs and Barnes, you start lower body today. The rest of you, upper. Time to get sweaty, gentlemen."

"Already beat you to it, Coach," Danny Tignall cracked, waving his hand beneath the crook of his floppity, drenched gym shirt.

Bennett Walsh joined in the act. "Burpees, not just what you get from birch beer."

Even Coach Schaub had difficulty avoiding a good laugh at that. To cover it up, he jammed his whistle into his mouth and summoned the class to the stairwell leading down into the weight room.

"I'll try not to embarrass you," Ricky Groff told Jason as they followed the rest of the guys. He put his hand out to Jason for a shake.

Jason inhaled for a moment, wondering how and why he'd gotten stuck with the one guy in Weightlifting class even lesser regarded around school than Jason himself. Jason had started to swell out from the single station exercises he'd done in class so far, and already Jason was wondering if being paired with Ricky Groff would slow his progress. Chris Majors and Kyle Boula wore their respective 300- and 250-pound bench club shirts again today, while Bennett Walsh had earned himself a 200 shirt on Friday when Coach Schaub invited an early-on contest for the achievement shirts.

Feeling a nudge of inspiration, Jason set his long-term sights on gaining one of those 200-pound club shirt for his own.

Deciding a handshake was dorky, Jason grabbed Ricky's slender forearm and bent it upwards, not with the intent to harm, though Ricky flinched in reaction.

"Dude," Jason said with a touch of aggravation as he held his free palm upwards.

"Oh," Ricky responded with a hee-hawish gape to his mouth. He extended his fingers into a palm in receipt of Jason's flesh-smacking high five before yelping, "Yow, man!"

Jason shook his head back and forth as did Coach Schaub, who was standing at the exit door of the upstairs gym. With Jason and Ricky bringing up the rear of the queue, Schaub added, "Sometime today, boys."

The basement-positioned weight room was so cold many of the guys' nipples were pushed through their slickened gym shirts. Some guys carried leftover summer belly fat that was also transparently exposed.

It smelled worse than it did upstairs. The only way it could've stunk even greater was if the guys had been working out in their socks only. It didn't take long for the collective body heat to warm up the compressed room.

The weight room stirred with sounds of clacking steel plates ranging from five to forty-five pounds being slid onto barbells and curling bars. It had taken no time for guys who already knew Coach Schaub's system to get into rhythm. This was not only an easy credit class to them, it was bonus time to bulk up for their respective sports.

Jason was surprised to see an Emerson boom box sitting on a desk hijacked from one of the classrooms upstairs. Chris Majors went over and flipped the power button on and nobody, not even Coach Schaub, dared say otherwise when he left it on the local rock station, 93.4, WRIM. Heart's sexy slide-and-stomp groover "Straight On" filled the room.

"Much better than that sappy love crap they're doing these days," noted Bennett Walsh, though nobody validated nor refuted his opinion.

Schaub only needed to point Jason and Ricky to the one empty station in the upper body section, a lone bench with an unfilled bar. As Schwarzemajors had already assumed a back flat position on another bench with Brad Stone loading up three 45-pound plates on each side, Ricky assumed they'd likewise drawn bench press.

"Let me start with just the bar," Ricky said as loud as he dared to Jason, lying down with his hands reaching up to grab the bar.

"No, man," Jason told him, sighing as Coach Schaub materialized like a pervasive gym genie.

"Military press, Groff," Schaub said firmly before moving on to the next station, where Craig Brunner and Justin Necker were carving the air at their hips with fluid, tandem hammer curls.

"Oh," Ricky muttered with a flush to his face that wasn't from exertion. "Um, I forget how that's done, Jason."

"Alright, lemme in there," Jason gnashed.

"Sorry."

"Forget it, just watch me. You *sit* on the bench facing the bar, okay? You plant your hands beneath the bar. Lock your wrists upwards so you don't bend them back, see?"

Ricky nodded as he watched. So did Craig Brunner and Justin Necker. So did Coach Schaub, for that matter.

"I feel like I can add some weight to this," Jason bragged as he pushed the bar off the rack. "The bar's only 55 pounds, like Coach Schaub said last week. So, you push it up into the air, flexing your straightened arms. When you do the rep, bring it back down to your chest. Repeat. Don't do it across your shoulders like I saw other guys doing. I tried it already, and it's a total bitch on your neck."

Jason loaded the bar back onto the rack and got up, inviting Ricky back to the bench with his hand.

"Good form, Hamlin," Coach Schaub complimented him. "That's some fine teaching, too. I'll be keeping my eye on you to make sure you don't try and steal my job."

"Thanks, Coach," Jason responded with the second biggest smile he'd had today. For a quick second, he let his mind dally to the vision of Lori's swaying skirt.

The next station was dips, which Jason nailed a solid eight reps, shaking with fatigue on the last two for each set of ten. By contrast, Ricky, still the least conditioned guy in the class, was wobbly as he inched himself downwards, his wrists threatening to capsize at the support bars. He could only do three reps per set, and each time, he dismounted sloppily. It was more like a desperate shove free.

After that were arm curls. Jason was able to squeeze off sets of twelve with 25-pound plates cuffed to each side of the EZ curl bar. Ricky needed to drop to tens and only peeled off seven curls per set. Bench was the final station of the day, and when the changeover cycle moved them there, Jason couldn't wait to see what he was capable of.

Ricky asked to go first, taking just the bar itself, finally cranking out an easy ten reps, though none of the other guys paid him any attention. It was when Jason hoisted and slid on a 45-pound plate to one side, then the other, when heads turned their way.

Oblivious to the attention he was getting, Jason thought again about Lori Phillips and how her boob had grazed him. Yeah, he'd felt more sponge than flesh from her bra beneath her shirt, yet he had to wonder if she'd scuffed him on purpose? He hoped so, especially after feeling an erection puff inside his pants earlier watching her swerve her hips as she left him. Had *that* been for his benefit as well?

Jason felt the same stirring downstairs right now and he quickly commanded himself to focus on the bench press, lest he be persecuted for pitching a tent in his shorts in front of the Weightlifting class.

Lori vanished from his mind as Jason only thought about that 200-pound bench press shirt dropping onto his newly chiseled shoulders.

Nobody but Jason could hear female metal vocalist Doro Pesch's lofting summons cast toward him through her robust, Dusseldorf-bred pipes, as if she was leaning smack into his ear to spur him on. As one of the few ladies performing in the heavy metal circuit, Jason had a bit of a crush on her, sure. Most metalhead guys did. Yet it was Doro's class and her humility setting a precedent and separating her from the eye candy blitz of tit-tumbling women who sugarcoated mediocre to awful glam rockers in their million-dollar prefab videos.

Jason wanted to move his lips in time, but instead he let Doro spool inside his mind "All we are, all we are, we are, we are all...all we need..." from her band Warlock's fist-pumping anthem, "All We Are." As if she could hear him say it, he mumbled "Respect," for her benefit only. Ricky heard him but made no indication of it beyond a stupefied expression.

Ricky then shifted behind the bench into the spotter's position, though Jason had very little confidence of Ricky being up to the task of hoisting the weighted bar off his chest, should his attempt at 145 pounds fail.

Jason squirmed until his butt felt comfortable on the rectangular, padded plank beneath him. He planted his feet and grabbed the bar with both fists, remembering to give just a slight arch to his wrists. He looked up, not at Ricky, but at a granite-patterned tile in the weight room ceiling, a couple inches below where he judged his chest to be. He inhaled and held onto his breath, letting it out slowly. He no longer felt sweaty from those annoying burpees, which, combined with the dips, had made his arms a little rubbery.

Despite that, Jason was able to push the 145 pounds off the rack and into a solid holding position in the air. He slowly eased it to his chest, and though he struggled with it a second, Jason found the starch needed to shove it upward again. His wrists began to tire, but he let the weight come back down before completing a second rep, then a third. It took the last bit of his reserves to hoist a fourth before notching the barbell back onto the rack.

"Nice, man," Ricky praised him. "I'm gonna be a while catching up to you."

Jason lingered in his spot on the bench as Curtis Fisher, Merriweather High's JV second string running back, barked at the junior football team's defensive tackle, Gunnar Salmond, to hump up his load of 285 pounds to a full standing position at the squat rack.

They were only outdone by Billy Joel shoving around his verses on the snide and pouty "Big Shot."

"It's not a contest," he told Ricky.

"Tell *them* that," Ricky said sardonically.

The boys finished class to a fitting cool down number on the radio filled with long, opening bars of acoustic guitar and a Mellotron flute. Led Zeppelin's "Stairway to Heaven." As the song built and picked up its electric-bombed crescendo, nearly every guy (Jason included, but not Ricky) was singing along and aping Robert Plant's raised pipes like goof-offs while wiping down the stations:

"And as we wind on down the road...out shadows taller than our soul...there walks a laaaaady we all know...who shines white light and wants to show..."

"There's one for you, metalhead," Bennett Walsh said in front of Coach Schaub, giving Jason a harmless knock on the arm once the song ended. "You're doing alright in here, man. Keep it up."

"Thanks, dude," Jason responded, trying to sound tough, but feeling far too happy inside to project any needless return machismo.

"I agree," Schaub said to Jason once he and Ricky had split up on their way to the locker room. "And I think you're the right guy for Groff. I've seen scrawnier kids than him turn superstar in my class. Both of you, keep your eyes on the big picture."

"We'll see, Coach," was all Jason could muster without coming off like a dork when inside, he was exploding with delight like the joy-spreading Kool Aid Man pummeling his way through an obstructing brick wall.

Chapter 19

"LET'S TALK ABOUT RISK."

Rob shifted in his chair, halting the rapid pump of his knees once he'd drawn the attention of his Economics Teacher, Sandra North. Rob recalled long ago advice passed by his mother to make sure he addressed his teacher right in the eyes, since it was clear she'd targeted him.

"Mr. Martino," she said, keeping a straightforward look at him, all business as it were. Was she looming upon Rob because he looked ready to rocket from his seat, as opposed to the unified slouching and head propping of his fellow students? Was she going to give him grief in front of everyone for his antsy knee-jerking?

"Yes, ma'am," he replied dutifully, even going so far as to straighten his posture. A strand of bangs tipped over his eyebrows, but he would leave it alone until he could get himself off the hook.

North smothered an apparent urge to laugh at Rob's hair spillage as she went on. "Suppose I asked to borrow a hundred dollars from you. Would you loan it to me?"

"I'd need to earn a few paychecks before I'd be in the position to do that, Mrs. North," Rob answered, grimacing at his own satirical response.

The class, however, gave its approval with a communal laugh.

"Hypothetically speaking, of course," Mrs. North said, pushing her left palm in the air to underscore her point. If Rob had offended her, she'd shown no sign of it. Instead of perturbed, she appeared amused. The only sign of any impatience was the way she shifted from right to left and arched her left heel backwards, elevating the foot off the pump of her tan, open-toed leather shoe. No doubt bought at Fayva, since Rob's mom had the exact same footwear. He glanced down only long enough to spot the aquamarine nail polish spread across his teacher's toes.

"Sure," Rob told her, post haste, flashing his eyes right into hers.

His mother would be proud.

"What criteria about me suggests I'm able to pay you back?"

"Well," Rob fumbled, "I don't know. You've been nice since school started up. It seems, anyway."

"It seems. You don't really *know* me, though, do you, Mr. Martino? It's only the second week of school. We're just getting to know one another."

"No, ma'am, I don't."

Rob felt the stares around him without even looking at his classmates. The only one in his eyeshot right now was Marcie Barone next to him. She tilted her head at him, then up at Mrs. North, then back at him. Marcie's teased, brunette hair poofed out so much Rob wondered how Jesse Reinheimer could see past her from his desk behind. A gold crucifix dangling at Marcie's neckline glowed between the collar of her floral pattered blouse. It shined ethereal. Divine, even.

"Would you say I'm a *risk* to loan money to, then?" Mrs. North asked Rob, summoning his and the entire class's concentration by accenting the word "risk."

"Maybe," Rob said, unable to come up with anything as clever as his first response to her.

"Maybe," she said, with a firm nod as she pulled away from him, drifting back to the front of her classroom. "That's exactly right, thank you, Mr. Martino. We all face certain risk in our life decisions. For those of you entertaining the thought of going to college once you get out of high school, that entails risk. You buy a car, there's always a risk element involved. Lord knows I should never have bought that '78 Malibu for all the heartache it gave me."

Nobody laughed, but the smiles around the classroom were as noticeable as the swift interest in their teacher's presentation.

"So too, and *more so* is it with money. Putting your money into a savings account is sensible, and if you're not doing so already, I suggest getting into practice now for your adult lives. There's minimal risk in savings, but I've seen enough mergers and fold-ups in the banking industry to know I want a solid, reputable bank offering me a significant enough interest return on *my* money. Supporting small local banks versus large corporations and conglomerates is honorable, and I can't say enough about building your community from within. Not so cut and dry, though, when it comes to investments."

Marcie Barone swung her head back at Rob long enough for him to take his eyes back off Mrs. North, who turned to her chalkboard and handwrote the word "INVESTMENTS" in block letters.

Feeling even more put on the spot, Rob sent Marcie a silly, crease-filled expression he figured rang of a poor man's Stan Laurel. He blew his bangs off his brows to give them room to bob up and down at her.

Marcie's mouth crinkled bemusedly at Rob before she turned her head forward again. That saying about butterflies floating around in one's stomach during a moment of nervousness or overwhelming curiosity...it's what Rob felt, replaying the crinkle of Marcie's mouth at him inside his head.

"When you're investing your money," Mrs. North went on, glancing again at Rob, then Marcie, as if she'd had a set of eyes peeking through the back of her auburn sculpt, "you're concerned about yield."

She paused again to write "YIELD" on the chalkboard beneath "INVESTMENTS."

"Yield is the return of earnings you get on what's called stock. A stock is a buy-in to a business, which means you own a *part* of that business. There's preferred stock and common stock and I'll get into the differences in a moment. The more stock you own in a company, the bigger you develop your portfolio, which is an overview of all your invested money, the base capital you have to play the market if you're so inclined. My husband gripes I'm always checking the Dow and Nasdaq at day's end before starting dinner, but I have nice chunks dropped into Helene Curtis, Liz Clairborne, and MCI Communications. Hasbro, too, and that's just the inner kid in me. I'm seriously thinking of dumping Tosco since they're starting to tank. The thing to always remember with stocks is there are no guarantees of return, which entails what, class?"

"Risk," answered more than half the class, including Rob. Which also included Marcie, who gave Rob a second passing glance before settling forward the remainder of the period.

"Very good," Mrs. North chirped, once again shifting her stare back and forth between Rob and Marcie before there was no need to.

Chapter 20

IT WAS THURSDAY, cool outside and the sky a slate palette feeling ominously of rain, though the forecast hadn't projected any precipitation until the weekend. For the time since sophomore year, Jason had walked to school without Rob. In fact, Jason had gotten out early, ahead of his mother, who at least remembered to wish him a good morning before retreating into the shower for nearly twenty minutes. He'd counted it before leaving her with a shout into the bathroom. Her return voice had sounded flat, weak, even, but she'd left Jason an apple flavored Nature Valley granola bar, which he'd gnawed gone before he'd ever gotten out of the development.

He'd risked upsetting Rob's parents by calling him at 9:42 after getting home from work last night, letting his friend know Jason had a reason for wanting to get out to school early, but leaving it open-ended. When Rob had pressed Jason for more information, Jason swapped subjects by letting Rob know he'd left his headphones off during the trek home from Super Thrift. Better yet, there'd been no emergence of Sam Shaffer's Nova. Shaffer and his crew had been absent from school most of the week, considering a typical suspension from school lasted three days.

Despite flying high from his success in Weightlifting, Jason had grown irritable at work last night to the point he'd nearly snapped at a customer. A woman suffering from acute adenoidal flaring had asked Jason while he was loading Del Monte peas in the canned fruits and vegetables aisle where the baked beans were located. The answer was a mere few feet away with an easy seven different brands to choose from, including the store's in-house version he considered bland without a couple of chopped hot dogs dumped into them. Miffed as he'd been, Jason had to marshal his best customer service smile instead of blasting the nasally lady as a blind idiot.

When he'd arrived home, Jason found his mother yet again passed out in bed. Same as before, he'd found the bottle of valium, this time tipped over on her nightstand. A handful of pills was scattered across the white doily splayed beneath her bedside lamp. She'd managed, at least, to slip into her red-and-black-checked nightgown, though it was all bunched up on one side up to her hip. She'd tucked herself in only to her knees in bed, giving Jason a glimpse of something no son should ever see of his mother. She'd passed out with her alarm clock radio playing, which Jason had snapped off in the middle of Neil Diamond's "Song Sung Blue" before covering her up.

She'd left him no dinner last night, much less made any meal at all, judging by the empty dish rack. Jason had made himself two grilled cheese sandwiches, this while calling Rob with a film of butter on his hand. Forgetting about it overnight once getting caught up in a late playing of *The Boogens* on HBO, he'd managed to wipe down the slippery receiver before his mother found it this morning. Of course, she'd been in the shower so long, Jason could've left for school at his normal time of 7:10 a.m. and been able to cover his tracks.

Leaving today at 6:40 a.m., Jason had gotten to school with more than half an hour to spare, and yet he'd found a few other early birds who had beaten *him*. Skate rat Kevin Fisher and BMX tricksters Wayne Holcomb and Roger Paquette, the latter two looking like junior pitchmen for Fox Racing in their long sleeve shirts, the wily fox mascot squinting between the block-styled letters F and X.

The trio was having their way in the mostly empty parking lot. Under the overcast sky, Kevin glowed in his oversized yellow shirt with a red *Thrasher* magazine logo blazoned across his underweight frame. He kept his thin brown hair shoved to a waterfall on the left side. Kevin was gliding casually until he shifted to scoop the tail of his board with his back foot, clad in burnt orange suede Vision Street Wear. Altering his front foot on an angle, Kevin popped the rear of the board and jumped in correlation with the motion. He was airborne for a couple seconds, his cascading follicles lifting with him, before planting back down with a hollow "clack!" His rear foot landed on the skateboard first, controlling the front with no problem as he rolled forward cleanly.

"Nice Ollie, dude!" Roger chirped as he pedaled his aluminum frame Redline bike, freestyling into a bunny hop before feathering a few quick snaps of his caliper brakes to halt, then hoisting his stance upwards and atop the contraption. Like a motocross magician, the front bike wheel was pointed between his legs, a scant few inches from his balls. Using the side pegs, Roger pumped his ankles on repeat to pull off an impressive pogo. Jason counted eight bounces as he passed by them.

"Rad!" Wayne called out once Roger slipped out of the bounding position and onto his seat, pedaling once again. It seemed as effortless, to Jason's eyes, as making a packet of Oodles of Noodles in the microwave. Wayne was not so fortunate. He snapped Jason quick a wave, loosening his right hand from the Powerwing handlebars of his P.K. Ripper. The gesture cost Wayne as the bike collapsed on its side, taking him to the pavement with it.

"Yowtch!" Jason called out as he flicked a horns-up at them. He could hear Roger check on Wayne's embarrassing though harmless biff, then Kevin grumbling out of nowhere about the trucks and wheels locking up on his Nuke Boy skateboard. Kevin's contemptuous dismissal of his board as "an utter piece of shit" made Jason dip his head to hide his grin. He and Rob had long shared an unspoken treaty with the freestylers, and he didn't want to offend any of them by laughing at the comedic scene. Wayne saved face by vaulting to his feet and telling Kevin he should switch to Powell Peralta boards.

Jason then saw the metal shop teacher, Mr. Bowers, further down the parking lot, barreling from a plum-colored Dodge Challenger. For whatever reason a shop teacher would need one, Bowers was carrying a briefcase on his way to the south entrance of the school.

Today, Jason had done another first by nixing his heavy metal vest, instead opting for the gray, zip-up hooded sweatshirt he'd worn on the trail with Rob last weekend. No band shirt either. Instead, he'd pulled out an old burgundy Grand Canyon tee his Aunt Peg had brought home for him four years ago. Amazingly, it was still a good fit. He'd even given his hair an extra minute with the hair drier this morning, letting it hang after a more thorough combing than usual until it settled. Any other day, he could've cared less if it frizzed.

Bounding up the steps to the senior patio two at a time, Jason was hoping to spot to Lori Phillips there. He wasn't sure how early she got to school, only that she'd been on the patio before Jason and Rob all week thus far.

Early to a fault, perhaps, Lori wasn't there. In fact, Jason had the entire patio all to himself.

"Seniors rule," he cracked at a murmur, as if needing to hush himself. Words he never expected to cross his admittedly jaded lips.

He took a seat on one of the concrete benches and watched Kevin, Roger and Wayne loop around each other and the lot, wondering why Roger and Wayne would risk chaining their expensive trick bikes at the rack in front of the school. Kevin, who would be forced to dump his skateboard into his locker once school began, pulled off another Ollie then a 360 kick flip moments later. The BMXers were in competition to see who could tailwhip the gaps from the back-sweeping soles of their respective red and black checkered Vans loafers.

After a few lazy minutes, Jason grew bored watching them and he nodded off in his spot. Having gone to bed exhausted just before midnight and with the early start this morning, his body rebelled on him.

He'd dozed a good twenty minutes until he heard the ruckus of his peers and tasted their blown-about cigarette smoke. With cars beginning to fill up the parking lot, Kevin, Wayne, and Roger had long made their exit.

"Good morning, Princess!" razzed Jake Gallagher once Jason shook himself awake. Jake twinkled his fingers at Jason without dropping the lit Marlboro between them. His friends chuckled with him as if on cue.

"Shit," Jason hissed, scrambling off the concrete bench to the heckling laughter from Jake and his Cooler Than Thou Brigade as they finished their smokes and flicked their butts over the landing. Today, their matched concert shirt du jour was Rush's *Power Windows* tour from '86. They filed into the school in a single line, all snorting and cackling at Jason.

Jason carried his bookbag in his hand instead of slinging it across his back. Already the hallways were thinning out, telling Jason without looking at a clock the Homeroom bell wouldn't be much longer. He sprang up the stairwell and without Rob to chat up and most kids already where they were supposed to be, Jason again took every other step, despite the throbbing in his legs. Had Rob even seen him on the patio?

For once, Jason had a direct shot leading to his locker. Only a few daring people were idling about in conversation. Noel Orem, who'd never said one word to Jason all these years and who hardly looked the metalhead part, flicked a horns-up gesture in passing. Noel had given Jason a simple nod in transit. It appeared totally devoid of sarcasm. The telltale connection Jason could see was the Death Angel bumper sticker plastered across his paper bag-wrapped textbook.

"Rock, man," Jason said, loud enough for Noel to hear as Jason flicked him the horns.

On Jason's locker was a small package fastened by a large piece of masking tape. Though it was somewhat covered, he could see his name written in thick black cursive. Feminine writing, which helped thwart the assumption someone, most likely a guy, was pranking him.

He pulled the package free, and he could tell it had just been put there by the easy release. Masking tape tended to make a yucky sound when peeling it away after a long seal. This was a stealthy and sleek parting.

Unwrapping the paper around it, he found a Certron C90 cassette tape without a case. He could see the words **"MUSIC FOR JASON"** scrawled in black marker across the bottom section of the tape, which was colored white, save for a quadruple blue wave cutting from the top before straightening out at the bottom. He had many similar Certrons at home dumped into a shoebox containing concerts he'd recorded from the radio during the King Biscuit Flower Hour program.

A squared, folded piece of loose-leaf was stuck with reversible Scotch tape to the back of the cassette, which repeated the content title of the first.

Unfolding the paper, Jason found a handwritten track listing:

Side A:

The Violent Femmes	*"Daddy's Gone"*
The Clash	*"All the Young Punks"*
Circle Jerks	*"World Up My Ass"*
Ultravox	*"All Stood Still"*
Depeche Mode	*"Fly On the Windscreen"*
New Order	*"Thieves Like Us"*
Psychedelic Furs	*"Into You Like a Train"*
Oingo Boingo	*"No One Lives Forever"*
The Smithereens	*"Blood and Roses"*
Sisters of Mercy	*"Lucretia (My Reflection)"*

Side B:

Pseudo Echo	*"His Eyes"*
The Cure	*"The Figurehead"*
The Smiths	*"Unhappy Birthday"*
Missing Persons	*"Walking in L.A."*
Bauhaus	*"Dark Entries"*
The Cramps	*"Beautiful Gardens"*
Siouxsie and the Banshees	*"Sweetest Chill"*
The Mission U.K.	*"Wasteland"*
David Bowie	*"Lady Grinning Soul"*

There was also a card with the package. It was smooth and glossy, like a playing card, only this was different. The back contained a cross figure of sorts with red, yellow, blue, and green points, set to a background kaleidoscope of symbols. The Rose Cross, Jason would later learn.

The front bore an Egyptian god, Hadit, the Secret Seed, the Fire of Desire of the Heart of Matter. The core spirit of mankind. The card depicted Hadit on a throne, with an apparition of a nude female figure representing infinity, the goddess Nut. At the top was the Roman number "XX" and the bottom, "The Aeon" was printed overtop a transparent word, "TRUMPS."

A handwritten note had also been included:

Made you a copy of my go-to mixtape to expand your horizons. May this Tarot I drew for you represent closure and a new rebirth with endless possibilities. As a heavy metal guy, you might find it interesting the card from this Thoth deck is derived from the writings of Aleister Crowley. Call me sometime. Lori. 410-238-2247.

Chapter 21

WEIGHTLIFTING CLASS SEEMED pedestrian all the way until showers.

Jason had found he could squat 225 pounds without a struggle, while Ricky wobbled and bobbled with a twenty-five found plate on each side of the bar for a total 105. The back and forth loading of plates for Jason's sets had grown irksome, but he'd kept his mouth shut. Everyone did, surprising enough. Nobody even bothered turning on the radio in the weight room.

Though Jason was on a personal high after finding that note and tape from Lori, something felt wrong inside the weight room, a palpable tension exacerbated by, but having nothing to do with the restrained grunting, red-faced plowing and the occasional clumps of dumbbells upon the floor.

In the locker room, nobody saw the friction sparking between Neil Harper and Justin Necker down one of the benches between the second of four rows of lockers where nobody had been. Nothing was said between them to alert anyone, yet amongst themselves, Justin mutely dared Neil to make a move with a widened, contesting glare from his eyes.

Shucked out of his uniform, Jason wrapped one of the white towels the school provided around himself, feeling a need to complain only to himself about the hard chafing of the fabric around his ass. It felt something not quite like sandpaper, but not mollifying like one could imagine from one of those Ivory Snow ads, either. The ones leading you to believe your towels would be soft enough to swaddle an infant using the detergent. Super Thrift ran out of that brand nearly as fast as Tide and All.

Ricky was already done his business in the shower and was struggling to knot the towel at his waist. He'd left his not-so-tighty-whiteys draped on a banister adjacent to the spritzing nozzles and he gave Jason a nervous grin as he snagged his underwear.

Jason was about to unfurl his own towel when he heard a rumpus bearing down upon him.

"Fight! Fight! *Fight!*"

Jason had little time to process the whirlwind of punches that would later remind him of the whirligig bedlam of the Tasmanian Devil from the Looney Tunes shorts.

Neil Harper and Justin Necker traded punches like barbarians set to task in an arena without any flails, swords, or maces. They went at it just as fierce, swinging wild and missing each other, then connecting. Each boy was so enraged, any strike made was nowhere near enough to stop the other. Neil jabbed Justin in the mouth twice. Justin, not even fazed, socked Neil in the gut. Likewise undeterred, Neil folded just enough to absorb the blow to his abdomen before firing a finishing cross hook any pro fighter would've loved in his arsenal. Having avoided this with an instinctive recoil, Justin spotted an opening and seized the moment, burrowing his head down against Neil's chest and driving into him, wailing into the latter's ribs.

"Get 'im!" shouted the onlookers, nobody really favoring either of the combatants. The brawl itself seemed enough to appease their hobnailed lust for violence.

Neil dropped an elbow upon the back of Justin's head, approximately where Jason had been struck the other night. It was enough to separate the two, and yet the pause was secondary as Justin gathered himself again, quick enough to shove Neil off balance, sending him crashing into Jason.

"What the hell, man?" Jason exclaimed, as he tumbled to the wet floor. Both his left side and forearm smarted from the impact.

His protest was unheard, and Jason was fortunate to have enough presence of mind to predict the launching of Justin's foot. Jason rolled out of the way, feeling the whoosh of Justin's kick, which also missed its intended target. From his sprawled position, Jason could see Neil scamper to his feet, then tackle Justin with enough potency to rouse the football players into a shouting fightgasm. Both guys collapsed to the floor with a flurry of fists while everyone but Jason and Ricky egged them on. Ricky was nowhere to be seen.

Jason next saw both of Neil's feet launch into the air as he was jerked backwards. Of all the times to think of a silly horror movie, it reminded Jason of those cabin demons roughhousing Bruce Campbell to a pulp in the *Evil Dead* movies.

"That's *enough*, goddammit!!!"

The reverberating pandemonium not only settled, it fell into immediate silence as the weightlifters looked collectively stupefied to see Coach Schaub with his arms latched around Neil's, hoisting both atop the youth's frizzled, sopping hair. Neil was locked in place by the coach, who showed his entire class how formidable a 5'9" 45-year-old man could be, when needs must.

Justin scrambled to his feet and for a moment, it appeared to everyone he was going to take a cheap shot with Neil in such a vulnerable position.

"Don't do it, Necker!" Coach Schaub bellowed. "I don't care if you clowns lose your shots at All-County, I'll have you both expelled if you don't settle down *right now!*"

It was as if Schaub had opened a secret trap door beneath Justin. He was now afraid to budge an inch.

"Show's over!" Schaub shouted, taking things down a notch before releasing Neil.

"I'll get my parents to sue you, old man," Neil spat, whirling to face Schaub. If he had any intention of carrying out his threat, however, the boy cowered just as fast as he'd thrown down.

"Do your worst, punk, and make my day," Coach Schaub challenged, closing in on Neil so their nose tips were within centimeters of touching. "I *dare* you."

Jason used a nearby wall for leverage to push himself to his feet as the spraying showers served as backdrop to this new confrontation.

"You ain't Dirty Harry," Neil said back, attempting to sound tough. His face yielded twin crimson splotches on his cheeks and a yellowish mark was already forming beneath his right eye. Said eye darted back and forth in fear within its socket, mirrored by the same action in his left.

"That's Hollywood bullshit," Coach Schaub growled, inching his face closer to Neil's the more Neil tried to pull away from him. "I'm just me and I promise you I'm more than enough. *Punk.*"

Danny Tignall had to be the tension breaking jokester by peeling off a ridiculing "Oooooooohhhhh!"

"Can it, Tignall!" Coach Schaub ordered, never taking his eyes off Neil Harper.

Neil had nothing else to say. Like Justin, he carried the collision of fright and shame about him.

"Smart move, Harper," Schaub said with the same authority and wherewithal he did on the gridiron. "You and Necker, get your stuff and come with me to the front office. The rest of you guys, get dressed and clear out. See you tomorrow."

Kyle Larson was the last guy other than Jason to shower. Both looked at each other and shook their heads as if in mutual agreement to skip showers altogether.

"Hamlin, turn 'em off!" Schaub called back with Neil Harper and

Justin Necker shuffling instead of walking in front of him. They looked like juvie prisoners with a firm, guiding hand planted upon each guy's shoulder.

"Okay," Jason whispered instead of projected. Kyle Larson turned away from the shower room and went back to the lockers.

Four of the six shower heads were still engaged. Jason padded along the squishy floor tiles, feeling a small pain in his side mate with a renewed crashing inside his head. It was nothing like what he'd suffered at the hands of Lee Metcalf, but its uninvited return pissed Jason off all the same.

Lori Phillips came to Jason's mind for a fleeting second, but he batted her image away, not because he wanted to avoid her, but because he couldn't get his head around anything good she might offer him at the moment. Right now, all he saw was himself getting tagged as collateral damage between two track stars with a beef against each other, and a redneck brawler who could smear all three of them along the shower room tiles without a blink.

Turning off the first three nozzles, Jason splayed his hands, wetted them beneath the fourth, and rubbed his gritty face with them. He dunked his head under the spray and let the hot water cascade down his scalp before pulling away and turning it off. All the care he'd put into his hair this morning, as useless as a two-cent postage stamp.

Jason whipped his towel away long enough to half-dry himself. As if he needed to, all alone in the shower room, he covered his nudity in a hurry to the likewise frantic sound of castoff spigot spatters.

Most of the guys were already dressed and leaving the locker room. They said nothing to Jason in passing, not even Ricky, not even Danny Tignall and Bennett Walsh, though all three gave Jason a bob of their heads, universal unspoken language for *take it easy*.

Only Kyle Larson remained in the locker room, and he was on the other side of the blue steel locker partition separating himself and Jason. Jason said nothing to Kyle, whose back was turned anyway. Coming to his side of the lockers, Jason gasped.

"*Motherfuckers...*" he grimaced.

On the bench in front of his locker, Jason found his bookbag, opened.

He'd left the bag unattended on the bench. His padlock, which got used just as much at work, was still dangling from the hole bored into the metallic door lift. Jason hadn't thought to put everything back and relock it. He also hadn't thought a brawl was going to break out.

Jason's deodorant had been uncapped and *used,* it appeared, spotting the black armpit hairs clinging to the milky white stick he knew weren't his.

This was bad enough, but not like finding his Memorex cassette on the floor, split down the center, and flung like trash. The filament ribbon had been unspooled and left extracted in a tangled mess. It hadn't been the tape Lori had just left him, thank God. Her mixtape was tucked all the way down the bottom of the bookbag and covered by textbooks like it was classified.

No, whomever had raided Jason's bookbag had taken the time to dig out his Walkman and at least *that* had been left unscathed. What had been extracted then vandalized was the tape sent to Jason by his New Jersey pen pal, Jennifer. The one which she'd recorded Voivod and Possessed for him.

"Hell to pay," Jason seethed.

Chapter 22

AT THE END OF HIS Creative Writing class, Rob had his mind dancing on his freshly divvied assignment, a 500-word max short story based on the open-ended prompt, "Hillary got the news today..."

Mr. Morrow looked downright devilish as he dismissed his class with a wide grin, citing, "Now we'll see who the optimists and the pessimists are in my class."

A bohemian transplant from Manhattan who'd read his own writings on open mike events during the Seventies at some famous poetry haunt in New York (so Mr. Morrow had claimed to his class) called The Nuyorican, Paul Morrow surrounded himself and his students in a flower power classroom unlike any other in Merriweather High. Creative Writing students were kept in company by psychedelic rock legends Jimi Hendrix, Janis Joplin, and Jim Morrison (all dying, in some ruthless grind of the universe, at the unfathomable age of 27) and legendary beat poets Allen Ginsberg, Jack Kerouac, Amiri Baraka, and William S. Burroughs.

Mr. Morrow may not have looked the part of a peacenik with his swapped-out brown and beige slacks and lighter variations of blue button-down dress shirts, but he'd pulled the clock out of his room on purpose, so as not to focus on time. Instead, a splatter-painted lacquer peace symbol was mounted in its place above the chalkboard, marking instead a time past still holding reverence and verve from a never-say-die hippie-at-heart. Jackson Pollack holding as much a domain in Mr. Morrow's classroom as counterculture civil rights fighters Ralph Abernathy, Anna Julia Cooper, and Malcolm X.

Rob glanced over at Marcie Barone, who met his stare like she'd been caught stealing. She'd kept her head turned from him in Economics, but right now, she froze in her spot, only her arms moving to gather her notebook, pencils and a paperback copy of V.C. Andrews' second sequel to her bestselling *Flowers in the Attic* series. *If There Be Thorns* tumbled out of Marcie's grasp, breaking the link between her and Rob as she stooped down to retrieve it.

"Rob," Mr. Morrow intercepted him. "I'm looking forward to seeing what you come up with for this new assignment, given your last writing. I can't agree enough that music is relative to the generations it plays to, but anyone with an aesthetic ear can appreciate what's come before and what's to come as much as living in the moment."

"Thank you, sir," Rob said, trying to focus on his teacher's glowing praise. Less than two weeks in his class, Rob decided Mr. Morrow was the best teacher he'd ever had at any school level.

"'Sir' is not necessary in my class," Mr. Morrow said in perhaps the kindest voice Rob had ever heard from an adult man. "'Sir' makes me think of unstable times in our nation's history. I should know because I lived it. New York was of the many hotbeds for American turbulence during the 1960s. Freedom Day in 1964 will always stick out in my mind. That's when people walked out of New York schools to protest segregation. Anyway, best I stop now before I hold you up for your next class. Do you have any ideas rolling for the next assignment yet?"

"I might have something," Rob lied, taking a secondary glance over at Marcie Barone as she double-timed her way out of the classroom, her cheeks flushed with embarrassment. Marcie gave Rob a quick shot glance before leaving, her perm bouncing about her neck like her curls were trying to catch up with the rest of her.

"Good," said Mr. Morrow. "I also wanted to approach you with a possible proposal. You probably know I'm the senior advisor to *The Cougar's Tale*. Right now, we're overstaffed, so I can't make any recommendations yet, but it's always that way at the beginning of a new school year. Some kids, not all, tend to lose interest or burn out, and by December or January we're often doubling up the remaining writers. When that time comes, I'd like to put your name in the hat. If you're interested?"

Now it was Rob who was locked in place, a euphoric wash cascading down his body the same way a pleasing foot rinse at the beach took all the grit away as he asked, "You think I'm that good, really?"

"Really," Mr. Morrow told him with a warm, wrinkled smile. "It doesn't pay, of course, but if you ever want to be a serious writer, you'll find yourself doing freebies to build your name. I'm happy to be paid for the few articles and essays I publish out there and teaching about writing not only gives me income; it gives me joy."

"You had to do a lot of freebies on your way up?"

"Absolutely. Those were my salad days."

"There's a song by the same name from this punk band we talk a lot about, Minor Threat, down in D.C. They've gotten pretty big around the country, by underground standards, anyway. 'Salad Days.' You've probably never heard of them."

"You'd be surprised," Mr. Morrow said with a wink. "My son, Tad, is friends with their guitarist, what's his name? Brian... Brian Baker, that's it."

"No *way!*" Rob exclaimed.

"Tad's in his second year at Georgetown, and he's always going to shows at the 9:30 Club, D.C. Space, and The Bayou."

"Wow," Rob said in awe.

"I don't need an answer right now, Rob, but give it some thought. I'm being proactive this year about the inevitable turnover. I'm as laidback as they come, but I've been known to clear a room when I've been caught with my pants down. Metaphorically speaking, of, course."

With that, Mr. Morrow turned toward his chalkboard in preparation for his next class, Expository Writing. Picking up a piece of yellow chalk, he wrote, big and bold: "FACTUAL, NOT SUBJECTIVE."

Rob hadn't even realized he'd been in the corridor leading out of the English and Language Arts wing, he'd floated more than strode. Even Marcie Barone's sudden skittishness became an afterthought.

The traffic was thinner for once in the corridor, often compared to a cattle chute by most students in those critical first couple minutes between period changes. Hanging behind in Mr. Morrow's room gave Rob a direct shot through, and he picked up speed, now with the realization after a dap of his wristwatch he had only three minutes to make it to his Civics class.

As Rob swung into the main promenade, he was jolted back into a holding pattern as he spotted Emily Haney and Lee Metcalf. He tried not to gasp with a sudden dawning, after all this time, just how huge Lee was compared to Emily. Ridiculous to think, Rob couldn't imagine the two of them having sex, not without Emily taking top. Lee would've crushed her missionary style.

"You absolute son of a bitch!" Emily trumpeted at Lee, jabbing a forefinger within inches of Lee's nose.

"It ain't mine," Lee said, as if he were on the defensive side of a court trial. "I'm not paying for it. Besides, you said you were on the pill, so tough shit, Emily."

"I haven't slept with anyone else, Lee!"

"What about Steve, huh?" Lee challenged, swatting Emily's hand away.

"Fick?" she barked incredulously, waggling her hand from an apparent pain Lee had inflicted from his whack. "That was at the end of tenth grade, and you *know* it, you bastard! I made him wear protection, too! How dare you?"

"How dare *you?*" Lee fumed, cocking his hand backwards in a threatening gesture.

"*Do it,*" Emily snarled. "Go on, you coward, hit me. Word of warning, though, not even your hot shit daddy'll protect you from me if you do. Hell, you shouldn't even *be* here, you're suspended! If Newton or anyone from the office catches you, you're toast, you dumb ape."

"Fuck this," Lee growled back at her, dropping his hand back to his hip. "And fuck *you,* Emily."

"Yeah, you did that already, Lee Metcalf. Biggest mistake of my life."

"Take a hike, Martino!" Lee yelled at Rob upon spotting him. "We'll see you and your headbanger honey later, don't you worry none!"

Lee stomped away from Emily and out of the school, the tail of his FFA jacket rising and falling above the lower tier of his enormous back.

Emily glowered at Rob for a moment, then her face slackened. She opened her mouth to say something, but the tears cut her off as she darted the opposite direction for the senior patio exit out of the school.

Chapter 23

"AND HE DIDN'T GET CAUGHT by the school?"

Jason and Rob were walking headfirst against intermittent gusts whipping their faces along Route 62. Still with as dreary a sky overhead as the morning, the wind had picked up after the first mile since Rob and Jason left the school premises.

"Hell no, man," Rob said, pushing his voice through the heavy surge. "I think I heard the whole conversation between Lee and Emily, and he wasn't there but a minute, if that. She reamed him out pretty good and he couldn't have been a bigger jerk to her. I can't believe I feel bad for her, but Jason, self-preservation rules more. I'm worried about Lee saying the farmers are coming for us."

The squall was made worse by cars zipping by, no one observing the posted 40 miles per hour speed limit. A tractor trailer hauling Miller and Miller Lite barreled by them, the blast knocking both Rob and Jason off balance. Despite the escalatory agitation of their dialogue, they'd still boyishly thrown their right arms into the air and made tugging motions at the freighter's driver on his way by. The boys may have been jostled off-kilter, but they'd been rewarded for their efforts as the truck driver snapped his bullfrog-ish horn for them.

"What, you got a secret boner for Emily Haney, all of a sudden, Rob?" Jason derided with a disparaging scrunch of his face, as if they'd been blown by a garbage truck instead of a beer rig. A small part of him wished he could've taken it back, since he himself had given Emily his train of thought a number of times this week. Not in the same way he thought of Lori Phillips, though. Nowhere in the same dimension.

"Oh shut up, ass face," Rob lanced back. He wanted to mention the seeming interest brewing with Marcie Barone, but in light of this exchange, he decided he would keep Marcie talk on the back burner.

"I do hope she cuts Lee's balls off, though," Jason added, with less of a dagger thrust.

"Aren't you worried what Metcalf, Shaffer, and their goons plan on doing to us?" Rob raised his voice against the increasing gusts.

"Fuck 'em," Jason returned, taking Rob's cue and drifting back enough to flank him as his pace had begun to accelerate with a spike of adrenaline charged by the mere mention of the farmer gang. "After what Lee did to me, all bets are off. I mean it."

"Like you can take him, much less the whole lot of them, on your own."

"If you won't back me up, so be it, but..."

"I never said that," Rob fumed. "I think you're talking suicidal, though. You need me, I'm there, but I'm in no rush to die. I'd like to get laid at least twice in this life before I'm pushing up daisies."

"Alright, man," Jason relented with a flippant wave into the air. "You got my back, cool. I got yours. Those sons of bitches better not try any shit, is all I'm saying."

"I wish I had your confidence."

"How pissed would you be if someone smashed *your* tape, Rob? I feel fucking violated! If I could prove one of those dick licking children of the corn did it, I'd...whatever, man. I find out who *did* smash the cassette, shit's going down. I don't care if I die."

"You *do* have a chance of getting laid, though," Rob shouted, doing his damnedest to outroar a cement truck rumbling by them.

"Tell the whole damn world, Martino!"

"Speaking of cassettes, I'm curious about the one Lori made you. I mean, dude, anyone knows the power of the mixtape between a guy and girl."

"I'll let you know," Jason said back without the need for a yell with the shopping center coming upon them. "A lot of it's this alternative rock I only know about, though she put a Circle Jerks song on it."

"I like Lori more and more."

"You can have Emily Haney," Jason roasted. "Though she's damaged goods. I can't imagine slipping the sausage to girl who's already had Lee Metcalf inside her."

Rob gave no response as a white Chevette faltered too close to the shoulder from another blustery whip ramming into it from the driver's side. Like everyone else, the subcompact mini car was blasting down 62, easy prey for the rampant winds. Rob skittered behind Jason in time to avoid being clipped.

"You worthless piece of shit!!!" Rob screamed back at the Chevette, which chimed a dweeby blat from its dinky horn back at him.

"The self-entitled pricks in this town," Jason bristled. "My father should never have left Bradenton. He belongs here. I can't believe I traded shifts with Dave Carlisle to have off tomorrow and go see the motherfucker."

"You're going to have to forgive him sometime, Jason."

"Give me one solid reason why, and I will."

On that, the boys remained silent until they arrived at the shopping center and Curry's Music.

Chapter 24

JASON AND ROB WERE GREETED by the blare of Queensrÿche's "Revolution Calling" first by Bud Curry and then by his assistant, a college-aged, thin girl in black jeans and a scarlet blouse. As if her last name was some protective secret she held from the public, she was only known around town as Dawn.

Dawn, who fledged her dusty hair with a part down the middle, had been Curry Music's cashier and ordering clerk the entire time Bud had been in business, a mere year-and-a-half to this point.

A large section of Curry's Music was devoted to Harley Davidson and biker accouterments, a partial "Biker Boutique," Dawn called it. Leather chaps, jackets, gloves, vests, and wallets dominated the rear of the store, along with Harley-themed t-shirts, most with a screeching imperious eagle spotlighted in some fashion. Two countertop spindle racks of designer shades and key chains (some toting rock bands, others being biker brand) were found at the register. Inside a glass case was a row of expensive metal lighters to offset the cheap sterling rings sculpted with skulls and headdress-sprinkled Indian profiles.

The main bulk of the store was devoted to 33 rpm vinyl albums and cassettes. 45 rpm singles slowly on their way out, Bud only ordered those on special demand from customers since there was no profit in them.

Though Bud Curry carried many of the popular selections as counted down on Casey Kasem's Top 40 and the local country stations, he was a rocker at heart, and his inventory leaned accordingly. His pride and joy mementos hung upon the walls were a Thin Lizzy subway poster autographed by the late Phil Lynott, a drumhead scrawled on by Ratt percussionist Bobby Blotzer, plus an original concert placard for the 1970 Isle of Wight Festival.

"I used to trust the media to tell me the truth, tell us the truth..." Queensrÿche vocalist Geoff Tate wailed from baritone to his higher registered pitches around the store. The volume was jacked high

enough to blow out even the school auditorium. To Rob's ears, it sounded crisper and richer than his cassette copy of Queensrÿche's *Operation Mindcrime* album from which the song rang. *"But now I've seen the payoffs everywhere I look...who do you trust when everyone's a crook? Revolution calling, revolution calling, revolution calling youuuuuuu...."*

"Heyyyyy, my two best customers!"

The decibels dropped notches as Bud Curry shambled from the rear of the store. He'd shucked off a brown Gibson Marauder with its electric humbucker off his curved shoulder and substantial paunch, resting the guitar neck against a swivel stool he'd been on. Dawn was fumbling to firm up a minor chord on the Marauder's production successor, a candy apple resonwood Sonex-180. After frowning at her finger-crinkled bungle, she toodled to the boys.

"What's up, Bud?" Jason quipped, pumping hands with Curry, who did likewise with Rob. Handshaking was a ritual the store owner observed with repeat clients.

"Ahh, you know, man, trying to stay afloat."

"How's business?" Rob asked, scouring the store and finding a rectangular box leaning against the cash register next to a taped sign yielding the handwritten message "NOW PLAYING." The longbox featured the extensive cover art to Queensrÿche's *Operation Mindcrime,* normally folded in half on other format packaging. Rob's eyes widened as he reached to examine the sprawling, full panorama, splitting the depicted conflict between the concept album's core protagonists, the brain corrupting demagogue, Dr. X and prostitute-turned-nun, Sister Mary.

"Ehhh," Bud answered, trying to stifle a burp leaking through his pursed lips which ruffled his scraggly bird's nest of a beard. "I'm selling a lot of Tracy Chapman, Dwight Yoakum, and K.D. Lang. There's this group of gals who cut their hair shorter than the Marines calling themselves the Valencia Roses who are always asking me for that Melissa Etheridge album. I keep selling that one out to the point it's my only unit on back order. Only you guys and some skater kid's bought Jane's Addiction, much less Living Colour, who fucking *rock*. Funkadelic meets Bad Brains. *Rolling Stone's* off their goddamn rocker, they're a five star band, easy. Living Colour *could* change the world. Maybe not George County, but yeah."

"Kickass," Rob said, pumping a metal proud fist at Bud. Beneath the gesture was a print of the devil pointing at all mankind in swaggering condemnation, the album cover of Mercyful Fate's *Don't Break the Oath.* For a moment, Rob wondered how he hadn't drawn the same condemnation from his peers the last two times wearing the shirt.

Even the seemingly devout Marcie Barone hadn't been put off by Jesus Christ's arch-nemesis splashed across Rob's slight pectorals.

"You two were the only ones who got a copy of Living Colour from me," Bud said with a crinkle of his mouth still seen amidst the smothering facial hair. "These guys have a viable radio hit, man, yet nobody else around this unsophisticated hick town is buying them any quicker than they're buying the new Sugarcubes offa me. I say it as a card-carrying hick myself. Not even the Valencia Roses will touch those Sugarcubes and their pipsqueaky, Icelander singer-shrieker Bjork, or whatever her goofy name is. I should've left that alternative rock crap to Tower Music or Sam Goody's. You shanked that call, Dawn."

"It's a grower," Dawn nattered back. "People will come around."

"Not in *this* town," Bud grunted.

"I have someone who might be interested," Jason noted with the excitement he'd lacked the entire walk to Curry's Music. "She made me a mixtape I'm sure is probably the same genre. I'm half afraid to listen to the tape, but... hell, I'll send her down."

"I'd appreciate it, brother," Bud said, adding, "I've been offering guitar lessons, but my only taker so far is hardly in the *paying* customer category."

"Love you, Bud," Dawn called back, nodding without a care to his gibe as she nailed her chord this time.

"I'll be your next student," Jason vowed. "As soon as I get some wheels first. Mom's not having it with a guitar until I'm driving."

"I'm looking forward to it, dude," Bud said with a nod pushing his scruff all about like a Viking might look speed-drinking ale from a horned flask.

"What's this, Bud?" Rob queried, holding up the cardboard *Operation Mindcrime* longbox. "Other than the potential Album of the Year."

"Ahh," Bud answered, taking the longbox out of Rob's hands for a moment while dipping beneath the register and coming up with a plastic jewel case half the size of the cardboard packaging but twice the size of a cassette tape. Rob and Jason saw the same cover art for *Operation Mindcrime,* only half the size of the outer container. Like the tape and album version, the central figures were folded away from each other, separated by interceding staples.

"This is a compact disc, a CD," he rambled on, opening the synthetic, protracting vessel. "The actual disc holder looks like this, and it flips open like a tape, but check it out. These discs are actually cool. They say the sound output is better than vinyl, and I'm on the fence about it, since I'm more a vinyl guy. Digital transfer versus analog, though, I get what they're doing; it's pretty awesome."

"Seriously?" Rob quipped. "This is the new format I've heard about, then?"

"You bet," Bud said back with another nod rustling his shaggy chin wag. "Mark my words, the CD is gonna take over the world. Tapes will become obsolete. Vinyl, I dunno. Many audiophiles out there still swear by records. They outright refuse to get on board with CDs. The industry is not only doing new albums on compact disc, guys, they're going to reissue *everything*."

"Christ, I'm not replacing my whole collection," Jason scoffed. "I can't even begin to add up the money I've already spent."

"Me neither," Rob agreed, "but I *am* intrigued, at least. Look at how much of the artwork you can see on this cardboard."

"A waste of trees, if you ask me," Bud said. "Who am I to argue, though? If it helps move units out of my store, then kill the trees. I'm perfectly comfortable as a hypocrite."

"What're you playing this on?" Rob asked, poking his head over the counter to scout the store's stereo equipment. It took him a moment to find the recently added black compact disc player (it had the word "disc" spread in lowercase bubble letters with the word "compact" smooshed in tinier characters above it) straddled atop a set of equalizers which had long been there, hooked up to the rest of Bud's sound gear. The CD player had a sheer window counting off the final 40 seconds of "Revolution Calling's" 4:42 running time.

"It's a Realistic 3200 from Radio Shack," Bud said with a hint of pride. "Normally I wouldn't be caught dead buying anything but a calculator or a CB from there, but these things are starting to flood the market and nobody else in bumfuck George County had one. See this, I'm getting CD promos of upcoming albums."

From behind the counter, Bud pulled out another longbox, this time with a partial profile of well-detailed skull with ripping fangs and an upward swooping horn, like a Texas longhorn or worse, Satan himself. The exact logo last seen in full on the funereal punk band, Samhain, led by former Misfits vocalist, Glenn Danzig. There was a glaring slit cut into the side of the box.

"Whoa," Rob cooed in recognition. "The Danzig solo album."

"Right?" Bud smirked, tilting the cardboard packaging to let the CD slide out. Like the cardboard, there was a gaping nick in the jewel case holding the disc. He pointed to the face of the disc to the boys, which bore the same image as the cardboard, only with an imprint in gold letters stating, **"FOR PROMOTIONAL USE ONLY: NOT FOR RESALE."**

"It was supposed to be the fourth Samhain record," Rob declared without a doubt of himself. "The gang's all there with Glenn, Eerie Von, Chuck Biscuits, and John Christ."

"James Hetfield of Metallica, too," Bud said in a smart tone meant to trump his young customers.

"Ahh, get outta here," Jason jeered.

"Dawn has a tremendous ear," Bud proclaimed, putting his chunky arm around her to show off his pride. "She's the one who brought it to my attention on 'Twist of Cain.' It's him. Hetfield played on it."

"I'd bet Rob's entire comic book collection you're wrong."

"Hey!" Rob protested, elbowing Jason in the sternum.

"Sucker bet," Dawn called out, gliding another perfect downstroke on her Gibson. "Def American gave us the album release fact sheet."

"If you have any *Moon Knight*, *Power Man and Iron Fist*, or *Legion of Superheroes*, I'll make you a hell of a trade," Bud interjected hopefully.

"I'll be damned," Jason said as both he and Rob raised their eyebrows with conceding nods of respect. "And you still got that new Riot album, Bud?"

"It's been here all year with your name on it," the grizzled biker-rocker replied, pointing to where Jason could find the album in question. "It'd be the first sale of the day, and we've been open since eleven."

"It's really that tough, Bud?" Rob asked compassionately as *Operation Mindcrime's* title track rumbled on.

"Dude, I sell more biker gear than tunes, if you want the truth, and that's through word-of-mouth direction only. All the gangs riding past here on the throughway and they don't know about my store. It eats me alive. Music's my passion, but riding's my *life*. I've been hoping to make enough bread here to ride all the way to Deadwood for the Sturgis ride. Right now, a ride to Dairy Queen seems like a pipe dream. I'm thinking about a store rebrand."

"And I thought Jason and I had problems," Rob said, twisting the Danzig CD in his hand over and over. "Got this on cassette?"

"I do," Bud said with enough cheer to his voice to sound alight. He pointed to the wall of cassette tapes for sale branching from where the biker wear stopped. "You know your way through the racks. What's going on with you guys?"

"Farmer trouble," Rob replied. "Sam..."

"Shaffer, yeah," Bud finished for him, shaking his head back and forth. "His old man and I used to go to Merriweather High a lifetime ago. If you can believe it, *I* was a bumpkin kid once."

"Get outta here," Jason repeated himself, carrying the vinyl recording from Riot to the register.

"Yeah, I'm serious. My folks used to own a hundred forty acres of wheat. They had a government contract and everything. What they didn't produce under agreement, they'd bale up and sell off to horse stables, though some of the neighboring farms bought straight from us for their barns and livestock. Fall to winter, you'd see those big ol' round bales around the land. My brother Chet and I used to try and climb 'em. We'd fail miserably and my old man always threatened to take a switch to us, though he never did."

"Uh huh," Jason said, placing Riot's *Thundersteel* album on the counter while Rob came up next to him with a copy of the self-titled Danzig tape.

"Anyway, Sam's dad was as much of a prick as his kid."

"Truth," Dawn affirmed from her spot, now lazing an arm over the stock of the guitar.

"Before all you suburbanites came out here, it was pretty much *all* farmer kids, give or take some of the middle-class snots in the few pocket subdivisions there were back then. We all used to beat the shit out of each other, us farmers."

"*Why*, man?" Jason asked, snider than he had on the walk with Rob. "That's dumber than the *Mac and Me* movie. Stupid *E.T.* rip-off."

"Because we were all a bunch of cocky backbreakers used to getting a steamy pile of shit slid down our necks by folks thinking they own us, or worse, they're *better* than us hayseeds, you know? You never really get used to it, though you pretend it doesn't bother you. There's more than 53,000 acres of tillable land in the county today, though it used to be 82,000, you get me? All this new land acquisition and development, people looking to get out of the urban chaos to move out here. My dudes, farming's just one big pissing match like rival street gangs, only we brawl when the beer hits us too hard instead killing each other over a dumb piece of asphalt or drug deals gone south. It's only gotten worse with all the new arrivals from Baltimore — or Balti-*ho,* as we used to call it — who don't know a thing about farming, much less have enough couth to throw their damn trash where it belongs, instead across of a man's way of income."

"None of what you're saying gives guys like Sam Shaffer the excuse to terrorize us, though," Jason burned. "Lee Metcalf, that bastard, he beaned me with a full can of Pabst! I mean, how do you justify *that* shit, Bud?"

"I don't excuse any of it," Bud said with a faint sigh, punching in the cost of the record, $7.99, on his register, then hitting the 5% Maryland sales tax button. "Lord knows I tangled with Shaffer's pap a few times to know one rotten egg begets another. His kid's been getting in trouble since Sam jabbed Luke Reed in the ear with a sharpened pencil back in fifth grade. I know Sam and company got busted earlier this week. The town's all been talking about it, but Jason, do your best not to provoke the crazy son of a bitch, is all I'm saying."

"Too late," Rob said before Jason could. "Sam and his crew stalked me at my job the same night they attacked Jason."

"What'd you do to piss him off, if you don't mind me asking?" Bud asked, bagging up Jason's record and handing him a receipt, then waving Rob to hand over the cassette for ringing out.

"Being born one county over, apparently," Jason spat. "I thought getting beat up in Perry Hall through sixth and seventh grade had been an endless nightmare. Just the mere mention of the area sets me off."

"If I'm not out line, Jason, you're looking a lot fitter than when you dudes started buying here," said Bud as he rang the same price for Rob. "I think Sam Shaffer and those punks have another thing coming if they try it again."

"Thanks," Jason said with a bare creak of a smile. "Cool Priest reference."

"I gotta go, guys," Rob blurted, spotting his father's car in the parking lot in front of the store. "My ride to work's here. Bud, see ya. Dawn, see ya. Jason, gimme a call later tonight, Slim."

"Sure, man," Jason muttered as Rob bounced out of Curry's Music and slid into his father's car. To Bud and Dawn, he said, "Stay in business, guys. I'll never forgive you for pawning that Tigertailz album on me, but I'd miss you if you went under."

"I *told* you, caveat emptor, Jason," Dawn heckled from her side of the store. "Not my fault you bought it anyway."

"Traitor," Bud jabbed right back at her. "I'm up here doing your job for *what* reason?

"For my working out an F sharp, B and C sharp minor progression. Slash, I am not."

"Next lesson, I'm charging you."

"Ouch," she cracked with an artificial moan.

"Hey, kid," Bud said to Jason. "I know you do a lot of walking back and forth from Super Thrift. You might want to start doing the same as your friend until this mess blows over with Shaffer. Get a ride."

"Yeah, alright," Jason sighed. "I gotta clock in soon. I'll catch you guys on the flipside."

"We'll be here," Dawn called out. "Hopefully."

"That's enough from the peanut gallery!" Bud shouted over her. "Jason, best advice I got for ya?"

"What's that, Bud?"

"Don't let the bastards grind you down."

"I like it," Jason said, snapping off a nod and half-saluting Bud with an upwards jerk of his bagged album before leaving the shop.

Unbeknownst to Jason as he walked the corridor leading past Carlton Cards, Zoe's Floral Boutique, and the Radio Shack Bud had scored his compact disc player from, he never saw the Metcalf brothers emerge from the latter store. They stopped and watched Jason go into the grocery store before Lee swatted his sibling on the arm and mumbled something into his ear before they headed off in the opposite direction.

Chapter 25

THE NEXT EVENING at his father's condominium, Jason was finishing the last slice of a sausage and pepperoni pizza from Di Nitti's Pizzeria.

"You eat so goddamn fast," his dad gnashed from the opposite end of the sofa, chomping into his third piece with a sickening slurp of the cheese. "And you get on *my* case."

On the tv, Latino fireball Tito Santana was putting the screws to some fall guy going by Len Kruger on WWF wrestling. Santana whipped his pretend-arrogant, chrome-domed adversary across the ring (or "squared circle" as commentator and grappling legend Bruno Sammartino was fond of saying), waiting for the return dash off the bouncing fiber ropes. Santana extended his forearm out, and though he'd connected below Kruger's windpipe, the staged clothesline had the bare minimum force to exert Kruger's hokey backwards crash upon the bouncy wrestling mat.

"At least make it look good, man, sheesh," Jason said, ignoring his father. He wanted to say how much his dad looked and sounded like a hog nosing into a trough trying to cram his pizza slice into his gummed-up mouth, but he had the good sense not to.

"I'd swear that meatball was going by *Hans* Kruger once," Jason's dad went on after clearing his emptied mouth with a chug of Schlitz. The glug from his greasy lips across the beer can sounded nauseating. "I like Santana, but he'd be a better heel than good guy. I'd like him even more if he'd get that stupid sombrero off the back of his trunks."

"*Dad,*" Jason muttered with a sigh after swallowing his last bite.

"Dad *what?*" his father sent him through clenched teeth. Pizza-stained teeth, at that.

"You were on autopilot driving us here from Laurel racetrack," Jason said with another perturbed exhalation. "I'm gonna have to stay the night here, since this is your fourth can of Schlitz since we got home. Never mind all those beers you took down at the track."

"You didn't have much to say all day," his father growled, licking his teeth, which looked downright insidious with his reddened cheeks puffing in and out to accommodate the inside darting of his tongue. "I had better conversations with the shoeshine guy, Manny, since you had your nose down in that *Outsiders* book the whole time."

"We were there all nine races, Dad, and you lost on all nine," Jason countered, feeling his defenses mount and beginning to care about showing his father respect as much as he cared about *The Young and the Restless*. "You were in the pisser five times and back with a fresh beer each time, Dad! You want the truth; you looked like you were on Planet Mongo all day! I could smell the beer on your breath when you'd picked me up this morning. Do you use Schlitz for mouthwash, or something? Jesus, Dad!"

"You're not my mother!" his Dad glubbed with rancor. "You sure as hell's not *your* mother, either! I'll be goddamned if I put up with your needling, the same way she did when I was still with you two."

"She obviously had a reason!" Jason fired back, picking up his plate to take it to the kitchen sink. "For the record, I have to be at work tomorrow by 10:00 a.m. since I had to trade shifts to get today off! If you were just going to drink the day away and pay me no attention, why are we even bothering with any of this?"

When Jason came back into the living room, his father was on his feet. He'd tossed his blue button down Cross short sleeve on the couch. The sight of his engorged, bloated gut was appalling to Jason, but nowhere near as alarming as the wrapped fists his dad held in the air.

"You've got some kind of balls on you these days, kid. You think you can take me, smart ass?"

"Jesus, Dad, sit down," Jason returned, staying in place as a whirlwind of fear and anger spun inside of him. Part of him wanted to go ahead and drop his old man since he had an easy target. The man looked like a fat Fred Astaire on a bad night at the ball; he could hardly balance himself.

"Come on, tough guy, let's go!" his father roared.

"No, Dad, what the hell's wrong with you?"

"Don't you cuss at me, you little prick! I see you getting some muscle to you. About goddamn time, too. I was worried you'd be a pansy all your worthless life. Come on! Show me what you've got!"

"I'm not gonna fight you, Dad, stop it!"

Jason was feeling less stoic and more upset the longer this stunning throw-down went on.

"Okay, let's take it down a notch, then," his dad said in such a relaxed voice it worried Jason even more. His father couldn't stand worth a damn right now, but he had an alarming control of mood navigation. "I'll bet you whatever's in my wallet you can't pin me."

"Say what?" Jason asked, feeling a squeak puncture his voice. He hated himself for it on the spot.

At least Jason's father hadn't heard that rasp, as he loosened his fists and splayed his fingers out in a silly, would-be wrestler's stance. Tito Santana made short work of Len Kruger for an easy three count behind his dad on the tube.

"Do it!" his father barked, teetering so bad now Jason might be able to push him to the floor with two fingers.

"No," Jason said, nonetheless, taking a step back from him.

"Let's go, Mr. Mouth! Come on!"

"You can't even stand straight, you drunk!"

"Come *on*, goddamn you...you...*pussy*..."

Something then snapped inside of Jason. He thought of the busted cassette. He thought of Sam Shaffer. He thought of Lee Metcalf's ominous laughter after hitting Jason in the head with the Pabst. A can of beer, like the one on his dad's coffee table. A different brand, but still the same thing. Alcohol, working its ugly self into ugly people, making them do ugly things.

Jason lost it and charged his dad.

His father had no time to react beyond the startled expression on his face as he went down to the floor.

Jason tugged his father's calves in reverse, and in his dad's inebriated state, he came down easier than a toddler taking its first steps.

Just like the WWF wrestlers, Jason rolled over and pulled his father's legs up into the air. He planted his forearm forcefully against his dad's shoulders, keeping them pinned to the floor.

"1! 2! 3!" Jason shouted, letting go of his dad. He'd finished off his dad in much faster time than Tito Santana himself.

Getting to his knees, Jason felt his body quake. He was upset with himself, and in the moment, he felt sudden, unexpected pity for his dad. Jason's eyes blurred with tears, and he hadn't seen his dad get up from the floor and vanish for a moment.

Wiping at his eyes, refusing to cry in front of his father, Jason said, "I'm sorry, Dad, I hope I didn't hurt you..."

When he could see, Jason found the barrel of a .22 rifle aimed into his face.

"Not so tough *now*, are you, you little shit?"

"Dad!" Jason shrieked. He was paralyzed, the question of whether the gun was loaded or not irrelevant with that barrel so close to his nose.

"*Are* you?!?" his father raged. His sweaty, swollen torso and hate-splashed face poured indignation, making him twice as fearsome as Lee Metcalf. There was murder raging inside his dad's glassy eyes. Actual murder.

Instinct prevailed and Jason flung himself to the carpet, rolling as many times as it took to get out of harm's way.

When he felt safe to look up, Jason saw his father in the same position, leaning the rifle down where his son had been. He'd been so trashed he had yet to see Jason was gone, backpedaling on all fours and trying not to let his terrified heaving give him away.

Jason willed himself up with a terrified push and he bolted for the wall phone in his father's kitchen.

It took him a few tries with his fingers shaking and making him misdial, but he finally got the numbers right for his house.

The dial tone rang, then rang, then rang...ringing over and over with no answer.

"Oh, my God, Maaaaaa..." Jason shrilled. "Please don't be asleep, I need you..."

He disconnected the call and tried again.

No answer.

Yet again and no answer.

"Shit, shit, shit," he whispered, as he snuck a bold peek into the living room.

His father was now sitting back on the couch, taking another drink of beer. The rifle had been left on the floor. To see it was to believe it, but Jason's father looked just as composed as he had enraged moments before.

For a split second, Jason thought about tearing into the living room and snatching the gun. Would he turn it on his old man? His Daisy air rifle being one thing, would Jason have the stones to pull the trigger of the .22 if he needed to?

Jason pounded the digits to his home a fifth time and got the same results.

"Lori," he blurted, plunging his hand into his pocket, since recalling her phone number by memory right now was like trying to learn Chinese on the spot. Thank God he'd put her note inside his pocket. He'd felt stupid doing it at first, like some desperate, lovesick puppy. Right now, he couldn't congratulate himself enough.

He hammered Lori's number precisely and it only took two rings until he heard her voice.

"Lori? It's Jason," he pushed out as if it would be the only chance he had.

"Hey, man!" she chirped on her end. "Wow, I'm glad you called. I..."

"You drive, right?"

"Yeahhhhh...."

"Do you have your own car?"

"No, I borrow my folks' Bel Air when I need to. What's wrong? Are you in some kind of trouble?"

He didn't answer for a moment as the reality of all that had just happened to him crashed between his ears and into his brain.

"Y-yeah," he stammered.

Chapter 26

"I WOULD'VE CLEANED HIS WALLET out, the damn fool," Lori said from behind the wheel of her parents' Skyline blue 1975 Chevy Bel Air, a far cry in style from the sleek, fin-cutting classics of the late 1950s. She'd left the window open as she held her lit cigarette close by, letting the outside air suck the tendrils from the car. "But that's just me. A bet's a bet and you won fair and square."

"Ehh, *Richard Simmons* could've taken him in his condition," Jason said, wishing he could've savored his own roast.

"Or Jazzercize your pops to death," Lori added, glancing at Jason with a hopeful expression that fell into a hypothetical sinkhole where failed jokes went once she saw she wasn't making a dent with him. "I've never seen a man carrying that kind of stomach. A woman, yes, in her third trimester. I'm surprised you didn't wake him up to tell him I was taking you home."

"Screw my dad. I never want to see him again."

"I'm no Ann Landers, Jason, and I know you're in shock..."

"Even Ann Landers would call that an understatement."

"You're going to need some time to get over this, Jason."

"There *is* no getting over it, Lori."

Inside the Bel Air, Henry Rollins barked like an insurrectionist with his ball sac being crushed through the car's already strained speakers. The chunky guitars of Greg Ginn whirled a buzz saw din which ignited Lori into a seat-bouncing groove. Widening her mascara-bombed eyes like she'd been possessed by a punk rock ghost who rubbed elbows with Sid Vicious in the afterlife, she sang in a deeper octave than her speaking voice. Lori was a fair contralto growler in duet with Rollins' ferocious woofing on Black Flag's "My War."

"My war!" Lori yapped on the dime, seizing her opportunity to reach through to Jason. She leaned over toward him like she was about to kiss him. Instead, she budded her eyes into nearly all-white saucers, penetrating the shadowy interior. "Why you're one of them? You say...that you're my friend, but you're one of *them!!!*"

Lori shut up and put her right palm out in a gesture for Jason to pick up the song from there.

"You don't wanna see me live!" he screamed. "Yeah, I know this one!"

"Yeah!!!" Lori shouted with a squeal of delight.

"You don't want me to give!" Jason roared, balling up his fists. "Cause you're one of *them!*"

While the song trundled in full anarchy mode, Lori accidentally swerved over the median line as she matched Jason's pitch, wailing with him. She tugged the steering wheel back to their side of the road without fishtailing, just as the searing headlights of an oncoming vehicle emerged in the opposite lane.

"Turn down your high beams, dildo!" she bellowed with a lunatic giggle.

"I appreciate you coming to get me, Lori, but let's make it home alive, okay?"

She resumed her lyrical pulse while flooring the accelerator, pushing the Bel Air to 60 then 65 miles an hour before taking a drag on her cigarette.

"Don't you worry about a thing," Jason heard her say, even with the condemnatory hardcore punk cataclysm rattling the car. "This tank may be a last year model, but she gives three cylinders worth of turbo-hydromatic lovin'. She was my mom's first. Mine also. I'm talking automobiles, of course."

At that, Lori gave Jason a testing the waters glance he could only think of as seductive, as she aimed her secondhand toward the cracked window. Her eyes sagged, not in a sleepy way, but in that racy, come-and-get-me-if-you-dare manner some people called "bedroom eyes."

"Yeah, sure," Jason teased, playing along just in case she was baiting him. It felt good, as much as odd, to switch gears from the horror he'd just been through.

Lori pushed the spent cigarette out the window then switched hands so that her left now grabbed the steering wheel.

Still singing, she lurched her right hand out to Jason's inner left thigh. Even with it being nighttime outside, he could see Lori's black nail polish as she glided her way slowly down towards his privates.

As if he hadn't been shaking enough at his father's, Jason was quivering in his legs and abdomen. The mere thought of Lori's hand contacting his penis through his jeans fired it into a screaming erection. He bucked his waist to meet Lori's hand as she spread her fingers out overtop, but not touching his bulging crease before pulling away from him.

"You're one of them, *fucker!*" she yelled at the song's conclusion. "Myyyyy waaaaarrrrr!!!"

Jason cocked his head away from Lori, dropping a sigh marked somewhere between frustration and an odd form of relief. A gamut of other concerns related to sex, or at least the suggestion of sex, rammed into his brain. He was a virgin. How would he perform? *Could* he perform with the lingering image of that .22 pointed in his face? If Lori had the intention of going all the way with him tonight, where would it go down, here in the car, her home? Would she pull over next to a secluded patch of woods to just drop trouser and go for it? If she even did let him inside of her, he had no condom. Would he be able to pull out in time? How long could he even last as a first timer? He'd heard so many guys at school brag about being ten-to-fifteen-minute studs on their first go, only to see their girlfriends shake their heads in refute of such claims behind their backs. Jason was suddenly more concerned about shooting his wad than getting shot in the face by his dad.

"Feel any better?" Lori asked, and not in a derisive way.

"Umm, that's a loaded question," Jason responded, trying to cool down his erection since it appeared her toying with him was as close to the line as Lori was planning to go. She'd done it without a thought, he mused.

"Most dangerous song ever recorded," Lori said, turning down the volume. She gave no indication she'd known Jason was battling a boner in his pants. "I play it nearly every morning getting ready for school. Kind of like a personal ritual. Have you listened to the tape I made for you?"

"Ahh, well," he fumbled, feeling his dick start to wilt. All it took was that question.

"It's okay," Lori said, reaching out to him again, but only patting his knee before switching back to her primary driving hand on the steering wheel. "I didn't expect you to call me so soon, much less dig into the music."

"It's been a day," Jason said. "I'm sorry, but I will."

"I know you will," Lori said with a smile that made her dusky lips seem virtuous instead of maudlin. "We're fellow castaways from Merriweather Island, and it's a shame we've never had a class together all these years, but I can tell. You're no bullshitter. I wouldn't have driven twenty minutes to get you if you were."

"I appreciate that," Jason whispered, glancing over at Lori, who did likewise with a smile unfastening her dark lips apart. It sounded corny to his mind, but Jason thought an angelic beam protruded from Lori's immaculate, whitened teeth. He didn't care if whatever lipstick she used turned his mouth into flapping licorice; he wanted to kiss her.

"I can't altogether relate to what you're going through, Jason," Lori said, turning back to the road. "But we have our own family skeletons in the closet whom we seldom see, thank the Goddess."

"Say what?" Jason quipped, her last word sounding ludicrous, though there'd been no accident to it. Lori had meant it, sure as she'd meant every single lyric of "My War" she'd bellowed.

"Goddess."

"Not God?"

"Well, yeah, there's God, but not the *Christian* conception of one, almighty masculine deity known as 'God.' A Lord and a Lady, to be pluralized. I'm talking about a compound, vast number of gods and goddesses collectively working as a divine unit to amplify the magnitude of the universe. We, in turn, give them glory and work with them in harmony to raise our personal energies and to stockpile energy to be returned to Mother Earth. It goes in-hand with the Tarot card I gave you, which I see you using as a bookmark, oh the humanity… Forgive him, Lord Thoth, he knows not what he does, even if *The Outsiders* changed my life."

"Yeah, I don't read as much as I should, but it's a hell of a story."

"If you want to know more about what I do, we can talk about it later. My mom's a Wiccan high priestess and she's been teaching me the path of magick."

"Uh, okay," Jason murmured. "I don't know what a Wiccan is, but sure."

"All that pagan-based heavy metal music you listen to," Lori joked. "For shame. I've seen that Ronnie James Dio button on your vest before. I'd be shocked if he wasn't one of us."

The more she spoke, the more turned-on Jason was getting. It didn't even have anything to do with sex this very minute, since his member had shriveled down to snail size as it did whenever it was cold out, during Weightlifting class, or if he was downright spellbound as he was right now.

"The universe told me to reach out to you," she said, taking a deep breath. "I had Mom do a reading on me last week and I was excited by it. If I'm boring you with this, just tell me to fuck off…"

"No way, go on."

"Alright, so I drew the Archangel Sachiel oracle card. He's connected to Jupiter, the planet, and he represents good fortune. The Essenes were a sect who worshipped Sachiel and they connect him to the element of water."

"So he can walk on water like Jesus?"

"Not so much like that, and I know this stuff is complicated. Believe me as a 17-year-old baby witch, polytheism is harder to learn than anything Merriweather can throw at us."

"You're a *witch*?"

Lori chuckled then said in an empathetic instead of disturbed manner, "I'll quote *The Wizard of Oz* here. You say that like it's a bad thing?"

"Uh, no, not really," Jason rummaged. "I thought there really weren't witches anymore. I mean, who does potions and spells in this day and age?"

"Ask the thousands of pilgrims who hit Salem every year."

"I stand corrected, then. The turn into my neighborhood is coming up."

"I know," she said, and before Jason had time to process how Lori *could* know, she went on. "Mom and I work with light magic. None of that evil stuff I hear praised in your music sometimes. Makes me sick, sorry. We shy away from voodoo, and we don't believe in Hell or the devil. How does that grab you?"

"I couldn't be more mind-blown after today, even if they decided to do another *Re-Animator* movie."

"Okay, how about this? The horns-up sign you metalheads do? That's a symbol to call in the god energy. Hardly a contemporary hand gesture. Anyway, not only is Sachiel looking down upon me in a positive light, I also got an Ace of Pentacles once Mom used my Thoth deck. You know, the same one as your Aeon card."

"Cool, do you want it back?"

"When you're done with *The Outsiders*, yes I would," Lori jested, turning in to Jason's development. "The Ace of Pentacles also says I'm looking at upcoming blessings of fortune. I need to put out good energy to receive it back. A basic rule of magick, what you put out comes back threefold. We call it the power of three. Even though I use an Egyptian tarot deck, I've been working with the Germanic and Norse deities, Odin, Freyja, and Hulda. Freyja is the goddess of love, beauty, sex, fertility and, funny enough, war."

"If Henry Rollins is one of you, no doubt Freyja's his gal."

"Don't mock, Jason," Lori cautioned in a warm tone as she pulled up to Jason's house. "This evening hasn't gone the way I expected, but it's been…"

"Better," he finished for her. "Better than the rest of my day, anyway. There's my house."

"Yeah, *much* better. You saved me from a *Waltons* marathon, for a little while, anyway."

"I'd invite you in, but there's no telling what my mom's like right now."

"What do you mean?"

"I'll call you tomorrow, is that alright? Whether she's awake or not. I need to tell her what Dad did today."

"She's asleep at 8:12 on a Saturday night?" Lori asked, checking her wrist. Funny how Jason only just now saw she wore a watch. Black banded, like the rest of her attire. "That's just obscene."

"I'll tell you about her more tomorrow," Jason said. "It's why I needed you to get me. Thank you for coming to my rescue."

"It's what I do," Lori replied, reaching for Jason's fingers and squeezing them twice before letting go. She then planted her palms on both sides of his cheek. "I also do *this* when a guy has an aura like yours that jives with mine..."

She leaned in and pecked Jason on the lips once, then pushed firmer against his. Her breath tasted of tobacco and mint, telling Jason she smoked menthols. Her tongue flashed out and hunted for his, slinking back the instant she'd connected. She was a master of the tease, Jason thought, not that he was upset about it. Lori's kiss may not have had the most pleasant taste, but it was the passion behind it ringing chimes of bliss inside Jason's head before she let him go. He felt something rise inside his chest this time, not down below. It was the sudden warmth and a teeming confidence he'd last felt tearing down the track in Weightlifting class.

"This could work," he told her dweebishly as he got out of the car.

"So mote it be," Lori said back.

Chapter 27

THAT SUNDAY, ROB found himself at Kerry's Family Pharmacy on the other end of town.

His dad needed a run to the drug store to pick up some Excedrin for Rob's mother, who had been dealing with a migraine refusing to give up the ghost since hitting her Saturday afternoon. An adjuster for Dunford Insurance Group only three blocks down from Kerry's, Rob's mom had gone in for half a day yesterday, only to be slammed with a bizarre, high number of roof damage claims. A Category F rope tornado had spanked the Union Hills subdivision in neighboring Howard County on Friday afternoon at an estimated 63 miles an hour. With the home office of the national insurance carrier, Allstate, operating on a weekday only schedule of 8:00 a.m. to 6:00 p.m., the anxious and sometime abusive callers barraging Rob's mom looking for immediate action on a Saturday had plunged her into a stasis.

It had been enough to knock her down for the night, leaving Rob and his dad to fend for their own dinner and now breakfast this morning. Accordingly, Rob's dad had been making run after run from the house all weekend, picking up cheesesteak subs the night before, pastries from Rondell's Bakery this morning, with side trips between to the post office, True Value Hardware, and the video store. Instead of poring through a return read of Marvel's three issue *Contest of Champions* miniseries yesterday like he'd initially planned, Rob had joined his dad in the living room for a viewing of *The Seventh Sign*, which his dad had rented and passed out on. He'd cracked his son up afterwards by saying about the film, "The Book of Revelation's enough to put *anyone* to sleep."

While chomping on a blueberry pastry, Rob had written his paper for Creative Writing class, making the painstaking effort to count each word with the tip of his pen three times to ensure a word count of 492. He was positive Mr. Morrow would appreciate Rob's interpretation of Harriet's "news." He might even call Rob up to the front to read again like last week.

Right now, Rob had a twenty inside his Levi's folding wallet with its red base and tan borders hatching an escape plan past the Velcro barrier. Since starting his job at Grigsby Tools, Rob had dumped $376.50 into a savings account both of his parents had insisted he open at Provident Bank, with no coincidence, next door to Kerry's Family Pharmacy. The lead teller there, Bella, was a heavyset woman with a winning smile that could swing a climate of change in the way Deng Xiaoping was doing for post-Mao Zedung Communist China. Bella was already on a first name basis with Rob after opening the account for the teenager. She'd complimented his early-on ability to deposit more than cash out his earnings.

Still, Bella had teased Rob for keeping the twenty from his last paycheck, but it didn't matter right now. His dad had long found the Excedrin and one thing Rob knew about the man was how he would use any excuse to drop into Kerry's to poke through the latest issue of *Field and Stream* each month. Rather than buy a copy or get a subscription.

Thus, Rob pounced on the chance to join his dad with the pharmacy's spindle rack of comic books in mind.

He'd freaked out upon the sight of one last copy left of the first issue of the Canuck X-Men Wolverine's new solo series. Commonly referred to by comic book nerds as "Logan," Wolverine was snarling overtop a pile of soldier corpses on the cover, his adamantium claws extracted, sending Rob into such a fanboy frenzy, he'd done a quick-snap victory dance to score the lone issue. From the top folds of the latest *Field and Stream*, his dad teased, "Worst happy dance I've ever seen, aside from that dumb 'Day O' bit in *Beetlejuice*."

Thinking about the money he had on him, and the money he'd only just gotten started stashing for a future car, Rob tried to forget Jason was leagues ahead of him toward purchasing a vehicle. On their walk to Curry's Music yesterday, Jason had let slip he had $3,100 in savings since starting work at Super Thrift earlier in the year. This with their periodic drops into Bud Curry's shop and, in Rob's case, every other week comic grabs.

The squeak of the spindling comic book rack enthused Rob but was getting on his father's nerves, judging by the random glances of annoyance sent to him from behind the magazine cover depicting a lake in South Carolina where trout and small mouth bass reigned. Rob next grabbed a copy of *The Punisher* #13 and, in keeping with theme, *X-Factor* #34, though he passed on the second issue of the X universe tie-in, *X-Terminators*.

Rob hadn't seen her stop at the far end of the aisle until Emily

Haney started her slow approach toward him. His father had finished reading *Field and Stream* a lot earlier than usual or he'd merely skimmed through it this time, as he'd disappeared from the magazine shelf.

Rob flinched upon spotting her from the corner of his eye. He dropped his comics to the floor with sudden clumsy hands. Feeling like a dork but not as much as he used to in Emily's presence, Rob gobbled them back up. There was something different about Emily's bearing, yet he never took his eyes off her, nor could be let his guard down. Echoes of Emily Haney's past denunciations of "Geeeeeek" from her grimacing teeth taunted him.

As she had lately at school, she'd ditched her FFA jacket, this time wearing a lighter, rainbow swirled windbreaker.

"Peace, dude," Emily said, flicking the universal V sign with her left middle and forefinger. "I'm not here to give you grief, though you *are* a geek. Comic books? Seriously?"

"What do you want?" Rob huffed.

"Look," she sighed at him. "I know you caught that scene with me and Lee. I'm not with him or any of those guys anymore, just clearing the air. I've known those jerks since kindergarten, and I can't believe what an idiot I've been all this time."

"Okay," Rob said warily. It sounded more suspicious than if she'd told him he was good looking.

"It's been hard," Emily said, making a phantom semicircle with both of her hands overtop her belly. "I got rid of it yesterday."

"And you're telling me this, why?"

Emily looked aggravated for a second, then she moaned before saying, "See you around school, Martino."

"It doesn't burn your tongue to use my first name, does it?" Rob blurted impulsively. What brought *that* on?

"Rob, then," Emily said, spreading a flutter of a smile which evaporated with the rest of her.

Another push of the squeaky rack after Emily left, and Rob fished out *Fantastic Four* #314, *Silver Surfer* #13 and *Detective Comics* #592.

A new female voice came behind his back.

"I like Wonder Woman and Cloak and Dagger and though it's been a while since they put anything out on her, Amethyst."

Rob turned to find Marcie Barone, looking more assured of herself than she had the past couple days in school.

She reached in and pushed the spindle rack. Her hair had been trimmed and permed again and she smelled like White Diamonds. The crucifix was in its usual spot, shooting a small beacon of light toward the side like a goad. Marcie leaned as close as she dared without letting her lurching, heavy breast touch Rob as she spun the rack again. "You can make mine Marvel all you want, and I buy a couple of their books, but give *me* this…"

Marcie snagged a copy of the rebooted *Wonder Woman* # 22, illustrated and written by George Perez, including the cover depicting Princess Diana in midair, her magic Lasso of Truth swirling about her and the clouds. A flock of doves anointed her mission to vanquish all injustice in the name of love.

"Don't tell anyone," Marcie whispered to Rob. "You know how judgmental people in school are. Comics are for elementary school kids, blah blah blah…"

"Sure," he said, just as quiet. "Your secret's safe with me as long as you return the favor."

"Punisher is too barbaric for my tastes," Marcie said, keeping her mouth close to Rob's ear without panting too heavily into his canal. "I prefer comic heroes with an agenda that doesn't involve killing."

"Wonder Woman killed the Hitler clone in the old tv show," Rob commented without trying to sound rude.

"Well, *duh*, that was for a good cause," Marcie countered. "And she took out her patron Roman goddess in Issue 192, when she had no powers. She also cut the head off Ares' son, Deimos, but that was to save the planet from a full-on calamity."

"So, you're saying killing is justified if the needs must," Rob parried.

Marcie fell silent a moment before uttering in deflection, "Okay, wise guy. Is Storm in that Wolverine comic you have?"

"Don't know, I just cherry picked it as soon as I spotted it. Last copy. You prefer female protagonists to male in your comics, I take it?"

"Estrogen power," Marcie replied, waggling the Wonder Woman comic at Rob. "Monica Rambeau, the new Captain Marvel, she rocks. She-Hulk, Elektra, Valkyrie, Batgirl, Huntress, Firestar, Catwoman, Rogue, even Abigail Arcane in Swamp Thing…bad…you *know*. My mom's hovering around somewhere, so I can't say it."

"Ass," Rob said it for both of them, as low as he could. "Holy cool girls, Batman, I had no idea you like comic books."

"You're rotten," Marcie said, fanning her comic book a second time. "I can't believe my luck running into you."

"Bradenton's never going to challenge Baltimore or Annapolis for population growth," Rob joshed. "A town this small, I'm surprised we don't run into each other more often, especially if you like comics. If you keep flapping it around, though, you'll take the value down to fine before you get to the register."

"You really know your stuff," Marcie said, still wagging her

Wonder Woman comic despite.

"*There* you are," a stern, heavyset woman blustered, cutting off their conversation. "You said you would be right back after looking over those dreadful pieces of pop art."

"My mother's a collector and curator of fine art," Marcie divulged to Rob as low as she could, but it wasn't enough to avoid being heard by all three of them. "Comic books are beneath her."

"Dalliances," Marcie's mother said in a stale voice. Like her daughter, Marcie's mother wore a matching gold crucifix, only hers was encrusted with tiny Herkimer diamonds.

"*Okay*, Mom," Marcie declared more than said as she flicked her free hand out in Rob's direction. "This is a guy I know from school, Rob Martino."

"Mr. Martino," Marcie's mother recognized by name. "My Marcie has mentioned you a few times. Good to put a face to the name."

"Ma'am," Rob said, inadvertently bowing a smidge and feeling dippy afterwards. The bigger thing crossing his mind other than trying to make a good impression was finding out why Marcie had been talking about him at home. Going perhaps too far in his imaginative capacities, Rob conjured a flash picture of he and Marcie reading comics together on the back of a deck. A handful of burgers smoking on their outdoor grill. On the deck of their new home, glinting like the wedding bands tying their futures. Marcie Martino. It had just as much verve as her maiden name, if not more.

"Time to check out," Marcie's mother said in a smug tone, breaking Rob's far-flung trance. "I have my lithium prescription, so let's say goodbye to your friend and depart. Channel 11 is running *Whatever Happened to Baby Jane?* and I haven't seen that in a few years. Mr. Martino, take care of yourself, though I would advise you not to err, even on the side of caution, as my daughter is not one of your breed."

"*Mother*," Marcie groaned in humiliation. "Rob's not a dog."

"Therefore," Mrs. Barone continued, flouting her daughter as if it were only the elder woman and Rob to themselves. "I recommend you keep a far berth from her. A good day to you."

"Yes, ma'am," Rob responded before his dad came back to check on him, adding as he looked straight at Marcie with a focus on boosting his dialect, "However, with all due respect, if Marcie wishes to engage with me in the future, I am more than open to the proposition. She's an intelligent young woman and I think having the independence to choose her friends should weigh heavier than it does."

"You're well-versed, but far too trifling," Marcie's mother said, straightening her corpulent posture and fluffing the dead fox wrapped across her shoulders. "Your manner of attire also leaves a lot to be desired."

"Excuse me," Rob's father interjected. The fire in his eyes said he would've vaulted and cleared both the oral hygiene and cosmetics aisles in a single bound to get in front of Marcie's mother. "If you plan on continuing to insult my son, you can give *me* your grievances first. 'Not one your breed?' How dare you? No offense, Miss..."

"Marcie," Rob said on her behalf, feeling a burst of joy inside. His father was holding it together, but he was also on the verge of hitting the napalm level fueling one of his Vietnam tirades. Rob more than appreciated the defense his father was giving him right now; he felt something akin to worship.

"A pleasure to meet you, Marcie," Rob's dad rolled on, giving her a polite nod but his intent toward her mother became like a verbal equivalent of his M16 in the field. "Let's say I had the same lack of couth as you, a lack of *pedigree,* if you will. Then I give the same snotty dismissal of your daughter without getting to know her. I wouldn't do that, ma'am, because I'm not some lowbrow gutter trash trying to elevate herself with some tacky dead animal slung around her shoulders. Where'd you get that thing anyway, you pretentious windbag, mashed on the road in Hunt Valley? We had days in Vietnam when we were out of rations and starving. We would've given our small toes for a fox to eat. Crickets often got us through the next supply drop. A snake could be like Christmas had come to the DMZ. I've gone off-topic, I apologize. As to the matter at hand, say one more disparaging word about my son, we *will* have a problem."

"Well, I never..." Marcie's mother gasped, her rubbery cheeks rippling with indignation.

"*Exactly,*" Rob's dad pressed. "And you'd be a more likable person if you did."

Marcie gave a silent gesticulation offering both surrender and acceptance of the situation and she followed her mother away, taking the Wonder Woman comic with her.

"Cute girl, Rob. Her mom's an asshole, though."

Rob had nothing but an affirmative nod for that.

Chapter 28

EARLIER THAT SAME MORNING, Jason woke up before sunrise at 6:38 a.m. For a weekend, unholy. Even yesterday his dad hadn't picked him up until 9:12 a.m., twelve minutes late, since the drunken son of a bitch couldn't be on time for anything except for his next beer, it had become sparkling clear. Jason had risen at 8:00 a.m. yesterday and was ready for his dad a half an hour early while his mother had slept through the entire pick-up event.

She'd also been asleep last night after Lori dropped Jason off and bed was where she still lay. Awake himself mulling over Saturday's events, both good and awful, Jason had heard his mom shuffle-scuff at 2:46 a.m. to go to the bathroom. He'd heard her tinkling, a clumsy chunk-a-munk unfurling of some Charmin, then the *baaaaaaah-gooooossshhh* flush of the toilet. She hadn't washed her hands afterwards, which was way out of character for her. She'd made a thing all these years the entire household should wash their hands after any trip to the bathroom, villainizing genital sweat and germs which could linger upon the fingers without a proper scrub. Jason had heard the word "unsanitary" enough to despise the infernal word.

The fact his mother wasn't observing one of her resolute house rules not only added to Jason's concern, it was also making him downright pissed.

As if he wasn't pissed at his mother enough after being unable to reach her last night when he'd needed her. Somewhere in the day, she'd been up, and she'd made herself scrambled eggs, since Jason found the cracked open shells in the trash can. She'd also heated up a Stouffers frozen lasagna for herself, the half-crumpled box and slashed open cellophane left upon the counter giving her away. She'd left all her dishes in the sink, unwashed, the crusty frying pan sitting without any pre-soak dish soap and water. All out of character. She'd had milk, the stinky white residue clung around the bottom and edge of a glass which had an emblazoned black spinnaker printed across one side. The sailing ship glass had belonged to Jason's dad, left behind and forgotten about by him, but not by Jason's mom. She'd been using it a lot since his father moved out.

What infuriated Jason the most to find, however, was a shattered wine glass in the sink, the shards scattered all over everything else. He could see a crimson stain in what the bottom of the glass would've been, still intact as a giveaway she'd been drinking yesterday. Not that it had been needed, since the telltale evidence of a three-fourths emptied bottle of cabernet sauvignon, '83 vintage, was left in the open with a paper towel wad jammed into the nozzle.

Jason wished he'd invited Lori in last night, and it taken all he had not to call her again. Yeah, she'd come to get him at his dad's without question other than to ask if he'd been in trouble. Yeah, she'd flirted with him, and *hell yes*, she'd kissed him. There was more to it, though. Lori had confided in him to profess herself as a neo-pagan witch, one of many things Jason had tried to process much of the night.

All being said, he would've felt mortified running to Lori a second time the same night. He would've been exactly the pussy his father had branded him. Of course, it was his father himself who had proven to be the pussy. It was the only comfort Jason took from the rifle incident.

Jason's dad had tried calling, but that wasn't until 11:26 p.m. Jason had let the voice message recorder get the call, knowing full well who it had been. He could hear his dad breathing heavily, like he'd run outdoors to his brink, reminding Jason in a weird way of how Tony Beckley had tormented Carol Kane during *When a Stranger Calls*. Jason had given his father's slurred, infuriated voice the finger upon hearing *"I don't know how you got home, Jason, but I'm sorry, goddammit. I'm sorry, okay? Jesus. Don't make a federal case out of it with your mother."*

Jason had deleted the message before cleaning up the kitchen. He'd nicked his right forefinger with one of the wine bottle shards, the blood spattering all over the white ceramic plate his mother had used for her eggs. A quick rinse with peroxide and a band-aid wrap, and Jason finished his tasks, which he'd called to himself in reservation, "cover-up dirty work."

He'd been so angry with his mother he'd only leaned his ear against her bedroom door to make sure he could hear her snuffling, instead of going inside to check on her.

As much as he'd wanted to listen to Lori's mixtape, he was in too ripe a mood to listen with an open ear, much less an open mind.

Over and over, a replay of his dad pointing the gun at him spun inside Jason's mind. A couple times, the tears returned.

Jason had forgotten all about *Headbangers Ball* on MTV, of all things, droning through more than watching a flusher of a hospital horror movie from 1982, *Visiting Hours* on HBO before he passed out. He'd been so exhausted Jason hadn't remembered moving from the living room to his bed. By the time he'd laid down, he was upset to find himself wide awake again until drifting off after his mother's visit to the commode.

Less than four hours later, Jason was back up.

His digestive system mounted an insurrection, even with Jason eating just a bowl full of Utz barbecue potato chips while half-watching tv. A lot of his stomach discomfort, he figured, was the sausage and pepperoni pizza souring inside his guts. As much as he wanted to poop, nothing would come. He was bound up and counting the numerous reasons why as he tried going back to bed.

Jason lay back down with his feet near the headboard, relocating his pillow to the front end of the bed. This, so he could put his headphones back on, now with Lori's mixtape playing.

Jason wasn't quite sure what to make of the mod swish and the twinkling xylophones of The Violent Femmes' "Daddy's Gone," but it took no time to rid himself of his troubles and nausea once he fell in love with the urgent and soaring melody of the anthemic "All the Young Punks" from The Clash.

Jason had gone into a fleeting state of jubilation with Keith Morris' manic raving on the hardcore crash of the Circle Jerks' "World Up My Ass." It dawned on Jason, Morris had once been in Black Flag, to which he and Lori had been howling along last night. The song had become a minute-plus adrenaline rush about society mores burning up Morris and how much he wanted to chew, spit, and tear all of it to oblivion. It had been enough to seize Jason, throttle him without upsetting his guts again, and unexpectedly send him back to sleep.

Three hours later, Jason woke again. Pulling the headphones off with a gross, sticky sensation affixed to his ears, he grumbled, knowing he'd missed the rest of the songs on the first side of Lori's tape. Also knowing he'd have to rewind it all back to hear them — or play the second side and let it spool for a rerun of the first.

He smelled something like raspberries and, once his hearing readjusted, he heard plates clattering in the cupboards.

His mother was up. Making breakfast, no less.

Part of Jason wanted to rush downstairs and open fire on his mother about last night. He wanted to grab her shoulders and shake her out of this funk she was in. He wanted to scream in her face, much like Keith Morris of the Circle Jerks, to make her understand what she was doing to herself, much less to Jason.

Instead, he swung himself out of his bed, letting the tight coil yank his headphones off him. They skipped across the carpet and limply settled there on the floor. Jason whirled his pillow back to where it belonged on the bed and he took a deep breath, before turning the power off his stereo.

Downstairs in the kitchen, his mother was in the same red and black flannel nightgown she'd been wearing the past few nights. Jason knew it hadn't been washed in quite some time, since the laundry basket had been overflowed to the point he'd considered starting a load himself last night.

"Hi, honey," his mother called out to him without turning. She had a wide-mouthed griddle on the stove, hissing as she spooned out lumps of pancake batter with chopped raspberries in them. "Thought I'd make my little guy his favorite French toast with raspberries this morning. You'd like that, wouldn't you, Jay?"

To Jason, the cutesy question came off condescending. It was the way his mother had spoken to him as a child, all the way through elementary school. It was pandering, discomfiting, and at Jason's age, unsuitable. Worse, she'd called him "Jay" instead of his full name. The abbreviation was something he'd enjoyed when he was younger, but he'd reached a point, around age fourteen, where he'd grown turned off from it, and he'd asked his mother to cease using "Jay" in favor of "Jason."

"Thanks, Ma," he said, cautiously, feeling gratitude to see his mother making him his favorite breakfast, which she hadn't done since his father was still living with them. At the same time, she seemed way off, as if that should be any surprise these days. Addressing him as "Jay" and in a sickening sweet tone, made Jason wonder if, coupled with the sleeping pills, the wine binge last night and the general neglect of herself, she'd gone off the deep end.

"Sorry Mommy's been under the weather so much lately," she told him, dropping a dollop of butter upon the griddle, then plopping a couple pieces of bread slavered by egg whites behind it. "I feel better now."

"I haven't called you 'Mommy' in a long time," Jason said with a stern tone, having enough of this…whatever it was…reversion to nearly a decade back in time.

"How'd it go with your father yesterday?" she asked, ignoring Jason's slight admonition.

"You want the truth, Ma?" Jason asked, feeling his body geyser with resentment. Facing a near-death experience with his father and now this embarrassing display by his mother, he didn't care what came next. He was ready to blow.

"Of course, I do," she responded, still using her throwback saccharine voice yet facing him with an uneasy, counterfeited grin. It all confirmed what Jason was suspecting. She'd lost her grip on reality.

"What's *wrong* with you, Ma?!?" he blared, knowing the answer, but having no choice but to shake her up.

"What do you mean?" she asked, looking heartbroken on the spot. She was confused and fragile to the point people fifty years her senior might. It almost stopped Jason in his tracks, but he pushed onward, nonetheless. This had to come out. It had to be done.

"I hardly see you these days! You're always sleeping! I *know* you're taking pills, Ma!"

"I am not..." she croaked at him in a tinny, wounded voice. The toasting bread on the griddle was starting to burn.

"Ma, flip them before you start a fire!" Jason yelled, dashing to grab the spatula out of her hand.

"Get off!" she exclaimed, pulling the spatula away from Jason possessively, this time playing the child instead of the parent. "I'll do it!"

"You can't lie to me, Ma! I've seen valium on your nightstand!"

"You're spying on me?" his mother asked in shock as she jabbed beneath the darkening toast, slapping the uncooked sides down against the hot iron as if she was trying not to get caught doing it.

"Ma, I *needed* you last night!"

"Why?" she asked, this time in a firmer voice telling Jason he'd finally gotten through. It was time to strike while the proverbial — and literal — iron was hot.

"You wouldn't pick up the phone because you were *sleeping,* for Christ's sake! Ma, I had to call a friend for help! I come home from work all this week, you're sleeping! The week before, you were sleeping! I was so scared he was gonna kill me!"

"*Who* was going to kill you?" his mother asked with a furious mashing away of her ridiculous puerility. Her countenance flushed pale. Her senses were now on full alert. This was the mother Jason was looking for.

"Dad!" Jason bellowed.

"Your *father?* He may be a complete jerk, but he wouldn't..."

"Come on, Ma, you haven't only been sleeping too much, you've gone clueless! You know how Dad is with his drinking..."

"Yes," his mother responded, her expression hardening even more. She scooped off the French toast that was now well-done and crisp black around the edges, laying them on an empty plate before turning the stove off. "What'd he *do,* that piece of shit?"

An hour of recollection turned into reconciliation between mother and son, culminating in Jason's mother ripping his father apart over the phone. He could hear his dad's pugnacious squawks of protest since she'd kept the phone off her ear while they waged a five-minute war of words. His mother gained leverage to such success she'd threatened, "You ever pull anything like that on Jason again, I'll have you arrested, or worse, I'll hunt you down and feed you your balls, you sorry bastard! Don't *even* think I'm letting him in any car you're driving ever again! You need help, Mac! Get it now!"

Taking full advantage of this momentum, Jason burbled, "I never want to see you again," into the receiver before his mother plunged the call disconnect button.

She'd heard Jason out in full, not only about his traumatic experience yesterday, not only his trials in and outside of school, the smashed tape, the brewing hostilities with Sam Shaffer and his friends, getting struck upside the head with a full can of beer. Jason also dished his objections to her excessive sleeping.

She'd tossed out the first batch of French toast and restarted a new, perfectly griddled set while they talked. With all cards proverbially laid out, his mother tossed the still-full bottle of valium pills into the trash can in front of Jason and hugged him for a near minute.

They'd eaten all the French toast gone and worked together to clean up, his mother washing the dishes and Jason drying and putting everything away into the cabinets. She'd apologized for leaving her mess the night before, explaining she'd grown upset thinking about Jason's dad and spiking the wine glass into the sink. She'd made a joke about kissing Jason's "boo boo" on his bandaged finger. Despite his misgivings earlier, he let her, just for fun.

She'd also apologized for "checking out," her words, adding how good it had felt to torch her ex-husband. They agreed to play the board game *Pay Day* in the afternoon when Jason asked if he could have a friend join them. His mother had been pleasantly surprised to hear a name other than Rob's.

His mother went on a house cleaning frenzy while Jason's call to Lori turned from a quick minute offer into a full-fledged discussion about her pantheon of spiritual envoys and what food, drink, color, and crystal stone offerings she gave to appease them.

Lori later kept all talk relegated to fond childhood memories in front of Jason and his mother over glasses of 7-Up as she proceeded to wipe them both out in *Pay Day*.

Chapter 29

"MY DAD TRIED CALLING twice more after you went home, Lori," Jason said, scouting around the school promenade before tilting his head back to her. Something seemed off to him right now, even if he was chalking most of it up to all he'd been through. The whole onslaught enough to put even a statuesque Buckingham Palace guard on visible alert. "Ma only picked up once. He threatened to stop paying child support if she didn't allow me to see him."

"What a maggot," Lori sneered, swinging Jason's right hand back and forth with Rob keeping pace on her other side.

"My mom's coming out of a tough place, but I gave her a big hug when she'd come at him with, 'What good is child support if you kill our child?'"

"Classic," Lori said. "I like her more and more."

"Don't you have a say in the whole thing?" Rob asked. "I believe the legal age is sixteen to decide how you want to interact with your parents, especially divided parents. Besides, I've known you and your family long enough to know your dad's full of shit."

"If my father hates me so much, he should've pulled out of my mom years ago."

"And they call *me* dark," Lori joked dryly, bumping Jason with her hip using enough force to convey her displeasure at his self-deprecation.

"Actually," Rob said, addressing Lori more than Jason. "I see you growing into a refined Barbara Bel Geddes type."

"Miss Ellie from *Dallas?*" Lori cackled. "Oh, you give me way too much credit, Rob."

"She also appeared in a few episodes of *Alfred Hitchcock Presents,*" Rob stated like a seasoned Hollywood critic. "I'm pretty sure I saw her in a rerun of *Journey Into the Unknown* as well. Keep an eye out for those shows sometime and tell me I'm wrong."

"The next Leonard Maltin," Lori kidded. "You're a complete

weirdo, though very sweet."

"You may be the only dude in the whole school who knows that crap," Jason mocked.

"I'm the King of Useless Information," Rob boasted as if he had a crown to back up the claim. "Forever may I reign."

"Long live the king," Jason chortled.

"I'm surrounded by idiots," Lori moaned, rolling her eyes up.

"I also lip synch the Pledge of Allegiance," Rob noted, out of nowhere.

"Ever since I saw *Red Dawn*, so do I," Lori added with a feigned shudder. "I don't care how hot Charlie Sheen is, that movie's embarrassing."

"I *like* that film," Jason protested.

"Of course, you do," Lori sighed, swinging Jason's arm again and giving him a girlish wink.

Conjuring a sunny verve collected amongst themselves which hadn't been there the first near month of school, Merriweather High students began to take notice the trusty duo of Rob Martino and Jason Hamlin were not only buffered by a third party, but Lori Phillips was also latched onto Jason. Hot juice for scuttlebutt feed.

"Look at 'em, gaping like Ringling Brothers came rolling into town," Rob said, jerking his head in the direction of other teenagers shambling by. "You two are gonna be the talk of the whole school."

"How's it going with Marcie Barone?" Jason asked, this time without any snidery. The threesome cut around the bend past the administrative offices. Vice Principal Newton was standing at the entrance into the offices, on guard for any morning shenanigans. He took the time to notice Jason and Lori holding hands and he let a thin smile leak from his otherwise serious visage.

"Like a preppie and metalhead should never mix," Rob said, this time with noticeable flatness.

"What? How?" both Jason and Lori quipped in tandem, already showing the signs of a tight, if still new, couple.

"Ehh, I ran into her at the pharmacy yesterday," Rob said. "At the comic book rack."

"Let me guess, they were all out of the latest issue of *Tiger Beat*," Lori teased.

"Funny enough, Marcie digs comic books," Rob refuted with a courteous laugh at Lori's jab. "Her mom took one look at me, though and, well, you know. I think the whole Marcie Barone prospect's over before it ever got started."

"Her loss," Jason grunted. "Stuck up…"

"No need to finish that thought, babe," Lori intervened. "I don't have anything against Marcie Barone other than her once looking down at my triple moon goddess pendant and telling me I need to be saved."

"Mom used to make us all go to church every week for 8:45 morning mass," Jason blurted. "I don't miss the up and down and kneeling motions and the Last Supper recitals, but if Jesus really saves, why are there assholes on the planet like my father, Lee Metcalf, Sam Shaffer, and those pricks?"

"Doesn't matter," Rob said to both, and he meant it. "If Marcie Barone bothers speaking to me after yesterday, I'll testify to the truth of miracles and renew my faith."

Taped to the school trophy case was an advertisement for an unusual charity sporting event the school was hosting a week before Homecoming. The headline screamed **"RETURN ENGAGEMENT! VARISITY GIRLS' VOLLEYBALL VS. BALTIMORE BLAST."** Flushed center were two pictures of indoor soccer sensations, Yugoslavian defenseman Mike Stankovic and the team's fleet-footed forward from Serbia, Stan "The Magician" Stamenkovic. The game was designed so the school's varsity volleyball team, which had won state the year prior, would play their sport against the Baltimore Blast, winners of the 1984 MISL championship.

"They're doing that stunt again, huh?" Lori quipped.

"What's the big deal?" Jason asked. "Other than volleyball versus soccer and minors taking on twenty-somethings."

"I went to last year's match," Lori stated.

"Really?" Rob asked. "I didn't think sports was your thing."

"They're not," she said. "I went with my older cousin Renee, who never attended school here. She graduated from Liberty in '82, but she's big into soccer and she'd have any of the Blast's babies if they'd offer. The gimmick, and I admit it's a good one, is the volleyball girls get to use their hands and arms, their full arsenal. The Blast players can only use their feet to return the ball."

"You can't be serious," Jason said, smirking instead of frowning at the description of the game.

"The girls won last year," Lori remarked. "Barely. It was cool. Those Blast guys held their own and only a couple times lost points for their hands touching the ball. The Blast kicking returns over the net were something to see."

"Grudge match," Rob joked, his subsequent guffawing picked up by Jason and Lori.

"I stood out like a sore thumb there," Lori added. "If you can imagine *that...*"

Jason and Rob continued laughing.

"Renee also rolled me my first joint after the game. We snuck up to the track and —"

"Well, look at *this* freakshow!" the trio heard behind them as they'd approached the east side stairwell.

Rob tremored in immediate recognition of the voice. Lori clamped her eyes shut, as if trying to will it all away, knowing something awful had found them. Jason's free hand balled into a fist, while his attached hand tightened to the point Lori shook hers free of his without sounding off about the sudden pain she felt.

The farmers had been gone all last week, but the suspension had run its course. They were back in school today.

"Corpses need love too," they heard Lee Metcalf sneer as all three turned to find him and Sam Shaffer, their own fists crunched at their waists. Even without the rest of their gang, their blue corduroy jackets looked like an indigo force field.

"Good for you, fuck faces," Sam jeered. "You like to do the ménage-a-trois, Lori? You should trade up. Me and Lee, we've got more dick than you can handle."

"Then go jerk each other off," Lori spat back at them. "And Lee, shame on you. Emily could've done a hell of a lot better, you absolute prick."

Lee's cheek flushed red, yet he was inexplicably smiling. Sam took the bait, though, as his entire face screamed louder than he no doubt wanted to from his throat.

"I don't hit girls unless I have to," Sam hissed, "but I'll make an exception if you don't shut the fuck up right now."

"You'll have to get through me first, Shaffer!" Jason barked, losing any composure he might've had, launching his palms forward and planting them against Sam's chest. There was no longer any fear. He thought about how effortlessly he'd taken down his father, and that clown was drunk.

Both Rob and Lori gasped in awe as Jason launched Sam off his feet by shoving him against Lee Metcalf. The collision and subsequent bounce off Lee toppled Sam to the floor.

"You and me, motherfucker!" Jason screamed down at Sam, pointing his right forefinger into Sam's face, the same way Jason's dad had pointed the rifle into his own. He didn't look at Lee, though he could just as readily turn in his direction, no matter being outclassed by the mountain of a man. "You started this shit, Shaffer! I dare you to fight me without your backup!"

Lori didn't need an invitation. She instantly stepped into Lee's path as he lurched toward Jason with his fist up. Rob tremored at the sight of the acceleration in conflict, but he wasn't about to flake out. He stepped up next to Lori and planted his shoulder against hers, blocking Lee from getting at Jason.

"Come on!" Jason provoked Sam, who remained on the floor long enough for Vice Principal Newton to come barreling into the scene. None of the participants other than Sam noticed a crowd had gathered around them.

"Break this up right now!" Newton thundered. "Who started it?"

Rob and Lori sagged together, her mouth gaping in relief. Lee backed away from the two of them, suddenly trying to distance himself from the whole incident.

Only Jason looked culpable as he'd had yet to simmer down.

"Mr. Hamlin!" Newton demanded in the same accusatory voice. "Who started it?"

Jason looked up at Newton, then at Sam Shaffer, who had the unequivocal stones to grin in triumph at him.

"Shaffer tripped," Jason lied.

The kids watching kept mum, despite whatever they may have seen.

Even Sam seemed in favor of this evasion as he said, "Yeah, that's right. I tripped. Lee's such a bear, you know. Watch yourself next time, you ox."

"My mistake," Lee parroted, going along with the act.

"First day back from suspension, you two hooligans can't stay out of trouble," Newton said in a lower tone. "I also know horse flop when I hear it. Consider this your only warning, all of you. Metcalf, Shaffer, I see you even hitting *each other*, you're expelled. The rest of you, get going. Homeroom bell is in three minutes."

As the crowd dispersed, Lee gave Sam an upwards, silent jerk of his head, indicating he'd see Sam later in the day. Sam, getting to his feet, returned the gesture in unspoken parting.

After Vice Principal Newton disappeared, Sam whistled a summons to Jason through his teeth.

"I'm gonna kill you, Hamlin," he threatened.

"Not if I kill you first," Jason replied in a deep churn.

Sam's eyes burst open, as if he'd been threatened by real, authenticated death itself. He scanned Jason, then Lori then Rob.

Back to Jason, Sam said, with far less bravado before slithering off, "You're crazy, man. You freaks deserve each other."

Chapter 30

"YEAH, SURE, AND ROGER Moore does all his own stunts."

"I'm not kidding, Jason. I heard talk of a sweet Christmas bonus coming this year."

"Come on, Fan," Jason groused, pulling the oily fried skin off the chicken breast he'd been smuggled and stuffing it into his mouth, resuming after he'd crunched, chewed, and swallowed it gone. "It's not even October yet and you're talking about Christmas bonuses? Merle's alright, I guess, but I don't see it happening. I wouldn't complain, mind you, since I've never been given a bonus of any kind in my life."

"Last Christmas, the big spenders," she uttered low but wittily, "they gave us $20.00 gift certificates to the store with a 10% discount."

"Nothing like keeping all the money in-house."

"The managers all get a free turkey for Thanksgiving, screw us peons."

"I'd be happy with a box of Good and Plenty."

"And they write off our holiday purchases as lost or damaged stock, how about that?"

"Where'd you hear all this, Fan?"

"Well, you didn't get this from me, per se, but—"

The swinging door leading into the employee lounge burst open, almost as if it had been bashed into.

"Miss Parsley," they both heard, this after Fan had already jumped in her chair from the sudden eruption.

"Oh, hi Todd," Fan acknowledged him, waving her hand in her face to calm herself.

"That piece of chicken," Todd said sharply to both of them. "Do you have a receipt?"

As if he'd been caught masturbating, Jason was mortified chewing on a hunk of breast meat.

"Todd, I..." Fan blurted. "I mean, they're getting ready to throw it out. I figured..."

"The price of a single breast of chicken is $1.89," Todd interrupted. "If you don't have a paid receipt, Mr. Hamlin, that's no problem. I'll make sure to deduct it from your pay this week. As for you, Miss Parsley, clock out now. You can come pick up your final check on Friday."

"Seriously, Todd, you're firing me? I'm sorry!"

"After all you've stolen from the store, be glad I don't dock your entire check," Todd said frigidly. He glanced at Jason in apparent scrutiny before turning away and yanking the door open with equal force as his arrival, adding, "Break time is over, Mr. Hamlin."

Jason let the chicken breast sit on the wobbly foldout card table the store provided in the break room. He stared stupidly at the gaping chunk from the chicken breast, then at Fan, whose lips quivered faster than her tears gushed.

"Sorry he…"

"Shut up," she sobbed, almost leaping from the table, and dashing into the unisex bathroom, locking it behind her.

"What a day, Christ," Jason gnashed, pitching the leftover chicken and the emptied bottle of Mello Yello that he *had* paid for, into the steel trash can with the push-in receptacle which always sprang back too fast, sometimes trapping hands inside. This time, Jason was more than a match for the confounded thing as the contents dumped from his hand into the waste bag with a *sliiiide-thunk!* before it could snag his hand on the return.

Back on the floor, Jason saw Todd bossing Dave Carlisle around at the front of Aisle 8, and together they loaded Mueller's spaghetti, macaroni and lasagna noodles as if the end of the world counted on having pasta as its final meal.

A part of Jason wanted to say something to Todd in Fan's defense, if anything, to maybe offer more of his check for all the other chicken pieces he'd consumed. Jason knew Todd better to leave well enough alone. Especially after needing Lori's help to escape his dad, Jason was more determined than ever to buy his own car. Jason had socked enough money now he was considering asking his mother to take him car shopping soon. He knew he'd be responsible for his own car insurance, much less gas once he scored himself wheels. Getting on Todd's bad side would only cripple this endeavor, much less getting himself a guitar. The latter felt less important, given all which had happened of late in Jason's life.

Jason swung into Aisle 7 and returned to his rolling U-boat only half cleared of the baking goods he'd brought out before break. He'd left the heaviest, if quickest to load sacks of sugar and flour lined across the bottom of the rolling stock carriage. This after spending his first two hours on shift filling the shelves with cake and corn bread mixes, spices, baking powder, alum, and frosting.

Pulling out a flat piece of metal with a retractable razor that slid in and out, Jason nudged the blade free so he could slit in squared motions the tops of the cardboard packages containing rainbow sprinkles and chocolate jimmies. In no time, he'd sheathed the blade back into its casing and slipped it into his jeans pocket.

Jason had no sooner dropped the cutaway lid onto a growing pile of cardboard toward the right side of the U-boat when Jason took a gander down the end of the aisle.

Terror slapped him upside the head to see Lee Metcalf leaning against the shelving. He was tossing a bag of brown sugar up and down, the contents sagging around his substantial palm before being launched up again and again.

"Holy shit," Jason emitted as faint as he could. He wanted to scream, for equal parts fright and fury.

Something directed Jason to check his other side, since he knew one bad thing usually came with another. At the risk of putting his back to Lee, Jason swiveled his head just enough to spot Sam Shaffer hovering at the other end of the aisle. No slasher movie with its unseen POV stalker finally revealed was as horrific as Shaffer right now. He was holding a bottle of Perrier, of all things, by the neck. If they hadn't been in an open public store, Jason had no doubt Sam's intent would be to crack that bottle over Jason's skull.

As much of a stand as he'd made this morning in school, now Jason was seized by panic. There was no Vice Principal Newton to hold Sam and Lee in check right now. Rob was at his own job. Lori, at home studying for some upcoming Wiccan sabbat called Mabon, the autumn solstice. Weird as the whole thing sounded to his ears, Jason wished he could be there with her learning about it instead of where he was this instant.

Without saying a word, Jason reached back into his pocket for the case cutter as Lee started in on him from his direction. Billy Metcalf manifested right behind his older brother, as if he'd been waiting for the green light to show from wherever he'd been hiding. Billy had to appear peculiar, shady even, depending on what other customers had taken notice of him.

From Sam's end, Butch Hill and Steve Fick joined him, as if the ceiling had opened and dropped them into position like a S.W.A.T. squad. They too drew closer to Jason. Their strides were not so much nonchalant as calculated.

Jason's heartbeat spiked. This morning it had been only two of them. Now it was *all five* of the farmer heavies. He felt only a portion of the courage he'd had at school. Jason's only defense, should they jump him right here and now in the grocery store, was his case cutter.

Jason extracted the cutter and flicked the razor out. Scowling as best he could while flipping his head back and forth in a game of cat and mouse he was about to lose to five bruising tomcats, Jason raised the case cutter up so he could let them all see it.

"Now hold on, Chief," Sam said, the Perrier liquid swishing and gurgling with each step closer he got to Jason. "I just want to ask you where the canned meats are."

"*What?*" Jason retorted incredulously, holding the extracted blade out in front of him and moving it from side to side. Lee and his brother had slowed down, but it all seemed like part of a prolonged master plan to unhinge Jason. So far, their ploy was working.

"Yeah, the canned meats," Sam said again. "I wanna know, motherfucker, 'cuz that's where your head's gonna go later."

The Metcalfs chuckled, then Butch Hill. Steve Fick looked perplexed for a moment until he caught up with the gag, then he giggled almost as hideously as their former comrade, Emily Haney.

"Steve, you need to do something about that stupid laugh," Sam jeered, not looking at him.

"Whatever," Steve answered, champing down on his preposterous snigger.

"Think you can cut us all before we take you down, Hamlin?" Sam taunted.

Sam took a step closer to Jason. So did Lee, Billy right after him. Steve and Butch hung back, now looking over their shoulders, searching for any interlopers.

"If I get *you* first, Sam, that's all I care about," Jason wrangled from the same indignant place giving him strength this morning. Finally. Something to work with. "Lee, I owe you one as well. The rest of you pricks can do whatever you want. I went through worse in middle school."

"You buff up, you get yourself a girl, you got a blade, you think you're all that," Sam went on, burrowing his voice to a place betraying a hint of his own panic. "You ain't shit, Hamlin."

"And you're a poser without these guys having your back," Jason broiled, swinging his blade in the direction of the Metcalfs while he shot daggers into Sam's eyes. "Offer still stands, Sam. You and me. *Only* you and me."

"I'll be outside waiting, then," Sam said, extending both of his arms outwards with an open challenge.

"What's going on here?"

Jason was moderately relieved to see Todd march down Aisle 7 with Dave Carlisle in tow. Jason only now appreciated how big Dave was, sized up against the farmer guys. Only Lee Metcalf matched Dave's girth and weight class.

"I warned you gentlemen before," Todd snapped. "Cause a problem in my store, and I'll..."

"I'm buying something, man," Sam reacted, waggling the Perrier bottle at Todd and Dave. The seltzer water glugged comically inside the green glass cylinder. Pointing at Lee, who held up the brown sugar sack for effect, Sam said, "His mom's making a sweet potato pie. We're here as customers, so get off our case, Todd."

"Seltzer's hardly your beverage norm," Todd said with a sarcastic arrangement of his face. "Though I'm sure you'd all be wanting to avoid the police, given your recent run-in with Deputy Bohager. All of you, ring up and get going."

"Yeah, yeah," Butch mocked Todd with a wave of dismissal.

The Metcalfs brushed by Jason, then Dave and Todd. To Dave, Lee Metcalf sniped, "What're *you* looking at, dick cheese?"

When all five boys made their way to the registers, Todd placed an out-of-character comforting hand on Jason's shoulder with no further word as he moved on. Dave Carlisle lightly jabbed Jason in the same arm. Truth be told, Todd's attempt at solace felt just as yucky as assuring, given the short time it had been since he'd fired Fan Parsley.

In a state of anxiety knowing Sam Shaffer would be good to his word by waiting outside in the parking lot with his buddies, Jason ground through his tasks with twenty minutes to spare. He couldn't slow down even if Todd ordered him to.

Instead, whatever spirit of kindness Todd exhibited earlier by chasing the farmers out had become a fleeting thing. Not one to waste the opportunity to economize, Todd assigned Jason to help wash pans and trays for Bonnie Graff, the bakery department manager who'd been kept overtime. No doubt lonely from manning the bakery counter all night, Bonnie hummed to Jason about her recent trip to New York to catch *Phantom of the Opera* at the Majestic Theatre on Broadway. Jason feigned interest, drowning her out with his own concerns while scrubbing and spraying the elongated, sugar-caked serving trays inside the bakery department's galvanized steel sink.

When it was time to punch out, Bonnie thanked Jason, who gave her a nervous grunt as he left. Jason cut through the rear entrance into the stock room instead of the open windowed front of the store where Jason could have a view of the parking lot to confirm if Sam Shaffer's Nova was still there. His bravery had ping-ponged throughout the day and Jason found whenever he focused strictly on Sam, he could rally the fortitude needed to take him on. With Lee, Billy, Steve, and Butch, however, Jason felt his chances of winning a fight, much less surviving, were stacked in his favor only by pulling the pin to a live hand grenade and tossing it at them from fifty feet away.

"I don't see them out there, Jason," Dave Carlisle said from behind a pile of Alpo dog food so high he'd been camouflaged. In his heightened state of fear, Dave had startled Jason.

"Your words to God's ears," Jason muttered, feeling his right hand, by an out-of-practice instinct, swoop up, and touch his forehead. It had been quite some time since Jason had performed a Catholic-styled Sign of the Cross, but now was as good a time as any to resurrect it, regardless of what ancient religion his new girlfriend followed. He completed the ritual by swinging his hand down and tapping his stomach, then his left shoulder, finishing with a swing to the right one.

"I figure they bailed or I'd give you a lift home. I don't get off until 11:00 though."

"I don't trust it," Jason said, pausing in front of Dave a moment. "Unless they got collared again, I know something's going down tonight."

"You gonna be alright, man?"

"Hell no, Dave, I'm a loose fart away from totally shitting my pants!"

"If you didn't lug your schoolbooks with you, you'd have a better chance of outrunning them. Maybe."

"Gee, thanks, man," Jason said, a discharge of frustration fleeing his lips.

"You need to get a car and stop walking back and forth, dude. You've been here most of the year, you should be able to afford one now. Get yourself some wheels, pronto, Jason."

"Working on it," Jason returned, giving Dave a halfhearted wave goodbye, feeling like it might be the last one he gave anyone.

Having punched out, it was Todd instead of Merle (the big boss having the night off) handling the front door locking duties. Jason felt his guts not merely roast but incinerate. It was worse than the time he and Rob had a chili eat-off with a shake of Tabasco sauce per spoonful, round-by-round. Jason had won, 19 shakes to Rob's 18, but Jason was the bigger loser that night in the bathroom.

This is what Jason felt like as he peered past Todd, working up the mettle to look for Sam Shaffer's car.

"They're gone," Todd said with a composure only he felt between them. "I'm going to call the sheriff and let him know they've been stalking you. I know what I saw, Jason. I'm glad you didn't swing that case cutter, or I'd have to turn you in after letting you go from the store. We've had enough employee turnover for one day, I think."

"Right," was all Jason could say, only now realizing Todd had addressed him with his first name. That courtesy didn't last long.

"Be safe out there, and we'll see you tomorrow, Mr. Hamlin," was Todd's next sentence.

"I guess," Jason replied, absent-mindedly. In his haste to search for the Nova outside, Jason found himself going toward the left exit instead of his usual right. The left aimed into the corridor leading to the other stores in the shopping center. Jason heard the mechanical wheeze of the automatic doors as crisp air massaged face. It felt terrific, but it was a false security. He next heard the sickening click of the lock behind him as Todd sent him a firm nod before turning away toward the right exit. Jason wondered, in delirium, if untrained, non-Roman gladiators felt the same way being locked into the Coliseum.

Outside, it was just as Todd and Dave had said. There was no sight of the Nova in the Super Thrift end of the lot, since the employees were required to park around the rear of the store. Only a Toyota sedan and a dented white van that once had a company logo or something across the side were found. An off-white splotch covered up whatever had been there prior on the van, making it look not only tawdry but sinister.

Jason saw other cars in the further reaches of the shopping center, none of them being the Nova.

"You got this, dude," he told himself. "Double-time it."

Jason took a step off the sidewalk when he heard it, freezing him from going any further.

The grotesque gunning of an engine, the horsepower sounding as pissed off as its master. Even from around the bend where it had been hiding, Jason could hear a voice shout "Hurry up and get in, dipshit!"

Jason suddenly wanted a quarter and a phone booth. The phone, he could've used in the store. *Should've* used. Why Jason hadn't called his mother for a pickup was only expounded by what had happened only last weekend. She'd thrown away the sleeping pills. She'd told Jason she was done trying to escape her worries and she pledged to be there for him. So why didn't he call her?

Too late now, even as Jason scurried into the parking lot. The Nova snarled a second retort, capturing Jason in newfound hysterics. He began to run but felt his legs revolt as the headlights bore down on him and something like a rebel yell called through the Nova's bellowing.

The car screeched to a halt, mere feet away from Jason. The sudden sprint and peal of Sam Shaffer's Nova had alarmed the owner of the Toyota, who narrowly avoided dropping her milk jug and bag of bread.

"Go on, Hamlin," Sam goaded, leaning out the window. "Take a chance?"

There was a maniacal flare to Sam's expression, and he revved the Nova another time as his cronies sounded off in their own way. Steve Fick again cackled, pricking his friends' nerves.

"Monkey man," Billy Metcalf groaned from his spot next to Steve in the back seat.

"Screw your mama," Steve returned, and despite what was happening to *him*, Jason could see a conflict mounting in the rear of the Nova.

"Had yours first," Billy smarted off. "Let me come inside her, even. Hope she's on the pill or you'll have a brother or sister who looks just like me."

"Will you skids shut the fuck up?" Sam ordered them, never taking his eyes off Jason. He put his open palm out by way of goading more than invitation. "Be my guest, Hamlin. We'll see who's faster."

Jason's hand shook inside his pocket, trying to get a hold of his case cutter.

"Go for that blade, I'll splatter you where you stand," Sam spurred, seeing what Jason was doing.

"That Nova needs a serious paintjob, Sam!"

In the heat of things, nobody had seen them arrive. Sam looked shaken of all a sudden, like Deputy Bohager had surfaced with the entire State Police barracks behind him. The other guys winced and shook their heads in what Jason could only read as a mix of exasperation and defeat.

Jason all but turned to goo with alleviation to find Bud Curry and Dawn standing behind him.

"Bud," Sam said, taking his voice down considerable notches.

"That's Mr. Curry to you," Dawn insisted with a scowl upon her face and her arms folded beneath her slight bosom. She looked every bit the scrapper as Sam and his troops right now. If the situation hadn't been so dire, Jason would've smiled in wonderment at her.

"What's the problem here?" Bud asked, as if he needed to.

"No problem, Bu...I mean, Mr. Curry."

"My ears told me different. I know your Nova anywhere. Everyone in town does, especially the local fuzz, am I right?"

Sam gave no response, only exchanged glances of apprehension at Bud and Dawn and his wilting aggression toward Jason.

"Steve, tell your old man I got that Best of Dean Martin album he ordered, you hear? He can pick it up when he's ready. It's not going anywhere."

Billy Metcalf snickered at that, as did Butch. Lee Metcalf looked undecided whether he wanted to get out of the car and take his chances with his fists or lean on Sam to drive off.

"Dean Martin," Billy repeated with a guffaw, planting his mouth against his palm to avoid making the scene worse than it had become.

"I don't care who your old man is," Bud sneered at Billy, then Lee. "The town planner position will be up for a vote next year. I'll raise whatever stink I need to get someone else in there."

"I doubt *that*," Lee mocked.

"Well, I also know he's a mean bastard at home. Wasn't much better when we all went to Merriweather at your ages. Your papa swings a mean belt, doesn't he?"

Both Lee and Billy not only fell silent, they turned pale.

"That's what I thought, and the man owes me a favor from back in the day I've never used. He knows I'll call it in sometime, and now, I think, would be a good time."

Lee and Billy now looked petrified in their respective spots.

"You boys get outta here and you leave my friend here the hell alone. And *his* friend. I see any of you bozos giving these guys grief any longer, I'll teach you the meaning of the word. Now *git*."

Sam's eyeballs pinballed in their sockets and his mouth fell agape. He was looking for something smart to say and coming up empty. Instead, he placed both hands on the steering wheel and turned toward the right to angle the Nova away from Jason, Bud, and Dawn.

"And you tell *your* papa hi for me, Sam," Bud added with a smirk so wide his facial hair looked more intimidating than the rest of him.

From behind the right side of the grocery store, Todd flashed a thumbs-up.

"Yeah, have a good night, Todd, you weenie," Bud grumbled facetiously. "You alright, kid?"

"I was a dead man," Jason uttered, his insides cooling down but feeling sicker than ever.

"You need a ride? Dawn goes your way."

"Yeah, no problem, sweetie," Dawn offered. "I can take you home."

Only by seeing Bud and Dawn lift their heads past him did Jason take note of the brisk clopping of boots behind him.

"He has a ride," Lori said, planting a kiss upon Jason's cheek and firing a wink in Dawn's direction. "*Sweetie*."

Chapter 31

"SHORT OF HIRING a hit on those rat bastards, what do we do?"

Rob looked even antsier than Jason and Lori, and he hadn't been through what Jason had tonight. By contrast, Rob's night at Grigsby Tools had been the exact opposite. Mundane, even. Four hours in, four hours out, only a minor shakeup to his routine in the fact the president and other top company brass had lagged for an afterhours meeting in the conference room, which Rob had to double-back and clean before quitting time. He'd seen that young bigot come out of the conference room, which had been clogged with cigarette smoke and a tang of leftover Chinese grub from Hunan House. Most of the food had been left to waste, albeit a score of fortune cookie wrappers littered the conference table, along with the crumbs and discarded paper fortunes. It had made Rob wonder if that junior dogmatist he'd met before was the one who'd taken a single forkful of shrimp fried rice and given up on the rest.

Finding Jason and Lori in his driveway after his dad had come to get him had been a surprise to both son and elder. Though used to Jason being a fixture around their house, Rob's dad had let slide the impromptu visit with the minor warning, "It's a school night, just a reminder." Assuredly because there was a girl in the mix this time.

"Well, Rob, Jason says you're quite a writer," Lori said, knocking her knees over and over from her seated position on the sofa in his room. "But this isn't *The Untouchables*. Let's get in the real world, huh? We have a problem we can't rely on as solved just because Bud Curry was able to put those 'rat bastards' in check. Can't you see Jason's scared out of his mind?"

"Am not," Jason protested, but the tight wrap he had around himself and the numerous times he'd plunged his fingers into his mouth to nibble on his nails said otherwise.

"Yeah, alright, babe," Lori said, patting his knee a couple times with pretend sympathy. So soon she'd given Jason the pet name, "babe." "You tell yourself that if it makes you feel better."

"It didn't happen to me, and *I'm* scared," Rob blurted. "After this morning, I was sure they'd come to my job again and shake me down."

"I'm the prime target," Jason said, imploring to Rob. "Put on some music or something. I'm about to crawl out of my skin."

"No," Lori said without being overly bossy. "We can't deflect this, and my parents will give me the riot act if I don't get home soon. I made the excuse I was going out for maxi pads to get the car and I have none to bring home."

"I pity you, then," Rob blurted.

"Now first and foremost, you're not walking to and from school, Jason," Lori said, taking control of the situation, considering her company was two shell-shocked boys. "That goes for you too, Rob, not until this all blows over. I'll borrow my parents' car as long as need be."

"*If* it blows over," Rob said without certainty. "I mean, tell us, Lori. You've been through this before with Shaffer. When does it blow over with him?"

She took a deep breath, glanced over at Jason, who was still nibbling on his digits.

"Stop that," she told him. "It's a bad habit."

"So's smoking," Jason retorted, continuing to gnaw on his right middle finger.

"Ouch," Lori growled at him. "And if you're flipping me off, *I'll* kick your ass a lot sooner than Sam Shaffer will."

It was a good tension breaker as Rob chuckled first, then Lori. Jason ceased his nail biting and forced a cheesy grin before plugging both of his hands beneath his legs.

"Seriously, though, Lori," Rob went on. "I'm sure I can answer my own question, but what kind of animal are we dealing with? We've heard the stories, but what actually happened when they came after you and the punkers?"

Lori sucked in again and exhaled as she picked up a paperback copy of Anthony Burgess' *A Clockwork Orange* left by Rob on her side of the couch. A torn slip of paper served as a lazy page marker, showing Rob had finished more than a third of the book. Lori flicked the would-be marker a few times, fanned the pages tightly with her thumb so as not to lose Rob's place, then she spoke.

"Great book. You won't know what to do with yourself when you get to the ending. A lot different than the movie. If Malcolm McDowell was a god, he might be something between Eros and Sarutahiko."

"Mars," Rob said with a nod of recognition.

"I'm impressed," Lori said. "Are you on the path?"

"I don't know what you mean by that, Lori, but my grandfather passed down to me an entire library on mythology. See?"

Rob pointed toward the bottom tier of his bookshelf where a handful of books were lined up, spanning Greek, Roman, Celtic, Persian, Norse, Judaist, and Egyptian mythos.

"I'm gonna be forever reading them all," Rob said. "It took me two months just to knock out *Bulfinch's Mythology*."

"I would've dug your grandfather," Lori said. "Screw a monetary inheritance. Leave me something that says who you were."

"Personally, I think Malcolm's character, Alex, is Azazel incarnate," Jason nudged.

"Again, I'm impressed," Lori said in appreciation. "Is Alex DeLarge a scapegoat fallen angel in league with the devil? His dumber-than-dirt 'droog' accomplices sure managed to absolve themselves and swing their sins all back unto him as their fall guy."

"I have my moments," Jason said, flickering the same wacky grin as before.

"To answer your question, Rob," Lori continued, "the farmers didn't do a thing to me. I know what Sam said this morning in school, but I think they have a code against roughing up girls. At least *I hope* they do."

"Knocking them up is a different matter," Rob cracked with a comical shrug.

"I wouldn't count on any code, Lori," Jason cautioned, keeping his hands tucked beneath his legs.

"They couldn't stand us just because of how we looked," she said, putting the book back where it was. "Called us freaks, clowns, *perverts,* of all things. After Sam and the guys chased us down to that turnout overlooking the brook on Gill Road, they went for Greg first since he was the most outrageous in appearance. Of course, they'd do the same if he'd been running around in tumbled jeans and Bally shoes. They hated Greg, like I hate football Fridays and an unsolved Rubik's Cube."

"You still haven't heard from him, I take it," Rob stated more than asked.

"Nope. I gave up trying. I see the cars leave and return at Greg's house, so I assume he's there. He must be really messed up. If he comes out at all, he must go vampire-style in the night or something."

"Listen to them, the children of the night..." Rob goofed.

"Yeah, yeah, what music they make," Lori tacked on, now with impatience. "Alright, Bram Stoker, you wanted to know what happened, so zip it a minute and let me get this out."

Rob made a silent zipping gesture across his lips. Jason stared off into space, while Lori crinkled her lips into a faint smirk before inhaling so deep her chest thrust and stretched out her shirt with its neon-accented depiction of the scraggly-haired lead singer of The Cure, Robert Smith.

"They got more physical with Greg and the other guys than you two," she recounted. "There was none of these head games they've been playing. They simply came right up and called Greg a faggot and accused him of butt slamming Scottie Siegel from our group. Then they chastised Scottie as a 'green-haired Jew-Who,' you know, like in Dr. Seuss' Whoville?"

"Pathetic," Rob said, shaking his head. "What's wrong with this country where people feel a need to attack others' race, religion, or sexuality? Or in our cases, dressing a different way, listening to music outside of the mainstream, even reading a freaking Thor comic."

"Let me know when you catch up with the actual origins of Thor, along with Odin and Freyja in your grandfather's books there," Lori said.

Jason snapped himself out of his momentary daze, blurting, "Odin? Oh yeah, that cool band in the *Decline of Western Civilization II* movie. Only played in one theater in all of Maryland at the Charles in Baltimore. My mom took one for the team and drove us downtown to see it. Of course, my dad told her to take his Baretta with her and shoot any squeegee kids we ran into."

"Your dad's already established what kind of man he is," Lori scoffed, "and for the record, the first *Decline* was better."

"If you say so," Jason countered with equal cynicism.

"*Anyway,*" Lori gnashed through her teeth impatiently, "Shaffer and Lee Metcalf went after Juan Juarez first…"

"Let me guess, because he's Hispanic on top of being a punk rocker," Rob grimaced.

"I never thought of it that way," Lori granted. "You're right though. We *did* have a kinda-sorta melting pot in our group, though Greg, myself, and Jimmy McDermott at least pass the local color test. Ian Barnett, too, but his folks moved to Marietta, Georgia and he transferred out. Took my Suicidal Tendencies tape with him, though, the thief. As I think about it, the whole thing started when Lee blindsided Juan by slamming him into the lockers. Just like that. Juan hadn't provoked Lee or Sam or anybody. No words were exchanged before or after. I was pissed, not just because of what they'd done to Juan, but they'd high-fived each other and Lee said, as loud as he could, 'A burrito sounds good right about now!'"

"Sounds like those pricks," Jason fumed.

"Greg was the most upset of us all," Lori resumed. "He'd gone up to Shaffer and Lee, and all the rest of their gorillas were there. Greg was riled up about what had happened to Juan, but he'd kept his temper under control. That's one thing about Greg, he's never lost control in school, so a lot of people have the wrong impression about him. Outside, a much different story. Greg's no wimp, I promise you. He's a bit of the opposite, a loose cannon. In front of us, Greg Boedecker could lose his shit over the dumbest things, like banging his knee against a bedpost or..."

"Wait a minute," Jason interrupted. "How would you know that? Did you and Greg hook up?"

"Of course, we did," Lori exuded. "Jason, that was more than a year ago. Old history and he couldn't hang in the pocket, so our one time wasn't much to speak of. Don't be a jealous spaz. It's a turnoff."

"Alright," Jason slunk in retreat.

"You get the picture. We've all seen Greg go into a complete rage over a spilled soda or having to change a flat tire. He was downright inconsolable earlier this year, to a point it was disturbing, when Dag Nasty traded Dave Smalley for Peter Cortner and went all melodic on *Field Day*. Don't mess with that guy's hardcore bands. Honestly, I think Greg has genuine emotion issues, nothing I could help him with."

"And this all has to do with Shaffer and Metcalf in what way?" Jason sassed.

"My point is," Lori prodded, again through her teeth, "I haven't been with you long enough to compare you to Greg, but after what happened at your dad's and what you did to Shaffer this morning, I do see parallels."

"So, is that why we're dating, then, Lori? I remind you of Greg? I hope I'm not some charity case to you."

"Alright, I'm done," Lori snapped. "You want to get your face caved in, be my guest! Greg couldn't get a punch in the day they chased us down. They avalanched him first because he'd had the audacity to stick up for Juan. Hear me good on this, guys; those redneck sons of a bitches play for blood, and they won't stop until they get you down to the ground, unable to move! It's no joke to them."

"So, what we do?" Rob interceded.

"Todd, the weasel assistant manager at my job, said he would call the police tonight," Jason offered, reaching over to Lori's thigh, who pulled away from him in spite.

"Do you believe he'll actually do it?" Lori asked, folding her arms across Robert Smith's shoegazing countenance, pushing her breasts overtop her forearms.

"Who knows?" Jason whispered, dropping his hand in pouty way. "He fired someone tonight for giving me chicken they were going to toss out. In his own way, Todd also saved me like Bud did. And you, of course, Lori. Not sure how you knew to come for me, but I'm grateful you did."

"Me and my mom call it our 'witchy ways.' I just knew."

"You got through today," Rob said delicately. "Tomorrow's another story."

"Tomorrow may be too late, Rob," Lori said, relenting her leg and pulling Jason's hand over to it. "Can we use your phone? I think all of our parents should be brought into this. This shit's gone on long enough."

Chapter 32

"IN LIGHT OF RECENT events, I think we should go straight to our homerooms this morning instead of tooling around the halls," Lori said, plunging the door lock into place on the driver's side of the Bel Air, then tsking at Jason and Rob for leaving the passenger side unlocked.

"Sue me for living," Jason mocked her, making sure he threw her a smile, albeit an antsy one. He reopened the door against its creaky resistance and locked it up, shutting the door again before Lori could bump him out the way with her outthrust key.

"If we get through today, I just might," she half-teased him back, bumping him anyway. Like Jason and Rob, she was on edge this morning. She looked around the school parking lot, already getting filled.

"Any sign of the rat patrol?" Rob quipped, whipping his head around. He carried as tense a look about him as he did at final exam time.

"All quiet on the western front so far," Lori replied, gesturing the boys toward the school.

They fell into a brisk rhythm from the parking lot toward the steps up to the senior patio. They'd had to pause to let the Social Studies I teacher, Mrs. Sandusky drift at a snail's pace in her cumbersome Volvo station wagon before they could cross.

"At least it's not Shaffer," Rob noted feebly.

Instead of swinging Jason's hand, Lori kept a snug grip on him. The trio scanned their surroundings again. So far, so good. There was only the less hectic sight of teenagers loafing around their cars, cutting up, wriggling about in dreadful dances and in the case of Jeremy Popa and his younger cousin, Sonny, tossing a Nerf football around. They could hear Jeremy chatter loudly, "Montana has it on the Philadelphia 11, third down, game on the line with four ticks left... Number 16 takes the snap, it's a clean transfer. He stands in the pocket. He has *all day* with this sturdy O line which hasn't given up a sack the entire game. Montana finds Rice in the end zone, he's wide open...the throw..."

The spongy ovular ball sailed out of reach of Sonny's outstretched fingers, bouncing off the concrete and far enough Sonny had to sprint to retrieve it.

"Joe Montana and Jerry Rice get traded to the Tampa Bay Buccaneers after blowing it," Jason chawed under the circumstances. He was the only one laughing and it resembled more of a series of dry coughs.

"Did you need a minute to smoke?" Rob asked Lori as they pumped their legs double-time taking the steps.

"Noooo," Lori replied. "That's very thoughtful, but as my new boyfriend pointed out last night, it's a bad habit. I'd only been experimenting with smoking a few weeks anyway. Going cold turkey'll be a cinch, and my pocketbook will thank me down the road. Let's just get our butts to our homerooms. There's no telling how long it'll take our folks to file the orders. The good news is my dad knows the circuit court clerk, Pauline Dougal."

"Aww, hey, Lori, I didn't mean anything by it," Jason pleaded. "I'm not out to change you or anything."

"That's good," she said with as much defiance as Leslie Gore telling the world her stipulations to all male prospects. "No man will as long as I can help it, but you made a good point and I'm willing to change for myself."

"Okay, Lori," Jason said, wisely avoiding any rebuttal as a hoot went up behind them from Jake Gallagher.

A spread of merriment sounding like one of those fake laugh tracks on tv sitcoms followed them as Gallagher badgered even further, "Alright, Hamlin, and Phillips! Sink the pink, dude!"

"Further proof Darwin was right," Lori snarled, pulling the door open for the boys, beating Rob to the handle. As Jason and Rob went inside, she tossed Jake Gallagher the finger. Jake's catcall response of "Ooooohhhhhh...." followed behind her.

"You said it would be a temporary protection order first, right?" Rob asked Lori once they'd banded back together.

"Yeah," she replied over the usual morning commotion greeting them. Lori snatched Jason's hand again, then slung her free arm around Rob's shoulder, partially draped across his bookbag. "I kinda blanked on what my dad was saying, but I think there's a peace order and a protective order. A peace order goes for thirty days. Protective, there's no set limit. Once the judge reviews our complaints of harassment against Shaffer and company, the order should take effect pretty quick. Until then, we've gotta stick together as much as we can and avoid those bastards. Hopefully your boss called the sheriff last night, Jason."

They'd closed the distance to a slow-moving pair of sophomore girls, who were engaged in a discussion about tampons.

"I've been using Playtex," the first girl said. "I'm not feeling so hot about it, though. Whatever they use to control odors, some powder inside, it's making me..."

"Girlfriend," the other interrupted, "you want to switch to Kotex right now. My older sister has a friend who had to go the hospital during the summer. Kept using those, especially for swimming, and she ended up getting toxic shock from a serious staph infection. Lost a lot of her hair over it, no less."

"Whaaaaaaat?" the first one replied, freaking out.

"The second girl's right," Lori muttered, as the trio passed them. "Even guys can get a staph infection. Bacteria of the damned, my mom calls it."

"Brutal," Jason said with a cringe. "You know, there's a part of me feeling like a coward, letting our parents fight our fight."

"You need to get over that," Lori gently admonished him. "Unless you can rally a backup army, you don't stand a chance against those guys. *We* don't, even together. This is the right move."

"Don't you think it's going to set them off even more?" Jason dissented.

"It's too late now. We brought in the grown-ups, so we've got to play it out."

"As long as we look out for one other," Rob said to console Jason more than Lori.

"Even the Three Musketeers needed help," Jason said dryly.

Upon spotting her, Jason hoisted Lori's hand up to their shoulders as they swung by Heather Belanger, back at her SGA recruiting post in front of the school store. Heather was still pushing her school spirit buttons, but to Jason's surprise, instead of her jeering him this time, she sent him a smile and a gentle laudatory clap as they passed.

"What was *that* about?" Lori asked, scrunching her face at Jason, having missed his silent exchange with the class president. She dropped her arm off Rob, who gave her a warm smile passing all the thanks needed.

"Nothing," Jason said with an unpredicted bashful grin.

"My folks will be calling the school anytime time now to report the farmers," Rob said as they took the stairwell up to second floor. "I don't know if it's enough to warrant expulsion like Vice Principal Newton threatened, but at least the office will be on alert."

"If we don't get our asses handed to us before he catches them, of course," Jason droned.

"Okay, that's enough gloom and doom, Mr. Hamlin," Lori decreed. "Do something more useful with that mouth and give me a kiss."

Jason did just that as they climbed the final steps, never missing a beat between.

Upstairs, the racket and clamor rolled at its normal hum, and another check around them yielded no sign of Sam and his gang.

Lori stopped in her tracks, however, locking her forearm so stiff Jason jerked backwards and crashed into her hip. Rob saw what Lori did, and he went stationary as well.

"What's up, guys?"

Emily Haney stood in front of them, meaning to impede their way, and yet it didn't feel the same as she might were she still with her one-time band of farmer friend set.

"I'm not setting you up for an ambush," Emily said, recoiling from Jason's panicked swirls. "I swear I'm not. Just like I told you at the pharmacy, Rob, I don't even talk to those slimeballs anymore. Hell, look at me. You see anyone lining up to be my friend these days?"

Lori and Jason gave Rob a curious glance and were answered with his quiet shrug. Lori turned back to Emily with a flash of mistrust in her eyes.

"Yeah, look, I can be the bigger person and admit I've been a complete bitch. To all of you, but you, especially, Lori. I can't apologize enough for what we did over the summer. I don't make any excuses, and I don't expect any forgiveness. Watch yourselves, is all I'm saying. Once Sam and Lee start something, they won't let it go until it's finished and usually they're the one who finish it."

"Thanks, doll," Lori responded with a whiff of scorn as Emily nodded down to the floor before taking off.

"That's one for the books, wow," Rob discerned, exhaling with a loud wheeze.

"Alright, guys," Lori said, pulling Jason over and dropping another full puckered kiss upon him. "We'll meet on the senior patio after school. I'm taking Jason to work, Rob. I can drop you off at home as well."

"You know what? Under the current situation, sounds like a good idea, thanks, Lori. See you guys later."

"Alright," Jason said back.

They broke up and went to their respective homerooms just as Sam Shaffer and his crew had reached the second floor. They'd been keeping a purposeful slow lurk to avoid detection.

"They're all dead meat," Sam vowed to their shadows.

Chapter 33

IN WEIGHTLIFTING CLASS, Jason was putting on a show without meaning to. Trepidation had every bit to do with bulling through his chest and shoulder reps. By the time he and Ricky had gotten to bench press, many of the other guys had paused to watch.

"You're starting to pull away from me, dude," Ricky whined as he struggled to bench 105 pounds for a total of four reps. "Sorry you have to keep switching plates. I think we've become a mismatch."

"Forget about it, man," Jason counseled as he and Ricky reloaded a thirty-five-pound steel plate to either side of the 105 pounds already on the press bar. "Don't worry about me or any of these guys. I'm only competing with myself. You focus on getting stronger. I've got your back."

"175 pounds, though," Ricky said in a tone of surrender. "Semester may be over before I get to that level. *If* I do. You've taken off like the Challenger space shuttle...uh, bad comparison, sorry."

"I've got a lot shit going on," Jason said in dismissal, assuming a horizontal lying position beneath the bar. "It's given me motivation."

"Nice about you and Lori Phillips, though," Ricky said with a raunchy smile.

"Wild, right?" Jason responded, reaching up to grab the bar.

"Dude, spot him!" Danny Tignall shouted from the dead lift station, where he'd dropped 395 pounds to the mat with a loud THOOM! Only Ricky flinched at the raucous slam against the buffered floor.

"Yeah, yeah, okay," Ricky fumbled before scurrying behind Jason's head and spreading his hands out in preparation of a task he wasn't up to. If Jason struggled to push the 175 pounds back up, Ricky would hardly be the man for the job to lug it up.

"Oy," Danny groaned, bumping Ricky as Jason lifted the bar off the rack. "Out of the way, Groff, I've got him."

Jason's arms wobbled a little before he locked himself in, then let the bar down to his chest, inhaling as he did so. He pushed all his breath out along with 175 pounds with relative ease. He repeated the press six more times.

"Yeah, boy, that's right!" Danny hollered. "Another rep!"

"One more!" he heard from the across the room, the chant picked up by many of the other guys along with Danny Tignall. "Get it, Hamlin! One more! You've got it!"

Caught by surprise, the bar dipped to Jason's chest faster than he expected and for a second, he thought he might need help.

"Let's go, Hamlin!" he heard, closer to his face. A quick glimpse found Bennett Walsh now on Danny's left side. For all intents and purposes, Ricky had become useless.

"Push!" Bennett shouted. "Do it, dude! One more!"

"One more!" Danny repeated. "You've got this!"

Out of nowhere, Jason pictured his fist slamming into Sam Shaffer's jaw and a rush swelled throughout his chest, amping his forearms as he pushed the bar back up a seventh, then an eighth time, no assistance needed, before dropping it back to the rack.

"Hell yeah!" Danny exclaimed, clapping his hands. Bennett picked up the applause, as did a handful of other guys.

"Nice set, Hamlin!" Bennett cheered, giving Jason a congratulatory swat on his outer thigh.

After the boys showered, Jason found himself again edged by Danny Tignall and Bennett Walsh as he was slipping into his jeans. His back and chest were still damp, and the chill in the room licking his wet skin was warmed by their presence.

"Hey, man," Bennett said. "You're kicking ass out there."

"Thanks, dude," Jason responded with a hesitant grin. "I want that 200 bench club shirt."

"Keep it up, you'll get it by next month," Bennett encouraged. "I'm not gonna lie, I wrote you off the minute I saw you in this class, but…" He stopped there, trying to come up with something good to finish his thought. He simply ended with a nod, which Jason interpreted as a token of respect.

"We know who fucked up your tape," Danny said. "On my little sister's life, it wasn't us."

"Heh, you *hate* Caitlin," Bennett teased.

"Semantics," Danny joked back passively.

"That's been the least of my problems," Jason answered them with his hands splayed out, the silent gesticulation meaning *What's done is done, what're you gonna do?*

"Yeah, we know," Bennett said. "You take on Sam Shaffer, you take them all on. We know the deal."

"We used to play youth soccer with Sam," Danny added. "And he was the same punk ass he is now. Same with Lee Metcalf and Steve Fick. I had my own run-in with Sam and his gang, and Christ, we were only 10 back then. I tripped Sam by accident scrumming for the ball. No penalty was called, and I scored on the play. Sam lost his mind in the middle of the game and took a cheap shot at me from behind. He and Lee kicked me a few times while I was down. I'll never forget it. They were booted out of the league, so I never had any get-back, you know?"

"What he's saying," Bennett took over, "is we know what you're going through and it's out of control to the point we're *all* of sick of them. You want to take down that prick, we'll keep the monkeys off your back if you want."

"Wow," Jason said astounded.

"You can add me to that list," Ricky said, appearing from around the other side of the lockers. "I'll probably go down before everyone else, but hell, whatever."

"Me too," a surprise arrival said.

Brad Stone tottered into the small gathering.

Both Danny and Bennett looked as speechless as Jason, but the two lacrosse aces put their fists out for him to bump from overtop.

"*I'm* the one who wrecked your tape," Brad confessed. "It was for all that dumb bullshit between us on first day, but you know what? I suck for that. Let me make it up to you if it comes down to it. We cool?"

"Yeah, we're cool," Jason said, dropping a round of plunged fists over a full circle of new allies.

Chapter 34

THE END OF THE DAY came without much incident for Jason, Rob, and Lori. Only Lori had seen Steve Fick coming out of the boys' room between fifth and sixth period classes, which she'd recounted to Jason and Rob. Fick had given her what she'd called "the mother of all stink faces" before double-timing the opposite direction from her.

"I wish those jerks took VoTech the second half of the day," Lori said. "I'm not going to lie, fellas; my witchy ways are blazing off the charts right now. I want out of here, like yesterday."

"Your own Spidey sense," Rob said with less staunch than he normally would making a comic book-themed metaphor.

"Something like that," Lori granted, grabbing both Jason and Rob's hands. Together, they snaked through the mob of kids exiting through the senior patio, hands locked, wriggling past most of the humanly obstructions with efficiency.

"Well, eeeeexcuuuuuuse meeee!" they heard behind them as Lori bumped into a junior girl, Franny Woodward, cutting through the patio with a swarm of teenagers using it, since Seniors Only rules really only applied during lunch hours.

"Sorry, Franny!" Lori called back without looking as she added, "Steve Martin, though, *really?*"

"Eat it, pus bag!" Franny chirped back. A few kids in the vicinity laughed their approval of her comeback.

"I don't have the patience for this nonsense," Lori muttered, tugging Jason and Rob like she was trying to slingshot them more than keep them in a protective row.

They'd found a clearing to burst through at the top of the steps, then it seemed like some mysterious force had zapped the trio into momentary immobilization.

"Hecate, be with us," Lori whispered, clenching her fingers so tight against Jason and Rob's the latter winced from the intensity of it.

At her parents' Bel Air were Sam Shaffer and his full cadre.

They had their butts planted against the Bel Air and for once, they weren't screwing off or nyuking amongst themselves. Each one looked the highest level of angry, Sam taking lead honors.

To Lori, he was what she perceived Hades might look like having to let his part-time wife, Persephone, return above ground at the spring equinox. To Rob, Sam looked more menacing than Two-Face from the Batman comics, the disfigured side *and* non.

To Jason, Sam had become the most hateful person on the school grounds, save for maybe Lee Metcalf next to him. The only thing startling Jason now was a flash image of himself twisting Sam Shaffer's head in a death grip until his neck snapped. It was seventh grade all over again. Four boys then. Five boys now. The opponents now being double the size and with far more imperative stakes, it would take more than a loss of control on Jason's part.

"What now?" Rob squeaked. "They've got us."

"If the protective order's in effect," Lori blatted, her fingers crunching so hard both boys shirked free of her.

"Nobody's told *them* yet," Jason finished for her.

Other kids in the parking lot, having spotted Lori, Jason, and Rob, glanced in their direction, then at Sam and his friends. No narrator or announcer was needed to spread the word. The gathering happened in such organic fashion it was as scary a prospect as the fight to come.

The anticipation dotting across all the faces on the east end of Merriweather High was so great it alerted Lee, who followed their trail over to the senior patio. He bumped Sam in the arm and pointed up at their targets. Steve Fick, Butch Hill, and Billy Metcalf followed suit. Together, they looked like a starving band of wolves detecting a pock of frightened rabbits.

Sam could've given even The Grinch a run for the vilest grin in this county or any other. He lifted himself off the Bel Air, and without looking at it, he reached for the car's radio antenna. He bent it down to an approximate 90-degree angle before lurching with both hands and wriggling it free altogether. He held the antenna like a trophy before winging it away like a boomerang that would never return.

"Jesus," Rob gasped, but that wasn't the end of the destruction.

As if they'd rehearsed ahead of time, Lee Metcalf raised his elbow and then plowed it down against the driver's side mirror. It lopped off as easily a guillotine decapitation.

Groans of shock came from both the patio and the parking lot.

It was Jason who snapped out of their collective freeze, and he'd shucked his bookbag off without a care of where it landed.

He'd left his friends at the top of the stairs. He stomped down the first few steps in powerful piston motions before the rest of his body reacted with rage, propelling him into the air. Jason cleared the remaining steps and he never felt the thud of his feet at the landing. He'd narrowly avoided knocking into a couple of kids carrying their books and their cased reed instruments.

From his peripheral view, Jason saw Brad Stone spark to life. It was as if he'd been prodded into action at the mere sight of Jason, running without a care of who or what was in his way. He saw Brad wheel around and shout something behind him before charging in the same direction as Jason.

"It ends *now,* dammit," Jason snarled, as he pounded the pavement, picking up speed once crossing into the parking lot.

He barely heard his girlfriend scream, "Jason, no!"

Chapter 35

THOSE WHO'D BEEN THERE to witness the series of events would use imaginative similes around school like "parking lot battle royale" and "Metal Fu Theatre." One of the freshmen, Stu Harris, called Jason "Sugar Ray Longhair," and those who'd come to his aid in what would've been an otherwise lopsided suicide run, his "guardian angels." Stu's description of the melee had rung, "The most epic fight I've ever seen that didn't have Roberto Duran in it."

Just about everyone described Jason's dash from the senior patio to Lori's car where the farmers were waiting with readied fists as the most impressive sprint the school had ever seen, even with junior varsity track star Hank Gill setting a county record at 10:19 in the 100-meter dash last season. One of the people Jason had nearly clipped before dropping her clarinet, Jeanette Bosch, tagged the explosive fracas "The Chuck Cranston Squad spanked by a metalhead Ren McCormack and his improbable coalition."

Ty Sharpe and Cesar Hernandez, two of the school's few Kangol-topped students of color, would later create a rap called "Merriweather Massacre." Even though no fatalities occurred this day, Ty and Cesar got the gist of the brawl better than anyone, starting with *"David met Goliath, he couldn't take no more, he took his first swing, Goliath hit the floor..."* It became a bigger Merriweather High hit than DJ Jazzy Jeff and the Fresh Prince's "Parents Just Don't Understand."

There'd been no floor to speak of, but the first punch thrown by Jason had sent Billy Metcalf to the pavement. Billy had the disastrous stupidity to throw himself in front of Sam Shaffer as Jason charged the whole lot of them, his swing faster than any of them could've anticipated.

With a frenzy in his eyes captured by Ty Sharpe as "colder than the Terminator," Jason lunged for Sam, only to be knocked off balance by Steve Fick, who also darted in front of the leader of his posse.

Fick lowered his shoulder, ramming into Jason's ribcage and

sending him staggering backwards. Jason somehow managed — with a tiger's intuition and agility in the heat of combat, perhaps — to put on the brakes before he could topple to the asphalt. It drove him past the flaring pain in his left side and gave him focus. Mimicking Lee Metcalf with the mirror on the Bel Air, Jason planted a hard elbow across the back of Steve's neck. The blow had been severe enough to drop Steve.

Again, Jason reached for Sam Shaffer, who reached for him as well, only to be cut off by Lee Metcalf, who socked Jason in the gut so hard, Jason's momentum abandoned him.

"Sh-shiiit," Jason cursed, sagging to his knees. His stomach, just that fast, hurt so goddamn much from Lee's undercut. The guy was an oaf who'd likely graduate no further than his own bedroom, but all assumptions of Lee Metcalf's strength were spot-on. Jason couldn't fathom a stomachache worse than this, yet it was nothing compared to Lee's follow-up strike into his right eye.

Jason's vision blurred a moment, and he could feel the immediate swelling on his face where he'd been hit. Hunched on the ground, he heard more than saw Sam Shaffer blast his foot at him before Jason roared in pain, his protest cut off by a sudden lack of oxygen. Shaffer kicked him in the same spot Steve Fick had.

The kick to his ribs had shaken Jason's vision clear, at least.

"Get off of him!" Jason heard from behind as Lori skittered past him, slapping Lee in the face.

The cracking sound against Lee's cheek further roused the built-up crowd in the parking lot, as if they hadn't already been hollering their bloodlust at the fist-filled pageant of violence.

"You alright, man?" Jason heard Rob in his left ear.

"Fuck no," Jason gnashed back through a wheeze before seeing Rob duck a swing from Sam. Another swing was too fast for Rob, connecting against Rob's chest. Being nowhere near as developed as Jason had become in recent weeks, Sam's blow had sent Rob comedically to his butt.

On his other side, Jason saw Lee hoist Lori off her feet, her back crunched against him. His thick forearms pulled her upwards from beneath her chest. Despite the agony in his stomach and ribs, Jason bellowed to watch Lee snatch Lori's right breast, squeezing and digging into it like he wanted to tear it off.

"Aiiiiiiiieee!!" Lori screeched in pain before Lee tossed her to the side like a discarded puppet. This done in reaction to the next arrival into the fray.

"You sick son of a bitch!" Jason heard.

Emily Haney pushed Jason out of the way, not to add to his troubles, but to clear her launched foot which caught Lee square in the balls.

"Ohhhhhhhhhhhhhhhh!!!!" moaned the crowd.

"I would've named it after you if it was a boy!" Emily screamed into Lee's face. "Leigh if it was a girl!"

Before he bowled over from being nailed in the crotch, Lee swung at Emily, tagging her across the cheek. Being tougher than any of her prior friends realized, she didn't go down.

Nonetheless, Emily teetered only feet away from getting hit again. She'd been on the verge of accidentally getting clocked by Brad Stone, who'd already swum into the brawl. He'd taken on Butch Hill, and the two had engaged in a savage battle of their own, trading hit after hit into one another's faces. Butch's was cut up from the pummeling Brad gave him, led by the latter's silver class ring, now missing its centerpiece gemstone.

"Watch out, Emily!" Brad shouted, swerving away from Butch, who'd gained his second wind despite the scores of blood pouring from his cheeks, forehead, and chin.

Brad managed to grab Emily by her hips and shove her out of harm's way. For his efforts, Butch served Brad a return favor under his own chin, sending the Merriweather lineman to the pavement. Seeing an opportunity to finish him, Butch lifted the shank of his right Coleman work boot with the intent of pulping Brad's head. Brad had the clarity of mind to roll away as Butch's foot came down, missing his mark.

Rob, in a complete panic, swung both of his arms like a wildcat with little clawing action to offer. He looked as inexperienced as he really was, windmilling more than punching, but Rob connected twice, both times against Sam's left temple. With a surge of excitement he hadn't expected from himself, Rob hoped he'd stunned Sam, judging by the loopy expression on Sam's face. It hadn't been potent enough, however. Sam shook his head back and forth like a wet canine before snagging Rob by the collar of his Kreator band shirt and headbutting him.

Rob's head careened before the rest of him. Punch drunk from a single ram, Rob was too dazed to proceed.

As if high on epinephrine after watching his friends get mauled, Jason welcomed a renewed, reinforcing energy. He pumped his legs, not in Sam's direction, but after seeing Lori struggling to push herself to her knees from being tossed like a bag of rags, Jason set his sights on Lee.

"Piece of shit!" Jason thundered as he threw all his strength into a punch which only slowed his prey. The crunch of his fist against a skull with the same apparent properties as a cement block nearly shattered his fingers. A scorch of pain lit up Jason's hand and raked his entire arm.

He had no time to worry about the throbbing, as Jason felt a sharp tug of his hair from Sam Shaffer yanking him backwards and sadistically crinkling his neck. Jason had only a moment to see two fists flying in his midst, not at him, but at Lee Metcalf.

Danny Tignall and Bennett Walsh had just arrived, the freshest fighters in the clash. Jason would later learn Brad had spotted Ricky Groff and told him to go find Danny and Bennett. For his shaky volunteering, it was the only role Ricky had played in the brawl.

The lacrosse stars bashed Lee from both sides, hammering on him until Lee pulled his arms over his head to protect himself from their relentless tag team attack. This left Lee's midsection wide open, and Danny and Bennett went wild, jabbing, and socking Lee down both of his sides. It was only until Bennett rabbit punched Lee in the kidney before the big guy capsized to his knees.

Not above another cheap shot in this free-for-all, Danny disengaged from Lee long enough to box Sam Shaffer's ears to break the neck-snapping hold he had on Jason's hair.

"Take his ass, Hamlin!" Danny bellowed before turning back to Lee, who was being pulverized by Bennett until he finally went all the way down. Without further thought, Danny whipped away to help Brad Stone, who himself was close to done in.

Sam looked stunned and in incredible pain as he plugged his hands against both ears.

"Fucking cheaters!" Sam screeched, squinting in anguish as Jason launched a flat-footed kick into Sam's chest. Jason's follow-through downswing was far less impressive than his assault as his planted foot betrayed him, causing him to tumble back to the ground.

His strike had been effective, though. Sam spilled across the hood of Lori's car. It was evident he'd sprained his back as Sam winced from this new pain, attempting to right himself.

Jason first thought was to release a knockout punch from his right, but his hand and arm were starting to go dead. Instead, he balled his left hand up and swung backwards, catching Sam in the nose.

"Gahhhhh!" Sam cried. Nobody would've believed it if it hadn't been on public display, but Sam Shaffer *cried*. "By dose!!!!"

His blood splattered on the ground in front of Jason. It took Jason a moment to feel a new pain in his left hand. His own body beginning to sag and flare up in light of possible victory, Jason wanted the whole thing to be over.

"Byyyy dooooose!" Sam exclaimed, clamping his hands to the center of his face. Blood squibbed through his fingers, and the look of horror in his eyes was something Jason would remember for the days to come. In triumph and, weirdly enough, in shame. To break another person's bones was a profound thing to Jason. It was a binding, culpable action, even in the heat of combat.

There'd been such a clamor from the onlookers a parade of faculty and the office administration stormed the scene from the patio and the rear of the school.

"Go, man!" Bennett yelled to Jason. "Get the hell outta here!"

Bennett and Danny ducked and put their shoulders underneath Brad's, lifting him up while forcing all their heads down, using the crowd as a shield to escape.

"Lori, let's go!" Jason yowled as he shook on Rob. Every nudge hurt like hell. "Come on, man, we gotta roll! WAKE UP!!!"

Rob's head was crying a four-alarm fire from the headbutt Sam had planted above Rob's right brow. He knew without touching it a goose egg had formed there. Less woozy, Rob laughed with delight once he could piece together the sight and sound of Sam Shaffer howling over his busted, bleeding nose. The next thing he heard was Lori starting the engine to the Bel Air.

"Move your asses!" Lori blared to them before slamming the door closed on her end. The broken side mirror lay uselessly within inches of the driver's side front tire.

"Go, go, go!" Jason ordered Rob, who, with his wits reinstated, scampered on all fours into the passenger side of Lori's car. Rob dove into the back seat, his head chastising him once again as she'd nudged the door open from inside. Jason, for all the pain he was in, forced his way into the passenger seat.

"Dis ain uvvvver!" Sam shrieked at them as Jason slammed the door shut. "Gon ki youuu ahhhh!"

Lori honked her horn before a clearing was made for her to drive away as the Merriweather High staff poured into the fight zone. Kids were cheering while parting a gap for Lori to squeeze through. A few patted the Bel Air like it had become the ultimate winner in the bout.

Sam Shaffer's entire bunch had been left, punched up and broken down. Only now did Billy Metcalf wake up to see the havoc wrecked upon his brother and friends.

"They'll see my car for sure," Lori squeaked in dread.

"Fuck it, we're alive to deal with the consequences," Jason groaned. "You alright, Lori?"

"That creep nearly tore my tit off, but I'm alright otherwise," she hissed. "You look like shit, both of you."

"You should see the other guys," Jason fumbled weakly.

Chapter 36

"WHAT DO YOU MEAN he's fired if he doesn't show up tonight? He's in the *emergency room,* you ruthless bastard!"

The waiting room at George County General Hospital was frantic with a heavy load of customers for a Tuesday night, many of them pale, moaning older people holding their sides or their abdomens. One man with dried, fetid urine splotching the crotch of his olive pants muttered "UTI" over and over, adding as footnotes, "I just know that's what this is...a UTI." It came off like a lyrical hootenanny. If anyone noticed the suggestion of urine hovering over said patient, they were kind enough to keep it to themselves.

A young mother was cuddling her sick son fiddling with a Mattel Electronic Baseball game in his shivery hands. He was wearing an outdated Hefty Smurf ball cap and the top to a pair of Incredible Hulk Underoos, also obsolete for 1988, suggesting bargain chic from the Goodwill racks. The mother, who appeared flattened and alone to her task, had to remind him to flick the sound switch on his game to silent as the boops and squawks had gotten on the nerves of many around them, in particular the *da-deet! da-deet! da-deet!* knell indicating a home run. The kid may have looked green in the gills, but he was a dinging digital Daryl Strawberry if there ever was one.

Jason both saw and heard Lori slam the receiver against the mounted pay phone near the vending machines, this before tuning in to the scrum his mother was engaged in against Carl Shaffer and Jeb Metcalf.

"You have the nerve to file protective orders against our boys, Pam?" Carl protested with broiling self-entitlement.

"With good reason!" Jason's mother snapped back. "Your sons have been harassing mine and his friends ever since school started!"

"Seems to me I should be the one filing against yours, Pam!" Carl grumbled haughtily. "He broke Sam's goddamn nose!"

"Your oakie of a kid hit mine upside the head with a full can of beer last week, Jeb!" she fired back, looking past Carl Shaffer. "You guys want to keep this going, I'll file aggravated assault charges next, starting with Lee!"

Behind his father, Sam was standing, his reset nose bandaged, looking angrier than the rest of his mashed-up face. Sam stared at no one, so long as no one was staring at him. Whenever he could get away with it, though, he shot Jason one odious glance after another. Jason made no bones; his vengeful gaze lay strictly upon Sam and Lee Metcalf beside him. As much pain as all three boys were in communally, they looked ready to go another round.

"Just who do you think you are, Pam?" Carl drove on. Jeb Metcalf had the good sense to say quiet.

"A fed-up mom who won't stand for any more of this violent persecution," Jason's mother smoldered. "Speaking of which, those boys are in direct violation. One hundred feet, Carl!"

"We were here first!"

"You can be compliant by getting on your way, then."

"You can't order us around!" Carl spat.

"Can't I?" Jason's mother defied. From his slumped position in one of the pink, polypropylene waiting room chairs, Jason couldn't believe this was the same woman who'd been recently sleeping away her free time. Nor did he see the defeated divorcee he'd had to prop up more so the other way around. His mother not only surprised Jason right now, she was earning his respect. "Roll the bones, I'm begging you."

"You're a goddamn lunatic," Carl fumed at her.

"Language!" chirped one of the elderly patients-in-wait.

"Excuse me, ma'am," Carl said to her in a far gentler, if patronizing tone.

"I'll have these ridiculous restraints lifted in no time," Jeb bragged out of nowhere, clapping Lee on his shoulder. Lee, already in enough pain, winced as much as he dared in front of everyone, first and foremost, his father, who now had his balls up and out on display.

"Ridiculous?!?" Jason's mother exclaimed.

"Why don't you lower your voice, Pam?" Jeb coaxed with an arrogant grin. "You're making a scene in front of these people who no doubt have their own…"

"Jeb Metcalf, I don't care whose pockets you line, the entire town knows about Sam Shaffer and his merry band of hellraisers, which includes two of your own. They were waiting for Jason, Rob, and Lori after school. They were the ones who…"

"As I have it," Jeb interceded, "*your* kid threw the first punch against my youngest."

"One punch was all it took, as I have it," Carl kidded.

"Mine's not the one with the broken nose and boxed ears, Carl," Jeb scoffed, turning his bravado onto his purported friend. "Took more than one to beat my oldest. The younger one, he's still rough around the edges, but he'll come along in time."

"More dick pulling than gay porn," Lori said with disdain.

"That's uncouth, young lady," Jeb told her, betraying a faint smirk he was trying to squash down. "I understand you assaulted my oldest, Lee, this afternoon?"

"Assaulted *him?*" Lori tiffed, rolling up the right sleeve of her sweater. "He's built like a tank! Whatever I may have done to him was nothing compared to what he did to me! Your son, who the entire school knows got his girlfriend pregnant then ditched her, grabbed my breast before throwing me to the ground. Here's the scrape on my elbow."

"Oh, hogwash," Jeb blew off with a wave of indifference. "You can't prove a thing with that. You fell somewhere, you scuffed yourself on a doorjamb. Don't insult my intelligence."

"I'm not above flashing this entire hospital to show the bruise your degenerate kid left on me. I also have hundreds of witnesses at Merriweather High who watched it happen. If there was a cop here right now, I'd have him arrest Lee on the spot for rape."

Lee, who'd remained quiet to this point, began to whine. "You're full of…"

"Shut your mouth, boy," Jeb commanded Lee.

"The protective order is just the beginning," Lori pushed on. "You want to talk about aggravated assault? I'm having my dad file a complaint of *sexual* assault first thing tomorrow, and I'll win. So help me, I will. How's your nuts feeling over there, champ? Emily's become my new hero. Who woulda thought?"

"Face the facts, gentlemen," Jason's mom said, taking over. "Your kids are thugs. Criminals. They stalked my son, even at his job. They've been seen twice at Super Thrift hassling Jason. I reiterate, they threw beer cans at him! Minors drinking and driving, which they've already been busted for! Juvie's too good for you, Sam Shaffer and Lee Metcalf, but I'll make it my immediate priority seeing you get there if you don't back the hell away from my family, which includes Rob and Lori."

Jeb and Carl fell silent before their offspring did. Lori and Jason shared warm, fleeting glances trundled by the abhorrent glares shot at them from Sam and Lee.

On a mounted tv inside the waiting room, Alex Trebek sought the question-in-disguise-of-an-answer to the prompt under the category of NATURAL DISASTERS. "*This volcano was responsible for the destruction of Herculaneum and Pompeii.*"

However any of the onlookers may have been feeling in their waits to be seen, they were glued to the spectacle before them. One except for an obvious *Jeopardy!* fan who muttered at the television, "What is Vesuvius? Wish it was a Daily Double."

"Drama queen," Jeb fired at Jason's mom, oblivious to Trebek's confirmation of the televised and ER-bound contestant's correct answer of "Mount Vesuvius."

"Those teen felons nearly ran him over in the parking lot at Super Thrift, you egotistical worm! If not for Bud Curry…"

The mere mention of Bud's name froze Jeb and Carl so much Jason's mother used it to her advantage.

"That struck a chord, did it?"

"Enough, Pam," Jeb said, a look of iciness matching the sudden chill in his voice.

"What's Bud Curry got on you guys?" she pressed on. "The fear of God couldn't make you look worse than the two of you right now."

"I said that's enough!" Jeb barked. Both Lee and Sam jumped at the force Jeb projected. Jason's mother merely blinked at it.

"I say we go down to Curry's store tonight, then Super Thrift and talk to the assistant manager, whatever his name is…"

"Todd," Lori spat before Jason could. "He just let you go, by the way, Jason."

"Whatever," Jason droned. "Just take the damn x-rays and let me out of here."

"He *what?*" Jason's mom asked like she couldn't take any more bad news tonight.

"Fired him!" Lori cried, shifting the attention of the conversation away from their adversaries. "The smug prick had the nerve to say Jason should have called out 'instead of having his girlfriend do it.' After I explained what happened and where he was, Todd still fired him."

"He can't do that!"

"Ma, don't worry about it," Jason sighed. "I've got worse problems than my stupid job."

"Uh-huh, I see what they're doing, clear as day!" Jason's mom shouted, much to the annoyance of the others in the waiting room. They'd now grown disinterested in one-sided bantering.

"Shhhhh!" someone hissed at her.

"Oh, bug off!" she sassed back before turning to Carl and Jeb, and of course, their sons behind them. "Super Thrift doesn't want any more part of this…this…dumb feud your boys started! This whole thing's their fault, and now it's cost Jason his job. End this now, or I'll name all of you together in a harassment suit…"

"Back off, Pam," Carl sneered, pointing his index finger at her. "I'm warning you."

"And I'm warning *you*, Carl Shaffer, a hundred feet is a hundred feet! The judge's signature says so. Take your sorry carcasses out of here right now before I have the sheriff on the other end of that pay phone."

"Consider it ended," Jeb said to Jason, his mother, and Lori before giving Lee a hideous stare making his beaten heavyweight son cringe in front of everyone.

As the Shaffer-Metcalf contingency slipped out of the sliding doors of the emergency room, everyone concerned about it caught Sam flare his choppers back at them.

"Mr. Hamlin?" they heard a nurse call from the triage station next to the waiting room. "Jason Hamlin?"

"Yo," Jason muttered, struggling to wave.

"You okay, honey?" his mother asked with concern, her voice soft and motherly.

"I didn't think anything could be worse than Perry Hall," he told her as he received a kiss on his right cheek from his mom, Lori on the left.

"You can say that again," his mother said.

Chapter 37

A COLD RHUMBA SHIMMIED across Rob's forehead from the icebag felling the swollen knot doing its damnedest not to go down.

Finding himself in the middle of his first fight since walloping Davey Norris back in second grade after Davey had stuck paste in Rob's hair, Rob's assessment of his performance today would be lower than greenhorn.

It was through blind luck and his absurd swing machine chopping (barely different than what he'd used to send Davey away crying) any of his squally punches landed upon Sam Shaffer. The way Rob had vacillated like a banshee, less with raw power and more of desperation, it drew down a personal shame hurting worse than his head.

If Sam had felt Rob's blows at all, he'd never shown it. Rob had been far less impactful than Jason, who'd been so *metal* out there with his punching, kicking, and at times, dominating force. Jason had been a sword cleaving Manowar song come to life, personifying a "sound of charge into glory ride, over the top of their vanquished pride…"

Rob, in the meantime, had been vanquished like a swatted gnat with Shaffer's unpredicted headbutt. His pride departed right thereafter, still lost on its way back.

After Rob called out from work tonight with his dad present to smooth things over with Chuck, his mom gave him three hits of ibuprofen with a glass of orange juice and a banana. Though he would've preferred Colt Cola and a pack of Tastykake butterscotch Krimpets, Rob popped the pills and forced the banana down in more bites than most people needed to, as his mother nagged him all the way to the spent peel, "The potassium will do you good."

Rob's head was thudding so much he was finding it difficult to read. He'd tried a back issue western comic from 1977 starring the Confederate-turned-bounty hunter whose gnarled, scruffy face looked like he had made out with a wood chipper, Jonah Hex. Issue number # 32, titled "Gunfight at Murphysburg," the cover showing the grey-coated, former cavalry lieutenant antihero caught in a standoff on a burning farm, one of the cowpoke gunslingers in the foreground purportedly getting the drop on Hex. The comic's usually amusing southern-drawled dialogue, filled with a lot of "Ah" for "I" and "kin" for "can," was adding to the throbbing in Rob's head.

The crash of Danny and the Juniors' "Rock and Roll is Here to Stay" thrumming from the basement wasn't helping.

Having the night off wasn't such a bad thing, Rob deduced, though he wished it had been for fun purposes. He wanted to fall asleep, yet his thoughts pestered him as much as his headache.

Last night, the president of Grigsby Tools had been working late again and as Rob rolled by his office with the rolling trash can, Rob had given the bigwig a cordial wave. The president had been on the phone, but he'd flicked Rob a halfhearted snap of his hand in scant acknowledgment. When Rob had gotten further down, he'd heard the president garble without a care to his volume, "Don't know if that janitor was a guy or girl who just went by. Christ, what a world."

His easy fall in the fight plucked him for countless minutes, but the next item on Rob's worry list became Marcie Barone.

She'd kept her back to him in Economics class, her head straight and away in Creative Writing. Even when Mr. Morrow had Rob come to the front yet again yesterday to read his A-plus answer to what Harriet's "news" was (he'd concocted a short story in which Harriet was a biophysicist who'd been rubbed out by the government upon finding a cure for cancer) Marcie had kept her head turned toward the Wall of Psychedelics until Rob sat back down. Her visible rejection felt worse than Rob finding himself sucked into a parking lot brawl he didn't want to be at but couldn't *not* be.

"At least you have a new friend," he told himself aloud, pushing the ice pack against his forehead. "Even if she's Jason's girl and not yours."

The longer he dwelled upon these feelings of inadequacy from his prone stretch across his bedroom sofa, the angrier Rob got. Which, in turn, jacked his headache to such measures he was counting down the two and a half hours until he could have another round of ibuprofen.

"I'll do a hundred push-ups a day and cut my damn hair if it'll change anything," Rob grumbled.

Calling a stop to his self-pity session, Rob's bedroom door thrust open, startling him where he lay.

"Rob," his mother said in a calm voice doing its best to offset the agitation in her face. It failed to have effect. "Your father and I have been called up to school. Right now. The boys you got into a fight with, they're all being expelled."

"There *is* a God," Rob mumbled, springing his left hand to keep the sagging icepack from slipping off his head.

"That's the good news," his mother said, just as his dad manifested right behind her. Rob hadn't noticed the music had ceased playing downstairs until just now.

"The bad news," his father picked up for her, "is you, Jason and some other boys who helped you guys are being suspended."

"What about Lori?" Rob asked, grunting through an ostensible flame tearing from one temple to the other. "Or Emily Haney?"

"As far I know, nothing's happening to Lori," Rob's dad said. "Don't know an Emily Haney."

"Never mind," Rob said, closing his eyes and shaking his head despite the crashing reverb. "Do I have to come with you? I called out of work over this."

"No, son," his dad told him in a surprising sympathetic voice. "They can't seem to reach Jason and his mother, but we're going. I don't approve of the fighting, Rob, but I've also known this was coming, just as soon as you'd asked me to lean on the school about the Shaffer kid and his bunch."

"My part in it wasn't much, but none of us saw things going down like it did," Rob mumbled. "I wish it hadn't."

"Which makes me feel a little better about it," his mother said softly, slipping away beneath the crease of his dad's elevated leaning arm. She patted her husband twice on the belly on her way through.

"Are you going to be alright, Rob?" his dad asked, still leaning against the doorway frame.

"Jason got it far worse than me," Rob answered. "I'm pretty sure he went to the hospital to get checked out."

His father nodded before saying, "A suspension is no easy thing to just let go, Rob."

"Yeah, I know, Dad," Rob said once again prodding the icepack back into place.

"We'll figure out your consequence later. You've been through enough at this point. All of you."

"Thanks, Dad."

"Right."

"And Dad," Rob blurted before his dad left. This time, the icepack slipped clear off, clunking to the floor with a cube-dancing squish. "Can you take me to Al's Barber Shop on Saturday?"

"He's not a stylist, you know. He's more buzz cut than feather and perm."

"I know," Rob said, slinging the icepack back to his head. "He'll have a field day with me."

Chapter 38

"HEY, JENNIFER:"

Only two words penned and already Jason's right hand was smarting. To crunch his achy fingers around his pen was far harder than squeezing one of those springy stress balls his mom used to bring home pressed with the company logo for her old job, Snyder Construction. She'd traded hats this past summer doing the same job at seven dollars more an hour as a receptionist and filing clerk now in an upstart software company, Oni Tech. Still a young corporation, there were no trinket squeezy balls, key chains, coffee mugs or other marketing paraphernalia to pinch beyond the aquamarine company t-shirt she'd passed on to Jason (which he was wearing for the first time) along with a handful of company pens. The font along the shaft of the Oni Tech pen he was using to write his New Jersey-based pen pal with was done in a brushy Sonnyfive typeface seeming more at home in a metropolitan art school or on a B-movie horror poster.

"Excuse the sloppy handwriting. I've had a way to go lately. Whattya listening to these days? I picked up the new Riot album but haven't had the time to play it yet. It's because...and I can hear you laughing right now...I'm getting my head around the Psychedelic Furs, The Smiths and New Order thanks to my new girlfriend, Lori. Yeah, I've got a girlfriend, can you believe it? And I got one before we go DEFCON and the nukes drop. You ever wonder if the reds will reinstate Operation RYaN and just go ahead and hit the button? We'll be total shit stains across the United States map if that happens."

The muscles in Jason's right elbow twitched repeatedly as he wrote, shuddering beneath the skin. The nonplussing throbs reminded him of those nasty space slugs slithering inside their human hosts in *Night of the Creeps* he and Rob had watched a few weeks ago. Before school started. Before all of *this*.

"If it wasn't for Lori, I'd be a complete mess right now," he continued scrawling, ignoring the continuous pain in his hand. *"I really dig her. I*

can't say the "L" word yet, since she's my first girlfriend and it's all still new, but I kinda do love her, between you and me. She has my back, and that's what counts the most in life, you know?

Things with my dad couldn't be worse. Story for another time, but it's been <u>bad</u>. Mom was a disaster for a little while, but she's come around. She's all mama bear now after coming out of a long hibernation, you could say. I feel bad she's been shoved into the single mom bit, but I doubt I'll burden her for too much longer.

No, I'm not gonna snuff it, don't worry. I'm talking about after graduation. I'm not the brightest glass in the China cabinet, so I doubt I can hang with college. I don't feel like getting my balls blown off in a war, so the military's out. I'm gonna buy a guitar soon and take lessons, find a band to join, and kick some ass on the road. Maybe I'll play in front of ya at Starland Ballroom or even up the shore in Asbury, you know, the Stone Pony. A guy can dream, right?

Of course, I need a new job since I lost my old one. Another story for another day. I have a good stash of money I was putting away for a car, but I may go ahead and find me an axe to play soon. Then again, my hand has to stop killing me first. Why, you ask? Blame it on this fucking farmer tribe I got into a huge scrap with. More details in the next letter. It's been an odyssey, as Lori would say.

Unfortunately, the tape you made me got destroyed. As with everything this month, an odyssey. Trip on this...one of the jocks in my Weightlifting class owned up to smashing up the tape since we'd gotten into a little mouth-off the first day of school. THEN he offered to back me up in the big fight, if you can believe it. He was good to his word and showed up, along with two other guys from Weightlifting, Lori, Rob, and this girl, Emily Haney, who turned on her own farmer friends. A real dramarama, right?

Don't worry about making another copy of the tape, I'll get the vinyl for each at some point. They both shred.

Do you ever wonder if our music is gonna last, you know, like, in ten years or so? Will heavy metal still exist, or will something else take its place? I look at some of our bands changing their look, slowing down their sound, catering to the party crowd. It makes me wonder if I should even bother trying to play guitar. There's a bad omen out there and not just on Sunset.

Until next time, stay true. Metal strong.

Your friend, Jason   \m/ "

Chapter 39

"YOUR MOM HAD THE OFFICE hold your homework for the new few days," Lori said, patting a small handful of ditto sheets on the edge of Jason's bed.

"And she also deputized you to bring them home for me, I see," said Jason, rolling his eyes to match his acerbic frown.

"Yep," Lori answered as she breathed once all over her knuckles then ran them up and down her breastbone. "I'm the epitome of awesome, what can I say?"

"Best girlfriend ever," Jason mocked, dropping her a second eye roll.

"Where doesn't it hurt?"

"Why?" Jason asked, at last dripping a smile in expectation of Lori's response.

"So I can smack the hell out it, doofus," was the unwanted, teasing answer Jason got.

From his slouched position propped against a three-pillow buffer, he pointed at his frisky, widening lips.

"Slick move, Indiana Jones," Lori said, scooching across the edge of Jason's bed and swatting his headphones to the floor, which bounced and bobbed a couple times from the yank toward his stereo. Face-to-face, she baited Jason, drilling her gaze into his, creaking her mouth and letting steam coat his lips. Her breath smelled pleasingly of Big Red cinnamon gum instead of tobacco.

He had no time to balk at her intentional dragging out once Lori planted her lips against his. There'd been no lipstick this afternoon to cover the plushy pinks of them. The shock to Lori's hair remained, accenting her autumn brown tweed sweater, unbuttoned at the top to give Jason a glimpse of her cleavage as she'd drawn close to him. He could see a splotch of purple down there and for a second, he frowned once more.

"What?" Lori asked, easing back from him. "I think I'm a damn good kisser."

"It's nothing," Jason said. "You kiss great."

"My third eye just told me something's bugging you," Lori said, following Jason's eye trail toward the opening of her sweater. "Oh, *that*. Lee Metcalf's stamp of accreditation."

"I don't care how big he is, the fucker ever touches you again, I'll find a way to kill him."

"You can have whatever's left when I'm done with him, sweetheart."

"How was school?"

"Well, I'd say it was just another day, but that'd be a lie."

"We're the talk of the town, no doubt."

"People were talking about the fight everywhere I went," Lori said with a steady nod. "Emily and I have become celebrities. I can't get my head around it. You and those jocks who backed us up—not sure what influence of the universe put *that* in play—you're all Merriweather High icons now. Even Rob, who looked kind of silly out there, but at least he took on Sam Shaffer. It won him enough cred."

"I'm still on the fence about Emily," Jason said in a drab tone, "but she did save me a blow by pushing me out of the way, and launching one into Lee's nads, that was impressive. So were you, Lori."

"Oh, hell, the walking mountain never even felt my slap, and I put everything I had into it. I know your hands must be hurting something terrible."

"They're getting better," Jason said, picking up both hands and scrunching his fingers in and out, repeating the motion in the direction of Lori's chest. "All the better to molest you with, my dear."

"The boobs are out of commission a while, sorry," she told him, intercepting his fingers with hers. "I sure hope Lee's father beat his worthless ass after they left the hospital last night. It was the first time I ever saw him so frightened."

"Seems to me the rotten apples don't fall far from the tree," Jason said, tightening his grasp just enough to show Lori he was on the mend.

"Okay, guy," she chuckled. "The x-rays didn't lie. Nothing broken, you'll make a nice recovery, keep icing them anyway. Show Jeb Metcalf's demon seeds they couldn't break you."

"Billy was no problem, at least," Jason joked lightly.

"You were amazing, Jason. I don't know how else to put it and I hate fighting. If it had been anyone else but you or even Rob, I would never have been in the middle of it."

"Thanks for having my back again."

"As I said before, it's what I do, and you know what?"

"Hmm?"

"Emily Haney's not such a bitch, after all. We found each other in the halls before Homeroom and believe it or not, she came up and gave me a hug."

"Get outta here."

"True statement. She called us 'The Lee Metcalf Hit Squad.'"

"That's actually funny," Jason said, pursing his bottom lip over the top to grant Lori her point.

"We talked for a few minutes."

"About what?"

"Girl stuff, it wouldn't interest you, but, crazy enough, Emily asked me to recommend a Depeche Mode album for her to try."

"Wow, *Little House on the Prairie* goes new wave."

"I told her to cut her teeth on the newest album, *Music for the Masses,* but any Mode fan who's really a Mode fan would go with *Black Celebration.* 'Fly On the Windscreen' on the mixtape I made you, it's from that album."

"With all that's gone on lately, I…"

"Shh, it's alright," Lori whispered, leaning in to give him another kiss. "I see it in your tape deck, so that pleases me. You have another two days off from school, though, so chop chop, huh?"

"Alright," Jason chortled. "I promise."

"I also brought you this," Lori said, leaning back to the printed sheets from school and coming up with a rectangular bookmarker featuring a panorama of the Grand Canyon stretched down the face. A printed slogan across the canyon skyline read *The Possibilities Are Infinite.*

"Cool," Jason said, examining the bookmark with fascination. He went straight there in his mind to the South Rim of the Kaibab Plateau, holding onto Lori from behind as they stared in awe at the multicolor sediments and the curving tributary below. "I appreciate this, Lori."

"I do have an ulterior motive, of course," Lori said, taking the bookmark from him and retrieving the library copy of *The Outsiders* from his nightstand. "You've made a nice dent in this, I see. I also see a little Ponyboy Curtis in you."

"I had a little time to catch up, and I think some of what we've gone through isn't far off from greasers versus the Socs, rumble included. If only I had a brother named Sodapop. Don't want no Dally, though. He's stuck on himself, no matter his being the acting father and all."

"Which is exactly the point S.E. Hinton was making, Dallas having to step into a role as dad to his younger brothers and his entire life being controlled by two rebels getting into constant trouble. Stick with him, babe. Dallas finds his redemption just like Ponyboy and Johnny Cade will. Johnny, well, I can't spoil it for you since you haven't seen the movie. It's too dramatic. Now me, I would've been done reading *The Outsiders* before lunchtime."

Lori fanned the book open to Jason's saved spot at Page 112. With a playful tweak of her brows, Lori retrieved the tarot card Jason had been using and inserted the Grand Canyon bookmarker in its place.

"Showoff," Jason cracked.

"I need this back, and I thank you," Lori said, leaning over the edge to grab her pocketbook she'd discarded upon arrival. She pulled out a boxed pack marked as **"THOTH TAROT DECK."** The artwork featured a snake coiled into a figure eight formation, two yin yang symbols floating in bipolar fields of black and white.

"Sorry if I offended your goddess," Jason said, reducing the humor in his voice in the event Lori's goddess had been listening in judgment. He had felt the need to return to his Catholic ways the other night at Super Thrift and he couldn't but wonder if it was Jesus Christ who'd sent Bud Curry and Dawn to his rescue, or Lori's pantheon, considering she'd had the second sight to drive up and get him. Perhaps both combined.

"Pish posh, as my grandma loves to say," Lori returned. "You *have* gained the attention of the Lord and Lady, though. Anubis and Isis seem keen on you. Sekhmet as well. She's the Egyptian goddess of battle. Also of healing, if you can grasp the dichotomy. You've pleased her greatly. Ask your mom to cook a steak this week so you can give Sekhmet an offering."

"Say what?"

"Stick with me and I'll open more than your chakras."

"What the hell are chakras? Sounds like a disgusting vegetable."

"I'm going to open you to the world of the esoteric, Jason. Chakras are focal points from your mind down to your...reproductive organs. It's a Hindu system of meditation referred to as Tantra."

"Aside from Stryper, there's some Christian heavy metal act called *Petra,*" Jason mentioned, not so much to mock Lori, but considering his immediate confusion of faith, it seemed topical.

"Shush," Lori said, pulling out the full stack of cards from the Thoth deck and shuffling them. "You're not ready for chakras, we've established that. If you become interested, however, I can have you come over. We'll get naked, skyclad, as pagan culture calls it."

"Okay, now you've sold me."

"Dork," Lori said with a giggle and a blush impossible to hide on her pallid cheeks. "It's not for sex, horndog. I would place a crystal on each focal point on your body and you would do a series of mantras and visualizations with me, imagining an inner energy traveling down your body. It's a cleansing. I do it with my mom."

"Naked?"

"No, bozo, eww. We use bathing suits. Now shut up and let me do this."

"What exactly are you doing?"

"A reading on you. We'll stick with a simple three card draw. I'm still learning oracle and tarot. A full reading is much more involved than this."

Lori closed her eyes and inhaled. She held onto her breath and raised the deck of cards to her face, resting them upon the bridge of her nose, the tip pointed square between her eyes.

"Lord Thoth, show me the truth I seek today," she murmured.

"If only *To Tell the Truth* was still on tv."

"Quiet," Lori sighed as she began shuffling the tarot deck once more. The cards moved rapidly, popping off a line of *chuff chuff chuff chuff* sounds. She repeated the shuffle, then a third time before a single card popped out and fell on the bed.

"You lost one," Jason said, reaching for the card.

"Exactly," said Lori, snatching the card before Jason could get to it. The card showed a pentagram with two sprouting lily pads at the ends of the northern two tips. Each point of the askew star shape was connected to a glass chalice, the bottommost dipped into its corresponding chalice. "This is what Thoth wishes you to see."

"I'll shut up and let you do your thing."

"Good boy," Lori said in a deep, officious tone telling Jason she would tolerate no more goofery at this time. "The Disappointment card, hmm. Can't say I'm surprised."

She shuffled again and another single card sprung free, bouncing off Jason's extended leg.

"Prince of Disks," she said, placing the card next to the Disappointment draw.

"What's that around the nude guy and the bull? Looks like a pair of headphones."

"It's a chariot, Jason, sheesh. As you said, let me do my thing."

"Shaddup, shuttin' up," Jason jested, unable to help himself. He was mimicking a snide, 1920's style gangster named Mugsy from a Bugs Bunny cartoon. Mugsy would've done better to shaddup himself, since the rascally rabbit roughed him up in brutal fashion as he did all his foes.

Lori grimaced in frustration at Jason, shuffling once more. It took her four passes of the cards this time until a card dropped out, showing a wheel with red spindles connecting to alternating rams' heads and doves.

"The Completion card," Lori said, her face finally relenting. "That's excellent."

"Yay me," Jason said. "Let's order a pizza and celebrate."

"You're incorrigible."

"I drive a chariot with my balls swinging. Of course, I'm incorrigible."

This time, Lori had no choice but to laugh.

"Alright, you comedian, listen up. The first card here is from the minor arcana, the Five of Wands. This is saying what you've been going through up to this point. Disappointment should be self-explanatory. Your dad, your mom's recent problems until she dug herself out. School. The bullying. You've been feeling vulnerable, depressed. You're ripe for the picking if you want to jump on the Goth train with me."

Jason let an amused puff of air blast through his nostrils.

"The second card, Prince of Disks. This is where you're at right now. It says you are the architect, the designer. Though there's a separate Chariot card in the deck, you drew this one. Essentially, they're saying the same thing. You are in the process of changing your life, but also rebuilding yourself. I know what you looked like before we started dating. You've buffed up in that weightlifting class. You're going through a transformation. It turned me on, if you want me to be honest, so I pursued you after the Goddess told me I should be investigating a relationship with you. The Prince of Disks stays solid in body and in command of his place in the universe. That's you, right now."

"Sweet," Jason said. "I turn you on, huh?"

"Simpleton," Lori smirked, giving him an air of dismissal wave, then patting Jason on the leg before picking up the final card. "The third card always says where you are potentially headed down the road, and it advises one for the future. You have The Four of Wands. Completion. This may seem obvious to you, but what the card is saying is before you can move forward with your life in a positive direction, you must prepare yourself to receive the goodness to come. You've been through hell the past few weeks, and stringing this whole thing together, it tells me you're not yet done going through it."

"Greeeeeeat."

"The Four of Wands does represent desire, if it's any inspiration to you. Emotional, sexual, intellectual. Call to Venus tonight, though I feel the Egyptian pantheon looming in on you. It's a wonderful thing if you choose to accept them. The Egyptian gods and goddesses are powerful, yet let's start with Venus. She represents fertility, beauty, power, and love. Fertility can come in many forms, not just belly slapping. Open your mind to her. You've got more to contend with, and I'll be here for you, but it's *your* journey, Jason."

"So, you're saying something else intense is coming my way?"

"Clairvoyance is a touchy thing and I'm still new at it," Lori answered, grabbing the cards and returning them to the deck. She shuffled a couple more times before putting them back in the box. "I can't predict the future, but I can be a channel for the gods and goddesses as much as they're willing to speak through me."

"Got it."

"I didn't make an impression with you," Lori said with faint disgust.

"No, no, you did," Jason said, reaching out to touch her shoulder with assurance. "It's mind-blowing, okay? I gave up on religion last year, though full disclosure, I did a Sign of the Cross the other night before Shaffer and his guys nearly ran me over in the Super Thrift parking lot. Kinda hard not to think I was answered, you know?"

"This can hold for another time," Lori said, rising from the bed and going to Jason's stereo. She unplugged the headphones from it and pushed play on the tape deck. "Let's see where you're at. Ahh, Oingo Boingo."

Danny Elfman crooned the chorus in time to a brisk-stomping groove, brought to soaring heights with screeching guitars, hammering piano strikes and a poky brass section.

"Let's have a party, there's full moon in the sky," Lori sang along. "It's the hour of the wolf and I don't wanna die..."

"I'm getting there with this music," Jason said. "This one slays."

"I'm so happy dancing while the grim reaper cuts cuts cuts," Lori went on as she pulled off her sweater. She'd worn no bra, and the bruise on her left breast was gruesome. Yet she appeared like she could've cared less. "But he can't get *me*."

"Whoa," Jason said, gaping at her like he was six instead of seventeen, mesmerized by the newness of seeing a naked woman in the flesh, all for him.

"The right one should be good to go," Lori told Jason, caressing beneath the unscathed breast. "Can you get out of your jeans, or do you need me to help?"

"I got it," Jason heaved, hurrying to shuck out of his pants. His erection was there before he got free of them.

"I know you're a virgin," she said.

"Your witchy ways told you that?"

"I got to pop Greg's cherry. Now I get the honor of taking yours."

In a blur, Jason found his underwear gone and his rigid penis inside of Lori's mouth. He could've climaxed right there, but she squeezed on him and said, "Ah ah," to make him settle down. He hadn't even seen her remove her skirt and panties, it all happened so fast. Lori was so stealthy he shuddered once again to feel the cool, sticky latex sheathing his member.

"You brought rubbers?" he asked foolishly.

"Duh," she said, smacking his hip. "Let's see if you can beat Greg's time."

"How long did he go?"

"A minute."

Jason went three.

Chapter 40

"THE END OF AN ERA," Rob said, gliding his hand all around the stubble on his head. He smiled at the practically bald reflection in the mirror though, truth be told, he was feeling more uneasy than satisfied at what he saw.

The return smile was at least as pleasant as the Autumn Leaves scented Yankee Candle burning next to him on the bathroom sink basin, swapped the other day for Ocean Air despite the close arrival of October. His mother, a relative fan of fall and no fan of winter at all, was a summer girl thick and true. She'd burned that Ocean Air candle down to the bitter end of its wick as a drawn-out farewell to the summer of '88.

Rob was putting on a show of geniality with both of his parents hovering outside the bathroom. In turn, their expressions revealed a contrast of mixed reviews of Rob's shorn dome. His father looked as proud as if Rob had cut all his hair off himself. His mother, who would no doubt enjoy a rousing conversation with Mr. Morrow over drainpipe jeans and crystal blue persuasion, looked half sick at Rob's shearing himself two inches down to the scalp.

"Reminds me of when they shipped me out to Okinawa," Rob's dad said. "In Basic, it was all the way down."

"Al seemed to take perverse delight in it," Rob marked.

"Said it was it his civic duty, no less," ribbed his dad. "I'm amazed you took it all in stride, Rob. Al's a jarhead from the Korean War days. 1st Battalion. You get your hair cut by Al on a regular basis, he'll tell you a few stories. The one which always gets him going is being aboard 'Happy Hank,' the Henrico which gimped its way into Potun. In polite company, he calls the ship's mechanical failures en route to Seoul 'unsat,' as in unsatisfactory. For military people like me, he uses more colorful jargon for the ship's engineers as 'cheesedicks,' which means guys giving means minimal effort. That, or 'fucknuts,' excuse my language, Julie."

"Which is why I would never fit in the military," Rob's mom stated with a not-so-disguised harrumph.

"My first time there and I can already tell Al's favorite saying," Rob noted. "Bravo Sierra."

"What does that mean?" Rob's mom asked.

"B.S." his father replied. "As in bullshit."

"I had to ask," she groaned.

"Semper Fi," Rob cracked still rubbing his bristly head. "Kids around school are really fond of 'FUBAR.'"

Rob's dad chuckled. "Of course, they are."

"It'll take some getting used to your new look," his mother countered, trying to be encouraging but sounding muddled, as if at a loss. "You had beautiful hair, Rob, if it means anything. I liked it."

"Thanks, guys," Rob told them, trying to avoid taking either side.

"You hit the weights like Jason, and you'll be an entirely new man," his dad added.

"He already *is,* Darren," Rob's mom contradicted before addressing him directly. "I haven't seen you wear a shirt without a band on it since you were in eighth grade. The long sleeve crew neck's a nice touch. On a Saturday, no less."

"Are you sure that girl I saw you talking to last week doesn't have something to do with this new change?" his father teased.

"Daaaaaaad…"

"Oh, a girl?" his mother chimed, snapping out of her momentary fugue.

"The bougie mother who thinks her shit doesn't stink. Do I have the right girl, Rob?"

"Marcie hasn't looked my way since last Sunday," Rob sulked.

"No accounting for taste, then," his mother said. "Move along."

"There's still time to ask this Marcie to Homecoming," his dad offered anyway.

"Yeah, right," Rob said, perturbed. "I thought she was cool. She's into comics. She *seemed* into *me.* My last paper I read in class the other day, Marcie couldn't even look at me up there."

"The Harriet bit?" his mother asked.

"Yeah, I got another A-plus."

"Well, yeah you did, it was genius. Whoever does find the cure for cancer, I hope they're knighted instead of assassinated."

"Thanks, Ma. The class gave me big applause again. Everyone except for Marcie."

"Prima donna," Rob's mother scorned before turning away for the living room.

"The girl's mother may be the problem, but the important thing is this," his dad said, seeming to wind up his breath as he did so. "Long hair, short hair, grubby clothes or spiffy. None of that makes who you *are*, understand? Don't chop your hair off because you're trying to appeal to some girl. There's lots of girls out there, Rob. If you're lucky, you meet the woman of your dreams like I did…"

"I hear you out there, Mr. Martino," Rob's mom called back. "A glass of Chardonnay with that sweet talk, you may get lucky later."

"Dudes!" Rob exclaimed, though he smothered a laugh he didn't want them to see. Bad enough he had a yellowish bruising to his eye he didn't want them seeing either.

"If you find yourself compromising for a girl before you've even had one date, Rob, then you're doing yourself a disservice."

"Never sell out!" Rob's mother hollered from the living room, sounding oddly like Jason. Coming from a parent figure, more than odd.

"It's not just Marcie," Rob added. "The kids at school have treated me and Jason like scum the entire time we've gone to Merriweather High. Pond scum, to be more exact. Creative Writing's the first time I've been given any kind of respect, you know?"

"Then that's where you win people over, Rob. Whatever reaction you get to your haircut and whatever else you choose to do to yourself in school, none of that should matter. Show them who you are by doing what you're doing. Embrace the good stuff. You've gone through the gauntlet, now stop, inhale, and point yourself in the direction of confidence. We believe in you, son."

"Zen from former Army?" Rob's mom shouted. "I also might just cook your favorite hot Italian sausages in tonight's spaghetti, Darren."

"I wasn't just livin' the dream in Ginowan City, baby. I did more than sloughing off watching *Ol' Yeller* a hundred times off base. Vacation before the 'Nam."

"Awful movie," she sent back to him.

"It teaches kids valuable life lessons! Loss, in particular!"

"I went down pretty fast in the fight," Rob interjected, rubbing above his right eyebrow. "This whole mess got started because of how me and Jason look. It's not just school, Dad! Nobody talks to me at work! It's like I don't exist other than to dump trash, pick disgusting tampons off the women's room floor, and spray ashtrays. The president, you know what he said when I tried to be nice to him earlier in the week?"

"Fred Gambrel's a bigger tool than the company's trade," his dad groaned. "He likes nobody, and nobody likes him. I'm not saying Grigsby will make or break your future, but stick it out, do the time, keep throwing your greenbacks into your savings account. We're both very proud of you. Forget about Fred, you be *you*, Rob. I'm serious."

"Thanks, Dad," Rob said, rubbing his head once again. "Not sure how Jason's gonna take this. We've been growing our hair out since we first met."

"How's he been doing since the fight?"

"I dunno, ask Lori," Rob replied with a shrug. "We've been off three days and I've called him each one. He got fired from Super Thrift, but he won't tell me why. I think we've spoken maybe five minutes total since the fight, Dad. Yesterday, he snapped at me and hung up. I could hear him and Lori, you know… Part of me thinks he was rubbing it in my face."

"Roger copy," his dad said with a chuckle. "Why don't you go over there now? It's not like the boy doesn't live three easy blocks away."

"If they're at it again…"

"Then you come back home. Rob, even the best buds have their friendships tested. I used to have lunch with Chuck all the time. Now, since he's become your boss, he doesn't say one word to me. It doesn't matter since he gets there right as I'm leaving. Regardless, I still consider Chuck a friend. Be happy for Jason and Lori. Your time will come. Bank on it."

Chapter 41

WHEN HE ARRIVED at Jason's house, Rob could hear the familiar *chunk! pffff!* flash of a discharged BB, then a *plink!* against the other side of the wooden fence. If there had been no barrier there, the BB would've dinged Rob upside the cheek.

"Is there anything better to do than picking off Skeletor, Ram-Man, and Man-at-Arms over and over?" Rob heard from the other side. "Albeit you missed this time."

"Could be that apple you keep gnawing on, Lori. Your crunching and slurping are affecting my aim."

Rob laughed from his side of the fence as he circled around and came down the other side.

"Apples are for love, magic, and immortality," Lori said with a hard dip in her tone. "If you believe the Welsh legends, the souls of kings, knights, and those performing heroic deeds were said to venture to Avalon in the afterlife, an island paradise loaded with apple trees."

"The commoners go in the ditch like anyone else," said Jason, shooting her down.

"I gave up an outing to the Amish market with my mom for this shit?"

"I know I would," Jason chattered at her.

"I'll pretend I didn't hear that. I even brought *The NeverEnding Story* and *Labyrinth* over to watch."

"The only thing I like about *Labyrinth* is Bowie and the farting bog," Jason returned as Rob came to the gate and tugged against the locked resistance.

"Yo, guys!" Rob shouted out to them. "Lemme in."

"Ahh, geez," he heard Jason grouse from the other side.

"Love you too, jerko," Rob called back, fuddling over his sudden feeling of rejection.

His reception from Lori was far kinder, and it was she, not Jason, who opened the gate for him.

"Rob?!?" she shouted, throwing her arms around and squeezing him before letting go. Over her shoulder, Rob saw a ruffled look spread across Jason's already perturbed face. "You should put an APB out for your hair!"

"Left for dead on the floor at Al's Barber Shop," Rob said with a reflexive grin. His attempt at humor, however, was undone by Jason's sour reaction to him. Rob didn't know if it was his haircut or just the fact he'd shown up, period.

"It looks *good*," Lori complimented, brushing her palm across the top of his head. "Tickles, too. What made you decide to do this?"

"Yeah, Rob, what's with the Mr. Clean look all of a sudden?" Jason spewed, making no attempt to hide his disgust.

"Don't mind him," Lori said with another swish of her hand over Rob's prickled dome. "He's been in a mood today. How've you been holding up since Tuesday?"

"A mood?" Jason yapped at their backs.

"Alright, I guess," Rob replied, glancing at Lori, then again at Jason.

"That goose egg's nearly faded," Lori said, reaching to Rob again and dragging her thumb across his upper brow.

"Don't act like I'm not here!" Jason blasted. "Why are you fawning over him, Lori? Are you his mother all of a sudden?"

"Damn, Jason, what's your malfunction?" Rob objected, fighting back something he'd never felt toward Jason before: complete displeasure. "You've been blowing me off since the fight, and now this? Sorry if I don't compete with your girlfriend. No offense, Lori."

"None taken," she replied, her face growing stony with mortification.

"Fuck off, skinhead," Jason burned. He sent Rob a vindictive stare which made its mark.

"Jason what the hell?" Lori whirled around, sending Jason a vicious glare.

"His haircut is bullshit," Jason fumed, ignoring Lori. "So's his dumb Ralph Lauren shirt. You sucking up to the Populars, then, is that it, Rob?"

"Don't..." Lori warned Jason.

"You traitor!" Jason spat.

"Grow the fuck up," Lori simmered at Jason, splaying her hands into the air, her tilted head following suit.

"Oh, so you're taking his side, then, Lori?"

"To hell with this," Lori grumbled, now shoving her hands backwards at Jason in a motion of removal. "I told you before; I don't deal with jealous assholes, especially when they have nothing to be jealous *of*. Rob, I have no explanation for your friend's behavior, I'm so sorry."

"Don't apologize to him!" Jason screamed, brandishing his Daisy air rifle with both hands.

"Really Jason?" Rob asked, feeling his body flush with consternation stinging him as much as Jason's unexpected betrayal. "All this because I cut my hair?"

"Death to false metal," Jason said in a murky pitch. "I think you need to leave, man."

"Just because I don't want to finish high school as a goddamn victim anymore doesn't mean I've given up on the music," Rob flared. "I'll always love heavy metal, but Jason, look what happened this week! I didn't last long out there."

"You sure as hell didn't," Jason taunted.

"Wow," Lori cut in. "The fight's changed you, Jason. I didn't really see it, but I can now, clear as Sirius on an August night. Rob's your friend. I mean seriously, Jason. Right now, you're no better than Shaffer, the Metcalfs and…"

"Shut up!" Jason roared.

"That'll be the last time I ever back you up, *dick*," Rob said, jabbing his forefinger past Lori in Jason's direction.

"I'm done here as well," she said, turning from Rob and veering past Jason into his house.

"Thanks for nothing, Rob," Jason growled, lifting the BB gun toward his chest.

"You want to get your dad back or you didn't get enough revenge on Sam Shaffer?" Rob hollered back. "It's just a harmless, stupid BB, whatever! Shoot me, if it makes you feel so mighty! Fire away, fucker!"

Jason shivered in his spot, and Rob could hear the BBs rattling inside the Daisy stock. The barrel came up, just enough to prompt a whoosh of the sliding door from the house. The purplish swelling around Jason's eye sprang apart with indignation before disbelief.

"What are you doing?!?" Jason's mother screeched. "Put that gun down now! Better yet, give it to me! Lori just stormed out of here and now I see *this*? What's gotten into you, Jason?"

Jason trembled as he assessed this new development. His mother had her arm outstretched to him and she was closing the distance between them in a hurry. She meant business; not only would she stop until she'd defused the conflict, she was going to confiscate and likely get rid of the BB gun.

"Rob, go home, please," she said without even looking at him. "I've got a handle on this."

She was good to her word, taking advantage of Jason's puzzlement and snatching the air rifle by its stock. She had to tug twice, but she pried it free from Jason and sent him an opposing look in case he dared try to snatch it back.

"Get outta here, preppie," Jason told Rob, his shoulders drooping at a loss.

"With pleasure," Rob snarled on his way back out the gate.

Rob went away through the front yard instead of the back, and the last thing he heard was Jason sobbing against his mother.

Chapter 42

THE FOLLOWING MONDAY, Jason, Rob, and Lori took their separate ways to school.

Jason walked and was beaten by Rob, who'd ridden the bus. After serving the three-day suspension, Rob had been greeted by the other kids with praise, and room was made for him in the back of the bus.

The most curious loaded around him, asking for his recount of the big fight. They also made a big to-do about Rob's haircut and his change in attire to acid wash jeans and a new, navy-blue crew neck his mom had picked up for him at Hunt Valley Mall over the weekend. Rob blended in with all the rest of the kids, no longer sticking out as a nonconformist, save for being the lone senior taking a school bus. He was too pleased by all the fuss to care about any of that.

As the bus passed by Jason walking by his lonesome, a handful of kids on the right side of the bus pushed the side windows down so they could stick their heads out and send him a cheer. Jason's hair fluffed out with each resolute stride, catching the crisp breeze like twin kites fluffing behind his ears and neck. Jason had strapped his denim vest back on. In fact, it appeared Jason had added even more buttons over the weekend, as if to make a point.

"Ultimate Warrior!" one of the sophomore kids, Brady Miller, shouted out to Jason, who didn't acknowledge any of it. If anything, Jason looked doubly pissed since Saturday, Rob noted.

Lori had arrived before either of them, stating to Rob she'd gotten a ride to school from her mom, as the Bel Air had gone into the shop for repair of the aerial antenna and side mirror and to buffer out a score of scratches lashed upon the hood from the fight.

Rob found Lori chatting with Emily Haney in the halls, and he put his hand up to flag Lori's attention.

"Hey, honey," Lori said, latching two soothing arms around him. "How are you holding up?"

"Since Saturday?" Rob returned with a gentle shrug. "Still feeling yucky about what went down. My dad and I caught *Elvira, Mistress of the Dark* at the movies yesterday while my mom raided Merry-Go-Round, coming out with two bags worth of new duds for me. We all met up for Italian at Donatelli's afterwards. I do these doofy short album reviews in my spare time, you know, pretending I'm a hotshot writer for *Rip!* or *Metal Forces*. I banged out three of those from my collection last night. It's good practice."

"I'm afraid to ask how the movie was," Lori said, pretending to be leery about it. "She's funny, sure, but those jugs of Elvira's don't exactly inspire any kind of a plot. You guys and your obsession with tits."

"Whaaaaat?" Rob asked, chuckling, feigning offense when instead, he was feeling the best he had since the last day of Junior Year. Even with Emily Haney present, Rob was hardly put off. "*Halloween 4* comes out this week. I'd be there on Friday with Jason if he wasn't being such a cock knock. I mean, Michael Myers is coming back. So's Doctor Loomis, however they manage to write him back after the end of *Halloween II*. It oughta be rad."

"Anything's better than that third one," Emily offered, surprising Rob more than Lori. "*Season of the Witch*, what dreck."

"It's a turd enchilada, but I'm kinda partial to it," Lori said. "I wish they sold the witch mask. I'd be the first in line to get one of those."

"You're both right," said Rob, embracing his unanticipated acceptance of Emily. After last Tuesday, it was becoming less weird.

"Who stole your hair, Rob?" Emily asked, but unlike the past, there was sincerity, warmth even, to her bantering. "I'd like to give the guy a reward."

"Nice," Rob returned, shaking his head at her.

"Seriously, though," Emily went on, taking a step closer toward him. Her eyes pranced all around his cropped head. "I approve. You clean up well, Martino."

"Thanks?" he returned, more in the way of a defenses-resting query.

Rob detected stares galore from people passing by them. He heard "Wow" gabbled at him numerous times in passing, followed by, "Is that really Rob Martino?"

"I was just giving Emily an inventory of Jason's meltdown on Saturday," Lori informed Rob, gesturing for the three of them to start walking around.

Emily lurched in his direction a second time, and at least to Rob's eyes, it seemed she'd given a decisive shove from her heels, calculating her hip and shoulder to bump into his.

"Sorry, man," she told him, but the nibbling on her lip said otherwise.

"Don't worry about it," Rob said as Emily joined his right side with Lori on his left. On friendlier days, he and Jason would've called this "being the meat between a girl sandwich." Jason had yet to be seen on the premises, though, and right now, Rob wondered what Jason might say if he could see Rob right now: the hypothetical meat between Jason's girl and a former nemesis.

"So did you hear about Mr. Chesney, the Political Science teacher?" Emily quipped, leaning into Rob's space to make sure Lori could hear her. There was something funny about Emily's body language to Rob, the way she was keeping a tight gap next to him and the way she was scanning him while trying to get Lori's attention over the stir of arriving students. As they turned a corner, Emily's knuckles tapped Rob's. This time she didn't apologize.

"No, what?" Lori called back. She'd been seemingly impervious to Emily's actions on Rob's other side.

"If you see Mr. Chesney today, then the rumors are false," Emily said, loud enough for two other girls to whirl in the direction of her voice, as if to catch what they could. The school consensus had changed in Emily's favor within a mere week. "If not…"

"What?" Lori asked again, more voluble.

"They're saying he and Francine Van Fleet…"

"Oh, geez," Lori groaned. "She's a sophomore!"

"She'd give Elvira a good run if you get me," Emily joked, elbowing Rob in the arm while making phantom chest extensions far from her own. Emily started in on one of those absurd laughs of hers, but she caught herself before it hit its nexus of obnoxiousness. No doubt Emily had given herself a complete re-evaluation of late. "Anyway, you get the picture. Total scandal."

"Oh, foul," Lori lamented.

"How's your head?" Emily asked Rob. When he stopped to think about it, neither she nor he were the same people they were only a couple weeks ago. This new Emily had exorcised the roughneck agrarian from herself by teasing her ear-length ruddy hair and ditching the corduroy in favor of cardigan. Maybe it was the sudden attention she was giving Rob, but there was something about Emily he was finding appealing right now. To think he and Jason used to call her a "hateful cooze."

"I'm fine, thanks," Rob said, meeting Emily's gaze, and for a moment, he forgot there was such a thing as Marcie Barone. *Is this really happening?* he asked himself, expecting Rod Serling to emerge from the upcoming corner in a pressed Botany 500 suit, hoisting a wave to Rob with a lit cigarette and jerking his head at the illusory signpost ahead telling him he'd just crossed into The Twilight Zone.

It was Lori who said what Rob had been thinking.

"Who would've seen this unlikely alliance?" she asked.

"Really," Emily said.

None of them saw Jason, who'd been swallowed by a throng of unforeseen admirers upon his arrival. He looked elated by the attention, yet beyond furious scoping his girlfriend and best friend in arms with Emily Haney.

Chapter 43

BY THE TIME economics class finished, Rob had grown irritated.

Not with all the interest in his new emergence. That much went swimmingly well.

Today was the most talking he'd done the entire duration he'd been going to Merriweather High, and it wasn't just Emily who'd given him a look over. Numerous girls passed by him with infatuated smiles, as had guys who'd known Rob but had never taken the time to engage him. Many asked him the same two questions: "What happened to your hair?" and "What made you cut if all off?" To which he gave the same noncommittal, if friendly-delivered answer, "It was time."

One of the drama club regulars, Brooke Gautz (a natural actress name with no need for an alter ego), dazzled Rob before he'd arrived to Economics by spooling the works of Sylvia Plath at him: "He felt purged and holy and ready for a new life..."

For all the fanfare he'd been receiving, however, Marcie Barone continued to stonewall him.

She'd given him a check-glance as Rob passed by her on the way to his desk in Economics. Marcie trying to check down her widened eyes told Rob he'd made an impact. Yet even so close to him, Marcie refused to turn his way. She kept a perimeter of avoidance with her shoulders. Her hair had poofed back out to its prior length. He'd stared at that mound on her head, jotting indecipherable notes from Mrs. North's lecture about diverting discourse on accelerations, as in demands for payment in full of debt yet to mature.

The longer Marcie snubbed Rob, the more he lingered upon her locks. Worse, it made him grieve the chopping of his own hair off, if only for a moment.

She'd been ready with her books to make the dash to Creative Writing, and Rob had, at first, prepared himself to cut her off to talk. No sooner had Economics been dismissed, though, Marcie rose and left like a jackrabbit, as if in anticipation of Rob's potential pursuit.

"Can't win them all, Mr. Martino," Mrs. North told him on his much slower trek out, catching him off-guard. "You were somewhere in La La Land during class, but your new haircut and those new clothes are a full one-eighty and I like it. Put you in a double-breasted suit with pinstripes, you'd make a considerable mark on Wall Street."

"Thanks," Rob said, feeling uncomfortable by his teacher's praise as much as validated. Still, he tucked Mrs. North's compliment away in his mind for future indulgence. He was almost as fast as Marcie Barone leaving class.

"Hey, Rob, wait up," he soon heard from behind as he shouldered his way through a backlog of kids.

"Emily," he said, whirling in her direction.

"I've got Brit Lit next door to Mr. Morrow's class," she said more like a pronouncement. "If you want some company for the walk down."

"Sure, I guess," Rob said, feeling his spirits pick up.

"Gee, the enthusiasm's too much to bear," Emily kidded.

"How'd you know that's where I'm going next? Are you spying on me?"

"Maybe. What's it to ya?"

"Uhhhhh," Rob flubbed, caught off-guard for the second time in mere minutes.

"Don't overthink it, Martino, I'm messing with you. I've seen you in Mr. Morrow's class reading. From where I sit in Brit Lit, you're impossible to miss. Star pupil, I take it."

"He digs my work, what can I say?"

"I'd love to read your stuff sometime, even though it's been all I can handle keeping up the chapter assignments in *Jane Eyre,* given my…you know, situation."

As strange as this whole thing felt, not only rubbing elbows with Emily Haney, and her possible coming on to him, what was even crazier was the bizarre draw Rob kept feeling toward her today. Was it because Marcie Barone had gone cold on him? Was it because he was reflexively jealous Jason had a girlfriend, and he didn't?

"I've gotta ask, Rob," Emily said, drawing closer to Rob. She held her textbooks, folders and the paperback copy of Charlotte Bronte's *Jane Eyre* clutched against her chest, her arms keeping the bundle pressed like she was defying anyone to pry it from her. Given what Emily had done to her ex-boyfriend, nobody was likely to try.

"I know, what made me cut my hair? Been having the same song played in my ears all day long. Call the deejays at B-104, it may become the next big hit, coast-to-coast."

"Funny guy," Emily said, cutting into Rob's space just enough to force them into dodging another cluster of jammed-up students. "Ever since I've known you, you had that crazy shag. Now it's gone. What made you do it? Did we get to you that much you just snapped inside and wanted rid of that head metal look?"

"It's *metalhead*," Rob corrected her as they approached the stairwell down to the main level. He made sure to lighten his tone, where it would have been in antagonistic security mode before last Tuesday changed everything between them. "Yeah, I suppose you can say that. Don't think for minute I'm not finding this is completely nuts you and I are walking together after..."

"Dude, I apologized already," Emily said in a borderline snippety tone.

"Yeah, you did, and you know what? After what you did to Lee, I'm more than alright with it."

"Don't mention my ex's name ever again in this lifetime or the next," Emily groused with an emphasized shudder.

"Never call me a geek or a grit again, and we'll make it a deal."

"Deal," Emily said with a wry grin. She bumped her hip against Rob's, this time with no excuse or apology. "What are people saying about it?"

"The haircut? Everyone seems overwhelmingly in favor. Unless you're Jason Hamlin."

"Sucks."

"Or Marcie Barone."

"That stuck-up princess doesn't even walk the same earth as the rest of us."

Rob paused before addressing that comment.

"It's true, Rob," Emily rolled on. "Why waste your time on an elitist like her? It wouldn't surprise me if Marcie has her bath water imported from Bethlehem. Everyone knows the girl's only had one guy in her life. Shane Fenton, and that's only because he was the junior chorus director and head counselor of the youth group at St. Luke's Methodist where her family goes. Once Shane turned eighteen and graduated, Marcie's narcissistic mother put the kibosh on the whole thing. You don't have a prayer with Marcie Barone, no pun intended. Take it as free advice."

"I thought there was something between us."

"You wanted to ask her to the Homecoming dance, didn't you?"

"A bit forward, don't you think, Emily?"

"No, forward would be *me* asking *you* to Homecoming."

"Yeah, alright, I get..."

"So how about it, Martino? You wanna go to Homecoming with me?"

"I...well..." Rob scrabbled, feeling put on the spot. Was this the same girl who'd once called him an "ape drape?" Was she the same one who'd pulled the trigger on her finger pistols at Rob the past few years like she'd wanted him blasted away for real? Now Emily Haney was asking Rob out to his first school function, of all improbable things?"

"I don't have cooties, Rob," Emily pressed on. "My undercooked bun went to Heaven, if there even is such a thing. I still ask God why He ever sent Lee Metcalf my way if He really loves his children as the scriptures profess. Look, I'm not playing any angles, okay? You want a certified statement backing me up, my dad knows a notary public. I propose this; we go see *Halloween 4* this Friday. Bring Lori and Jason too, and we'll call it a non-double date."

"Assuming Jason's talking to any of us then," Rob said, shaking his head. It was all happening so fast, it dinged his head faster than Sam Shaffer's headbutt.

"Yeah, Lori gave me the 411. She told me he popped his cork on you both over the weekend. She refuses to call him, but I can tell; that girl's hung up on him. I mean, look, this whole thing that went down last week, Jason was a total madman. What he did inspired me to jump in against Lee. He inspired me to approach Lori, even you. You're all pretty cool, and I mean it. I know now what you've been going through, and it reeks."

"You don't have to sell me."

"Then let me pitch you a horror night, then Homecoming. If there's still trouble in paradise between Lori and Jason, we'll hit the movies by ourselves. I'll spring for the popcorn, you get the flick. The new Rob Martino and the new Emily Haney. This school won't know what hit it."

Chapter 44

DRAWING AN F ON HIS Accounting test from last week would be the least of Jason's problems this day, yet he stewed about it for much of the way home.

He wasn't anywhere near as mad at Rob and Lori as he'd been this morning, spotting them circling the promenade with Emily Haney. He'd had a good purge of it by soaking his head under the shower head after completing the Mad Mile (as Coach Schaub had called it this morning) with Danny, Bennett, and Brad, all taking the same time of 8:46 side-by-side for completion. The new bonds Jason had forged with his fight mates had carried well onto the track. Ricky Groff hadn't been in school since the fight. The unofficial word had it Ricky was moving. Left without a lifting partner, Jason was welcomed by Coach Schaub to work in with anyone he wanted, and he had his three choices to work in with.

It was hard to put the past in the past, but if Lori and Rob were making nice with Emily, Jason figured he should be expected to do the same. If he still wanted Lori in his life.

Jason hoped to find Lori waiting for him after school on the senior patio. He didn't see her parents' car in the parking lot, which could've meant she'd already left, or her parents had taken the vehicle to get fixed. He assumed Rob had taken the bus home, since he hadn't seen him the remainder of the day. His new buddies from Weightlifting were all on the fields for after school practice in their respective sports. Bennett had offered to teach Jason how to lob a ball with lacrosse sticks, in the event of a long-term player injury. Jason declined his new buddy with a respectful high five.

There was talk flurrying around Merriweather about some teacher in Political Science Jason knew nothing about who was likely to be canned, much less arrested, for having intercourse with some 16-year-old-girl named Francine Van Fleet. Jason was grateful there'd been something else for the school body to talk about other than the big throwdown.

Cars honked at Jason with outstretched hands waving at him as they blew by. The whole thing had become surreal, how his life had changed so drastically in less than a month's time. Jason felt like the world's most dodgy, small-scale celeb as much as he felt completely alone. This, even with a car of junior guys slowing down to offer him a ride. Like Bennett Tignall, Jason passed on it with a polite flick of the horns, mustering the right amount of gratitude to send them on their way, no harm, no foul.

The intersection at Route 62 was clogged with kids from Merriweather High, all turning left, which cut into the crosswalk Jason needed to use. He'd been used to taking that direction and heading down to the shopping center since spring. In fact, he came close to panicking to see the flashing digital time of 3:16 p.m. on his wrist, knowing it took him close to forty minutes to walk the distance to Super Thrift from school. He'd be home in twenty instead.

Another car honked at him and again, Jason put up a cordial wave, muttering to himself, "Alright, guys, I'm not frigging Ghandi."

His bookbag felt heavier than normal, which he figured was due more to fatigue than content. A few sedentary days off, first spent in bliss with Lori, then in explosive frustration over the weekend; Jason was spent.

Jason thought about trying to call Lori once he got home, assuming she would even pick up. He could already tell she wouldn't be the first to cave, not as angry as she'd been at him on Saturday. Jason realized over the course of the day what a horse's ass he'd been, most especially to Rob. Rob's excessive haircut had more than concerned Jason upon sight of it; it had freaked him out for a reason he hadn't been able to get his finger on until later in the day.

Jason was feeling his own identity slip away, much as he could see a new one building. One which involved having a girlfriend and a new set of associates he could never have imagined coming onto his horizon. It had just been Jason and Rob these past few years, and now this carousel of change. For Rob to whack his hair away, it symbolized to Jason, not so much selling out, as he'd pegged Rob with, but a rejection of their entire friendship.

Such an assumption was crap, Jason finally accepted in last period. The more he tumbled this around his head as he got to the entrance of the development; he knew it was Rob he should try calling first. Jason picked up the pace, thinking maybe he could catch Rob before he left for Grigsby Tools.

Once Jason got to his house, though, he was surprised to find his mother home from work already, it being 3:35.

Was she sick? Did she have a migraine? Had she lost her job? Had she even left today?

Letting himself in with his key, Jason dropped his bookbag in the foyer where he usually left it unless he had homework. All the catch-up work Lori had brought for him, Jason had whizzed through it in Study Hall before Accounting, so there was no need to haul his books upstairs.

"Ma?" he called out.

She didn't answer him right away, shaking Jason up.

"Ma?"

A second time with no answer.

Jason bounded into the kitchen, but he didn't find her. Nor was she in the living room.

"MA!!!" he roared, raked by a sense of dread he was right to feel.

Only thing, it wasn't his mother he needed to worry about.

"I'm on the bed," she called out feebly. She sounded sick. Worse than sick. Like something so terrible had happened it had throttled her and dumped her into a slouched, trampled position on the edge of her bed where he'd found her. She'd been crying. She might have been pulling on her hair, it was in such disarray. Letting his mind run rampant, had Jason's mother been attacked?

"What's wrong?" Jason asked in a panic. "Are you okay? What happened to you?"

"Your father," she blubbered, fresh tears sieving out of both eyes.

"What about him?" Jason snapped. "I told you I want nothing to do with him. Did he come over?"

"Jason," she croaked at him. "Your father was drinking and driving."

"Oh, no," Jason gasped, no longer feeling any of the wrath he'd brought home. Nor any of the wrath towards his dad. His mother said it just as Jason thought it.

"He's dead," she said, leaning forward like she was going to vomit on the carpet, letting her hair plunge around her face to hide her grief.

Chapter 45

JASON WAS EQUAL PARTS livid, stunned, and wounded. Crying was relegated to the back burner. In fact, Jason would punch himself right in the jaw and reaggravate injuries from the fight, should a single tear loose emerge. He knew how foolish this thinking was, given the watering of his eyes.

Instead, Jason held his mother, the same as she'd done for him once Rob had left the other day. Part of this felt abnormal, that he should be the one consoling her. A new paradox occurring to Jason was sometimes a mother needed her child more than the other way around.

Jason pulled his mother close to him, resting the non-bruised side of his face against her head. He could smell a trace of apples in her hair, diverting his rampant thoughts to his mock debate with Lori about apples and Avalon. He wanted Lori here right now, hugging him while he hugged his mom.

Mother leaned into son, who had her in height these days by more than a foot and, since he'd begun working out, an easy twenty pounds on her. On Saturday, Jason found himself leaning down to plant the same side cheek upon her shoulder.

"Stupid, selfish man," she wept, sniffling against Jason's chest while wringing her hands in her lap. "If he were alive for me to do it, I'd slap him silly."

In her hysterics, she'd flipped on her alarm clock radio.

Todd Rundgren's "I Saw the Light" surfaced, further piercing his mother's sorrow. Jason remembered the starry-eyed tune from afternoon drives on back country roads to nowhere during his childhood, the frolicking, up-and-down piano, the back-and-forth cha-cha rhythm between snare and tom heads and the pensive love letter Rundgren doted to his unknown muse in song. Rundgren's swooning fret slides amplified collapse and suffering this time instead of divvying its intended romantic trance.

"God almighty, turn it off, Jason," she bawled. "It would have to be that song."

He broke away to flick off the radio as Rundgren serenaded, *"But my feelings for you were just something I never knew..."*

"I wish you could've known your father at the beginning," Jason's mom said, taking a deep breath and swabbing her eyes with the sleeve of her pine-colored blouse. "My biggest regret is you'll never get to. Your dad, he had charm. Boy, did he have charm. He was rugged like James Brolin though he had a temper enough to shame even John McEnroe if you pushed him into a fight. He could be seductive back then simply asking for a glass of water. When I met your dad, I got to see both sides of him. I was attracted to the man upon first contact. It's so true what they about love at first sight. I know you and Lori have really hit off and I'm so happy for you, Jay, but I can't describe what your father made me feel the minute we met. Hell, he's gone now, so why worry about prudery? He turned me *on*, Jason. I was hot for him. I felt alive being with him. You must know this for anything after to make sense. Do you get me?"

"Yeah, Mom," Jason said somberly, trying to accept everything she was telling him.

"The man I knew had a soft touch and soft lips beneath that untidy mustache of his. His kisses were one thing, but, even if I'm your mother...what that man could do with..."

She paused a moment, censoring herself through waterlogged eyes and quivering, devastated lips. When she could compose herself, she resumed.

"You've got to understand, baby, your mother didn't just pick any mutt out of the litter. Your father loved me once, enough to stand by me when we made love and conceived you. You weren't planned Jason, but we welcomed your coming. I hope you can believe me. Your father didn't run when I became pregnant. He stood tall and married me and willingly became your dad. I trusted in that, despite what he may have become later in life. He's done terrible things, but in the beginning and for a long time, you were the light of his life, even more than me. Trust me when I say it."

"I know we had good times," Jason relented, feeling his chest swell and his eyes fill up to their capacity. Tears were inevitable, yet Jason held onto his own anguish, as long as he could. He had to. For his mother.

"You were the *light of his life*, Jay, and I never took offense. The best day of my life was seeing that dopey expression on your dad's face when he got to hold you for the first time. It made me happy he loved you as much as he did, and he was such a good provider. For all his faults, he made sure we were taken care of. I know he didn't show it all the time, but the only way I can hope to console you is to make you understand he loved you more than anyone in his mistake-filled life."

"Don't sugarcoat it, Mom! He was a drunk, and it cost him his life!"

"I know, baby, and it's going to be so hard from here on out. You're close to legal age, and I don't know what happens to us, to *me,* since there'll be no support coming now. The bigger picture, though, I don't give a good goddamn what that divorce decree says; that's my husband going to the grave and I hope whatever demons turned him so ugly go with him. I'll always love your father, Jason. I hate him too, but we're both going to have to find it within ourselves to forgive him."

"I don't know if I can, Ma," Jason said, his lips shivering, his pupils washed in such a flood his mother looked like a squirming apparition.

"That Todd Rundgren song, Jason," his mother said, full of commitment as she snatched both of his hands with hers. "It was in the spring of '72. You were still a baby. Your father and I had the most spectacular sex with you in the bassinette next to us while that song was playing. I'm sorry to be so gross, but he took me *there,* not once but three times. You were asleep and I was quivering, I was so content. I asked him if he wanted a second child. You know what he told me?"

"No, what?" Jason asked, both of his cheeks feeling the heat of searing fluid. He'd forgotten just how strong his mother's grip was. She clamped onto him, shaking his hands up and down in single, vigorous motions. It felt tragic instead of reassuring.

"He said you were more than enough, and we'd gotten it right the first time."

Jason shrugged his hands loose and turned away from her.

"I need to be alone, Ma!" he yelled. "I'm sorry!"

"Don't be, sweetheart," she told him as he darted out of her bedroom. "You never have to be around me."

Jason scampered down the stairs and shot out the front door, nearly knocking over the standing coat rack in the foyer.

He was down the lawn and into the street in no time. Jason felt his legs cranking, but not the actual thuds of his feet as he increased his speed.

Jason's teeth rattled and his sore eye flared. Jason ran, faster than he did on the track to impress the Weightlifting class. No, to impress himself, which was far more important. He even ran faster than his now legendary headfirst tear into the fight last week.

Jason knew his destination, but he'd found himself, in a blur, well into the woods before it hit him where he was. He skidded into a pile of dried, dead leaves, a *fwashhhhhhh* sound pushing back like it was trying to shush him.

His heart minced in his chest and just that fast, his throat started hurting from the cold air he'd been ingesting. None of this stopped Jason as he spotted a broken tree branch next to the leaf-scattered trail. He seized it and ran to the nearest oak. For a split second, he thought of Lori's adoration of trees and how she'd told him in his bedroom they were living — if stationary — things.

"Sorry, Lori, sorry, tree," he gnashed, swinging the branch against the oak.

His first strike was met with resistance. For another split second, he wondered if the tree was fighting back against him.

Then he thought of his father asleep on the family sofa, an open can of Schlitz in his hand, tipped inwards toward the crotch of his already soggy-looking dress slacks. It was a revolting sight to Jason, now a revolting memory. How bad did the man suffer when he wrecked his car? Had he died, too shitfaced to know those were the final moments of his life? Or had he remaining seconds to realize the damage he'd done, to himself and to his family? Had he any final regrets before he expired?

"Damn you!" Jason hollered, taking a second swing into the oak. It splintered but didn't break up. "I don't care what Mom says! If you loved me so much, why'd you run from us and get yourself killed, you drunken bastard?"

Jason smashed the branch again, feeling it give. Another swing and another. He looked like a berserker lumberjack trying to chop down the oak with no axe in sight.

"Fuck you, Dad!" he roared, as the branch bisected against its will, it seemed. The split end twirled away, plopping into a sea of leaves gulping it from sight.

That was when Jason gave himself permission to cry in full.

It was more like an enraged yowl. Whatever Dustin Hoffman's character, Thomas "Babe" Babington Levy, had been going through in the Nazi-strung dental hell of *Marathon Man,* Jason projected the same feeling, only twice the torment. His scream ricocheted all around the woods, alarming birds, and a random chipmunk dashing out of nowhere across the path and out of sight on the opposite side.

The trees swirled around Jason, spinning as if returning the favor for banging up its brother oak.

"Were you ever proud of me, Dad?" he asked aloud, closing his eyes in the attempt to slow down the lightheaded pirouettes. "Or do you regret not pulling the trigger when you had the chance? Mom's heart's in the right place, but I'm not buying it. Were we so bad you had to resort to cheating and drinking?"

Jason opened his eyes and felt his bearings begin to return.

"You called me a dummy when I was a kid," he heaved, glancing at the leafless tips of tree branches reaching to tickle the belly of the skyline. "A *dummy!* Did it occur to you I was too scared to let you down when I didn't understand the concepts? Who cares what equation we were trying to figure out? It was second grade, you asshole! To this day, I still shit the bed in math. Is it any wonder I hate it, Dad?"

Jason stopped there, checking around in the event anyone had shown up to witness his ravings.

"Waste of a life," Jason snarled to his shoes, looking down into the dirt between the leaves. In the summertime with Rob, there'd been ants, beetles, and mites to watch mindlessly. Now it was quiet, devoid of action. He missed that as much as his friend.

Jason palmed away the crusting residue around his eyes and started walking instead of running. In a long, long distance, he heard The Cars' "Let's Go" from someone's vehicle. Distant, happily familiar, like the comforting wash of the Atlantic Ocean upon the Maryland seaboard.

He'd gassed himself with all his exertion, but Jason wasn't ready to go back home, not just yet. He didn't want to leave his mother alone for too long; there was no telling what she'd do.

On the opposite end of the woods was an open stretch of field, once used for agriculture, now left as a barren, untilled eyesore. Jason knew it was destined to join his neighborhood as an annexed subdivision. For the time being, though, with no crops and no houses, it served his purposes as an exposed, gritty gateway to the train tracks on the vista.

Jason slogged through the solitary pasture, not yet sure how far along the train tracks he wanted to go. Part of him felt like going to the shopping center, skipping past Super Thrift which no longer wanted him, and over to Curry's Music.

He hadn't brought any money with him and though he considered Bud and Dawn friends (especially after coming to his aid last week), he didn't feel right just showing up for no reason other than needing two comforting faces to talk to.

Even at half the speed of his usual pace, Jason got to the train tracks fast. He nicked a few pebbles between the slats and threw them sidearm toward the horizon. He could hear them land and skitter away, giving him slight satisfaction.

Jason balanced himself on the left rail without needing his arms to steady himself. He'd done this so many times that, even shaken as he was by the death of his father right now, he had no problem gliding atop the rail, foot in front of foot, for half a mile.

Jason was about to turn around and head back home, but something nagged at him upon spotting the Rill & Company textile warehouse which hadn't been used in years. From his spot on the tracks, Jason saw the scrambled blue graffiti mark of something looking like a "P," "X," "L" and M" sprayed atop one another. Assumedly a gang marking, which Jason had always thought weird, being out in rural George County. When he'd lived in the far rougher Baltimore suburb, Perry Hall, gang totems appeared everywhere in strip shopping centers, bridges, dumpsters, even across the middle school's outdoor basketball court. Here, the graffiti seemed as out of place as a Space Invader struggling to march through a Pac-Man maze.

All the times Jason had passed the shambled warehouse with its crackled, chipped paint and busted out windows on the way home from Super Thrift, Jason had given it little thought beyond the out-of-place spray-scribble. You could only see it from behind Rill & Company's abandoned storeroom planted yards away from Route 62, which ran parallel to the train tracks.

He dropped off the rail and down the craggy slope leading to the warehouse. Jason had to tramp through weeds, broken bottles, flotsam branded with a Burger King logo and other trash. Someone had left an old Christmas-themed issue of *Hustler* magazine behind, possibly caught and ditching it on the lam. It had been weathered and washed out by the elements, but Jason could still detect an image of a couple wearing parts, not all, of a toy soldier and ballerina uniforms. With bare breasts aloft, exposed, bushy nether region parted beneath the tutu and a stiff crank doubtless ever carved into a wooden toy sentry, they were performing The Nutcracker in a way Tchaikovsky never intended.

The lot housing the warehouse was besieged by broken glass shards and splintered skid slats like the palettes carrying freight into Super Thrift. However long it had been since Rill & Company used these facilities was hard to tell, but what was easy to ascertain was the owners had left in a hurry with no care as to cleanup. They'd placed two padlocks on the main doors, giving Jason pause to wonder if someone really did use the warehouse these days.

Out on Route 62, cars rustled by in intervals. Traffic was light right now, at a time when Jason would've been at work, prior to being fired. Lori had explained it to him numerous times, but Jason still couldn't fathom the store's decision process.

He took a slow roll around the front, figuring kids, maybe his age, maybe younger, had their fill smashing out the high perched windows with rocks. The damage had long been done, given the swishy cobwebs lobbing from the broken panes. One detailed spider web seemed recently spun, bouncing in and out, given the occasional gusts plinking it.

If Jason had been paying attention to the doings on the road, he would've spotted a familiar '69 Nova slow to a near stop in passing, then cut a hard turn into the warehouse lot.

Only the gunned engine alerted Jason. Unlike the last time he'd been this close to the same car, however, it wasn't stopping.

Chapter 46

"HOLY SHIT!" JASON SHRIEKED, diving out of the way of the Chevy-manufactured hood which would have sent Jason to meet his father in the afterlife on the same exact day.

Jason fell to the pavement, and not even planting his shoulder could save him from being gashed down the forearm by the sharp end of a clear green, half-shattered bottle of Sprite.

"Nyyyyyahhhh!!!" Jason wailed in pain.

The Nova fishtailed, the screeching rubber from an apparently new set of Michelins sending a death siren into the air. Jason could smell the awful pong of smoke from the burned off treads.

"You wanted me alone, motherfucker," was the next thing Jason heard out the rolled down window of the Nova. How Sam Shaffer had gotten out of his car and within reach of Jason's prone position would be a mystery to solve for later. If he lived long enough to hear anything beyond Sam's foreboding edict, "Here I am."

Sam's nose was still bandaged, but he was alone for a change. The confidence inside of Sam's eyes, however, shone as if he'd had his full entourage with him.

"Come on, Hamlin! Get the fuck up!"

"If I do, I might kill you," Jason growled, only now seeing his own blood smeared across the lot, running down his arm. "You have no idea what I've been through."

"Is that so?" Sam retorted, snapping his right hand into his back pocket, and just as fast snapping a switchblade into action. "What's that you told me before? *Not if I kill you first.*"

It wasn't quite the same scenario in the story Jason had been pecking through, a fictitious well-to-do suburbanite snot known as a "Soc," having a bone to pick with a greaser kid of yesteryear going by the handle "Ponyboy."

The image of Ponyboy getting jumped and not only threatened by a switchblade, but his head plunged into a fountain, swirled about

Jason's mind for a split second. He wasn't all the way finished with the book yet, but Jason had grasped with full comprehension of author S.E. Hinton's recurring theme: teenagers at odds with each other, teenagers from different walks of life…those teenagers fought, and some of those teenagers died. The switchblade had become a harbinger of havoc.

The instant Sam had snapped the lever to his Solingen Springer knife, which some referred to as a "shell puller," Jason saw the switch handle's pickbone scales before the actual blade itself. This was less an aesthetic thing and more a case of Jason watchdogging the motion of Sam's hand, which waggled the weapon.

Sam had the high ground on Jason. One blink, one lapse of concentration, and Jason could be gutted, Sam having enough time to carol a few bars of "Sweet Home Alabama" as he turned Jason's intestines to spaghetti.

A sidebar thought, Jason was glad he'd shucked his denim vest off when he'd soothed his mom, leaving it and all its heavy metal regalia on her bed. It would've only slowed him down right now.

"Got that case cutter on you, Hamlin?" Sam prodded Jason, his fingers tightening on the hilt of the switch. With his bandaged-up nose prompting a nasally intonation, Sam looked and sounded more comical than threatening. Jerry Lewis Goes to a Rumble. Those ignited eyes of Sam's, however, spoke of all the danger implied. "Better go for it now while you can, before I carve your ass to ribbons."

Inside his head, Jason heard an echo of his father, still alive, only a short time ago. The slushiness in his voice, the staggering, the ballooned stomach. It was like he'd never died and he was right there with him now, in a guttery warehouse lot, taunting Jason once again: *"I see you're getting some muscle to you. About goddamn time, too… Come on! Show me what you've got!"*

In anticipation of Sam's next move, Jason reached for the Sprite bottle shard which had cut him. The rounded base of the splintered bottle was still intact, enough for Jason to grab from beneath and use as a makeshift knife.

"Oh, no you don't!" Sam barked, sounding more like a nose-clogged *marf*, swiping his blade down at Jason. He'd pulled back nothing, the swish of his blade swanking just how narrowly it had missed slicing Jason a second mouth.

As he'd done at his father's apartment with the .22 rifle pointed in his face, Jason rolled for his life along the ground. He felt the grit and dirt seep into the cut on his forearm. Jason hollered as it felt like he'd rotated onto a hornet's nest. No time to give energy to the pain, as Lori would've put it. Jason didn't see it, but he heard the hiss of Sam's switch, and he felt a breeze along the back of his neck, now exposed with Jason's hair all helter-skelter.

Going right where he and Lee had left off in the big fight, Sam lifted his foot, this time encased inside a black, steel shank work boot, and he let Jason have it in the ribs.

"Aaaaugh!" Jason yelped, now at enough of a disadvantage Sam's third swing made its mark, carving into his left hamstring. Jason felt the scorching hotness of the incision, then a frightening chill, as blood flooded his back leg.

Jason spasmed on the ground, howling at his latest wound. The broken glass shard rolled out of his grasp. He was now in such terror he began to pull himself into a fetal position, as if doing that would repel any future damage.

Last time, Jason had been the aggressor, no fear. This time, Jason had been caught at the worst possible time with only Sam alone to deal with. In its own chilling way, it was a far bigger blindside than Lee pelting Jason upside the head with the Pabst can.

"Where's your balls now, huh, Hamlin?" Sam yelled, kneeling to Jason and grabbing him by the hair, just as he'd done in the parking lot at Merriweather High. "You ain't so tough now without your little army, are you? You goddamn pussy."

That was all it took. It had become a trigger word with Jason. All the times his father had derided him, rejected him. Being branded a "dummy" in his younger years was nothing compared to being called a "pussy" by the same man who'd helped bring him into this life.

Jason felt the chill of Sam's blade, already having feasted on his flesh once, prick the side of his neck. It should have submitted him, but instead, it sent Jason the essential alarm bells to fight back. *Thank the Goddess,* he found himself saying, and it didn't feel unusual. *Sekhmet, Isis, Diana, Brigid, whoever you are, whatever you are, be with me right now, please!*

Sam's face so close to Jason's head, Jason knew what he had to do, even if it meant taking another slash of the blade along his neck. Feeling Sam's grip loosen on his hair, it was all the leverage Jason needed. Jason snapped his head backwards. Thankfully, no cut came across his neck.

He felt the crunch before the scream pierced his eardrum. Not even the three days of ringing after attending the Monsters of Rock Festival the past summer could do outdo the deafening agony Jason had to gnaw through inside his ear canal, much less the sudden shock sent snapping into his brains.

It had been worth it, though.

Sam buckled and rolled away from Jason, though still grasping his switchblade, as if to lose it meant he would lose, period.

"Muddafugga!!! Nah aggnnnn!"

Pushing through the typhoon ringing through his head, Jason rejoiced to find Sam pawing at his rebroken nose, futilely trying to contain the blood.

"Goddamn, it works," Jason muttered as an image of a gore-fanged lioness skulked inside his awakened third eye. "Praise Sekhmet!"

Sam removed his hand to inspect the damage, going cross-eyed over the stained splint and bandages. He looked googly and Jason would've laughed in jubilation if he wasn't in dire need of finishing this fight and somehow seeking medical help before he bled out. He could see pools of his blood on either side of him, but now Sam was adding his own to the mix.

Cars continued to slink by on Route 62, but nobody caught what was happening a simple head turn away. Jason was still on his own.

"Ahhh kiiii youuuuu!" Sam yapped, taking another swing at Jason with his blade.

Jason was thinking more clearly despite the blood coming out of two points on his body. He'd predicted Sam's swing and rolled yet again, this time in the opposite direction. He lurched for the broken bottle piece and snagged it again, just as Sam dove after him, forgetting the gushing from his nose. Sam meant what he'd slurred; he was out to turn Jason into ground beef.

Jason dodged Sam once more, who'd driven the tip of his blade downwards in a stabbing motion. The blade nudged the ground, sending off a tiny spark. Jason hoped by missing, the knife would've dislodged from Sam's hand, but it didn't.

What did happen was a pause of frustration, giving Jason a golden opportunity. With the glass pointed outwards, Jason raised his own weapon behind his neck, then brought it down into Sam's free hand planted against the pavement.

"AHHHHHHHHH!!!!" Sam bellowed, even louder than when Jason had smashed into his already decimated nose.

The piece sunk into Sam's hand deep enough to open a pool of blood from the stab wound. Without thinking, Sam dropped his blade and yanked the glass free, caterwauling in horror as his blood fountained in hideous spurts from his hand.

Jason rolled away three more times before forcing himself to his knees. The back of his left leg was wet and sticky, and he could see the left denim pant leg turn ornate. Next to Jason was a broken off slat and though its point was duller than the glass shard, it still looked formidable.

"You're finished," Jason told Sam, grabbing the slat, and using it to push himself to one knee, then the other.

"Fugggg ooooo, 'ammmlinnnn!"

Sam had another trick up his sleeve, or rather from the upper tier of his jeans.

Jason winced as he saw two things manifest at once.

First, a Beretta 92 pistol which had been tucked into the small of Sam's lower back. How it had stayed in place, much less avoided firing in all the commotion, might've been further divine intervention from Lori's supernatural world. Or perhaps Jesus Christ had formed a pact with them on Jason's behalf.

The second thing was a new arrival to the scene. A white Ford Escort with red side piping halted mere feet away from Sam. The driver's side door thrust open.

"Over here!" they both heard.

"Greg?" Jason whispered, feeling elation, even more so to find Greg Boedecker was motioning with his right hand for Jason to toss him the split-off plank while he had the drop on Sam Shaffer.

"Buuudeeeckerrrrr?" Sam blubbered, his blood continuing to sieve down his mouth, staining his red and green checked flannel shirt. "Daaa fuuuuu youuu dooiinn eere?"

Jason needed no further prompting. He lobbed the slat, well out of Sam's reach, and nearly out of Greg's.

It became a thing of grandiosity, like King Arthur being tossed Excalibur in a deed of destiny from the Lady of the Lake. Again, Jason thought of Lori, and not just because her ex-boyfriend had drawn the fortune of coming to his rescue. When Jason thought of it, he had to thank, not just Lori's deific powers for watching over him in these battles with Sam Shaffer, but everyone from Bud Curry to Brad Stone and those in-between.

Add Greg Boedecker to the list, as he leaped and caught the wooden slat, and in one fluid motion, he swung it against Sam's face.

The pistol fell out of Sam's hand, clattering against the pavement. Jason braced himself for any errant discharge of the gun, but none came. Sam toppled to the pavement, woozy, barely conscious.

Jason saw Greg move in and kick the switchblade over to him. A simple lean forward and the knife was in Jason's possession.

All the tables-turning intervention, however, took a horrific plunge.

Having him at a disadvantage, Greg leaned down and grabbed the Beretta. He glanced over at Jason, then down at Sam. If Sam was capable of nullifying people with his unnerving smile, he'd met his match with Greg. Greg's eyebrows and his upward smirk looked like they wanted to reach out and congratulate each other. To Jason, Boedecker looked every bit as deviant as Ted Bundy.

"Aww, no, Greg, don't do it, man!"

Greg didn't hesitate.

POW! POW!

Jason closed his eyes to avoid seeing Sam Shaffer's brains and skull spread across the concrete, but he couldn't avoid witnessing the aftereffects. His stomach churned and Jason felt far dizzier than he had in the woods moments ago. Carnage scattered amidst the twinkling glass fragments, bringing to light the incisive Sprite bottle Jason had used, dashed with Sam Shaffer's blood. Jason recalled an easy hundred death metal lyrics commemorating such slaughter. To see it firsthand, it would be a long time before a Carcass or Morbid Angel album would sit right with Jason again.

He was so transfixed by the butchery in front of him Jason had nearly forgotten the instigator of it all.

Jason was dumbstruck to find Greg holding the Beretta, not by the handle, by the barrel. Furthermore, he had it stuck out to Jason. If he hadn't known better, Jason thought Greg might pistol whip him with it.

"Can you get up?" Greg asked, and unlike the psychotic face he'd worn before shooting Sam Shaffer, his voice matched the frostiness of his countenance. He held the gun out to Jason, his arm rigid, unwavering. Statuesque.

Jason used his good leg to brace himself, pushing with all his leftover strength to hoist himself to a one-legged standing position. His left side hurt like hell and the blood was still coming, spiked by Jason's sudden propulsion. Standing up, it was numb and practically useless.

Jason wasn't yet certain Greg was about to play a trick on him by switching his grip on the Beretta and plugging Jason right there. If he had any hard feelings about Jason and Lori's relationship, now would be the time for Greg to take him out. Jason had Sam's switchblade, but fat lot that would do against a bullet running at him faster than an Amtrak.

"Get in the car, point this at me," Greg told Jason, snapping the Beretta once to demonstrate his willingness to turn the gun over. "I'll give myself up and we'll get you some help. You're losing blood, Jason, so don't take too long deciding."

Dubious yet seeing Greg's point, Jason lurched forward, dragging his bad leg behind him. He brandished the blade in front of him, for the good it would do him.

"You don't need the knife, man," Greg badgered him. "Word of honor."

"Honor?" Jason quipped disbelievingly.

Nonetheless, he took a second laggard push forward, then another, and the Beretta was snug inside his free hand. Jason lowered Sam Shaffer's switchblade, then dropped it to the ground. The few resounding clicks it made was like finality itself.

Greg's arm remained pointed at him, his empty hand and a new, stupefied expression on his face reminding Jason of Michelangelo's fresco of God touching Adam's hand in the Sistine Chapel.

"Is this even real?" Jason blurted.

Wherever Greg had gone to that moment, he snapped out of it and let his arm fall slack. "Is anything?" he posed.

Aftermath

"THAT WAS HARDLY worth the wait."

"The third one's still better, you gotta admit."

"Let's not get carried away."

Rob and Emily shuffled through a tight crowd out the third theater of the Golden Oaks Cinema 6 with castaway popcorn crunching beneath their shoes and murmured mixed reviews around them of *Halloween 4: The Return of Michael Myers.*

"That was breaking taboo a little, don't you think?" Emily asked, hooking her forefinger into the back loop of Rob's khakis. "Stalking a child all movie long with the intent to chop her up."

"He didn't get her, at least," Rob ragged, tilting his head back to Emily.

"The whole thing was stale, just like the crowd," she commented, pulling Rob closer without mashing her chest into his back. "Remember how much fun it was going to the *Friday the 13th* movies?"

"It was party time," Rob affirmed. "Rocky Horror, slasher-style."

"Nobody shut up. It was loud, people carrying on, throwing M&Ms at the screen, at each other."

"Yelling at the victims for doing dumb stuff and balling each other before Voorhees whacked 'em."

"Guys scaring girls, their screams getting other girls to scream."

"Were you one of the screamers, Emily?"

"Hell no, I was too busy laughing at it all, it was so glorious. This snooze fest? Donald Pleasance should've said no."

Rob tossed their shared and emptied popcorn bucket and their finished soda cups into a rolling trash can manned by an usher they both recognized from school, 11th grader, Tim Daniels. Rob kept to himself how it reminded him of his own position in waste removal at Grigsby Tools, from which he'd played hooky on a Friday to take Emily to the movies. His father had given him a gentle reprimand, acknowledging it was for a good cause, at least.

In the lobby, Rob and Emily saw more kids from Merriweather High and nodded to them as they passed. Minus some goodhearted pushing and shoving by some rung-up middle schoolers near the concession stands, the exodus out of the cineplex had been rather docile.

"I caught you trying to hold my hand, Ace," Emily teased, slipping her fingers into Rob's.

"So does this mean we're officially dating?"

"Don't be a geek about it, Martino." Emily fired him a grin and a pogoing of her eyebrows.

"Mmm hmm," he said back sarcastically.

When they reached Emily's burnt orange '71 Plymouth GTX in the furthest end of the cinema parking lot, Emily pulled Rob closer and wrapped her arms around him, laying her head against his chest. The evenings were growing colder with Daylight Savings Time on the horizon, spelling earlier twilights and frigid temperatures. Cars all over the theater parking lot started, revved, took off in a hurry, then clogged into a queue at once.

"You know, I'm glad we did this. I can't make you feel what I went through, but it nearly made me swear off guys."

"I gotcha."

"Rob, so many people begged me to keep the baby. Some told me I'd burn in Hell if I went through with the abortion. They kept demanding I drop out of school in seven or eight months and become an instant mother. That's right before Graduation, Rob! Can you imagine getting this far but missing out on your diploma? Even with all their badgering, I thought about keeping the child. That was, until Lee told me he'd never accept it as his."

"I was there and Lee's a dirtbag," Rob sneered, tightening his hold on Emily. The heat of her hand placed against his pec, starting to swell now that he'd been doing 30 push-ups in the evenings before bed, was something he'd always longed to feel from a girl. *Marcie Barone, eat your heart out,* he mused, letting the thought float away where it belonged.

"When I said I was going to abort it, I had to listen to those fanatics call me a slut, a whore, a baby killer. Someone left a note on my car saying they were going to follow me all the way to the clinic and make sure I didn't make it inside."

"Damn."

"Who knows who'd left the note, but the rest of my hagglers were friends of my family, churchgoers, the clergy. Reverend Isaac was the nicest out of any of them, yet even he wouldn't hear me when I said Lee gave up on our child long before me and I shouldn't be expected to carry it to term. I'm different, but I think it's irresponsible to bring an unwanted child into the world. It's the child who always pays the price in the end. And in the end, Mr. Metcalf was the one who paid for his son's mistake."

"Well, hopefully Lee's learned the error of his ways after you kicked his ball sac into the next county."

"One of the best moments of my life," Emily said, looking up at Rob. "Better than having a box of ginger snaps all to yourself. Tonight's been up there, even if the movie sucked. I'm flattered you called out of work for this 'non-date' we agreed to."

"I don't recall agreeing to such terms," Rob said with a wry grin. "Though I'm with you on the ginger snaps. We can always share."

"Guess I'll have to hide my stash around you, since I *don't* share, but yeah, this has turned into a real date, I suppose, even though we went Dutch."

"How about we shared the expenses?" Rob said, dipping toward Emily and parting his lips.

"Getting a little ahead of yourself there, Martino?" Emily goaded, pulling her head back from Rob, but not too far.

"Are you baiting me, Ms. Haney?"

"Maybe. And any guy with the progressive thinking to use Ms. instead of Miss just may bunt his way on to first base."

"Kiss her already!" they heard from some goof poking his head out the passenger side of an inching Vauxhall Cavalier.

"First base only," Emily told him, receiving Rob's mouth with hers before swatting him on the butt in mid-kiss.

Second and third base would come the night of Homecoming.

– – – – –

"*Atreyu?*" Jason asked with a frown. "It might be a cool name for a metal band, but for some warrior kid who's supposed to be a what, 'greenskin?' The little shit has cool hair, but c'mon, Lori, seriously? Don't even get me started about a talking pile of rocks."

"Keep an open mind, will you? It's a fantasy story."

"It's plagiarism calling this schizo world 'Fantasia.' The Nothing just may consist of Walt Disney's legal team. They'll devour this thing far quicker than Bastian Bax can. Close the book already, dude, and end this suffering!"

"I must be getting used to your silly cynicism," Lori teased. "Sounds to me you've been paying attention a lot more than you're letting on."

"I owed you one viewing of *The Neverending Story*, but just one," Jason toyed with her in return, patting Lori on the thigh with his free hand. The other was holding an egg-shaped crystal with cobalt blue and copper swirls around it.

"Keep a tight grip on that lapis lazuli," Lori advised him.

"Pretty stone, but remind me again what doing this is for?"

She sighed and leaned back against Jason's good side. "In Wicca, we employ metaphoric crystals all the time. Different stones, different properties, different uses. There are so many that I don't want to overload you with too much information. Lapis lazuli is used for physical healing, which you can benefit greatly from. The ultramarine can be ground up for paints, though it's such a regal looking stone, most people wouldn't dare desecrate it. This stone was a common tribute to the gods and goddesses of Egypt, so when it's done its work on you, offer it to Sekhmet for answering you against Sam. By then, I'll move you on to malachite."

"Which does what?"

"It's transformative for positive change."

"I'll gladly welcome a new trend."

"Jason, look," Lori said, hooking her arm around his and clasping his wrist with a sigh to follow. "I applied to Amherst College near Boston. This was before you and I got together. I've received a pre-acceptance letter based on my 3.7 GPA, but it'll depend on how I do on the SATs if I'm locked in. I've got my heart set on a liberal arts degree."

"Seriously?" Jason quipped, taking his eyes away from the television and scrutinizing her. "Did you even think about this before getting involved with me? What if you get accepted? What about us?"

Lori had no answer.

— — — — —

The name Greg Boedecker became synonymous with "murderer," particularly with the farming community. After turning himself in, confessing he'd shot Sam Shaffer and letting Jason take the credit for apprehending him, Greg threw himself deeper onto the sword, claiming both Sam and Jason's wounds had been at *his* hands. All to exonerate Jason.

Deputy Bohager called bullshit to the story. So did Sheriff Walt Tanner, who'd locked Greg up until his parents had come up with $25,000 in bail money. As did the reporter from the *George County Regional,* who blew the roof off the entire region with a mystery nobody felt like solving. Forensics found two sets of fingerprints on the switchblade left on the scene, neither belonging to Boedecker. It meant nothing once Greg signed a full confession. The farmers wanted blood for blood. More than that, once it was determined Greg would be tried as an adult so close to age 18, they lobbied as many hardline Maryland legislators as they could petition to reinstate the death penalty.

After a few weeks, the death of Sam Shaffer became passé news to most in school, which had moved on, as people, places and circumstances will. The yearbook for the graduating Class of '89 would later feature a heavily contested In Memorium page dedicated to Sam as well as Cindy Wise, who would flip her car over and die in mid-January from a jagged, icy curve on the dreadfully windy Warehime Road.

– – – – –

Not only did the *George County Regional* blow up the arrest of Rory Chesney, former Political Science teacher at Merriweather High School, for his tryst with a minor, Francine Van Fleet, all the Baltimore network news stations had gotten their hands on the story. Everyone from the school hallways to water coolers in workplace offices statewide was aghast. Chesney was seen on the tv for his arraignment hearing, wearing a suit jacket over his head. Around school, the married ex-teacher was referred to by the students as "kid fucker," Francine Van Fleet as a "junior homewrecker." As would be Jason's fate in less drastic fashion, Francine would be forced into staying home and eventually transferring out of Merriweather High.

– – – – –

With no fanfare nor farewell, Curry's Music closed, a week before Halloween. Wherever Bud Curry and Dawn went off to, nobody knew.

"Maaaan, that's beat," Rob said in front of the locked, empty store with its taped sign, **"THIS SPACE FOR RENT,"** his mouth hanging agape. "Bud, where'd you go?"

Jason's mother waited for them patiently in her running car. She was staring off to the side out of her window, looking every bit as devastated as the boys for her own reasons. Jason, still using a cane to gimp through a long healing of his slashed leg, looked back at his mom with more pity for her than himself.

"I'd pinched enough money from my last check to get Anthrax's *State of Euphoria* and King Diamond's *Them* today. I got razzed about it at the bank and lectured to by my folks."

"There's a Record World close to where we're moving in Rosedale," Jason said serenely, leaning on his cane. He came off far older than he was by doing so. "Won't be the same as Curry's."

"When I get a car, I'll come down to Rosedale and we'll go there, I guess. You're right, dude, it won't be the same. Nothing will."

Jason rummaged around his pocket and came out with a lime-colored Bic lighter. He thumbed down on the spark wheel a few times until a flame emerged. Forcing himself to stand straight and ease off the cane, Jason held the lighter up to the smeared, filmy glass in salute.

"Thanks for everything, Bud," Jason said.

— — — — —

For his eighteenth birthday on October 27th, Jason's mom gave him a guitar, a black Epiphone Firebird 500. It had come used from Magnus Music, but Jason hardly cared about that. It had been one the greatest days of his life. His mother had taken an advance on her Christmas bonus and every dollar of it went toward the mahogany-based Epiphone with its synthetic ebanol fretboard.

She'd also chipped in a 1984 Carvin 30-watt tube compact amplifier. She'd given Jason a handful of tab books, two filled with intermediate beginners' songs, two filled with iconic tunes by The Beatles and Fleetwood Mac. Jason's mom had let Rob and Lori in on the whole thing and they gave him gifts of Judas Priest and blues tab books respectively. Lori's present contained patterns by Willie Dixon, Robert Johnson, Howlin' Wolf, Buddy Guy, B.B. King and Muddy Waters, Jason's future music pantheon. He stayed up the entire night of his birthday after Rob and Lori went home, devouring lingo such as "pickups," "vibrato," "frequency responses," and "spring tension."

— — — — —

If there was one song that brought kids together at Merriweather High, it was Club Nouveau's hip hop take on Bill Withers' "Lean On Me." With basketball an attendance flop for the year, the PTA grudgingly gave its vote on the installation of a jukebox in the cafeteria, with the provision it only be played before school and during afterhours. No song was played more; the Beastie Boys' rap-rock anthem "Fight for Your Right to Party" registered a near second. Though it was always the Populars beating everyone to the juke with their quarters, kids from all walks of life were singing along to Club Nouveau, no matter the separatist cliques which dragged on, same as it ever was. It was common to find kids bobbing back and forth, shoulder-to-shoulder, nodding their heads in time to the rallying song's clouting drum machine. Though it had been out a few years, the "Lean On Me" remake would become the Class of '89's theme song.

— — — — —

At the end of the first semester, Rob was asked to come to the front of the class in Creative Writing. By now, it had been all but expected of Rob to share his work, even with Mr. Morrow progressively hand-selecting other students to avoid favoritism. Rob had become an unspoken superstar of the class, and for his encore reading of the class' final assignment titled "Who Am I?" He had the eager attention of everyone, including Marcie Barone.

Rob also had an extra member of his audience. Emily had been standing in the open doorway leading into Mr. Morrow's room, having come to school late that day for a dental appointment. Everyone saw her lingering there and nobody said anything, not even Mr. Morrow. In fact, the amicable teacher gestured to an open seat for her to take, which she did. Emily sent Rob a double pucker air kiss as he started.

"Who am I?" he began, not looking at his paper, but at Emily, then the rest of the class before referring to his paper. "I think everyone here knows who I *used* to be. Withdrawn in action, louder than bombs with my external expression, which needed no words. I wore my convictions. This, before you all got used to seeing me up here on a regular basis, no doubt accusing me under your collective breaths of kissing our paisley-loving teacher's rosy behind on both cheeks."

The class split their guts over that one, even Emily.

"I was wondering what felt funny back there," Mr. Morrow larked, looking around the classroom with a hammy expression. "I can save myself the co-pay at my proctologist's office." This extended the laughter, so much even Rob had trouble getting back on point.

"You've seen me change," Rob pushed on. "I've seen some of you change. Sidebar to my paper, did anyone see *this* coming, me dating a one-time enemy?"

Some laughter continued, much of it sounding cautious. Emily flashed Rob the universal three-fingered "I love you" sign for the first time.

"The first month of school, me and my friend, Jason Hamlin, the one who didn't cut his hair nor change his wardrobe, we went through hell. Him especially. I'd only reopen a can of worms by rehashing what you already know. There's no point in that. What you may not know is that it takes courage to be yourself. Absolute courage. You can say, hey, Rob, don't preach to me; you're looking like anyone else these days. Yeah, that's true, and confession time; it's a reaction to years of being on the outs for so long. I'm metal true, but I paid a price. Me and Jason both did."

By this time, Rob left his paper sit beneath his hand at the pulpit. Now he was winging it.

"A wild, crazy fight in which we emerged kinda-sorta victorious, and with a lot of help, the way me and Jason are perceived now, well, it's awesome, but Honesty Time? It's just plain *weird*. I know many of you hated me in the past, just because I'm a heavy metal guy. Ask my girlfriend all about it."

"Guilty," Emily interrupted with a gleam in her eyes.

"If you all saw me now, how I look, would it change your overall perception of me?"

Rob held tight a moment to let that question sink in. Nobody answered beyond a few nods of awareness. None harder than Emily.

"Would you think the same thing of me for listening to Slayer or Iron Maiden looking like this in a striped Izod instead of the way I used to look? I'm sure it wasn't just Emily there who thought the word 'grit' when you saw me. Think about what Geddy Lee was trying to tell us in Rush's 'Subdivisions.' Be cool or be cast out. The saying 'never judge a book by its cover' is cliché, but it was probably derived in a high school, if not a middle school. The syndrome of hatred at what people don't understand never goes away. I'm sure Mr. Morrow can tell us a few gritty stories about discrimination and injustice from the turbulent Sixties."

Mr. Morrow used only an elevated Black Panther fist to reply.

"My point is, because I'm getting on my own nerves proselytizing, it's not a case of who am I. It's who are *we?*"

The applause Rob received was so boisterous the teacher in British Literature, Miss Eldora, poked out of her room. Spotting Emily next door, her eyes widened in disbelief.

Marcie Barone peeled her mouth with her fingers and blew.

Emily outdid her.

— — — — —

A week before Thanksgiving, the moving van loaded up with Jason and his mother's belongings. A placard marked **"SOLD"** had been stuck upon the Long and Foster sign on the lawn in front of 1752 Corinthian Way.

"Lori says she'll come down and see me," Jason said to Rob. "I know it's Amherst University or bust with her, though. She'll be moving out of state if she gets accepted. Now I'm the one who's moving before her. Who knows when I'll actually have time with her, you know?"

"Emily's already been accepted at the University of Miami," Rob said, patting the buttons on his denim vest for show. "So I'll be in the same boat as you. She's going for a degree in Marine Biology. Me, I'll be hanging statewide at Fulton Community College. My parents got the student loans approved, so it's a lock."

"Mine rattles more than yours," Jason muttered, flapping the bottom hems of his jacket. "You look ridiculous wearing that overtop a Tommy Hilfiger sweatshirt."

"One last time," Rob told his friend with a smile and a toss of the horns from both hands.

"I still find myself hating my dad," Jason sighed. "Every day I curse him we have to move. It's not mom's fault, but I'm mad we're leaving. Dad didn't take any life insurance out, which is shocking since she said he was always so pragmatic. The last memory I get to have of him is one I want to forget. Between you and me only, Rob? I still miss him."

"You're strong, man," Rob said. "Strongest mofo I've ever met. I'm going to miss *you*."

"This ain't the end, dude. I'll get a car before you do. We'll keep this train rolling somehow."

"Yeah, but it's a half hour drive one-way, Jason. You'll get sick of it in time."

"Like hell," Jason said, seizing Rob in a hug on the lawn. Their band buttons clacked against one another, making them bust out in laughter while holding their embrace a few seconds longer. "Here, dude, I have two of these. Add my extra to your collection before you turn poser."

Jason pulled a duplicated Dio band button off his jacket and handed it to Rob.

"Thanks, man," Rob said, examining the button. "Crazy I never noticed you had two. An agreement, then, here and now. We never lose touch. We try and get together at least once a month."

"Twice."

"Even better. We catch Queensrÿche, Overkill, and Armored Saint next time they're all in town. All of them, Jason, I mean it. Promise me."

"Done deal," Jason said, high-fiving Rob.

It was one of thirty-plus years' worth of promises they'd keep.

33 Years Later…

MetalLion02: Another epic fail by Martino. Hang it up, brah.

ShredGoDz: It's a Drop A when you down tune all six strings, Martino, not a D. The D is for one string only. Do you even *play?*

Doofendumb69: Actually, I think he was right on the money on this review. More progressions and less straight riffing than Kali Magic's last album.

MetalLion02: STFU @Doofendum69. Your handle's lamer than your opinion.

Doofendumb69: You're all balls behind a keyboard @MetalLion02

MetalLion02: Like Bon Scott, I've got the biggest ballz of them all. IMO. No, *IRL*

Doofendumb69: Get over yourself and then a spell checker after that. I doubt you've even grown your first pube.

MorrigansLust: Like Martino even matters anymore. Maybe when L.A. Guns still had all their original members. Can't believe he actually pulled *them* in for a reference, smh…

MetalLion02: LMAO @MorrigansLust Come and get a bullet, ya bitch @Doofendumb69 Ohhh, FTW!!! Go back to the 80's, Martino, bc your outdated references are calling.

IronEd2003: Really, Martino? A 7 out of 10 rating? This album's an easy 9. Whattya *really* listening to over there, Katy Perry? You ain't been metal a minute of your limp dick life.

PwrSheena707: This band's long past its prime, just like the reviewer. Take a hint.

"Shut it down, hon. You're getting worked up."

"What is it about this generation? Why are they such—"

"Cowardly, self-entitled little shits?"

"Something like that," Rob harrumphed. "What are they so bitter about?"

"Their music sucks?" Emily chimed back at Rob, ruffling his waning hair. "Kardashian envy?"

"Helicopter moms?" Rob guessed. "Or, the opposite extreme, coddled by X-box?"

"They're egotistical because they're allowed to be," Emily quantified. "They communicate with acronyms and emojis, they use a phone to listen to music, *eww*, and they're hopped up on Monster drinks. Schools don't even teach cursive writing anymore. Today's youth have twice the conveniences we did, but they're also getting cheated and exploited by a dumbed down regression. God help us in our retired lives, they don't even care. What do you expect of them, Rob?"

"Something better than digital DocuSign, TikTok, and cyberbullying."

"You ain't getting me to e-sign anything," Emily said, "except maybe an affidavit stating you've hit that point in life where you can do with some Just For Men gray reducing shampoo. Talk about regression. A lot better than that static-shocked clown in our Senior yearbook, though."

"Devotion is overrated," Rob griped, but not too much. "Is it too late to unfriend you on social media?"

"Oh, chill out, baby," Emily said, laughing at him.

"I'm used to your ball breaking, Em. It's what makes you tick, and it's a huge part of our success, being able to tease each other without it getting personal."

"Unlike the old days, it's *never* personal. I've always been salty and I own it. With you, though, it's…"

"One of the reasons I married you," Rob said with a swooning flip in his eyes.

"Awwww," Emily cooed back.

"Seriously, though, the disrespect those cocky bastards show me online is bad enough. They go after the bands without mercy, as if the artists owe them something just for being around. It's not like these bitchy cellar slugs are buying records. Downloads and streaming, it's the wave of the future, sure, but it's gotten soulless. Where's the joy of holding the artwork of the album cover in your lap and getting intimate with the music?"

"I used to stare at the cover of *Freeze Frame* by the J. Geils Band for nearly a half an hour whenever I'd listen to it. Always in the evening before bed. I can still hear Dad nagging me to get to sleep, since we'd be up at 4:00 a.m. without fail. We'd always start in the corral with the horses before tending to the rest of the animals then the fields by sunrise. The old homestead will always be home, period."

"I'm sure both of our dads are rolling strikes in heaven," Rob waxed.

"Makes me happy they got along in life, much less joined a bowling team together."

"Parents to two former adversaries who fell in love. We set the right example, you know, and not just for Lenny."

"I suppose we did," Emily sighed as if doing so might fix things in her boggled mind. "Been two months since the boyo's checked in. Christmas before that. It wasn't easy letting our kid go be a grown-up in New York. Bad enough my mom is still mourning her grandson wanted a life in the big city instead of leading the fourth generation in George County."

"Mine's not much better, though she was tickled Lenny called her up for her birthday."

"And missed yours altogether," Emily groaned.

"I'm not offended," Rob told her, pointing to the flat screen monitor of their shared PC. "I take bigger exception to this bullshit. You know, these kids, they're even worse to each other online. Makes me wish for the old days when everyone accused me of worshipping Satan."

"You sure about that, Rob? I was one of those doing the accusing."

"You came around."

"Thank Lee Metcalf. I saw him on FacePage last week, by the way."

"You didn't mention that to me."

"He's a tatted-up, sad looking, overweight hoss. His profile pic is more like a mug shot. I'm calling it karma. Seriously, Rob, put those Gen Z losers behind you, if they're even who they claim to be behind their *Grand Theft Auto* and *Call of Duty* avatars. Those spoiled brats would never have survived our day. A single land line for an entire family, slam and dunk."

"Can't even imagine what they'd do being held accountable for their big mouths with their fists," Rob said, reaching for Emily and pulling her closer to him by the waist. "Mic drop."

"Here, allow me," Emily said, planting her hand down upon the cordless mouse and rolling it along the synthetic resin of a pad showing the cockpit of the Millennium Falcon during a light-bursting jump into hyperspeed. One click, and the browser winked out, showing a wallpaper picture of Emily and Rob at Gautier Winery in West Virginia. They were each holding up a couple glasses of Moscato underneath a white wooden trellis snaked with grapevines. The glasses were tilted and touching each other in a cheers gesture.

"Somebody hadda do it."

"You can't let these jerk-offs get to you, Rob. You've had a good run and I don't blame you for getting out. Just don't make the reason you're quitting the music industry be due to those trolls. They're the ones who don't matter and they know it. Anyone with substance in their lives has better things to do than talk smack online. I have enough couth to do the smack talking right to your face."

"I love you," he told Emily, letting his hand drift down to her rear.

"Damn right you do," she said, kissing him on the top of his head. "Lot more butt to grab these days."

"Nonsense," Rob said, resting his head against Emily's hip. He felt her shimmy, but not enough to detach him. "Your butt is a work of art, especially at fifty-one."

"Meh, abstract, maybe."

"I've overstayed my welcome."

"No, your head and hand are fine right where they are. Leave 'em."

"I meant the music industry."

"Oh, gotcha, so you're shifting your focus to editing the *Olde Town Review* and putting the music industry behind you. You finished on a high note, though, a dinner interview with Geoff Tate for *Thunder* magazine. Well, not so much an actual *magazine* these days."

"Hello darkness, my old friend," Rob said with a gloom he did and didn't feel. As he rubbed Emily's fanny, he had a memory of Lee Metcalf doing the same thirty-three years ago. *All mine,* he thought greedily. *The good guys do win sometimes.*

"I've come to talk with you again," Emily sang in response, adding the second line of Simon and Garfunkel's timeless ruminating about the sound of silence circa 1964.

"Hundreds of interviews," Rob pined. "It was a blast and a privilege. I won't miss the transcribing, though."

"I won't miss all the hard copy promos clogging our mailbox every day."

"All these years interviewing bands, hanging backstage and on tour buses, covering live gigs, always a rush like each was my first professional assignment. Who, for the record, was Jack Russell of Great White."

"I know, I was there for all of it, hon. Made me proud to be by your side for your final interview."

"*Operation Mindcrime* was a big deal for metal music back in the day. Jason would've creamed himself to be there with us chowing down with Geoff Tate."

"He would've," Emily agreed. "You're closing this chapter the right way."

"Thanks, Em. We've had a quite a story of our own, you and me."

"And we'll keep on writing on it," she said leaving her shucked off bra on top of his head. "Happy Anniversary, Rob."

— — — — —

The sex had been fantastic, the anniversary dinner at Flemings unforgettable. Lenny had texted them both wishing them a happy twenty-second before they'd gone out.

"Score one for the kid," Emily had said in appreciation.

They'd each ordered a Cowboy Ribeye steak, medium for Rob, Emily taking hers more thoroughly cooked. They'd taken a chance over the dubious menu listing of MARKET PRICE for the ribeyes, and once the bill came, they agreed to never speak of the total again.

The following morning was a Sunday. Emily and Rob were hung over on three Moscow Mules apiece with two bourbons each along the way.

Cavalry Cemetery in Rosedale was busy this morning, it being warm, sunny, and unblemished outside. It felt like a brilliant Easter Sunday with relatives milling in obligatory holiday remembrance instead of it being an ordinary May weekend. Both Rob and Emily wore shades to block the sun which only aggravated their headaches even more.

"You never let me down when you make a pot coffee, Mr. Martino, but it didn't help this time," Emily grumbled. "I may have overexerted myself yesterday, you sex fiend."

"I believe you started it, *Mrs.* Martino."

"I can neither confirm nor deny."

Rob chuckled, taking Emily by the hand.

They wished good morning to a woman who looked even more tired than they did. She was sitting in a foldout chair, her ashen, wrinkled face tucked beneath a floppy sun hat. In her lap was a tray and two clusters of matched playing cards, one bundle facing the direction of the grave marker she was stationed at.

"That's 500 and gin, Harold," she said, nodding at Emily and Rob as they excused themselves behind her.

Approximately fifty yards down the same row, they stopped at their destination.

"Someone's been here recently," Emily stated, pointing to a mixed flower bouquet sprouting from an urn in front of a granite headstone bearing the inscription:

JASON F. HAMLIN OCT 27, 1971 – AUG 3, 2021

"His mother, my guess," Rob said, reaching down and letting the petals tickle his palm.

"When's the last time you heard from Pam?"

"Not since last fall when she had me come over to pick up his guitar and all his vinyl."

"*Five boxes* worth," Emily groaned. "You'd just ripped and purged your CDs onto that thumb drive. Jason, we love you, but you're a royal pain in the ass, just saying."

"Who else was going to take it?" Rob asked sardonically, dropping his head to the gravesite. "What's up, bud?"

"Hey there, sweetie," Emily added, touching the top of the headstone. "Hope you're jamming with Jimi or Prince up there."

"Well, dude," Rob said down to the grass plot instead of the memorial. A little more than a year after Jason's passing from pancreatic cancer, Rob still found it tough to look at the actual marker. "I'm moving on from music. Yeah, I can hear you calling me a poser. It's alright, go for it."

"He *is* a poser," Emily teased. "But he's all mine."

"Tighten your oxygen mask next time you're inside the shark tank at feeding time, Em. Your head's gotten a bit swollen."

"Oh, no he didn't."

"He did indeed," Rob cracked, feeling a genuine smile ease onto his face for the first time since they'd arrived at the cemetery.

"We saw Lori," Emily said, knocking Rob with their locked hands.

"She came down from Salem. You remember she opened that occult store on the main drag, Essex Street..."

"*Esoteric,* Rob. You're the writer of the family, come on."

"Yeah, well she told us we wouldn't exactly be welcome in the voodoo and dark magic shops if we're light magical beings, something to that extent. Not that we're burning cauldrons for kicks. Anyway, she looked us up and we treated her to crab cakes at Pappas. It's been so long since she's been in Maryland. She wants us to come up there and have the local lobster. She says it's not all rubbery and bland like down here. We rule crab cakes, inarguable fact."

"She asked about you, Jason," Emily said, closing her eyes.

"Lori's a Wiccan high priestess now, third degree," Rob went on. "She got married to a Cabot Priest from the UK named Clive about a decade ago. They missed out on the joys of parenthood, lucky jerks.

They've been focused on their shop. It's called Aeon Eternal. Lori said you would've loved that."

"When Rob told her you'd died, she bawled, poor thing."

"So did Em, don't let her fool you otherwise. After they calmed down, Lori went into some kind of trance for a moment, right there in the restaurant. That's why we're here today, bro. She said she could see you, the teenage you, the one she'd known. Lori said you were standing next to a goddess with a lion's head who had her arm around you, all protective-like. I remember Bastet and Sekhmet from my grandfather's mythology books."

"Which he refuses to part with," Emily said.

"Anyway, Lori wanted us to say she loves you and always will, in your guys' time and place, of course."

"She also said you're a snarky piece of work, since there really is a metal band called Atreyu."

"One of many bands I got to interview," Rob said for posterity. "It was an honor being in the industry, dude. It would've been a dream to interview you for publication. I never got a blues assignment, though."

Rob fished inside his right pocket and came up with an old button which had once been pinned to Jason's denim vest. It had the band logo **"DIO"** on it.

"Brought you something," Rob said, leaning to the ground. He pushed the button into the earth at the head of the marker. "Say hi to Ronnie for me on the flipside, man. Love you, dude."

Rob and Emily left the cemetery, still holding hands. Rob sang her Ronnie James Dio's "Rainbow in the Dark" all the way to the car.

Afterword

Ray Van Horn, Jr. circa 1989

WHEN I CAME UP WITH the concept for *Revolution Calling*, I was at the tail end of my 16-year run as a music and horror journalist. Considering most of my assignments were tailored for the things I loved, especially as a teenager in the Eighties, it was a no-brainer this would be the perfect vehicle to purge a few lingering bits of angst through the word. Angst from my life back then, and even as a journalist who later interviewed more than 300 bands, actors, and film directors. It was a glorious side career, but it wasn't always VIP.

I knew *Revolution Calling* would be for my brothers and sisters in metal. We may seem few in numbers on the surface, but you can't stop us as a vast global community. I also knew this story would be for my classmates at North Caroll High, though I made a strict point not to use direct friendships or relationships. Instead, this would be a time capsule for Panther Strong conjured by my observations and interactions. I do confess to choosing a few real people who flashed color into our teenage monochrome.

I didn't know how long it would take to organize all of this into something beyond a heavy metal retrospective. I will tell you after putzing along for a few chapters, distracted by intense life changes, it only took re-meeting my future wife, TJ, to give me the spark.

Babe, you have no idea what a gift you gave me, not just yourself and your soul; you gave me my verve back. That time in the cabin, our first away trip as a couple, two writers, two laptops, a fifth of Jameson. The trails, the snuggling, the porch after a smart rain, the rolling mountain fog, and the tang of wet earth revitalizing us. You asked me for my elevator speech for this book and I had it on my hip. This would be an *Outsiders* for Generation X with a heavy metal twist, based on actual experiences.

TJ, *Revolution Calling* was made reality because of Deep Creek Lake, and you fostered it. I love you so frigging much.

At the time of this writing in the fall of 2023, I have just been to my 35th high school reunion. A strange but rewarding kismet it should arise right before *Revolution Calling's* publication.

I was delighted to see grown-up versions of my rolling posse, even kids-turned-adults I'd been friendly with back in the day. Some of us looked like youth eternal in our early fifties. Everyone operated like there was no such thing as time, picking right back up where we'd left each other, even if for many, our friendships endured long beyond graduation. Even better, no curfew, no legal age limitations.

Through *Revolution Calling,* you got to know who I was back in the 1980s, but as I promised in the Author's Note, I have extra disclaimers to lay down.

Revolution Calling was my life: my friends and my enemies, my hopes and doubts, my failures and rewards. My fears and my ecstasy. My two jobs. My master Jedi in high school and at a record store doomed to fail. Yes, I bought a Bic lighter back then, not to smoke, but to salute Ron Curry's empty store after his third attempt to keep it running.

The Senior Patio was real, and as I announced the upcoming publication of *Revolution Calling* with a suggestion of its origins, the number one question people from my North Carroll past asked me was if I had included the smoking area on the Senior Patio. Roger that. Imagine, if you will, faculty and twelfth graders puffing on tobacco sticks in the same "privileged" common area, only at arm's-length.

I had one serious girlfriend in high school, and, for what it meant at age seventeen with reckless promises of marriage, she was my universe. It wasn't a Goth girl I was with, though one came along in 1989 as a brutal life lesson. Rule number one, never date a girl who says off-the-bat she wants to sleep with Robert Smith of The Cure because she views him as a father figure. Lori Phillips is the pre-shamanist Siouxsie Sioux I wanted and deserved, and I enjoyed her romancing Jason as the sorely needed homeopath Rob could never be to him. Nor did I have a Phoenix-risen firebrand like Emily Haney, albeit, *hint hint*, the adult knotted versions of Emily and Rob is a flirty glimpse into my current love life.

I had, for a year, someone similar to, but not altogether like Marcie Barone. 1987, my junior year, was one of the finest of my entire life. I became an emotional tampon when my quite-serious girlfriend went off to college a year ahead of me and I found myself scampering for a last-minute senior prom date which never manifested. Regardless, Monica, I appreciate you for the love and energy we shared. It was a rarity when a Popular hooked up with a grit. We tried to meet in the middle between our diverse interests and floundered, but as David Lee Roth sang in his solo career, we had some good times. *Damn* good times.

Ultimate confession, my time overall at North Carroll High was pretty terrific. I chose to condense the toughest times of my teen life and push it all together into a two-month quasi-fiction narrative. Yes, I was bullied in freshman year. Yes, I was accused of being in league with Satan for wearing the pentagram on a t-shirt with Motley Crüe's *Shout at the Devil* album cover despite openly slinging a crucifix and imploring to my persecutors to no avail I was a somewhat regular parishioner at St. John's Catholic Church.

I rose up and stood tall, using logic instead of my fists, considering I'd nearly killed five boys in middle school after suffering merciless

months of daily abuse. Scary Hall, you betcha. At North Carroll, I vowed to fight myself before I'd fight anyone else, since I'd seen what the darkest side of myself was capable of. Luckily, by junior year, I had no worries whatsoever. I grew deeply involved in Weightlifting and I really did all the extensive walking Jason does in the story. I loved sports already, which nobody knew until I showed what I could do like Jason did, and I could talk football, baseball, and hockey. I ran track, not for North Carroll, but myself, and I got up to 17 miles around that oval after graduation.

I had a loud and proud metal side with my crew of headbangers and our punk rock friends we'd bridged with during an age the subculture underground called "crossover." The punkers of our school indeed got chased down and beaten up. There was absolutely a case of Nazi punk racism in the slam pit at a show we were at. Rod Jones was very much a real metalhead of color and he got pulverized by a skinhead who showed him no mercy. We all ganged up on the skin, tossing him out of the pit to a bouncer who'd seen it all and quickly hustled the xenophobic prick out of the club. Cue Jello Biafra.

My father was indeed a compulsive alcoholic. Everything Jason's father does in this story happened to me, along with other mistreatment I attempted to rid myself of in my short story, "Dad's Notebook," which appears in my short story collection, *Coming of Rage*. My dad could be ruthless, and he attempted to buy my love as a child with baseball and *Star Wars* cards while getting crackered every night. He verbally fought my mother to the death when she called him on the carpet for his excesses. My dad jammed a finger against my forehead at age seven, barking at me, "Think, dummy, think!" when I couldn't solve my math equations. Thus Queen's "We Will Rock You/We Are the Champions" and my

Kiss albums were my lullabies in 1976 and '77.

To be fair, my father loved me more than anyone on the planet. We had a lot of good memories, especially Orioles baseball games in the late 1970s and 80s. He paid for a portion of my college tuition. He helped me out when we were financially shattered in my former marriage. He told me he was proud of me, and he meant it. Dad was frustrating and vicious at times, but I thank myself for forgiving him all his affronts the day before he died from COPD as a chain  smoker. A bittersweet flinch from his suddenly watered eye in his comatose state told me he got the message. I find myself missing the man a lot, but I feel his aura around me constantly.

Rob's parents are the same as my own mom and stepfather, the two finest people I have ever known. Pop is a greaser rock 'n roller to the end and his weekly lessons and recall with Fifties music trained me for my future in music journalism. Pop, in 1st Cav, survived the 'Nam at the DMZ, the infernal hellhole known as "The Rock Pile." This man who had to pull his torn apart brothers off the field of carnage had the mettle to take on someone else's child as his son. Same as I've done with my own. Mom is my soulmate, my dearest friend, the wisest, shrewdest, toughest woman who showed me how hard work can elevate a banking teller to Vice President of the institution. She is the essence of love and compassion, and she showed me how to bury the fangs that sometimes come peeking out.

I had lots of friends in high school, purposefully seeking others outside of my closest tribe, since I've always felt cliques and subdivisions in school is a self-defeating, though natural course of social development. I was often found in school with a girl at my elbow chatting away, even though none of them morphed into any kind of romantic relationship. Sure, I wanted dates with many of them, though I always kept such feelings private. Yet they all felt secure around me to convey their private thoughts, their inner workings, even personal details about their boyfriends. I valued that so much. It's not often one can earn such widespread confidence.

FOR ALL OF YOU MENTIONED here, thank you. You all played a part in some fashion in *Revolution Calling's* evolution. I especially thank my Creative Writing teacher, Paul Day, who I couldn't help but honor in this story as peacenik eternal, Mr. Morrow. Mr. Day remains the greatest teacher I ever had and there were many at North Carroll High School. I nearly bawled to find Mr. Day attending one of my open mike features more than a decade after graduation and he told me to call him Paul, like an equal.

Also, kudos to my Expository Writing teacher, Steve Hollands. Both men had me read every single assignment I wrote in their classes to gain a public conviction by reading my work to my peers. I had many classmates who hung upon my silly words back then and are still my audience today. Thank you, guys. Seriously.

Thank you to every single editor, publicist, record label exec, band manager, artist, and film director for giving me the side career of a lifetime. To list you all would take another five pages but know that I love every single one of you. Bori and Heather Krgin, you saved my life at a time when I needed to provide for my family with a bounty of freelance for Blabbermouth. You're good people to the highest. Liz and Dave Brenner, you turned my ballsy Megadeth vs. Metallica blog post into one of the most rewarding gigs I ever had. Of the headbanger readership who remembers me, it's mostly due to *Metal Maniacs* and my monthly column at *AMP*. Dee Snider of Twisted Sister, thank you for the riotous interview then offering me a slot chatting up other guests for *House of Hair Online*.

Geoff Tate, formerly of Queensryche, thank you for the dinner hang in DC back in 2006, bro. I told you then what *Operation Mindcrime* meant to me, and I hope you and your old bandmates feel it more than see it with *Revolution Calling*. I can only hope to have replicated a sliver of your magic.

Much love to the esoteric community for being such graceful healers, oracles, and sages, supporting both mine and TJ's endeavors. Lori was my gift to you and the Lord and Lady. Blessed be.

Thank you, tara caribou and Raw Earth Ink. This is our second go-round and I've put my baby in your hands. You have the common courtesy and respect to know what that means.

Thank you to my entire family. You are the reason, plain and simple. To my son, Nolan, I hope you read this someday when the piss and vinegar inside you settles down and you've found yourself. I pray for your success in life more than my own but let *Revolution Calling* serve as document of who your old man was at one time. Melissa and Nick, thank you for accepting me into your lives. You two are some of the hardest-working people I've ever had the privilege to know, much less call newfound family.

Special shouts to Paulette and Mark, the first friends I ever had on this planet from the time I entered it in 1970. Paulette, your support and especially our decades-long Stephen King for Christmas tradition hailing all the way back to *Pet Sematary* has been instrumental in my writing foundation. Now inclusive of the works of Richard Chizmar, also facilitated by you. My writing journey is hardly complete, but my path and the people who've come onto it makes it so much richer these days.

The Author's Note and Afterword were chatty, I'll admit, and I don't foresee being this extensive ever again in future works. It's because *Revolution Calling* was my bucket list project, but more than a mere check-off. This is my blood, my pain, my love, and I hope my legacy statement. I had lots to say, and I appreciate all of you for being a part of the ride. See you again next round.

~Ray Van Horn, Jr.

All photos from North Caroll High School, Hampstead, MD, courtesy of the author

About the Author

RAY VAN HORN, JR. is a veteran journalist and the author of *Coming of Rage*, released through Raw Earth Ink. He spent sixteen years covering music and film for outlets such as *Blabbermouth, AMP, Pit, Dee Snider's House of Hair, Music Dish, DVD Review, Horror News.net, Fangoria Musick, Metal Maniacs, Noisecreep, Unrestrained, Impose, Caustic Truths, Pitriff,* and many others.

Ray contributed essays to Neil Daniels' music biographies on Iron Maiden and ZZ Top. Ray's blog, *The Metal Minute* won Metal Hammer magazine's "Best Personal Blog" award. Ray also wrote NHL game analysis for *The Hockey Nut* and other sports articles for *Kid Shtick*.

He was a beat reporter and photographer for *The Emmitsburg Dispatch* and *The Northern News*. He was host of the forum "Comic Books" at *ReadWave* and the 1999 winner of Quantum Muse's fiction contest. Ray wrote serialized superhero fiction for Cyber Age Adventures from 1999 to 2001. His fiction and essays have appeared at Akashic Books, Atomic Flyswatter, The Rubbertop Review, Story Bytes, and New Noise, plus the anthologies Axes of Evil and Axes of Evil II. Ray was recently interviewed at and a guest contributor for Horror Tree.